MEGGIE'S REMAINS

MEGGIE'S REMAINS

JOANNE SUNDELL

FIVE STAR
A part of Gale, Cengage Learning

GALE
CENGAGE Learning™

Detroit • New York • San Francisco • New Haven, Conn • Waterville, Maine • London

LIBRARY OF CONGRESS CATALOGING-IN-PUBLICATION DATA

Sundell, Joanne.
  Meggie's remains / Joanne Sundell. — 1st ed.
  p. cm.
  ISBN-13: 978-1-59414-788-3 (alk. paper)
  ISBN-10: 1-59414-788-4 (alk. paper)
  1. Colorado—History—To 1876—Fiction. I. Title.
PS3619.U557M44 2009
813'.6—dc22   2009010477

First Edition. First Printing: July 2009.
Published in 2009 in conjunction with Tekno Books.

Printed in the United States of America
1 2 3 4 5 6 7 13 12 11 10 09

ACKNOWLEDGMENTS

I most gratefully acknowledge Tekno and Five Star-Gale, Cengage Learning, for keeping their expert, guiding hands ever outstretched to me. There are so many to thank but on the occasion of *Meggie's Remains,* I would like to thank, in particular, Acquisitions Editor, Tiffany Schofield, for her patience, energy, and unflagging mentorship in my Five Star releases to date. I would also like to thank Author/Editor, Alice Duncan, without whom my books wouldn't "be." For me to have the opportunity to learn from these genuine, top-level professionals in the writing industry is a blessing, indeed.

"*Jane, accept me quickly. Say, Edward—give me my name— Edward—I will marry you.*"

"*Are you in earnest? Do you truly love me? Do you sincerely wish me to be your wife?*"

"*I do; and if an oath is necessary to satisfy you, I swear it.*"

"*Then, sir, I will marry you.*"

"*Edward—my little wife!*"

"*Dear Edward!*"

"*Come to me—come to me entirely now,*" *said he: and added, in his deepest tone, speaking in my ear as his cheek was laid on mine,* "*Make my happiness—I will make yours.*"

Jane Eyre by Charlotte Brontë

CHAPTER ONE

1874 ~ Colorado Territory

The stench of death hung in the air, molded gray, dank, rotting. It was an unearthly place, a place Meggie had been before. She knew what was coming. Her heart hammered in her chest. Her breaths came quick and shallow, not enough to bring any ease. Her ears buzzed. She shook her head, struggling to stay conscious and keep her focus. She knew the fiend hid in the shadows, waiting. It needed her to be afraid. It fed off her fear. Cold, gray walls pressed in. She thrust her arms out to keep the devil away, but it was coming ever closer. It hissed and rasped, slithering toward her.

It was close now, so close she could see spittle hanging from its misshapen chin—drops of venom waiting to kill.

Then it was upon her!

A door slammed, waking Meggie. Heavy footsteps lumbered along the outside hallway. Had it left? Had the thing left? No. It had never left before. Meggie sat straight up in bed and whispered hard into the darkness. "Six feet under, six feet away, where to stay safe, the devil must stay!" The chant helped defend against her night terrors. Believing herself yet trapped in fitful sleep, she felt for the cross around her neck and whispered again. "Six feet under, six feet away, where to stay safe, the devil must stay!" The smooth wood warmed her icy hands. She ran her fingers over the cross for comfort and reassurance, but none came. The fiend was close, in the shadows, waiting to strike. It thrived in the dark shadows of her nightmares, fueled by her fear. But it couldn't thrive in the light!

Her cross forgotten, Meggie threw off her covers and sprang out of bed. Jolts of cold shot up her body the moment her bare feet touched the icy plank floor. The sensation sent a rush of air to her empty lungs. Frantic to escape her nightmare, she strained to see through the darkness and find the light. Light would protect her.

She saw a window and rushed over to it; nearly tripping on the hem of her nightdress as she did. Street lamps flickered on the snowy roadway below. They offered the protection she so desperately needed. There was a balcony outside the window, a balcony in the light. The latch wouldn't give! She tried the latch again. Forced to give up on it she quickly felt her way along the wall for another way out. When her damp palm slid over a handle, she turned the cold knob and pulled the door open. The moment she stepped into the dim, desolate hallway, she froze. The hair at the back of her neck stood on end. Each bristle pricked and hurt, each one signaled the danger closing in.

It was coming—*molded gray, dank, rotting.*

The thing was coming.

This time she'd get away. This time she'd outrun the devil!

Meggie took off down the narrow passage. The instant she came up hard against a door, she tried the knob. It wasn't locked! It led outside, onto a stairwell, then to an alleyway below. Ignoring the bitter cold, she scrambled down the flight of stairs and then quickly cleared the dark corner of the unknown building. She kept running, not stopping until she'd made it to the center of the deserted snowy street, until she'd made it into the light where she'd be safe. Spreading her arms wide, she tilted her face up into the welcoming snowfall and began to spin round as a child might—a child afraid of the monster after her—a child desperate to defend against such evil. Round and around Meggie turned, every turn washing away her sins and lifting the burden from her tainted soul, every turn sending the devil back to hell. Any moment now she'd awaken and be safe in her bed, her nightmare over. Round and around she turned, oblivious to everyone and everything, including the pair of watchful eyes fixed on her.

What the hell? Ethan couldn't believe what he saw. It was three o'clock in the morning. He'd only had two drinks last night, but he was dead tired. It couldn't be the whiskey talking. He needed a smoke. The familiar task of rolling the tobacco and licking the paper to seal it didn't help. The womanly essence of his mistress Samantha still lingered on his fingers. Maybe he should be back in the warmth of her arms rather than on a frozen street in the middle of the night watching some crazed female catch her death.

Easing back into the doorway of the First National Bank, Ethan wanted to stay out of sight. He lit the tobacco and took a draw before he studied the odd female again. At first he thought the woman might be one of Hannah's girls all liquored up. A second look told him she wasn't. Hannah didn't take to any of her gals overdoing it. Fired them on the spot. And he'd never seen anyone work in a saloon that wore whatever it was this woman had on. No. The harebrained female didn't come from any hurdy-gurdy or saloon.

What in Sam Hill was she up to? Had to be crazy. No one but a lunatic would be wandering around in the middle of the night in the snow, half-naked, and twirling in circles like some child. The unusual sight reminded him of the young girl who skated round and around on a frozen slip of ice in the glass globe on his study desk. Once upturned, the snowflakes magically drifted over the girl's revolving figure. A day hadn't gone by when he didn't overturn the familiar miniature and bring life to the winter scene. Ethan shrugged his shoulders and dismissed any association between that girl and the one in front of him now.

It was hard to see the woman's features clearly through the snowfall, but he could make out long, dark hair plastered over her shoulders and down her back. She didn't have much on, only a long white shift. And barefoot. No shoes or boots in all this snow. Fool woman apparently wanted to freeze to death. He started to walk toward her but stopped short the moment he spotted the cross around her neck. Ethan sank back into the shadows. The cross swung out each time she turned another circle. Figures, he thought. Only crazy people believe in God.

Gunfire from somewhere down Blake Street drew Ethan's attention. Until the shots rang out it hadn't occurred to him how unusually quiet it was. After a last draw of his smoke, he tossed the butt on the ground and pushed away from the doorway, intent on getting the woman out of the cold.

But she'd disappeared. Vanished?

Not a sign of her now up or down the snowy street. Maybe she was a ghost, a spirit from some other world. No. He shook his head at the thought. He didn't believe in them any more than he did in God. "Crazy fool woman," he muttered and turned for home.

Ethan was right. Meggie hadn't been spirited from some other world. She was very much a part of this one.

Snapped back to reality by the unmistakable sound of gunfire, Meggie was horrified to find herself in such a state. She wasn't in some nightmarish hallucination after all, but awake, outside in the snow, in her nightdress, with no shoes on! She started to run, despite her near-frozen feet and legs, but stopped. She'd no idea which way to go. Furious with herself for her irresponsible conduct, she didn't understand how she could have let herself get into such a compromising, degrading predicament! Peering in every direction, she hoped something might trigger her recollection. Nothing looked familiar.

Freezing cold, she had to get inside. The large building in front of her looked shut. Could she have come from there? She started for the building, intending to try the front doors, but something guided her around to the side instead, then up icy stairs, then through an unlocked door. Thankful to still be on her feet—so cold and stiff they burned each time she took a step—she padded down the shadowy hallway, praying for guidance, for some sign of which room might be hers. All the doors were shut. All but one. She pushed it open and then hobbled inside.

"This has to be my room," she whispered. "It *has* to be." Unfortunately, this wasn't the first time she'd found herself in such a pickle. It wasn't the first time she'd lost her way. She'd had nightmares before and awakened in strange surroundings, doubting her sanity more than once. She hated what she'd become—what she'd been forced to become.

Fighting her shakes and shivers, her teeth rattling so hard she could hear little else, she felt around the room for a lamp. There had to be one. Any kind would do. Whale oil, lard oil, or kerosene. Not gas. The room couldn't have gaslight. The chances of finding such a convenience in the West were slim, indeed.

The West. She remembered now. She was in Denver and had arrived last evening. Images and thoughts painted picture after picture in her mind. She put her hands to her temples to slow the dizzying recollections. She was chilled to the bone, and a reeling head only made things worse. She had to get warm. Fumbling around the still-dark room Meggie traced her fingers over the bedstead, glad to find a lamp. Matches, too. Quickly now, she lit the kerosene lamp. As soon as the tiny flame began to glow, she turned up the wick.

In the lamplight she hobbled over to the door and shut it,

15

then made her way to the bed. Gathering up the quilt atop it, she took painful steps over to the rocker by the window and gingerly sat down. Immediately, she hiked her nightdress up over her knees. She massaged first one foot and then the other to get her blood moving, pumping them in turn. Grateful when she felt the prickly needles tingle and shoot up and down her legs, she knew she hadn't suffered frostbite. She'd be all right.

Hah. Me, all right, she mused to herself. *Wouldn't that be a corker!*

Drawing the quilt closer about her shoulders, she nestled against the slatted back of the rocker. Her body began to settle but not her troubled thoughts.

She was far away from home now. Yesterday evening she'd checked into the American House, the largest hotel in Denver. Although she hadn't wanted to part with too much of her hard-earned coin, she thought it best to stay in the three-story, brick lodging instead of a boarding house. In such a big hotel, no one would notice her.

But what of the price? She couldn't remember. Very unlike her. She recalled the name she'd signed on the register: Rose Rochester. Her God-given name was Meghan Rose McMurphy, but for now she'd be Rose Rochester. Hopefully, the dear Lord would judge her lie only a small sin.

She pulled her knees up to her chest and settled farther into the rocker. It didn't matter that she was twenty-five years old, the childlike motion still eased her. Out of habit she pulled her cross out from beneath her nightdress and clasped the familiar wood between her hands, its size nearly filling them. Calmer and warmer now, she inspected her room.

It was a lovely room, much nicer than what she was used to. The wildflower pattern in the wallpaper reminded her of a garden. The iron bed frame had brass-trimmed rails. She stared at the flickering lamp on the bedstead, happy for the companionable light. Something drew her attention to the worn, maple washstand in one corner of the room. A white basin, pitcher, and stack of linen towels had been placed on it. The table was scratched. She could see the deep grooves even in the poor light. She could feel them. Jerking her gaze away, she spotted an oval mirror above the chamber set.

She didn't like mirrors.

What was the necessity of such a frivolity? Meggie knew she had red hair that always wanted to curl, violet eyes that changed color with her mood, a pale complexion dusted with freckles, an ordinary, turned-up nose, with nothing at all remarkable to say about her size or her height. What else did she need to know that any looking glass could reveal? Besides, she never took any pleasure from gazing at her own likeness.

No, she didn't like mirrors.

Meggie yanked her unpleasant thoughts from the mirror and finished inspecting the room. Next to a maple wardrobe was a settee. A braided carpet blanketed the area at the foot of the bed. The rug brought a cozy touch to the unfamiliar room.

This time had been the worst.

Maybe the exhausting train trip west had brought on her nightmarish episode. Yes, that was it. She knew she hadn't gone mad. She might be a lot of things, but mad wasn't one of them. But if anyone had seen her outside during the night, they could draw no other conclusion than to believe her insane. Surely no one lingered about at such an outlandish hour to witness her bizarre behavior. However could she explain herself if they had?

She couldn't.

Meggie looked out the window. A thick coat of frost created uneven frames around each of its panes. The lacy designs captivated her, as did the snowfall beyond. "No one better treat me as if I'm not in my right mind. No one better, ever . . ." Meggie whispered to the gentle flurries outside. That was her last thought before she fell asleep, cradled in the secure arms of the swaying rocker.

A rap on the door woke her.

"Mrs. Brenner. Mrs. Brenner." A youth called out. "Your comp'ny's here for breakfast."

Meggie didn't respond. Had she come inside the wrong room last night? Was this Mrs. Brenner's room, and not hers?

"Mrs. Brenner. Mrs. Brenner," the boy raised his voice. "Hope I'm not botherin' you, but I'm supposed to make shore you get the message, ma'am."

Meggie needed a moment to clear her head. She didn't want to make any mistakes.

"Mrs.—"

"It's *Miss Rochester,* young man," she called back, her body still in a tangle in the rocker. "I'm Miss Rochester, not Mrs. Brenner." She hoped and prayed the boy had been given the wrong room number.

Dead silence on the other side of the door.

"I'm powerful sorry, ma'am," the boy finally said. "Yep, shore am sorry."

He sounded nervous, bless his heart. Meggie smiled to herself. Youngsters had a way of making her smile. "Never mind, young man. You're not to worry," she consoled through the closed door. "And good luck in finding Mrs. Brenner."

"Well . . . well . . . thanks, ma'am. Yep, thanks," the boy mumbled back.

She listened as he ran down the hallway as only a boy can.

Breakfast. The mere suggestion of food helped Meggie unfurl her contorted limbs. Her stomach rumbled. Relieved to discover her stiff legs could support her, she padded toward the wardrobe and opened it. She let out the breath she'd been holding the moment she saw her things. Thank the dear Lord, she'd found the right room last night. Quickly now, she grabbed up the items she'd need and laid them out on the bed. First she must wash. Nothing was more important than the ritual of washing. It felt good to scrub her face and hands. Despite the frigid water in the pitcher, Meggie scoured her hands a second time. Replacing the linen, she cringed when she found herself staring at her reflection in the mirror. She didn't like what she saw. *I don't like mirrors.* She snatched up the damp towel and tossed it over the glass.

The room needed tidying. A clean room is a tithe to heaven, the sisters used to say. In no time Meggie was dressed, her hair pulled into a tight bun at her nape, with her bed made. A few russet tendrils always managed to escape her bun, but she paid little attention to the disobedient wisps.

Her stomach rumbled again. She looked around for her hooded shawl and her money. Offering up a quick prayer to express her gratitude for both, she thanked God for the wear left in the reliable, threadbare wool and for her twenty dollars. She reached into the bottom of the wardrobe to retrieve her indispensable. After she'd counted the coins inside the drawstring bag, she reassured herself that every penny was still there.

"No more than twenty-five cents for breakfast," she muttered in reminder.

The moment she saw her spectacles on the bedstead, she scooped up the wire rims. She wouldn't be caught in public without them, or her cross. Once the wire rims rested securely on the bridge of her nose, she was ready.

Delicious aromas from the hotel dining room greeted Meggie when she reached the landing at the top of the stairway. She felt faint, suddenly unable to remember when she'd last eaten. Still unsteady on her feet, she started down the carpeted staircase. No sooner had she reached the bottom, than she abruptly turned toward the hotel's front entrance rather than the dining room. On impulse, she just had to step outside and feel the cleansing snowflakes on her face. She didn't know why. Reassurance maybe—reassurance that she was all right this morning with no fiend from her nightmares in close pursuit. Bringing her shawl about her shoulders, she pulled the hood up until it reached the top of her forehead, readying herself for the cold.

The watchful desk clerk returned her nod as she crossed the lobby, and then out the doors of the main entrance.

One misplaced step onto the icy planked-porch landed Meggie squarely on her rump in the street. At once she found herself trapped in a bath of snow and slush. "Jesus, Mary, and Joseph!" It had to be her black lace-ups failing her on the slippery porch. She sucked in a self-conscious breath the moment she realized what she'd said. The sisters; what would they think of her?

"What the hell?" A husky voice swore from somewhere above her.

Meggie hadn't heard the man approach, much less feel the impact of someone practically stumbling over her. She held still, deathly still. At that moment her hood fell partway over her face. All she could see were two large, muddy boots sticking out from under the bottom of some kind of weathered greatcoat, only inches from her own booted feet. He was too close to her, way too close. Instinctively she whispered aloud. "Six feet under, six feet away, where to stay safe, the devil must stay! Six feet under—"

"Beg your pardon, ma'am?"

The stranger's deep, gravelly tone made her jump. It was difficult to hear anything over the wild thudding of her heart. To have the stranger so close terrified her. Gripping slush pinned her hands, keeping her trapped. Though instinct told her not to, she wanted to push her hood off her face so she could see the man. She wanted him to leave and to leave her alone! If she didn't say something soon, he might not.

"Ma'am?"

"Eh, yes?" She tried to sound matter-of-fact.

"Six feet what?"

Oh, dear Lord. She'd rambled on to a perfect stranger. Very unlike her. Willing herself to stay in control and to ignore her rising fear, she at last freed a hand. When she did, disobeying her instincts, she pushed back her hood and looked up.

That was Meggie's second slip of the morning.

The stranger's dusky scrutiny immediately penetrated the thick fabric of her brown woolen, exposing her, rendering her helpless. The falling snow offered little protection against him. What dark magic was at work? How else could she be so effortlessly imprisoned?

Afraid of the man, yet strangely drawn to him, she didn't understand what was happening. She tried to look away but couldn't. She'd never encountered any man before so handsome or tall or with such a formidable physique. The more she examined him, the more familiar he looked, almost as if he'd stepped right out of the pages of her favorite romance novel. She quickly dismissed such an absurd thought, and, compelled to do so, studied him up and down. Up the entire span of his oilcloth greatcoat, up over a presumably well-muscled body and broad shoulders, up over a clean-shaven jaw and firm mouth that twitched just enough to reveal a telltale dimple at one of its corners, and up over his straight, sculpted nose. No farther. It was his eyes, all slate and seductive shadow, that stopped her; that held her and dared her to look anywhere else. The ridge of his black Stetson rested low on his brow.

Flushed all over, Meggie didn't understand how she could feel so warm when she knew the day was not. More unnerved now than scared, she kept her gaze locked in his. Surely the stranger's disarming good looks were tools of the devil, meant to lure and entice, to wickedly tempt, and then devour.

Men are devils, *changeling* devils.

An unfamiliar quivering, a disturbance from somewhere deep inside her, threatened to shatter what was left of her already-fractured nerves. She was afraid of her own feelings as much as the man standing over her. Her defenses were down. She wasn't used to this feeling, and she didn't like it. The clear line between her nightmares and daydreams blurred. This scared her the most, making her doubt her sanity.

She had to get away, to escape this newest danger before it was too late.

CHAPTER TWO

Ethan didn't have time for this. He was late. His business meeting was important. He wanted to get to his downtown office early, before all the others; especially his partner, Uriah. He wanted to go over the details of the upcoming business merger with Uriah before their meeting. No, Ethan didn't have time for any delay.

He stared down at the woman keeping him from his office. Her garb surprised him. Who wore clothes like this? He'd only seen this kind of burdensome, plain dress on temperance women. With over fifty saloons and gambling halls in the city, this fool woman could be toting her signs up and down the streets for years. Ethan focused on the mud-spattered spectacles balancing on the tip of her reddened nose. A bookish temperance woman, to boot. The way she scrunched up her face just now to keep her wire rims on, struck him as something a child might do.

The snowfall picked up, but not enough to shield her luminous eyes from him. If he didn't know better, her eye color seemed to change a little each time her eyes opened and closed. Shades of violet deepened to black. It wasn't just the color that interested him. The way she looked up at him, vulnerable, like a snared rabbit, threw him off guard. Nope, that's one he didn't expect. And he didn't like it. The last thing he wanted was to strike fear in a woman. Something else reached out to him from those violet depths, something unreadable.

Ethan studied the curious female, from the wet strands of dark hair pulled well off her face, to the sprinkling of freckles on her cheeks. He stopped at her mouth, mesmerized by her rosy, full lips, and by the way she tugged on her lower lip with her upper one in little rhythmic motions. He ran his tongue over his own lips, then caught himself. What the hell was he doing? Comely or not, she was the most pitiable creature he'd run across in a long time. The sooner he helped her, the sooner he could get to his meeting.

"Ma'am, take my hand." Ethan extended his.

Meggie didn't take it.

"C'mon, just grab my hand."

"No." She spat out.

"No?"

"Yes."

"Yes? Then, let's have your hand," he said again.

"No!" she blurted, trying valiantly to get up and away from the unwanted assistance. Her efforts failed miserably. She couldn't even scoot backward in the slushy mire. Exasperation, weakness, hunger, the cold shudders, and sheer panic all joined forces, threatening to topple what little control she had left.

"C'mon, lady. Grab my hand." Ethan reached for her again.

"No! You don't need to help me. You don't need to come any closer." *Please, please just go away,* she pleaded silently. Others had begun to stop and stare. She felt walls closing in around her.

Ethan had had enough. He took hold of her.

"Let go of me!" Meggie yelled now and jerked her hand free. This landed her right back in the icy mire and sent her shawl flying.

That cross. With her cloak off, Ethan could see the cross dangling from its chain clear down to her waist. The woman last night wore a cross like that. *I'll be damned.* Why hadn't he realized it earlier? Same street. In front of the same hotel. This skittish, school-marm plain, temperance-preachy female was that same fool woman. Could be some kind of nun, for all he knew. Didn't they wear those crosses? He added Bible-thumper to his description of her. The idea of her being a Bible-thumper upset him the most. Ethan fought the sudden, overwhelming urge to leave the pathetic female in the street, wanting to be anywhere else. Now it all began to make sense to him. The reason the female had acted so crazy last night and still did was because she *was* crazy. He'd have to go real careful with her.

"It's all right, lady. Everything's all right. I won't come closer. That's a promise. You just take it easy. All right?"

Meggie bristled at the change in the stranger's tone and his choice of words. How dare he speak to her in such a way! "*I'm* taking it easy," she coolly replied, despite her fallen position. "You're the one who should take it easy. You're the one harassing me."

Ethan wasn't sure what to say next, what with the woman's mood switch.

"Stranger? Did you hear me? I don't want you to harass me any further."

"Harass you?" He couldn't believe it. "Listen, lady. I've been trying to help you out of a mess. If you don't understand that, then you're plum—" He managed to stop himself before he stated the obvious.

"Crazy? Plum crazy? Is that what you meant to say?" Unaware of her raised voice, Meggie struggled to get up, not a bit thwarted in yelling at him. "If you think you can practically knock down a perfect stranger and call her crazy, then . . . then you, sir, are the idiot!"

"Knock *you* down?" Ethan strained to hold his temper. A nutcase for sure; he didn't want to say or do something to further incite the irritating woman. The way she glared at him convinced him of her already-fevered state. Her eyes had switched colors on him. Now they were violet. How in blazes was he supposed to help her when she wouldn't let him? Tempted to leave her just where she was, he couldn't. He bent down and scooped her up.

Meggie panicked all over again. Her bravado of only moments before deserted her. Her heart pumped wildly. She couldn't breathe. The stranger's touch scared her to death. *Six feet under, six feet away, where to stay safe, the devil must stay!* On top of exasperation, weakness, hunger, and the cold, she'd no defense against the stranger! Where was that buzzing coming from? The dull vibrations in her ears picked up. Her vision clouded. Lightheaded, she shook her head back and forth, trying to get rid of the sudden, queer feeling.

"Sam Hill." Ethan swore under his breath when he realized the dang-fool woman was about to go into a swoon. His meeting was important. He didn't want to miss it because of some unhinged, school-marm-plain, sign-toting, temperance-marching, Bible-thumping female about to faint dead away on the street.

That's exactly what Meggie did.

Dammit! Ethan held the unconscious woman in his arms, surprised she didn't weigh much. Under all of her wet getup he'd expected her to have a fuller shape. Her spectacles suddenly toppled onto her breast, just catching the end of her cross. Ethan looked away, and, ignoring all the stares, made it to the entrance of the American House Hotel in several strides. The woman he carried stayed in a faint. He pushed the hotel door open with his heavy boot and presented his odd baggage to the clerk waiting behind the registration counter. The stout little bald man's head barely cleared the top of the desk.

"Does this belong to you, Cottswell?" Ethan spat his question to the surprised clerk.

"Why . . . why . . . mornin', Mr. Rourke." The clerk looked up at Ethan rather than at the lifeless female in his arms. He'd seen her leave the hotel earlier.

"Does she belong to you, Cottswell?" Ethan bellowed. He didn't try to hide his irritation with the whole situation.

The runty clerk looked at the female in question.

"Her? You mean, she? You mean Miss . . . Miss—" he stammered, then pulled the hotel register in front of him, quickly running a stubby forefinger down the list of signatures.

"Yeah, Miss Rochester. Miss Rose Rochester. She arrived yesterday. Registered last evenin'."

"Good. She does belong to you. Well, where do I put her?"

The clerk didn't answer.

Ethan's patience wore thin. The look he shot back indicated just that.

"But Mr. Rourke, is she—?" The clerk wiped beads of perspiration from his brow, apparently searching for his nerve. Once he'd tucked his handkerchief into a pocket, he clasped his hands together as if he were in a church. "Is she a goner?"

It wasn't unusual for a body or two to be found on Denver's rowdy streets, with almost every outlaw, card shark, cowboy, carpetbagger, gold-seeker and silver-hungry man in the Colorado Territory in town. It wasn't unusual at all. But a woman?

"Hell, no." Ethan wanted to say *you idiot,* but stopped himself. "Fainted dead away out front."

The little man appeared relieved.

"Her room key. Let's have it," Ethan ordered.

Receptive now, the clerk turned around and pulled the spare key from its hook on the panel behind the counter. He stepped up onto a stool to reach it.

"I'll show you, Mr. Rourke. Right this way." Scurrying from behind the hotel desk, he started up the stairway, already a bit winded from the exercise.

If he hadn't been in such a bad temper, Ethan would have laughed at the way the stocky little man held onto the lapels of his poorly fitted, tailor-made suit as if he were leading some important expedition for lost treasure. Ethan followed, all the while wondering if what he held in his arms was any kind of lost treasure. He guessed not.

The woman was still in a faint, and he reckoned she was much easier to deal with this way. He hoped she'd stay out cold until he left her room. The thought of her coming to and tearing into him didn't sit well. Once inside her room, Ethan gently deposited her on the bed.

Cottswell waited in the doorway.

"Mr. Rourke?"

Ethan turned to face him.

"Mr. Rourke, I'll just send the wife up to help. All right?"

"I'll wait," Ethan said.

Seconds turned into too many minutes. When the clerk's wife failed to show up Ethan decided he couldn't wait for the female nuisance to freeze to death, so he looked around for dry clothing. He spotted the wardrobe and went over to it. The wardrobe's meager contents surprised him. She sure didn't own much. He pulled out a cotton shift, quickly tossing it onto the head-rail, and then scanned the room for a trunk or some type of bag. He didn't expect to find a Saratoga exactly, but a little more than an old, empty satchel and a book. He picked the leather-bound volume up off the foot of her bed. It wasn't a Bible as he'd expected. It was something called *Jane Eyre*. He'd never heard of it. He tossed the book back on the bed.

Ethan had an unimpaired view of the disheveled, unconscious woman. A few particles of sleet still clung to her face. Closer now, leaning over her, freezing droplets from his weathered Stetson fell onto her face. He took off his dripping hat and threw it on top of the book he'd just tossed onto the bed. When he reached down to wipe away the wetness from her face, her skin was stone cold. He jerked his hand away and swallowed hard. Was she dead? Somewhere between the street and her room, had the fool woman died? He stared at her cross. Death wasn't a stranger to him. He'd seen men die before, but he couldn't take being around a dead woman.

Ethan forced himself to put his hand just over her nose and mouth. Warm little pants against his unsteady fingers convinced him she was alive. At least she'd done him the favor of not up and dying on him. Still, his insides turned. He ripped her cross away and tossed it onto the nearby bedstead, not wanting to look at it. Her wire rims fell onto the bed, but he didn't notice.

He studied her face. Her skin, less red now, had lost most of its ruddiness from the cold. He could see a few freckles pepper her delicate turned-up nose. Her complexion reminded him of morning cream lightly sprinkled with nutmeg. Should he touch it or taste it? Suddenly tempted to do both, he settled for a touch. When he ran the fingertips of one hand over her freckled cheeks, he discovered he'd been right. Smoother than cream. Reluctantly, he pulled his hand away. Didn't know if any woman had felt that soft before. He didn't like the fact that he liked it— that he liked touching her. He stepped back from the bed, puzzled by his unexplained reaction. Hell, he didn't even know the danged woman, and he for sure had no desire to get to know her.

Crazy female's making me crazy.

Ethan didn't have a choice. He had to get her out of her wet clothes. Still blacked out, she sure as hell couldn't do it. And the cursed clerk's wife apparently didn't want to do it. He'd have to do it himself. Grudgingly he yanked her dry shift down from the bed's head-rail where he'd tossed it. He'd make quick work of this. But as soon as he started to unbutton the soaked

29

woolen, he realized, like everything else so far this morning, things weren't going to go as he planned.

Undressing a female wasn't anything new for Ethan, but he'd never removed clothing from an unconscious woman, and never had he undone an outfit like this. All thumbs, he couldn't budge any of the tight little buttons at her neck. He'd have to start somewhere else. Why the hell would anyone wear such trouble? If she were awake, he could cut the thing off and give her money to buy something new. But if he ruined her dress now, he could predict the tirade she'd go into when she discovered the damage. He didn't want to chance dealing with that. When a few buttons finally gave way at her waist, he worked upward.

He inhaled a faint scent of something. Not perfume. He didn't think it was perfume. Wildflowers, maybe. He'd have to work past the distracting fragrance. Blasted dress. Another stubborn button. Intent on his task, Ethan didn't realize his hands rested just over her bosom until too late. Even through the thick layers of clothing, he fought the urge to splay his fingers over the soft mounds. Finally the last button of her high-necked costume gave way.

Still in a faint, Meggie was oblivious to his ministrations.

In no time, Ethan had her dress off her shoulders and pulled down below her waist. It was what she had on under her dress that surprised him now. Instead of a corset, it was another dratted, damp gown buttoned clear up to her neck. He glanced at the white cotton he'd taken down from the head-rail. Same thing, he figured. Once he had her dress off, he undid the wet, stiff laces of her boots and removed them before he tackled her undergarments. The buttons gave way far too easily this time. Ethan wasn't ready for what he saw when he pulled the shift off her shoulders and down to her waist.

He tried to avoid her partially-naked beauty, doing his best to ignore his own stirrings, and quickly trained his gaze downward to her feet. That didn't help him much. One of her heavy, black cotton stockings had slipped a little, revealing more of one comely knee than should be revealed. Before he realized what he was doing, he was staring at her naked loveliness again . . . at her perfectly formed breasts . . . at her tiny waist—no, sir! Won't touch any of that.

Ethan exhaled hard. There wasn't a spot on her that wasn't as alluring as the next. Nutmeg and cream all over. He'd never seen such a confection. She didn't look too crazy to him now. Anything but, with all those soft curves. Quick as he could, he pulled off the wet shift; leaving her in her pantalets and stockings, and then pulled the quilt over her. He'd get her in her dry shift but didn't trust himself just yet.

Meggie squirmed in bed, as if in pain.

Ethan didn't know what to do. The woman looked like she was hurt or something. Hell, he wasn't any doc. Maybe something was caught under her. Her wet hair. He'd never been so hesitant to touch a woman. Gently, he rolled her onto her side.

Son of a bitch!

Scars—her back was covered with them.

Ethan wasn't repelled. He was mad. Who would have done this to her? Beat her like an animal? No wonder she was hurting. Her wet clothes and hair must have aggravated her injuries. He ran his fingers over one scar and then another, trying to imagine what could have happened to her. The woman did act crazy. Maybe she'd been in one of those asylums, those places where they lock people away. Maybe she'd got the scars there. Crazy or not, she didn't deserve this. He angrily jerked his handkerchief out of his jacket pocket, then gently pulled her hair aside and dried her back. Then, just as gently, he eased her back on the bed and arranged the quilt over her.

Meggie settled. Her brow smoothed.

Scars or not, Ethan found her beautiful. Long, dark lashes fluttered against her creamy complexion. Her lids remained closed under soft, scarlet brows. His body stirred again. She moved slightly, a faint moan escaping her rosy lips. For the briefest of moments, he imagined her moaning . . . for him.

Aw, hell. He needed to get out of there.

Losing no time now, he slid the quilt down, and then managed to quickly pull the dry gown over her without waking her. Despite his haste, he made sure to get all of her loose, wet hair out from the inside of her shift.

Meggie squirmed again but didn't seem in pain. Quite the opposite.

Ethan pulled the quilt clear up to her neck, then backed away from the bed. Without warning, out came her arms from under the quilt. He should have headed for the door, but instead, he watched her pull her slender arms up over her head, and then stretch them along the pillow.

Moaning softly, Meggie nestled her whole body deeper under the quilt. Then, ever so slowly, she opened her eyes and looked right into Ethan's.

"Edward. Oh, Edward," she whispered to the figure standing next to her bed. "Dear Edward." She met his steel-gray gaze before hers traveled lovingly over his well-formed brow, then down past his sculpted, straight nose to rest on a strong, firm mouth. His lips twitched ever so slightly. Her insides fluttered, sending tremors to her very core. A telltale dimple appeared at one corner of his mouth, and her tremors grew as she drank in his handsome features.

I love you so, Edward.

How she wanted to run her fingers through his thick, dark hair; lingering to rub together the rough ends where it had been cropped off at the neck. How she longed to have his gentle, hungry lips pressed against her waiting mouth. To be gathered up in his strong embrace with his body against hers, the two of them melted together into one. Slowly and deliberately his dusky scrutiny worked its spell, exposing and fascinating her.

Oh, Edward, you are my love, my life. Touch me. Love me.

Tides of heated pleasure rhythmically pulsed the insides of her aroused body. Desire mounted and exploded into blissful ecstasy. "Edward. Oh, Edward!" she moaned at the height of her passion. In that instant she shut her eyes and prayed nothing would ever harm him.

Stay safe, my Edward . . . always safe.

Ethan was out the door and down the hallway in seconds, taking no chance on the woman opening her eyes again before he'd left.

"You all right, Miss Rochester?"

A woman's child-like voice startled Meggie. She blinked several times, and then stared blankly at the little woman standing next to her bed. Who was the woman and where was her Edward?

Edward?

Oh, good heavens!

Meggie realized she'd been dreaming about her romantic hero, Edward Rochester, again.

"Wh-who are you?" Meggie sputtered. "Whh-what happened? What on earth am I doing in bed? Did someone . . . was someone here?" She peered around the room and halfway expected dear Edward to reappear. How silly and foolish! Edward Rochester only existed on the pages of her beloved romance novel, *Jane Eyre*. She could hardly expect him to materialize in the flesh, in a hotel in Denver! "Whatever is going on?" Meggie asked, buying time to clear her fuzzy thoughts, all the while throwing off her quilt and trying to climb out of bed.

The little woman stopped her. "Now just hold on there, Miss

Rochester. You gave everyone quite a scare. Fainted right out in the street, you did," the woman said, and placed her small hands on Meggie's shoulders, attempting to press her back down in bed. "You should rest now. Why there's no tellin' what ails you."

Meggie bristled.

"I declare. You have to be very careful now, young lady. Could be you're carryin' and—"

Meggie would not tolerate this conversation, this insult, another second. She sat straight up in bed.

"Thank you, but I'm fine," she said through gritted teeth, not hiding her irritation. "Don't trouble yourself another moment. I'm certain you have better things to occupy your time rather than needless worry over me, Mrs.—"

"Well, well," the elfish woman pouted back. She straightened the lace collar of her blue calico dress. "My name's Mrs. Cottswell and I was just tryin' to help you, dear. My husband and I run this hotel."

Meggie softened, at once guilty over her unkind words to Mrs. Cottswell. "Thank you, Mrs. Cottswell. Truly, I appreciate your help, but I'm fine now."

"Well all right, if you're sure. I'll just be on my way then," Mrs. Cottswell kept on as she walked toward the door. "When you're up to it, come down to the dining room and get some vittles. A hearty meal should fix you right up. Food always does. Yes indeedy." She threw Meggie a bright smile before she closed the door.

Despite demanding hunger pangs, Meggie didn't get out of bed. She lay back down, nestling her head onto the pillow. *Imagine me carrying a child?*

Absurd.

Ridiculous.

Impossible.

She turned toward the frosty window, forcing her thoughts

onto the gray day outside rather than on herself. If it snowed like this in October, what must the dead of winter be like? Denver had been nothing but a puzzle so far. For so long her life had been fine. Things hadn't turned this upside down in years. Why now? She didn't like the obvious answer, knowing full well what had brought her to Denver. But then she thought of the stranger she'd encountered on the street. Most assuredly, her upset *wasn't* because of him.

Even if he were the most handsome man she'd ever seen in her life, why should that matter? Why should she care? She didn't. She made a point to avoid such men, to steer clear of any such "accidents" in her life. But something about this particular man niggled at her insides. She couldn't get it out of her mind that she knew him from somewhere. How on earth could she possibly recognize someone she'd never met? Frustrated, she turned onto her stomach and gave her pillow a thump before resting her head.

At that moment the oddest sensation hit her from her privates—a damp tingle. She quickly turned back over in bed. She didn't have time to be sick. She'd already had two serious brushes with cold weather since her arrival in Denver, and she couldn't afford any more wasted time in the hotel. Then she remembered her fall outside in the snow and slush. The wetness had soaked through her clothes right to her pantalets. Of course, her pantalets were still wet . . . yet . . . how could she feel so strange, so tingly, from a simple fall? And it wasn't even . . . it didn't feel . . . she didn't feel sick . . . *there.*

Immediately ashamed of such thoughts, Meggie bolted from her bed.

CHAPTER THREE

Meggie knew it was wrong to think about her physical body. It was sinful and wicked to think such thoughts. Setting her mind elsewhere, she quickly changed into dry undergarments, pulled on her other wool dress, this one gray, and brushed the mud off her soggy boots; all the while plagued with questions. How did she get from the street to her room? Who brought her up? Mrs. Cottswell couldn't have carried her upstairs. And it couldn't have been Mr. Cottswell. Why, he wasn't much bigger than his wife. Meggie couldn't imagine who—but then she thought of the man from the street—the darkly handsome, foreboding man who'd run into her.

Did he bring her up to her room and get her into dry under things, her inexpressibles? No man had any business ever, ever coming that close! She sank into the nearby rocker, closing her eyes, needing to calm down. Her heart pounded as she thought about the stranger, but not out of fear; not exactly. Something gnawed at her insides. The queer feeling was unfamiliar. She pushed out of the rocker. It was probably just hunger. She should eat a little.

Something else nagged at her. The hair on the back of her neck always stood on end, signaling danger, when she felt threatened. Why hadn't it happened when the westerner touched her? She remembered his touch and swallowed hard. Collecting her cross in both hands, she cupped the familiar wood before reaching up to reposition her now-clean wire rims on the bridge of her nose. Slowly, she moved her fingers to the back of her neck to feel the tiny bristles that surely were there. But no, nothing at all from the unsettling stranger's touch; nothing but the racing of her heart. She'd rather have her hair on end than this.

Meggie whisked *Jane Eyre* from the foot of her bed. *Jane Eyre* always brought her comfort. Surprised to find its leather damp, she rubbed her fingers, then the sleeve of her dress over the precious volume to help dry her beloved romance. A little moisture wet the frayed leather just like—*there,* in her privates. She thought of the stranger again. His handsome visage loomed in front of her. Meggie held onto *Jane Eyre* even tighter. She treasured the worn pages above all else in her desolate existence. Despite the differences in their lives, Jane's struggles were hers. Jane's successes were hers. She knew she'd never find the happiness in real life that Jane had found with Edward Rochester on the page. She wouldn't look for it. Meggie hastily tucked the novel under her bed pillow, then turned toward the wardrobe to take out the coins she'd need for breakfast.

Ethan hadn't enjoyed his own breakfast.

Usually he couldn't get enough of Nettie's breakfast, but not this morning. He didn't feel like eating what his devoted housekeeper had prepared. He ignored the likely reason—his earlier run-in with Rose Rochester. He poured himself a second cup of coffee; he'd needed to get back downtown. Uriah waited for him. Uriah wouldn't understand his delay. Hell, he didn't understand why he'd come home before going to the office. Uriah must be chomping at the bit by now.

Not a hair on Uriah's head had changed in all the years Ethan had known him. They'd met on the same wagon train west. Uriah wasn't more than fifteen at the time, only a year younger than Ethan. They partnered up right away. For two young rowdies with little education, they'd not done badly in their fifteen years together. Uriah had a knack for ferreting out gold from bedrock, and Ethan had a keen business sense. The two soon became known for their fairness and honesty, a rarity with so much valuable ore around. Their friendship had worked for a lot of years. Ethan could always count on his partner.

This morning the deal to complete the wagon road over Berthoud Pass, begun by Russell from Empire City back in '63, would be finalized. Ethan and Uriah were the key players and had invited a group of associate partners to come in on their enterprise. It made good business sense Ethan thought, although he was worried about two of the investors.

Bart Gentry and Angus Tritt.

Ethan couldn't figure why Gentry dragged his feet. Hadn't every deal he'd let him in on been a success? Hell, the Black Hawk find alone was a killing. Maybe running the stage line into Indian country gave Gentry cold feet. Ethan never pegged Gentry for yellow. Greedy, yes. Gentry had always been ready for a dollar. In the seven years they'd had dealings together, Gentry had never hid his greed. Ethan didn't know why he trusted him. Maybe he just wanted to because of Gentry's brother dying at Breckenridge. Too many lives were lost in that mine accident. Maybe it was because Gentry put all his cards on the table, or so Ethan believed. Bad idea or not, it was too late now. Things were already in play. Hell, Ethan even let that bastard Tritt, head of the First National, in on this one. He'd caved when Gentry leaned on him to include Tritt. Ethan already regretted it.

Tritt had turned into a greedy son of a bitch, dipping into his customers' pockets to line his own. He'd raised his rates at the bank, and made it harder for folks in need to take out loans. Same as Gentry, Tritt liked the money too much. This was the last time. No matter that Tritt had been an esteemed, and at one time, ethical banker. Ethan wouldn't do any more business with him after this, banking or otherwise.

Having already made his fortune, Ethan wasn't in this latest venture for profit. He wanted to help cut a path through the mountains, to be a part of opening up the West. It was important to everybody on the frontier. It was important to him for lots of reasons, not the least of which was staying busy. He liked it that way. Less time to think—to remember.

He took a last swallow of coffee. It didn't go down well. He scooted out his chair. It was high-time he got downtown.

"To our success, gentlemen. To the Colorado Overland Stage Company." Ethan's associates raised their glasses of whiskey to join him in the toast.

Bart Gentry didn't raise his glass.

Usually watchful, Ethan didn't notice.

By now a pair of distracting violet eyes blocked his vision. By now creamy skin sprinkled with nutmeg coated his thoughts. One thing was certain. The Rochester woman couldn't be any kind of nun. No nun would be moaning like that, fancying such pleasure with a man. The Rochester woman wasn't any stranger to passion. She sure felt it for "Edward." He couldn't decide if this Edward was a lucky man or not. Whichever way you looked at it, the female was trouble. Who'd be willing to saddle himself with such an armful?

I sure as hell wouldn't.

"Say Ethan?" Uriah broke into Ethan's thoughts. All the others had left.

"Yeah?"

"Ethan, what's gotcha lookin' so funny? The meetin' went off without a hitch. You look like you just ate somethin' that don't agree with you." The big man stood in front of Ethan's desk.

Ethan had to laugh. "You got that right, partner. I guess I did come up against something disagreeable."

"Like I said, what's gotcha goin'?" Uriah wouldn't let the subject go. He touched both sides of his thick, blond mustache with a beefy finger, content to wait for an answer.

Ethan leaned back in his desk chair. Its hinges creaked. He wasn't about to tell his old friend he'd run into a harebrained female who dressed like she was on her way to a revival and acted like she was in need of one. Besides, Uriah was almost as bad as his housekeeper; both meant well, but Ethan could do without their worries. If Nettie didn't fuss over him about this or that, Uriah tried to get him over to have that supper his sister forever wanted to cook up for him. Ethan always ignored Nettie's doting and always turned down Uriah's invite.

Ethan got up, still disregarding Uriah's question, and started for the coat rack by the front door. A thin layer of ice had built up on the inside of the glass panes. He pulled his heavy oilcloth slicker down off its peg and made a mental note to check the seals on the frame after this latest storm.

Uriah came up behind him.

Ethan took his Stetson from the shelf above the pegs, positioning it down low on his brow before he slipped his arms through the sleeves of his coat and turned to face Uriah. Neither man stood a hair under six feet four.

"Listen, what doesn't agree with me is whiskey on an empty stomach," Ethan finally answered his friend. "What do you say we head over to Larimer's?"

Uriah followed him out.

"Say Ethan, is Byers gonna stay up in Hot Sulphur Springs the whole winter? With us runnin' that first Concord up there tomorrow, it won't look so good if he idn't there," he gave voice to his worries, catching up to Ethan now.

"William isn't going anywhere, Uriah. He's not leaving his town and the hotel he just built. He's digging in right along with the other settlers. It's all set," Ethan reassured him. "After the stage clears Berthoud Pass, it's on past Grimshaw's haystacks to Junction House. We've Rollins to thank for the use of the stage stop. Then it's easy going to Hot Sulphur Springs."

"What about the Utes, Ethan? Think they'll give us any trouble?"

"No more than I'll give you, if you don't stop asking so many questions." Ethan tried to joke about something that wasn't a joking matter. He had the same concerns as Uriah.

Uriah smiled, but he knew better than to think Ethan wasn't worried, too.

The pair walked the rest of the way to Larimer's in silence.

Eternally grateful to see Mr. Cottswell occupied, because she was still embarrassed over fainting outside, Meggie walked silently past the hotel desk. Time enough after breakfast to face him. Before she confronted the clerk, she needed to put some food in her stomach. She kept walking toward the dining room, not risking a stop to admire the lacy glass shades of the chandelier overhead, or to sit a moment on the circular Victorian couch in the center of the lobby. She must take extra care now to avoid any more accidents.

"Good mornin' to you, lass."

A plump, apple-cheeked woman greeted Meggie at the dining room entrance.

"Would you be likin' a table now? Sure in that you would. Why else would you be a comin' in? 'Ere I am goin' on when you're likely 'ungry as can be."

Meggie warmed to the pleasant Irish woman. She smiled back. "Why yes. I would like a table. Anywhere will do. In the corner or just anywhere."

"Go on. In the corner. What are you sayin'? You think I'd tuck a nice Irish lass such as yourself away in the corner? Go on with you. Never a'tall."

"Irish? How do you know I'm Irish?"

"An' what kind of a fool would I be not to've noticed your red hair an' all? Gracious me. May the Blarney stone fall right into the sea if I'm wrong about you! Just because you don't 'ave a touch of the brogue in you don't a'tall mean you're not as Irish as the wee little people themselves."

Meggie laughed. "The little people. Yes, I know all about them. I may have brought a leprechaun or two with me from Boston for all anyone knows." Meggie was getting into the spirit of the conversation and enjoying it so much that she didn't realize she'd revealed anything about herself to the kindly hostess.

"Well, come along then. Let's find you a wee cozy table you can 'ave all to yourself."

The round woman's starched white apron made the queerest crunching sounds as she moved between the tables, making Meggie smile.

" 'Ere you go, lass. Right by the window an' near the Franklin stove."

Glad to be situated by the fire, Meggie sat down at the table.

"Came in on the Kansas-Pacific yesterday, did you?"

"Why yes. Yes I did," Meggie answered, surprised that the hostess knew.

"An' would you now be wonderin' just 'ow I come to know that? Well, most all our guests come on that very same train, they do. A good guess, don't you think?"

"Yes," Meggie said. "A very good guess, indeed."

"An' may I be askin' you if you came all the way west for our snow? Would you believe it? Snow already. We can only ask our blessed Lord to keep most of it away for a wee bit yet. Time enough for such weather as this." The woman at last seemed to remember why they were both there. "Now lass, what is it you'll be 'avin? We've got batter cakes, chipped beef on beaten biscuits, potatoes, sausage, bacon an' eggs, an' sure an' now the best fried pies west of the Mississippi River itself!"

Meggie moistened her lips. It all sounded wonderful. Then she remembered the silver dollar still clutched in her hand. She wouldn't spend any more than twenty-five cents out of it.

"Just some coffee and a biscuit would be very nice. I'm really not so hungry," she added self-consciously. "Just what I ordered. That's all I want."

"I'll be bringin' it out to you right away, with a little jam and butter, I will."

Meggie's stomach growled in anticipation of any kind of sustenance. Embarrassed over it and over her poor finances, she concentrated on the cheery fire in the nearby wood stove rather than look elsewhere. After a respectable interval, she raised her chin and glanced about the room. There were two other tables with customers seated. No one looked in her direction. The tables were covered in white linen and set with blue flowered china. The little blossoms provided a marked contrast to the snow outside. Meggie peered out through the window's tatted sheers. The designs woven into the curtains matched the lacy patterns of falling snow.

Just then she thought of her earlier encounter with the stranger in that same snow. The aggravating, annoyingly handsome man who'd so far managed to ruin her day. She hadn't even had her breakfast yet. *I guess he's trying to ruin my breakfast, too!* In protest, she yanked her gaze from the window; far easier to do than yank the notion from her thoughts that she knew him from somewhere.

" 'Ere you go, lass." The hostess returned and set down a platter laden with more than what Meggie had ordered. Bacon and eggs came with the biscuits and coffee, along with a plate of fried apple pies and jam and butter.

"I'm sorry. I'm sorry, but I didn't order all of this. There's been a mistake." Meggie protested. It all looked and smelled so good, but she couldn't allow this. She couldn't spend this kind of money on a meal. Was that pity she read in the kind server's eyes? Meggie's back bristled. After all, she had some pride left. "Please. I'm sure this is someone else's order," she repeated.

"No mistake, lass. All paid for. You've not a choice in the world. Now eat up. It's a 'earty meal you be needin' in this cold."

Before Meggie could say anything more, the woman had disappeared into the kitchen. All paid for? Surely this was a mistake. She shouldn't eat a bite until she'd sorted this out. But the hot food in front of her was too tempting. It smelled wonderful. Suddenly ravenous, she picked up her fork and dove into the eggs. Her silver dollar fell to her lap. She barely noticed. Had anything ever tasted so good? The biscuits, too. She spread the strawberry jam so thick on the biscuits that some oozed down her fingers. She didn't care, delighting in the flavor of the ripe berries when she licked her fingertips.

When she finished eating, she took up her mug of coffee. Holding it in both hands, she sank back against her chair, intent on enjoying every sip of the delicious brew. The instant she looked out the window, she saw two tall, formidable men standing in front of her, their backs turned. She stayed calm. After all, they were outside while she was inside. They were just two men talking, paying her no mind. She mustn't think every man she saw is a threat, out to get her, for mercy's sake. Then something about one of the men drew her particular attention. She watched as he raised an arm and placed a hand on the other man's shoulder. The simple movement triggered her recollection.

Him.

The stranger.

The same man on the street.

The same man in her room.

Meggie's heart raced. Her chest tightened. She felt sick to her stomach. The meal she'd just enjoyed threatened to come back up. But try as she might, she couldn't tear her eyes away from the stranger.

"So, what'll it be, Ethan? Back to the office or the First National?"

Ethan gave his friend a mild slap on the shoulder. "Well, pard, how about neither? Thought maybe you'd like to take care of that little matter. I'm not in the mood to deal with Tritt again today. That banker sours me every time."

"No problem, Ethan. I ain't been in a decent scrap all week. It'll be dessert after such fine fixin's."

"Thanks." Ethan reached inside the pocket of his slicker and took out his tobacco pouch. He made quick work of rolling a smoke, then fumbled around in another pocket and searched for a match.

"Say, Ethan?"

He knew what was coming before Uriah could ask.

"Wanna come over to the house tonight for supper? The folks are always askin' about you. And you know my little sis. She's bakin' somethin' special."

"Thanks, but I can't. Besides, don't you have plans with that gal from the mercantile?" he teased, changing the subject.

"Shucks. Me? Who'd wanna be seen with this ugly mug?" Uriah tried to make a joke of it. He'd never met any woman who'd been attracted to him. They all liked Ethan well enough, but not him. He never resented the fact. Wasn't in his nature.

"Denver's full of gals just waiting to be smitten with the likes of you," Ethan said. Uncomfortable now with the turn of their conversation, he resumed his hunt for a match. "I'm heading over to the train depot. That shipment of survey equipment should have arrived from Kansas City yesterday. See you back at the office."

"Sure thing," Uriah agreed. The First National was just across the way.

The wind had kicked up, making Ethan's task to light his smoke difficult. The snow continued. He turned his tall frame against the snowy gusts and looked for a dry place to strike a match. He leaned in toward the hotel restaurant window and lit his smoke. Once he'd taken a deep draw on the tobacco, before he pulled away from the window, he looked through it . . . through rivulets of pelting sleet . . . through little glass spectacles . . . right into Rose Rochester's unmistakable eyes.

Ethan recognized her all right. *Damn.* He turned away from the window and headed into the wind and the welcome distraction of the snowfall.

If only she'd been looking anywhere else. If only she'd been anywhere else, then maybe she wouldn't have seen him again. Meggie tried to take another sip of coffee, but her hands trembled so, she had trouble holding the mug. The stranger's steel gray gaze pierced through her still. With shaky fingers, she reached behind her neck to feel the hairs that would surely be bristled there, signaling danger.

Despite the fact that she struggled daily with not overreacting to every man who came near, she expected the hair at her nape to bristle at the mere thought of the foreboding stranger. He unnerved her. He unsettled her. She should be frightened to death of him. But again, just as before, her neck was smooth. None of this made any sense. Meggie didn't understand why she didn't react to the stranger. He was dangerous; surely he was. Was it his disturbing good looks that fooled her? They shouldn't. She never cared about looks.

"I've never cared," Meggie muttered aloud.

"What's that you say, lass? Would you be wantin' anythin' else?"

Meggie jumped at the question. She hadn't heard the hostess approach.

"No, I'm fine. I was just saying I don't want anything else now."

"Lass, if you don't mind me sayin', you look a wee bit peaked. Sure an' now, are you all right?"

"Oh, truly I'm fine. Thank you. Thank you for asking." Meggie managed a weak smile. Grateful when the hostess cleared the dishes and disappeared back into the kitchen, Meggie stared out through the frosty windows. She was relieved to find the stranger gone. Wasn't she? *Of course I am!* She shot up out of her chair. Her silver dollar clinked loudly when it fell to the floor. She'd forgotten all about the coin. And she'd forgotten that her meal had been paid for. Too drained to worry over it now, Meggie declared the mystery of the paid-for-meal a stroke of good luck. If her good luck held, she'd get the answers she needed now from Mr. Cottswell.

"I would appreciate a moment of your time, Mr. Cottswell," Meggie blurted out the moment she arrived at the front desk, before she lost her nerve to talk to him.

"Why, of course, Miss Rochester. Anythin' you want," the clerk gushed, grinning at her from ear to ear.

His ready use of her name and his solicitude threw Meggie off guard, making her almost forget her purpose.

"Schools, sir. Could you tell me about the schools here in Denver and where they are located?"

Heartened to hear of two schools, one on Stout Street and the other on Arapahoe, she listened carefully to Mr. Cottswell. She was so intent on the clerk, her back now to the hotel entrance, she didn't hear the door open. She didn't see the shadowy figure clad in dark pin stripe and wearing a black bowler, enter. She didn't turn for a look when she felt a chill breeze brush past her. Only when her fingers moved automatically to the back of her neck to rub over the hairs standing on end . . . only then did it register that someone, something wicked . . . *is here.*

Slowly, reluctantly, Meggie turned away from the counter to search the lobby with her gaze. Not a soul. Her mind must be playing tricks on her again. Relieved to discover no one lurking about, she tried to relax. She couldn't. The hairs on the back of her neck still stood on end. Struggling for composure, she faced Mr. Cottswell again. She had to find work and lose herself amid the many townsfolk in Denver. The sooner she disappeared into anonymity, the better.

Anything but anonymous in Denver, Ethan nodded at the wiry stationmaster once he'd stepped inside the depot.

"Afternoon, Mr. Rourke."

"Afternoon, Harold. Just stopped by to see if the shipment I'm expecting arrived on the Kansas train yesterday."

"It sure did, Mr. Rourke. I'll just go and make sure of your order. Won't be a minute," Harold said and disappeared into the back room.

Ethan stood in front of the caged window. He looked down at the open train register, just the other side of window. Curious, needing something to do while he waited, he slid his fingers beneath the bottom bar and turned the book. He saw a list of names and pulled the register closer. It appeared to be an account of the handful of passengers who'd come in on yesterday's train. The date at the top was right. He scanned it for Rose Rochester's name. All the passengers were men except one: *Meghan R. McMurphy.*

He looked the list up and down again to make sure of what

he'd read. The only woman who'd arrived yesterday was a Meghan R. McMurphy. No Rose Rochester to be found. So Miss Rochester wasn't Miss Rochester after all, but a Miss McMurphy. Hell, should he add criminal to his description of her? Well, sir, it wasn't his problem. She wasn't his problem. But for some unexplained reason he just happened to knock over the nearby bottle of ink which just happened to blot out all the names of the previous day's passengers—hers most of all. Ethan stepped away from the station window, wanting to put distance between himself and Nutmeg. Unaware he'd used the endearment, he'd wait outside the depot for Harold to return with his order.

Ethan pulled out his tobacco makings, suddenly needing another smoke. No, sir. Nutmeg wasn't his worry.

CHAPTER FOUR

"I don't have any place for you here."

"But you must," Meggie insisted, keeping a respectable distance from the headmaster. Not once during the entire train trip west did it occur to her that she would have difficulty finding work as a teacher.

"Miss Rochester, our school here at Arapahoe is fully staffed. Try the Stout Street School."

Too upset to reply, Meggie gave the headmaster a polite nod, then left, intent now on finding Stout Street. She didn't want to think about being turned away again, but turned away she was. There were no teaching positions available, and the Stout Street headmaster held open little promise for one in the future.

It had stopped snowing. Meggie barely noticed. She hadn't expected this. She hadn't expected to be shut out of a teaching job in a place as large as Denver. Only two jobs were available for women in the West: teaching or prostitution. She'd never become a prostitute. She'd die first. Since she wasn't married and never would be, teaching was her only option.

Meggie thought of the money she had left to live on. Less than twenty dollars. She had to be careful and make it last. Being alone was nothing new to her. Being destitute was nothing new to her. But being alone and destitute in the rugged west was something altogether new, and scared her almost as much as her night terrors. Almost. She couldn't go back to Boston. That wasn't an option.

The wind picked up. Meggie trudged aimlessly through foot-deep snow, mindless of the cold. The hem of her skirt, dampened and dragging her down, matched her mood. Her spectacles had frosted over. No matter. She didn't use them to see; just to hide behind. She pulled her spectacles down low on the bridge of her nose so she could see where she was going. Not that it mattered. Up ahead was an intersecting street. She took it. The moment she turned the corner, icy gusts forced her to seek shelter in the first doorway she could find. Shaking all over, almost as badly as last night, she pulled her thin woolen shawl closer and tried to get warm.

Here she'd just run away from one hell in Boston right into another one in Denver. No job meant no food, no shelter, and no safe haven. There was never a safe haven from her stalking nightmares, but she thought Denver would be more welcoming. It wasn't. She'd made a mistake in coming west. She might just as well have stayed in Boston and braved what was coming. A sudden gust of cold sliced across her face. She felt deserving of the insult, but turned her back to the biting wind to protect against another.

There was a sign on the door she faced. It took a moment to focus before she could read it: THE ROCKY MOUNTAIN NEWS—William Byers, Owner and Editor. Just below it, she read a separate sign posted, this one smaller, and this one fixed to the glass pane inside: Jobs available in Hot Sulphur Springs: blacksmith, carpenter, *s*table and saddlers, schoolteacher. *Schoolteacher!* Afraid she was seeing things, Meggie read the sign again. Once she was sure of it, she pushed open the door of the *Rocky Mountain News.*

The strong smell of ink and newsprint greeted her when she stepped inside.

"Help you, ma'am?"

A lanky young man with dark blond, slicked-down hair stood

behind a counter. She relaxed right away. The counter kept him at a safe distance. She thought he must be a typesetter, what with the smudges of ink on his chin. He stood with his arms folded, as if impatient for her reply. His ink-stained fingers made funny little prints on his boiled white shirt. He stared blankly at her as if nothing was amiss.

She relaxed more. "I would like to inquire after your advertisement. The advertisement about jobs in Hot Sulphur Springs."

The young man's brow furrowed. He rubbed his forehead, smearing ink all over it. "Oh yeah. My . . . uh, Mr. Byers' town," he said, at last brightening. "Right up the stairs there to Mr. Peabody's office," he directed. An inky finger appeared in front of Meggie's nose to point the way. "Everyone has to see Mr. Peabody."

A little uncomfortable, Meggie didn't like losing the security of keeping that counter between her and any men working at the newspaper. *I need this job,* she reminded herself as she took to the stairs, each step hard taken. Reaching the top, she peered through the door standing ajar to her left. A bespectacled man sat at a desk, bent over mounds of paperwork. The rest of the small office was as cluttered as his desk. The situation didn't look fearsome to Meggie. She cleared her throat to get the man's attention.

The man looked up. His look of surprise turned into a smile.

"Come in, come in, little lady. Come in and have a seat here." The man got up and freed the only other chair in the office of its stack of papers, then motioned for her to sit down.

"Are you Mr. Peabody?" She sat down, a little uneasy but determined.

"The very one. Ned Peabody at your service."

His scrutiny unnerved her. She didn't like anyone, any man, staring closely at her. Of course, she realized, he was a newspaperman, which was why he was staring. Still, she didn't like it.

Mr. Peabody said nothing and kept up his stare.

Meggie stiffened her back. She needed to get used to this. She wasn't in Boston anymore. She needed to get used to being around men.

"Now Miss—"

"Rochester," she answered. "Miss Rose Rochester."

"Well, Miss Rochester, what exactly can I do for you?" He leaned back in his chair and clasped both hands over his chest.

"I'm here about the job, Mr. Peabody, the job in Hot Sulphur Springs, the schoolteacher's position."

He didn't seem at all enthusiastic by what she'd said.

"Forgive my surprise, Miss Rochester. It's not every day we get anyone in here asking after jobs in Hot Sulphur Springs. Please go on. What is it again you specifically want to know? What job?"

The wood slats of her chair back poked into her already-unnerved backbone. "Mr. Peabody, I would like to be considered for the job as schoolteacher in Hot Sulphur Springs. I love to teach. I love children."

The wrinkled corners of Ned Peabody's eyes tightened just enough for her to believe she read his decision against her in them. She had to convince him otherwise. "I have a proper teacher's certificate from the East and years of experience. No one has ever questioned my professional abilities."

"I'm sure you're more than qualified, Miss Rochester. My concerns relate to other issues. There are things you need to consider, that anyone needs to consider, before heading into the mountains. How long have you been out west, Miss?"

"I've been in Denver for one day now."

"One whole day, have you?" Ned Peabody smiled a fatherly smile. "No offense, Miss, but you don't even know your way around the city, much less the hills. From the looks of you, you're a dyed-in-the-wool tenderfoot. The West is a whole way different from the East. Things are hard out here." He stood now. "Maybe after you've been out here a year or so, well then . . . then we can talk about finding you something."

Meggie stood, too; clutching the cross beneath her shawl. Her heart thumped against her fingers.

"Mr. Peabody, please. Please give me another moment of your time."

Ned Peabody sat back down, apparently willing to do just that.

"Mr. Peabody, how many folks who live here now were born and raised here? Were all of them? Was every single resident here now born in Denver?" she asked, taking her seat again.

Encouraged by his smile, she kept on.

"I daresay, Mr. Peabody, you have a few folks from the East who've managed to survive out here in the West. Surely there are plenty of miners and settlers who've done all right. Well, I'm one of them . . . well . . . what I mean is that . . . I'm not a miner or a settler, but—the thing of it is, Mr. Peabody, I'm just as able as the rest to make it out here. I've worked hard all of my life. Just because someone is from the East doesn't mean they've lived a life in the lap of luxury and never sullied their hands." Her insides shuddered at her own use of *sullied*. She ignored her upset and kept on.

"It doesn't mean they can't learn to live a new life. Why do you think we all come out here? Why do you think I came out here?" She shuddered again. She wasn't going to tell him the truth, of course. "Why, isn't this supposed to be the land of gold and golden opportunity for everyone? I just want a chance, Mr. Peabody. Just a chance." She'd finished. There was nothing more to say. Anxious, her hands clammy, she unwittingly ran them along the damp fabric of her skirt.

"I'll say one thing for you, Miss, you sure got spunk." Ned Peabody leaned back in his chair. "I bet you could talk the antlers right off a bull elk. Yes, sir. Well, I'll tell you what. You listen to me a piece, and then let's see what you think about this job you seem to want so much. All right with you, Miss Rochester?"

"Oh yes, Mr. Peabody. That's more than all right," she said, her enthusiasm obvious. From then on she sat at rapt attention; hanging onto Ned Peabody's every word about the perils of mountain life. If the blizzards and harsh winters didn't get a body, then the isolation might, he told her. And then there were the Indians. Thousands of Utes were encamped over the mountain passes. And there was illness to think about. With hardly a doc outside of Denver, she'd have to rely on her own remedies and nostrums, no matter what the ailment. Most likely, too, she'd come up against some ornery types of varmints who'd "decorate a cottonwood" if they could be caught. Not all the trappers and miners and such scattered throughout the hills were of the decent sort. With so few women in the territory she'd have trouble for sure if she met up with certain disreputable varmints. She'd be a woman alone in wild, rugged, and unpredictable territory with no husband or family to protect her.

"You are unmarried, right, Miss Rochester?"

"Yes, that's right." She shifted uncomfortably in her seat. She knew he wondered about that, but it wasn't his business or anyone else's that she was alone.

He cleared his throat as if dismissing the subject.

"So you see, Miss Rochester, not exactly a Sunday afternoon in the front parlor. Life in Hot Sulphur Springs won't be easy for you."

"Well, Mr. Peabody, since I didn't grow up whiling away my

time in some front parlor, I'll be just fine then." She tried to smile.

"All right then, Miss Determined Tenderfoot, you've convinced me. The job is yours. Besides, I can't sit here the rest of the day listening to arguments from you," he offered good-naturedly.

Grateful tears welled in Meggie's eyes. She held them back. How would it look? She couldn't cry in front of Mr. Peabody, or he'd take his offer back. The two spent the next thirty minutes in serious discussion over her upcoming journey. Folks had been settling in Hot Sulphur Springs since '69. Likely there were plenty enough younguns there by now needing to learn their three R's, Mr. Peabody had said. As the teacher, her salary would be twenty dollars a month. And she'd be provided with a cabin. Mr. Peabody didn't know what else his boss might have planned. He couldn't tell her the number of students she'd have or if there was even a schoolhouse built. He was sorry he didn't know what supplies she'd need or if the shelves of the mercantile in Hot Sulphur Springs had anything useful on them. The store had gone up last year. That he did know. All other answers would have to wait until her arrival, which brought them to the subject of how she'd get there.

Meggie would be taking the brand new stage line over Berthoud Pass and then on to Hot Sulphur Springs. The line would only be running for a short time, what with winter coming, and would pick up again come spring. "Quite the thing, you're coming in today," he'd said. "If you'd come in any later, no telling if you could even get up to Hot Sulphur Springs. The weather could prevent travel any time now." He advised her to pack up all her things and be ready to leave at sunup tomorrow. He'd book her passage on the stage.

"Of course, Mr. Peabody. I'll be ready to leave first thing in the morning."

"Very good. Be in front of the stage office on Fifteenth Street at six sharp. Old Bill Sykes will be ready to pull out on time."

"I'll be there at six sharp," she echoed.

"Good. Good. Everyone in the town will be tickled pink to meet you. I expect even a few of the younguns will be happy to have a teacher," he said, nodding his head to emphasize his point.

The thought of living among new people scared Meggie, but the thought of staying in Denver without a decent job, where she might be found out, scared her more. After she and Mr. Peabody said their goodbyes, Meggie rushed down the steps, past the lanky typesetter still behind the counter, and on out the front door of the *Rocky Mountain News*. This time she put her shoulder into the icy wind and braved the wet and cold to get back to the American House as fast as she could. There was little time before she'd be leaving for the mountains. This afternoon and evening were all she had in Denver. She felt light of foot and light of heart.

Adventure lay ahead of her, according to Mr. Peabody. She gathered together the loose ends of her tattered shawl with one hand, and stilled the sway of her venerable cross with the other as she hurried along, happy to be happy. Why, she could be anyone hurrying down the street now: an ordinary, normal person living an ordinary, normal life. The thought was . . . extraordinary.

Mr. Peabody worried unnecessarily about her, she believed. She'd embrace her new life, her adventure, the same way Jane Eyre had when she left Lowood. Hadn't Jane sought work in a strange, new place? Jane had to find a way to deal with trial and tribulation. If Jane could do it, so could she. If Jane could leave the horror of Lowood behind, Meggie could do the same with Boston. Besides, in the mountains she could disappear. No one would be able to find her in the remote town of Hot Sulphur Springs.

"You say you don't have an account of the passengers who arrived on the train within the past week?"

Harold had felt ill at ease the second the accusing stranger showed up at his depot window. He'd been in the business long enough to recognize the type. Didn't cotton to Pinkertons or snake oil salesmen. This guy was a little of both.

"Nope, don't have anything like that to show you," the stationmaster replied flatly. Even if a part of his list hadn't been destroyed, he wouldn't help this sleazy easterner sniff anyone out. "Sorry," Harold bit out and stepped away from his window. His business with the stranger was finished. He couldn't care less if the guy believed him.

"Well, that's too bad." The unwelcome man didn't take his cue and leave. Instead, he slipped a fifty-dollar bill through the bottom of the caged opening.

"I'm heading on to Colorado Springs, but I'll be back through here real soon. If you should find that passenger list, I'd like to know who's on it. I want to find a Meghan McMurphy. An eastern gal. A relative, actually." This last oozed out like a dollar bottle of phony elixir.

Harold wasn't fooled. But he was a little curious about the McMurphy woman. Fifty dollars was a lot of money to shell out for information. Fifty dollars was a lot of money, period! Somebody must want to know about Meghan McMurphy real bad.

"She's a redhead in her twenties. Remember. Meghan McMurphy," the stranger repeated in the same oily tone.

Harold slid the money back under the bottom bar. "Yeah, well, like I said, mister, I don't have a list," he said.

Scaly fingers shot out to snap up the bill. "And like *I* said, I'll be back."

Harold wouldn't look forward to it.

"I'll be in tomorrow mornin' first thing to handle the stage leavin'," Uriah offered energetically.

Ethan smiled to himself. How his friend could find so many things to act like a kid at Christmas about was a wonder. Like Uriah, he was also glad to see their project get off the ground. But unlike his partner, Ethan's thoughts turned to all the work ahead before the passage would be a smooth one. That and concern over the Indians.

The recent treaty with the Utes brought only an uncertain peace. Ethan was pleasantly surprised the government had received any kind of agreement out of their chief, Showahcan. Despite his youth, Showahcan was clan leader to the thousands of Indians living in the mountains. The Utes were a different breed from the red men of the plains. His trips to the Indian Agency at Fort Garland had told him as much. The Utes were fierce fighters. The Arapahoe, Cheyenne, and Sioux rarely succeeded in any raids on the mountain tribe. In fact most of the time, the Plains Indians would lose their own horses instead of being able to steal the Utes'. Ethan hoped the mountain Indians would stick to their agreement to not molest anyone traveling on his stage line. He had the sudden urge to check on things for himself.

"That suits me fine, Uriah. I'm thinking I'll head out myself at first light."

"What for, Ethan?"

"Truth is, I want to hook up with the agent Simon Pritchard at White River. Just making sure all is well." Ethan waited for the inevitable questions.

"Do you 'spect trouble, Ethan? Thought things were nice and

quiet. Has William told you there's trouble up there? Should I ride shotgun in the mornin'?" Uriah's earlier exuberance faded.

"Hold on, partner. No one said anything about trouble. Don't go and jump the gun on me. I'm just saying I want to get a firsthand look at things, that's all."

Uriah settled. "Makes sense. Yep, makes sense," his rugged features relaxed. "Ethan, are you gonna take the stage up?"

"No. I'm riding alone. Faster that way."

"I don't know 'bout that, Ethan," Uriah smiled. "With old Sykes drivin', he might clear Berthoud before you've watered Nugget in Empire City."

Ethan laughed. "True enough. Bill's the best. Can lead a team to hell and back, I expect." For some reason, the mention of hell took away Ethan's good mood. Damn, he hoped that wasn't where they were all going. Before the two men left their office, they agreed to meet back in Denver in a week's time.

Ethan set out for his home in Capitol Hill. His three-story brick mansion rose above the other stately residences. Granite columns decorated both sides of the front portico. Evergreens flourished along the approach, growing tall in the five years since the house went up. Ethan thought of his housekeeper Nettie, and scraped his muddy boots on the iron grate by the door before going in. No sooner was he inside than Ezekiel, Nettie's husband, appeared in the foyer to take his slicker.

"Thanks, Ezekiel." Ethan slipped his arms out of the heavy greatcoat. "Got a little work to do," he muttered to Ezekiel, and headed straight for his study.

"Ethan?" Ezekiel called after him. "How 'bout I have Nettie make you a bite. The wife's tellin' me you haven't eaten much fer a spell. You know how she gits after me if she thinks yer poorly."

Birds of a feather, Ethan thought; Uriah, Nettie, and Ezekiel. He paused in the doorway of his study. There was a time when he'd welcomed all their mollycoddling. Five years ago, maybe. And five years ago he might have wanted to live in his big, drafty house. He'd always keep his friends. Damned lucky to have them, he knew. And he'd probably keep rattling around by himself in his empty house, too. But there was a part of him he couldn't keep, a part that he'd lost years ago.

Ezekiel repeated his question.

"Tell Nettie not to bother," Ethan said, eye to eye now with Ezekiel. "Matter of fact, I'll be heading out when I'm done here. I'm going into the mountains to check on our new stage line and make sure things run smoothly. Would you let Nettie know? I shouldn't be gone more than a week."

Ethan turned around and walked over to his mahogany roll-top desk, forgetting all about Ezekiel. He didn't notice Ezekiel still in the doorway. He didn't see the sad expression on his loyal servant's wrinkled features.

Ethan sat in his swivel chair, intending to make quick work of the ledgers he needed to review before he left. He reached for the ledgers but came up with the familiar glass snow globe instead. He inverted the winter scene . . . remembering. The snow globe had been a gift. He loved to watch the snowflakes dance over the miniature skating figure. He loved to watch the slip of a girl spin round and around. The winter scene suddenly changed from ice to fire in his fingers. Ethan slammed the globe down on the desk. It didn't break.

The dancing form had transformed into a blur of nutmeg and cream. He thought of the girl—the woman—he'd rescued from the street. He thought of Nutmeg. He didn't like it, not one bit.

Unlike Ethan, Meggie was in a happier frame of mind. Still excited when she reached the hotel, she hurried inside the American House and took the stairs two at a time. She had respectable work now and would be on her way to a brand new life in the morning. If only she could share her good news with someone, with the sisters at the convent or with Pru, her dearest and only friend back in Boston. Yes, that's what she'd do! She'd send an express to Pru, sharing her good news before she left. There shouldn't be any harm in doing that. Pru wouldn't tell anyone where she was.

But the moment Meggie set foot on the landing, something made her hesitate. She looked around. Silly. There was no one lurking about, no danger. She reached the top of the stairs now, the entire hallway in view. It was empty. She thought of what had happened earlier, what she'd felt while talking to Mr. Cottswell at hotel registration, like something bad . . . *someone bad . . . was here.* Silly! She told herself again. She saw no one in the hallway. Rebelliously, she refused to check the hairs at her nape. She refused to think about any danger waiting in the shadows, here or in the mountains. Her trip tomorrow called for boldness, and bold she'd be. The thought of leaving town shouldn't ruffle her in the least. She wasn't leaving anything or anyone behind in Denver . . . or was she?

The image of the handsome westerner came to mind.

CHAPTER FIVE

Shrugging off the forbidding stranger's image wasn't so easily done. He kept returning to her mind's eye. Meggie envisioned him standing outside the restaurant window. She could see his hands raise and protectively cup the match while he lit his smoke—the very same hands that had placed her in her bed. Her body tingled where she imagined he'd touched her. She should be afraid of him, not . . . *not this.*

Out of instinct, she felt the hair at her nape, surprised to find her skin smooth. She should be relieved but she wasn't. Unable to push thoughts of the stranger away, she was forced to stare into his seductive, slate depths, held captive to his dark good looks. She easily remembered his tall, well-muscled frame, and the way his broad shoulders had blocked all else from view. Her eyes closed and she breathed in the scent—his scent—of musk and leather and new tobacco. Her nostrils flared gently as his masculine essence misted over her. She thought again of his hands on her body, imagining him putting her in her bed when she was in a faint. Thank the good Lord she had been in a faint! She'd no protection against such an impossible moment. Her eyes flew open.

The pleasure of it, of these new feelings, scared her.

To have any such thoughts scared her.

The stranger scared her.

Hurrying inside her room, she closed the door and leaned hard against it, hoping the closed door would keep thoughts of the westerner out. It did not. Her body still tingled, thinking of him. She quickly pulled away from the door. He seemed familiar to her, as if she knew him from somewhere before Denver, but to have feelings for this man—or any man—made no sense. Meggie tried to shrug off such worries, reminding herself that she really didn't have a problem. She wouldn't have to see the unsettling stranger again. This time tomorrow she'd be out of Denver.

Denver was dangerous. In such a well-known place, she could be found. She should have thought of that when she left Boston. Another mistake she'd made. Her mistakes were beginning to add up, and to catch up with her. She'd best take care. Right now she needed to live in a more isolated place; if, that is, she wanted to live at all.

It didn't take long for her to get her belongings repacked in her worn satchel and ready for the morning trip. She was nervous about tomorrow—nervous about going; nervous about staying. Writing Pru would help soothe her nerves. No need to rummage through her things for writing paper, pen and ink. She didn't have them. Mr. Cottswell. She'd go to the front desk and ask him. She didn't relish talking to him, still embarrassed about everything, but there was the matter of her hotel bill. Best she get this over with. Collecting her money from her indispensable and worried over the price of her room, she started for the door.

"Not a penny, Miss Rochester. Your balance is as flat as the open prairie." The little man appeared pleased with this happy retort.

"How can that be, sir?" Meggie was dumbfounded. "Surely you've confused me with somebody else?" It suddenly occurred to her that he might believe her a charity case. She'd never be that again. It offended her that Mr. Cottswell might hold such an opinion. "I have money, sir. I can pay my own bill. I insist that you tell me the sum owed," she finished, indignantly.

"Miss Rochester, you owe me nothing. Like I said, your bill's settled. Why don't you just call it good luck and leave it at that?"

Meggie wished she could. Too many questions already nagged at her since she'd arrived in Denver. Too many things had already upset her.

"Mr. Cottswell, you must tell me. Who paid my bill?"

"I can't answer that, Miss Rochester. No ma'am, I can't."

Meggie couldn't imagine why Mr. Cottswell wouldn't reveal who paid her bill. She turned around then, scrutinizing every part of the lobby. An uneasy feeling settled into her shaken bones. Had she been followed? Was all this part of some perverted game? She didn't wait to see the relieved expression on Mr. Cottswell's face when she gathered up her asked-for writing materials and rushed back upstairs. She'd not question the matter further. But unlike the insistent clerk, she couldn't call the episode good luck.

A familiar chill caught her at the top of the stairs. She'd felt it before. This time it wasn't an image of the westerner she conjured, but something more dangerous, more deadly. Steeling herself, she walked through the icy passage and kept on down the hallway. She'd walked through such graveyards before in her nightmares but not in the light of day. Her state of mind was tenuous at best and she knew it. Every day she got worse. What if . . . what if . . . No! She'd never go back there. *Never.*

Rushing inside her room Meggie slammed the door behind her, her writing materials forgotten. She prayed that tomorrow's journey would carry her far away from her nightmares and this stalking dread. Her chest hurt and her head ached. Unbidden, born out of new fears, she whispered hard into the oppressive air around her, "six feet under, six feet away, where to stay safe, the devil must stay!"

The night ahead would be long. Tomorrow could not come soon enough.

The Concord hit another rut. Meggie was jolted awake. Her wire rims had slipped clear to the end of her nose. She pushed them back up. Immediately uncomfortable under the stares from the older couple sitting across from her, she looked outside. Nothing but dusty terrain and scrub brush. No sign of any more snow as in Denver.

"Why, the mister and I had no idea of it."

Meggie stiffened, yet smiled politely at the woman speaking.

"I'm Minerva Markson, dear, and this is my husband. You fell asleep so fast when we left Denver, we didn't get to meet proper-like."

Her recurring nightmare had plagued her last night, but she thought she'd got some sleep; evidently not enough to stay awake and keep up her guard. Meggie straightened against the hard leather seating. She looked at the kindly couple. They appeared exhausted, too. They were dressed in unadorned, dark wool traveling clothes. Meggie wondered if they were with the church. The thought warmed her. Mrs. Markson looked spry enough despite her years, but she couldn't say the same of Mr. Markson. He looked ill. His face was pale, his eyes glassy, and his brow furrowed as if in pain. Meggie couldn't help but wonder why this frail man and his wife were making such a rigorous journey. Caught staring, Meggie quickly spoke up, at last remembering her manners.

"I'm Rose Rochester." She was surprised at how easily she could lie. It was a sin to lie. But there were worse sins.

"I can see by your look, Miss Rochester, you're wondering what us old folks are doing going up to Hot Sulphur Springs with you. And here it is winter coming on. It's the mineral springs. You see the mister." Minerva Markson placed an affectionate, gloved hand on her husband's arm. "The mister suffers from the ailments of old age, I'm afraid. Arthritis and the rheumatism. "We're going to the healing springs in Hot Sulphur. The mister will be cured, I'm sure." Mr. Markson nodded his head as if in agreement, but said nothing.

Surprised to hear of the healing mineral springs, Meggie wondered why Mr. Peabody hadn't mentioned anything about them. But then, something so important to her might not be so important to him. If the waters were indeed healing, maybe, just maybe they'd help her.

"And you?" Mrs. Markson spoke up.

"Me?"

"Yes, dear. You. Who else is in this big old rickety coach but the three of us?" she replied good-naturedly. "What prospect takes you so far into the mountains, Miss Rochester?"

Meggie shifted uncomfortably in her seat. A direct question deserved a direct answer, but perhaps not the whole truth. "I'm the new schoolteacher in Hot Sulphur Springs. I was just hired yesterday." The instant she said it, she was mad at herself for saying more than she needed to. She didn't have to mention details, for pity's sake.

"How wonderful, my dear. I must say I am surprised, you going all the way into the mountains, alone with no husband."

Meggie knew Minerva Markson meant no harm. She was just curious. Anyone would be. Still, Meggie must take care with her answer. "I'm happy for my new job. I love to teach, and so I took the job." To say anything more would be foolhardy.

The coach hit another rut. Relieved that Mrs. Markson paid no attention to her now, Meggie watched the way the Marksons held onto each other lovingly, hand-in-hand. Unwittingly, she picked up her indispensable from the seat beside her and put it to her breast. The drawstring bag held her money and *Jane*

Eyre. All she had for companion now was her treasured novel, ever a boon to her flagging spirits. Easing against the hard leather of her seatback, she gazed outside.

They'd begun their climb up a pass. Berthoud Pass, she remembered the driver had said. The journey over the pass wouldn't be easy. She was a little afraid, but more concerned about how the Marksons would tolerate the steep, rocky passage. The kindly couple, still hand-in-hand, had fallen asleep. Just as well. She was sure they needed the rest.

Meggie experienced something akin to exhilaration on the climb up Berthoud Pass. Evergreens as far as the eye could see, ascending ever upward over crags and bumps, toward ice-capped mountain tops. Occasional streams wound their way down the mountainside, the last ice-melt before winter. Meggie's heart picked up. It was all such a wonder. She could never have imagined such vistas, not in all of her born days.

At last the big coach made it to the summit of Berthoud Pass. Meggie thought of waking the Marksons up to see the wondrous site, but then thought better of it. They should rest. She wanted to yell out to the driver to stop for a bit, but did not. Bill Sykes might stop to rest the horses. Hopeful he'd do just that, she got ready to climb out of the coach, waiting for it to slow down and stop. The venerable driver did no such thing, heading instead straight down the other side of the pass. Disappointed, Meggie settled back against her seat.

The air turned frigid. It had been cold before, but nothing like this. Quickly now, Meggie grabbed up two of the blankets stored inside the coach and tucked them over the Marksons. Neither woke up, still-hand-in hand. Grabbing up a blanket for herself, she pulled it around her shoulders. Fighting exhaustion, wanting to fall asleep herself, she dared not. Besides, there was too much to see on the way down. She didn't want to miss any of it.

Once at the bottom of Berthoud Pass, the huge Concord continued along the wagon trail cutting through thickets of pine. On they rolled, for hours it seemed. The idea of traveling after sunset made her uneasy. The Marksons had awakened. They had to be hungry and thirsty, but didn't say anything. Meggie wondered if they were close to the stage stop, where the couple could get a hot meal. She looked back outside. The day grew dim. On the coach lumbered, past two towering haystacks, and then there was nothing but open valley. Tired and hungry herself, she wished they'd arrive at their destination before dark.

Suddenly the big coach lurched to a stop.

"Junction House!" Bill Sykes yelled, reigning in his team.

A plumpish, jolly woman opened the coach door right away, greeting them. "Supper's ready, folks. Just come on in and rest yerselves and have some vittles to warm you."

Meggie immediately liked the amiable, stocky, brown-haired woman. "Thank you, ma'am," Meggie said, waiting for the Marksons to disembark first.

"Hush all this ma'am stuff. You all just call me Martha. Now come right on in," Martha ordered and stepped back to allow the three to enter the two-story lodging.

A fire in the hearth crackled its welcome. The delectable aroma of beef stew emanated from the cast iron pot hanging over the flames. Led to a long wooden table in front of the fireplace, the exhausted travelers didn't hesitate and sat down on the benches.

The front door opened.

A man entered.

Meggie bristled. She wished she didn't think of every stranger as a threat until they proved otherwise.

"How do folks. Name's Jasper Wheatley. Reckon you've met the wife."

Meggie relaxed. Mr. Wheatley seemed friendly enough. He was as thin as his wife was round. Bill Sykes followed close on Jasper's heels.

"I'm hungrier than a bear after hibernation, Martha," the veteran stage driver pronounced and made a beeline for the stew. After serving himself a generous helping he took a seat next to Meggie.

Though uneasy, she forced herself to sit still. Mr. Sykes wasn't a threat. Heaven sakes, all he wanted to do was eat his supper.

"Where you folks from?" Martha pulled a rough-hewn rocker up next to the hearth. "I declare, it's a pure pleasure to see you all. Not every day we get folks in these parts. With winter comin', why it'll be next spring afore we'll be seein' too many more folks. I'll be as happy as can be to cook up a mess of fixins' fer each and every one." Martha beamed.

Meggie enjoyed the easy banter and finished eating, listening as the Marksons tried to answer all of Martha's questions in between bites. When Jasper and Bill Sykes started up their own conversation, Martha's attention turned to them. Meggie felt rescued.

"Jasper," Bill spoke up. "Have you had any trouble with the Indians in these parts?"

Meggie's insides gave a start. She'd forgotten they were traveling in Ute territory now. Mr. Peabody warned her as much, but she'd forgotten.

"Nope," Jasper replied. "Fact is, they're right friendly to the wife and me. 'Cept fer Grimshaw, we're the only white folks round here. No more settlers till Hot Sulphur Springs and on past. Them Utes love to race their horses. I'll tell you, Bill, some days the dust is so kicked-up out yonder you cain't hardly see yer hand in front of you," Jasper joked.

Bill Sykes didn't laugh, thinking of his relief team. "Have they let our horses be, Jasper?"

"Yep, shore have. No sign of trouble."

Meggie put down her fork. She hadn't thought about being in Indian country until now.

"Yet," Bill gritted out and got up from the table, heading for the door. "Think I'll bed down tonight by the corral."

Jasper got up and followed behind. "Say, Bill, how'd you do comin' up and down Berthoud? The road over Rollins Pass is in better shape but shore takes a far piece to get here on it."

The big driver turned around and stood in the open doorway.

"Pshaw. Nothin' to it, Jasper. 'Sides, Ethan's road will be better than Rollins' when things is finished."

"Ethan, did you say?" Martha suddenly broke in. "And just how is that handsome devil a doin', Bill?"

Bill grinned at this, but her husband just shook his head.

"Woman, yer too danged old to be chasin' the likes of Ethan," Jasper scolded.

"Why, I'm a doin' no such thing, husband," Martha huffed. "If I cain't ask after the very person that built the stage road so's we can take care of folks and make our livin', then just who can I be askin' after?" Martha glared at her husband, then turned to her guests.

"Come on, folks. Let's get you all bedded down and cozy fer the night. Just follow me." She got up from her rocker. Meggie and the Marksons had finished eating and got up, too.

Sleep didn't come easily to Meggie. It never did. The idea of falling into her nightmares kept her awake. Other things, too. She thought of the Utes and the danger all around. So far, she hadn't seen even one Indian. Jasper Wheatley didn't seem too worried. Bill Sykes did. She could tell at supper that he was worried. Meggie pulled her quilt closer. Something else kept her from sleep: the Wheatleys' earlier exchange about somebody named Ethan. Meggie was curious about who Ethan was to cause a stir between Martha and Jasper. She thought of the darkly handsome westerner in Denver, his face so close she could reach up and touch it. He was the kind of man who could cause a stir—he certainly had in her.

She rolled onto her stomach and gave her pillow a thump, then laid her check against the clean muslin. She'd almost prefer one of her nightmares to this turn of her thoughts.

CHAPTER SIX

Meggie stared out at the brown October fields as the stage lumbered toward Hot Sulphur Springs. This new day would take her to her new home. It gave her hope, the thought of a home. It gave her reason to think she might finally lead some kind of normal life. She'd try. She'd try very hard. The great Concord swayed back and forth on the rough wagon road. No matter for Meggie, but the Marksons held on to each other for support, clasping hands as they had the day before. How Meggie envied them. How she wished she lived in their world—no doubt free of stalking nightmares—and not hers. But it was the price she must pay for her sins. She prayed every day for God's forgiveness. Every day.

A narrow creek wound its way alongside the stage. Meggie studied it. She wondered where it led. Unlike the streams rushing down the sides of Berthoud Pass, this one pushed gently across the valley floor. Nothing broke the flow of the stream, nothing stood in its way. No animals. No houses. No peop— Meggie saw something, someone, in the distance. It was a child. A boy.

The boy stood, facing the oncoming stage. The gusty wind blew his coal-black hair away from his small shoulders. Close enough now to see the boy clearly, Meggie thought his stare belonged on someone much older. The dark-skinned child held what appeared to be a spear in one hand. Standing at the creek's edge, he was dressed in a hide shirt and breeches, with moccasins on his feet. Motherly-instinct made her want to yell out and caution the child about getting his feet wet. Something about the way the boy stood so proud and still struck her. Was it defiance she detected in the little fellow? She'd been defiant as a child, too. The memory made her feel an instant bond with the boy.

Not until the stage had gone well past did it occur to Meggie that the boy was an Indian child, a Ute. She'd finally seen an Indian. She'd heard about the Indians out west—how they terrified white settlers, attacking and killing men, women, and children. But the boy . . . the innocent little boy she'd just seen didn't terrify her. He looked like any child would, playing outside by a friendly stream in his homeland. Not hers. Not the whites'. She was supposed to fear and hate the Indians, but seeing the little boy just now . . . she could not.

"Hot Sulphur Springs!" Bill Sykes at last pulled the Concord to a stop.

Meggie waited for the Marksons to disembark. Sitting back against her seat, she shut her eyes tight and offered a silent prayer to God that when she stepped down off the stage, it would be a step well-taken. She prayed that she'd be safe in this new town and that the folks here would welcome her. The thought of meeting new people—more men—grated against her insides. She opened her eyes. She'd done all right since she'd left Boston, hadn't she? Yes, she had. Not one man had bothered her. Well, maybe one. The stranger in Denver had bothered her all right. He'd laid a hand on her, but she was still here, still all right. That thought, and that thought alone, gave her the courage to step down from the stage.

Hot Sulphur Springs Hotel, the sign read. The two-story log building in front of her had to be Mr. Byers' hotel. There was no sign of anyone about. The Marksons must be inside. She glanced down the main street, the only street in Hot Sulphur Springs. Townsfolk emerged from their cabins, no doubt curious about the stage. One woman held a baby, the other a broom. Two men stopped loading a wagon in front of Grady's Mercantile to have a look. The smithy stood in front of his shop, staring openly at her, while a group of children stopped their play and came running. Meggie warmed to their giggles and smiles, forgetting all about her nerves.

"Oh, my." She giggled herself, when one of the boys brushed past her in a rush to climb onto the stage. Another boy followed, and then another climbed inside the stage. A little girl followed the boys, all excited and all scrambling wherever they could inside and out the huge Concord. The team of six whinnied and snorted at the stir caused.

Bill Sykes came outside the hotel.

"All right, you little whippersnappers, off my stage," he barked out.

Smiles turned to long faces as each child grudgingly got down from the stage. They turned to leave, but the big driver stopped them. "How's about you all come with me and help get my team settled in for the night? I'll let you ride in the stage to the corral, all right?"

Cheers all around as the children scrambled back inside the stage.

The big-hearted driver looked at Meggie. "It appears I got a passel of little 'uns to see to now."

"It appears you do." She smiled at him, liking Mr. Sykes very much.

"Ma'am, I've moved your belongin's inside the hotel," he said, and tipped his hat before climbing back onto his coach.

"Thank you, Mr. Sykes," Meggie called out as the driver, team, children and all, pulled away.

It would be dark soon. She started for the hotel, but then she heard something and stopped. It was water, rushing water coming from out back of the hotel. Bill Sykes had spoken of the mighty Grande "spittin' and rushin' " right through Hot Sulphur Springs. Her heart picked up. The river sounded powerful.

"How do, young woman." A tall man pushed the hotel door open.

Meggie swallowed hard. "How do you do."

"Old Sykes just filled me in. Peabody hired you, did he? I've been in a pucker over whether we could get a teacher up here. Well, I'm glad to meet you Miss, Miss—"

The man seemed friendly enough. She relaxed as best she could. "Rochester. Miss Rose Rochester." She gave her practiced response. *Meggie girl, take care with your words,* she told herself. *Remember the danger of confessing too much—of secrets revealed.*

"Rose Rochester, is it? I'm William Byers," he introduced and put out his hand.

William Byers. The owner of the newspaper and this hotel. Meggie stared mutely at his hand, knowing all he wanted to do was shake hers in greeting. Should be simple enough, but for Meggie it was not so simple. With little recourse, she offered her hand.

He pumped her arm generously. "Welcome. Welcome to Hot Sulphur Springs."

"Thank you," she said, glad his touch wasn't so bad. Mr. Byers looked more like an easterner than a westerner, with his muttonchops and clipped beard. His wavy brown hair was trimmed at the neck. His gentle brown eyes twinkled. She read trust in them, yet stiffened a little when he unclasped her hand and took up her elbow.

"Come on in and meet the wife," he said, losing none of his enthusiasm. "We're just about to sit down to supper."

Meggie let him guide her into the dining room. A slender, attractive woman with blond hair arranged in a loose topknot looked up from setting the table.

"Hullo, hullo there. We'd almost given up thinking the stage would be in this evening. A lot of excitement for our little town," she declared, her blue eyes sparkling their welcome. In the next instant she was at Meggie's side, replacing William's hand with her own.

"I'm Elizabeth Byers. I'm that pleased to make your acquaintance Miss—"

"It's Rochester. Rose Rochester."

"And you're the new teacher, aren't you? Well, you're certainly a sight for sore eyes. The townsfolk will be that pleased, they will." She gave Meggie's arm a squeeze at this. "Our Frank is seventeen and apprenticing in Denver now. If he needs any more schooling, he'll have to get it at the newspaper," Elizabeth said lightheartedly.

Meggie thought of the lanky, absent-minded typesetter at the *Rocky Mountain News.* He must be their Frank.

Just then the Marksons entered.

Elizabeth unhooked her arm from Meggie's to help seat the worn out couple. "You folks come and sit down over here."

Meggie took a seat herself, at once worrying over the Marksons; Mr. Markson especially. He looked so drawn, so tired. After a good meal and a good night's rest, and soakings in the warm mineral springs, he'd be improved. She planned to soak in the waters, too. Tomorrow. She'd find out tomorrow if they were, indeed, healing.

"Have some pot roast, Miss Rochester," Elizabeth offered, interrupting Meggie's soulful reverie.

"Thank you." Meggie served herself from the platter of sliced beef and then passed the meat to Bill Sykes. She was hungry. Her mouth watered at the rest of the sumptuous fare. Carrots. New potatoes. And cornbread, fresh from the oven! Wafts of steam rose from the piled-high basket of warm bread. Before she realized what she'd done, she'd reached out and grabbed the biggest piece she could find. Embarrassed, she sat back against her chair, staring down at the slices of roast on her plate. She ran her fingers over the hand that took the bread.

No red marks. No one slapped it.

And no one had taken the bread from her.

She poured herself a glass of water from the pitcher set in front of her, and then took a self-conscious sip. The vegetables were passed next. She made sure to take tiny portions, not wishing to draw any notice, and kept her eyes trained on her plate and the table.

The table was made of cherry wood, beautiful and polished. The lanterns flickering atop the table provided enough light to admire it, and to admire the delicate rose carvings on the three vacant matching chairs. She'd never expected to see anything so fancy in the mountain hotel. Looking up now, she noticed two paintings hanging on the wall opposite her. Sconces helped illuminate both. One painting was of a child ice-skating across a village pond, and the other, a town gathering at Christmas. Meggie stared longingly at both, then caught herself and looked back down at her plate, listening now to the conversation at the table.

Tonight Bill Sykes had been assured that he wouldn't need to sleep in the corral at the smithy's. More watchful than a hawk, Zeb Kinney, the smithy, would be up at the first sign of any trouble, William told him. No one said anything more about the Utes, about whether they'd seen any near Hot Sulphur Springs, or about whether they made any trouble for the settlers. Silence around the supper table on the subject spoke volumes to Meggie. She guessed all had been calm between the Utes and the settlers. She thought of the little boy she'd seen by the stream, glad he lived in peace . . . so far, that is.

"And as for you, Miss Rochester," William said, turning to Meggie.

Startled, she did her best not to look as uncomfortable as she felt at his attention.

"Tomorrow I'll show you your cabin," he said. "It's a good one, I think, a good home for you and a good school for our children."

Home. *My home.* Meggie couldn't wait to see it.

"Tomorrow then, Miss Rochester?"

"Yes, tomorrow," she replied.

William got up from the table. With supper over, everyone followed suit. Meggie walked behind the Marksons and Bill Sykes up the narrow wood stairs. They all followed Elizabeth Byers who, tallow in hand, led the way. Meggie waited her turn while each guest was shown to his or her room.

"And here you are, Miss Rochester." Elizabeth opened the last door at the end of the hallway.

Meggie followed her inside, watching closely as Elizabeth Byers lit the tallow on the bedstead.

"Hope you'll be comfortable here. There's an extra quilt at the foot of your bed. You'll probably need it before morning. It's getting that cold now," Elizabeth said while turning down the covers on the pine bed. "Wash basin and all is over there." She pointed at the washstand near the window. "Necessary is out back."

Meggie, only now spotting her satchel on the floor at the foot of the bed, nodded her thank you to Elizabeth Byers.

"Breakfast's at seven. But don't worry. I'll keep something hot for you if you sleep in a little. Expect you will, what with the long trip up. Well goodnight, Miss Rochester."

"Rose. It's Rose." Meggie offered, surprised that she did.

Elizabeth smiled.

"Rose, then. And you must call me Eliza. Everyone does."

"Goodnight, Eliza." Meggie warmed even more to her.

Eliza paused in the open doorway. "There will be plenty of time tomorrow for us to get good and acquainted, Rose." She smiled again and closed the door behind her.

Meggie didn't want to get good and acquainted with anybody, no matter how friendly they appeared. She'd need to go over in her mind just what she could tell Eliza about herself. She must be very careful. No one must catch on to her masquerade. If found out, it would be dangerous for her, even up here in the mountains, far away from Denver and from Boston.

Quickly now, she shed her gray woolen and her black lace-ups, slipped into her nightdress, and then knelt down by the side of her bed. "Thank you, Father, for leading me to my new home. I'm truly grateful for this blessing. In Jesus' name, amen." Exhausted, she crawled under the covers, wanting to sleep, yet not wanting to. Happy for the companionable light, she stared at the lit tallow. Instead of snuffing it out, she'd let it burn. It helped her feel safe. Fighting sleep, her lids heavy, she kept her gaze fixed on the flickering candle.

Sunlight streamed across Meggie's face and woke her up. It felt wonderful to have slept all night with no nightmares plaguing her. The sun felt wonderful, too. She heard it then, the river out back. In a hurry to see the "mighty Grande" and the hot springs, she scrambled out of bed. Nothing remained of her tallow but a little pool of hardened beeswax. She'd make sure to ask Eliza for another one.

In ten minutes' time Meggie had pulled up her hair, dressed, and completed her toilette. Sparing herself a few moments, she washed her hands again. It always eased her to know her hands were clean and washed a second time. Meggie liked the Byers' hotel, all but one thing—the mirror over the washstand. She grabbed up a square of linen toweling and covered it. She didn't want to see her reflection. She didn't want to acknowledge the woman inside her. That woman died a long time ago. No, she didn't want any glimpse of what remained of her after . . . after—quickly now, she found her wire rims and put them on. Shrugging off the dark turn her thoughts had taken, she needed to use the necessary. She hurried out of her room, down the steps, and through the empty kitchen, quietly closing the door behind her.

The moment she stepped outside into the brisk air, she realized that much of the morning was already gone. Oh, faith! How will it look, the new teacher sleeping in, a layabout! She hadn't passed anyone coming outside and didn't see anyone now. Fast as she could, she used the privy, then washed up in the basin by the kitchen door. Instead of going back inside to find Eliza Byers, or at least to get her shawl, she walked to the edge of the river. It wasn't far from the back door, maybe thirty feet. Once there, the swift current overlapped its banks and soaked the toes of Meggie's boots. Instinctively she bent down and put her hand in the rushing water. The current felt strong, powerful, drawing her in. She quickly pulled away. No need to be so careless. One slip and she'd be gone with no one the wiser.

The opposite shore was some hundred feet across. Upriver the water took a bend, then disappeared from view. Downriver she spotted a bridge, hard to see through the foggy mist. Her heart gave a start. For some reason the mist reminded her of the dusk approaching when Jane Eyre first met Edward Rochester on that late, cold, January afternoon. It was hard for Jane to see then, just like now for Meggie. *Jane had been on her way to post a letter, and Edward was taking a shortcut to Millcote. The causeway was icy. Edward's horse slipped.* Meggie sighed heavily. Her romantic imaginings drew her to the footbridge, then the hot pools just beyond. The mist coated her wire rims.

She put them in her pocket. No one else was about. She wondered if the Marksons had already been outside, and if Mr. Markson had soaked in the hot pools as yet.

Drawn right away to the largest pool, Meggie began undoing the buttons at her dress front, giving little thought to her actions. She couldn't wait to immerse herself in the steamy bath. Her skin ached for it. Surely such an immersion would help purge her of her sin, wash away her shame and make her whole again . . . whole and worthy of God's blessing. So anxious to test the hot springs herself, she didn't pay any mind to the pile of men's clothes near the water's edge, nor did she think how improper it would be for her to strip down to her chemise and pantalets now. She bent down by the steaming pool and let the fine, warm mist coat her face. It felt wonderful. She shut her eyes to better experience the sensation. Something splashed in the water, making her open her eyes.

Jesus, Mary, and Joseph!

The impossibly handsome westerner from Denver, corded muscles and all!

The naked truth of her dire situation was heading right for her. His steely glare bore through her. Pulling to a stand, she'd no time to react other than hastily rebuttoning her dress and bracing against goodness knew what. The stranger didn't look any too pleased to see her. Well, she wasn't pleased to see him, either.

He was closing in.

She took a step back.

He was at the edge of the pool now.

She backed up another step. She'd never imagined such a man, all sinew and muscle and power. He was close—too close—yet she wasn't afraid of him; not exactly. She should run, but she didn't. Mesmerized by him she watched as he threaded both his hands through his dark, cropped hair. He didn't get out right away, but stood in waist-deep water. Not for a moment did he take his eyes from her. Steam rose from his powerful body and blended with the chill air surrounding them both. He looked to Meggie like some great lathered animal readying for the chase.

She held her ground.

"Well, you want to watch? It's fine with me, lady," Ethan spat out, breaking the uneasy silence.

"Whatever do you mean, watch?" she heard herself answer. *Does he mean the dimple by his mouth? Is that what he means?*

"Have it your way, lady," he said and started for the bank.

As soon as he began to pull out of the water, revealing his bare waist, hips, and—Meggie spun around so fast she almost fell. Blessed Saints! At least her back was to him now. Thank God she didn't see his . . . *him* . . . anymore! *That's what he meant. He implied I want to watch and see him naked. Of all the nerve,* she fumed to herself. Her earlier fear turned to anger. *The very idea I would want to see him or any man improperly clothed. Insolent, irritating man.*

She should leave this very instant. But she didn't.

"You can turn around now."

The rich timbre of his voice sent a tingling jolt down her spine. She assumed he was fully dressed.

"Well I know I can. I certainly can whenever I wish to do so. I just don't wish to do so," she said indignantly. "And you don't have to swear."

Ethan cursed under his breath.

"Stranger? Did you hear me? I said you don't have to—"

Out of nowhere it seemed, he grazed her shoulder as he brushed past. Startled yet unable to move from the spot, she mutely watched as he disappeared into the mist. It took several minutes for the hint of musk, deep woods and tobacco to clear from Meggie's disrupted, disoriented senses.

It took Ethan a little longer to throw off the lingering traces of wildflowers.

He couldn't believe his bad luck. The odd baggage came out of nowhere. He didn't think he'd ever set eyes on the trouble-some woman again in Denver, much less here in remote Hot Sulphur Springs! Once he reached his room at the hotel, he went inside and slammed the door shut.

Damn fool woman. *Damn Nutty Meggy.*

Of course she still had that damn cross on, like an albatross, he thought. What the hell was Nutmeg doing up here in Hot Sulphur Springs? Ethan didn't like being caught off guard like this. And he sure didn't like the way her eyes, one minute violet and the next turned to black, drew him in. No, sir, he didn't like that at all. He didn't want to be drawn in by any female; especially one with coppery hair pulled back to the point of pain. He could only imagine the wildfire started when she let it down.

Aw, hell! Ethan didn't like the turn of his thoughts. Not one bit.

He was angry all over again that he'd paid her bill at the American House Hotel. He didn't know why he'd done such a fool thing. Pitied her, he supposed, what with her scars and all. Hell. The moment a blur of savory cream sprinkled with tempting spice coated his thinking, he knew exactly why.

He didn't like it. Didn't need it. Didn't have time for it.

He didn't want anything to do with Nutmeg.

His instincts told him to head back over the pass right away. He should leave, and not just because of his run-in with Nutmeg. Winter wasn't going to sit around and wait for him to finish his business in Middle Park. Any moment a storm could hit and put an end to travel. He'd never regretted any of his business decisions, but he wondered now if this had been the right thing, scheduling a few trial stage runs before winter. No matter now. Ethan grabbed his hat and slicker off the nearby chair where he'd tossed them. If he hurried, he could make the White River Agency in two hours' time.

Meggie, who was all shivers, still held to her spot beside the hot pools. The disturbing mists had cleared. She didn't like being so unsettled, and had no urge now to immerse in the water. It had been years since she'd felt free from such an urge—years since she'd felt free of the desire to wash away any man's touch. Yesterday, granted, she'd let Mr. Byers touch her and the world hadn't come to an end. But that was yesterday. Today she didn't feel so blasé about her circumstances. Used to her routine, to her practiced habits, she was comfortable with them now. She'd adjusted to them. In a bizarre way her rituals provided security in an insecure world. To have anything or anyone shatter things in her ordered world frightened her. Then, once again, Meggie did something quite out of the ordinary. She leaned over the pool to see if she could catch her reflection. When she realized what she was doing, she almost fell in.

I don't like mirrors.

I don't like reflecting pools.

The chill winds picked up. Meggie hugged herself to keep warm. The hot springs would be warm, but all desire to bathe in them faded. She vowed to not let this happen again—to never let the stranger's presence affect her practiced routine and ordered life. He was nothing to her. *Nothing.*

A vow made easily enough, but just how to keep it . . . ?

CHAPTER SEVEN

Meggie stepped inside the hotel kitchen.

"There you are. I wondered what happened to you." Eliza smiled.

Meggie tried to smile back. She felt anything but cheerful.

"You've been to our hot springs, haven't you? Did you soak? The pools are so very relaxing." Eliza kept up her good cheer.

Meggie said nothing.

"Dear, are you all right? You look as if you've seen a ghost." Eliza's brow furrowed.

Maybe Meggie had. Maybe her mind was playing tricks on her again. Maybe the changeling demon from her nightmares had found her. No! She'd seen a flesh and blood man, that's all. The stranger from Denver. She was not crazy. She was not. Still, she needed time to sort this all out. Time she didn't have, with Eliza's gaze fixed so on her. She must not make Eliza any more curious than she already seemed to be.

"I'm fine. I just forgot my shawl when I went out and am a bit chilled." Meggie lied. Another sin. The sisters' condemnation echoed in her head.

"You poor dear. You must warm yourself. Come sit at the table and I'll pour you a nice hot cup of tea. It will put the color back in your cheeks."

Meggie eased a chair out and sat down.

"Did you sleep well last night, Rose? I hope you found your room satisfactory?"

"Oh, yes. The room is very nice." Meggie tried to concentrate on what Eliza was asking rather than on the stranger in the hot pool. She took a sip of the tea set in front of her, buying time.

"Did you see a friend of ours when you were out back? He's—"

The cup suddenly burned Meggie's fingers. She set her tea down so fast the cup rattled in its saucer. "No," Meggie blurted out. "Not a soul."

"Well, I'm that sorry you didn't meet him," Eliza said. "He was going for a steam but must have changed his mind. No matter. You'll meet him later, Rose, when we all have supper. You can meet him then."

Jesus, Mary, and Joseph! Meggie didn't want to see him at supper or any other time!

"Rose, you must be famished. I've got just the thing for you." Eliza got up and went over to the stove.

Meggie needed to keep herself steady. If she wanted to live an ordinary life so badly, she'd best try harder. Midday sun streamed into the cozy kitchen through cornflower-blue curtains, creating a far different atmosphere from the sensual, foreboding mists outside. Meggie followed the sun's stream on past the yellow pitcher on the windowsill, then across the calico napkins folded and stacked in front of her on the table. Putting out her hand, she traced the sun's rays across the napkins, feeling the warmth. She straightened in her chair and glanced around the kitchen. It was a pleasant room.

Cast iron pots hung evenly on their hooks along one log hewn wall. Just under the pots, open shelves of dishes, glasses, and cups were neatly organized. Under the window was a double-washtub sink. And a pump. Finding such a convenience in the mountains surprised Meggie. She studied the row of tins on a shelf over the stove. They were marked with the names of their ingredients . . . salt, sugar, flour, coffee, and molasses. A huge bin of firewood lay stacked by the stove. An open door leading to the larder was just to the other side. Meggie could see shelves stocked with glass jars of fruits and vegetables, kegs of vinegar and molasses, and sacks of flour and sugar. The store of goods impressed Meggie. The Byers didn't seem to lack for anything.

"Here you are." Eliza set a bowl in front of Meggie.

"Thank you." Meggie brought her attention back to the table.

"Hope you like rabbit. My stew's a favorite with most, if I do say so myself, Rose."

Rabbit! Meggie had never eaten rabbit. "It smells wonderful," she fibbed, taking up her spoon. She pictured soft floppy ears and a cute little pink nose. It took every bit of will she had to taste the stew. It wasn't bad, but still, she'd rather not eat it. Carefully now, she picked through the stew to eat only the vegetables.

Eliza pulled her chair closer.

"So tell me, Rose, where are you from originally?"

More lies to tell. She would have to remember precisely what she said now so she could repeat the same lie to others. "I'm from Ireland. I was very young when a family friend brought me to America to live with a widowed aunt who's since passed on. I just never went back home to Ireland. I went to school in the East and earned my teacher's certificate. After a time I wanted to teach in the West. And, well, the opportunity came to travel, and so here I am." Meggie tried to sound nonchalant. Uncomfortable under Eliza's close scrutiny, Meggie hurried with the rest of her lie.

"My family and I write back and forth. One day I hope they'll join me—my parents and my sisters. Yes. I have three sisters. All older and all married with children. It would be very hard for them to travel now, you know, what with their own families and the expense and all. It's that hard for us all to be apart but we must endure the pain of separation. Someday we'll be reunited. Indeed we will."

Meggie was quick to shove in another mouthful of stew. So quick, in fact, she was unmindful this time to pick out only vegetables. As she grudgingly chewed the tender meat, she hoped the strange look on Eliza's face was due purely to interest in her lengthy biography and not to recognition of the lies she'd just told. Unnerved, Meggie could do little but wait for Eliza to say something. She took another bite of stew, her stomach uneasy.

"And I suppose the reason you don't have an Irish accent is because you've lived in America so long?"

"Yes."

"Rose, how brave of you to venture west. A woman alone. Not many would, you know," Eliza declared, and then took another sip of her tea.

Meggie was relieved that Eliza didn't press her on the subject. How she hated to lie to Eliza. How she hated that she must lie to the townsfolk. She knew she committed a sin each time she told a falsehood. But she had to lie. She'd no choice.

"Good afternoon, ladies." William Byers all of a sudden charged into the kitchen. "How do again, Miss Rochester." He gave Meggie a quick nod. "Fact is, I was just about to come and find you. Want to head over to your cabin for a look-see?" Not waiting for an answer from Meggie, he gave his wife's arm an affectionate squeeze and served himself from the stove. "First I need to have some of Eliza's tasty stew."

"Dear." Eliza looked at Meggie. "You best put on a wrap. We can't have you coming down with the ague. There's that much of a chill in the air."

Meggie scooted her chair out. "Yes, of course. I'll just go up and get my shawl. Thank you, Eliza. You're very kind," she added as an afterthought. She meant it. The Byers were very kind. So were the Marksons and Mr. Sykes and the Cottswells back in Denver. Everyone she'd met since she'd fled Boston had been nice to her. She hadn't expected this amiability. It was a surprise that folks outside of the cloistered world in which she'd lived for so many years were just that: nice.

Suddenly she couldn't wait to see her cabin, her new home.

Meggie tried to keep up with Mr. Byers' brisk pace as they strode past all the town buildings, then down a roughed-out trail along the Grande River. She'd almost forgotten about her encounter with the unsettling, handsome stranger from Denver. Almost. She was so engrossed in the scenery along the path that she bumped right into Mr. Byers' back the moment he stopped.

"Par-pardon me!" Embarrassed and upset, she stepped away. Reflexively her hands went up in front of her face as if she expected him to hit her.

William looked at her, his expression blank, and said nothing.

Her face reddened. Old habits were hard to break. She thought she read pity on Mr. Byers' face.

"Well, young lady, we're here," he said, smiling now. "What do you think?"

Grateful Mr. Byers didn't say anything about her strange reaction to him, she looked at the cabin now. It was larger than she'd expected. The flat-roofed log cabin spanned nearly the entire length of the clearing. It was situated at the edge of the Grande, with tall pines thick all around.

"It may not be the fanciest place on the frontier, Miss Rochester, but it's built to be the sturdiest square-hewn cabin in these parts," William announced proudly.

"Rose," Meggie surprised herself when she said it. "Please, call me Rose."

"And you call me, William. All right?"

"All right," she quietly answered.

"Come on now, let's have a look inside, shall we?" he encouraged.

He didn't have to ask twice. Meggie was right behind him. Dark at first inside the cabin, the moment William propped open the wood shutters covering the two cabin windows, afternoon sun poured in. There were glass-paned windows beneath the shutters, not oilcloth as Meggie had expected. It was a fine surprise. She sighed, musty air and all. It was her air in her cabin. And furniture. She had furniture of her very own. She'd never, ever had anything of her very own before, and now she had a wood-frame bed with a feather mattress, and a sawbuck table and chairs!

"Pretty nice, isn't it? Feather bed and all," William said, correctly reading Meggie's thoughts. "Well, you don't have to go any farther than my wife to know how the feather bed got here. Eliza wasn't about to let any new teacher sleep on straw ticking."

Meggie nodded mutely, unable to find her voice yet to thank him. Pivoting, she turned to look at the rest of the cabin interior. A pine washstand sat next to the head of the bed. A chamber pot rested beneath it on the puncheon floor. She blushed and quickly raised her gaze to the ivory basin and pitcher that finished the chamber set. There was a small mirror.

She'd soon take care of that.

On the wall above the sawbuck table there were three shelves. One contained a little grouping of white crockery, another held empty mason jars for drinking, while the bottom shelf had tins marked with cooking ingredients. Just like at the hotel, Meggie thought. One quick glance, and she spotted a store of goods in the corner nearest the table, convenient to the table and to the cabin's open-hearth, stone fireplace.

"Sorry there's no stove here yet," William said. "Eliza's been after me to get another one up here. In the meantime, hope you don't mind cooking over an open flame," he apologized.

"No," Meggie managed to say, albeit absentmindedly, her focus on the brass kettle hanging suspended from one of the hooks on the pivot crane. A collection of iron pots had been set to one side of the mantel with a large pail of tallows pushed to the other. A supply of firewood had already been stacked in a wood box next to the hearth.

"The bucket you'll need to fetch water is over there." William pointed in the direction of the door. "There's a natural spring just out back."

Meggie saw a washtub next to the bucket. For clothes and bathing, she supposed. She liked her new home. She liked William. He was so kind to her. He spoke to her with all the gentleness of a father, with all the concern of a father, with all the care that she'd imagined a father would have. She'd never had anyone pay her such attention. She'd never had a family to speak of.

"Rose." William wasn't finished showing her around. "Rose, over here we've built benches and tables . . ."

Meggie followed him to the other side of the spacious cabin.

". . . which will do nicely for desks I should think." William put a thoughtful hand to his chin.

Meggie stared at the slates already placed on the tables. She counted ten, deciding that must be the number of students she'd have.

"As for your pupils, Rose," William spoke up, "what with having to help on their ranches, attendance will be hit and miss. I hope you understand. Families do the best they can."

"Of course," she acknowledged.

"Rose." William suddenly strode over to the fireplace. "You need a good rocker here. I'll bring one over from the hotel."

"No, you don't need—"

"To bother?" he finished her sentence. "Of course I do. You

need at least one comfortable chair here."

She did love a rocking chair. It ever soothed.

"All right then." He surveyed the room one last time, then looked at Meggie. "Don't be late getting back for supper, Rose. Don't even think about staying here tonight. Eliza would have my hide. She's a mother hen, you know, not happy unless she's clucking over someone. Right now that's you." He reached for the door latch. "Tomorrow is time enough to move your things here. School can start Monday next. I'm sure Eliza and the other womenfolk will have you all settled in by then."

Meggie suddenly thought of the painting of the Christmas village she'd seen at supper last night. The townsfolk in that village must be just as nice as the women in Hot Sulphur Springs.

"See you this evening," William said, then shut the door behind him.

"Goodbye," Meggie said, too late for William to hear. This was all such a wonder. Unwittingly she began to turn round slowly, taking in every detail of the cabin. She turned round one time, and then two, much like a child might—much as she'd done on the frozen street in Denver, but for a far different reason.

Ethan hadn't sworn so much since that bronco bucked him off back in '64, laying him up for weeks. Didn't have time to be laid up then. Didn't have time to be laid up now by some priggish, Bible-thumping, redheaded female. Why in blazes was Nutmeg here? Why was she here instead of off somewhere with her Edward? Ethan's insides churned at the name, Edward. He thought of Nutmeg again. She was beautiful, all right, even though she covered it up. He wondered why she kept her looks hidden, but then caught himself. She sure as hell didn't keep herself hidden or covered for Edward. Sure put her Bible away for him! Ethan remembered her passion in Denver when she cried out for Edward. Ethan jerked his greatcoat off its peg. He didn't have time to sit around and worry over this. Other matters demanded his attention.

He made it from Hot Sulphur Springs to the White River Agency in less than two hours. He liked the Indian agent there well enough. What Ethan didn't like was hearing what the agent had to say.

"I'll tell you, if them folks in Washington knew what these Indians can do—hell, will do—all them white folks would steer clear of 'em fer shore."

Ethan listened carefully to Simon Pritchard.

" 'Course there won't be no more ruckus now, I don't think. Showahcan's done got his revenge, fer now. Cain't say as I blame him. If one of mine was raped and murdered, well . . ." Simon took another sip of bitter coffee and gazed out the window of his modest cabin.

Ethan wanted to know more, realizing again how smart the government was to assign the rugged old pioneer to the White River Agency. Simon knew the mountains. He knew the Utes. He had experience written all over his weathered features, from the bottom of his full-bearded chin to the top of his silver head of hair.

"Don't expect I'll be tellin' the folks in Washington what happened yesterde', Ethan." The leathery agent shook his head. "Damn stupid sons of bitches. Showahcan got to 'em good. Their days of trappin' is over, shore as shootin'. Never seen three bodies cut up that-a-way. If'n you was to ask me, I think them trappers done worse to that poor Ute girl. Plain downright mean and nasty, they was." Simon took another sip of coffee. "Them varmints didn't deserve it, but I done buried the sons of bitches anyway. Leastways what I could find of 'em."

Ethan could only imagine what the unknown Indian girl had suffered at the hands of her white tormentors. No one, red or white, deserved to come up against such fear—to die in such a gruesome way. He'd have left the sorry bastards for the buzzards.

"So I ain't gonna say nuthin' 'bout this, Ethan. I'm a hopin' yer gonna do the same."

"Don't worry, Simon. It wouldn't do any good. It would just stir things up. Are you certain the Utes won't go after the settlers now?"

"Humph. You young fellas what go round a thinkin' the answer is that easy. There ain't no guarantees 'bout nuthin' up here, Ethan. The best we can hope fer is an uneasy peace. Their Chief don't want any of his people havin' nuthin' to do with us white folks. That there gives us an edge. Odds is on our side, too, that there won't be no more ruckus over this, seein' as the Utes are aplenty in these parts. Numbers is on their side. Ain't enough of us white folks up here yet to worry 'em. Don't know as any of us wanna be here when things change. Washington won't be happy until the Utes are run clear out of the territory. When things start up, the Grande will be runnin' with nuthin' but blood!" Simon slammed his empty cup down on the table and walked over to the cabin window.

Simon's prediction forced Ethan to think on the coming storm.

"I know somethin' none of them tenderfoots pushin' pencils back in Washington know, son." Simon turned to Ethan. "These Utes ain't a gonna ever let themselves be rounded up and corralled on some reservation. If you wanna know somethin' fer certain, there you have it. String me up on the nearest cottonwood if any of 'em ever sees a day on any reservation. Every man, woman, and child of 'em will fight till their deaths afore that happens. I know 'cause I know Showahcan. I know how he thinks. Showahcan idn't fooled by us. He idn't fooled by promises or treaties. No sir. His people ain't a gonna end up jailed on the poorest land what can be found in the territory. I'll say it again, son. The mighty Grande will be spillin' over with the blood of red men and white."

The finality of the aging pioneer's words fell like a blow across the tiny cabin.

Simon turned back to the window, staring out at the thick forest. "You take care, son," he said, then grabbed his hat off a nearby peg and went outside, quickly disappearing from view.

Ethan understood Simon's upset. He believed every word the old pioneer said. The truth of it sank in like a downed bottle of bad whiskey. His guts churned. He scraped out his chair and got up. If he left the agency now he should make it back to Hot Sulphur by nightfall.

Nugget pinned his ears back and whinnied.

Ethan didn't need his horse to signal. He sensed danger, too.

"Easy boy," he said, trying to calm the skittish animal. "Easy." He stroked the powerful horse's neck as they rode. When Nugget quieted, Ethan moved his hand away, to the butt of his reliable Winchester rifle. Ethan couldn't see them, but he knew the Utes were following him. They hadn't attacked. He didn't think they wanted to, or he'd already be dead. Still, he kept his hand on his Winchester. The sun was setting. The outskirts of Hot Sulphur were up ahead. Easing his hand off his rifle, he guided Nugget over the rough, rutted trail to town.

The Indians worried him, but then so did another potential problem.

Nutmeg.

It would be dark soon. Meggie tensed. She should have left for supper by now. She shouldn't have whiled away the afternoon daydreaming about her new cabin, wandering around exploring outside as if she'd not a care in the world. Most definitely, she had a care now. She needed to get to the hotel before dark. Quickly, she lit the kerosene lantern. It might not help ease her case of nerves, but at least she'd see her way. Even when she found her way to the hotel, she wasn't sure she wanted to go inside. She wasn't sure if she could sit down and eat with the stranger there. She wasn't sure if she could get the picture of him out of her mind . . . *half-naked, his body steaming and—*

Oh faith and bother! Hadn't she promised herself that very morning that she wouldn't let the stranger upset her anymore?

Meggie forced her thoughts away from the unsettling man and onto the pathway to the hotel, going over the way in her mind. She'd walk along the river, then follow the bend. And then where the path met the steep hill, there was a wood rail marking the trail up the hill to town. She could do this. Gathering her shawl about her, she took up the lantern and unlatched the cabin door, re-latching it behind her.

The wind kicked up, making the little flame in her lantern dance. Her feet crunched over pine needles. The river roared past. But then she heard something over the water's roar . . . something off in the distance . . . something able to pierce the night air, like the howling of a wild animal—the howl of a predator ready to stalk, ready to hunt.

She started to run, screaming when she bumped into something right away. It was too dark to see who or what it was.

"Rose! Rose! It's only me, Rose." William put his hands on her arms to calm her.

"William?" She needed to make sure.

"Eliza sent me. She was afraid of this very thing; that you'd get lost in the dark. I can see you found your way. You're on the right path." He took her lantern from her. "Come on. Just follow me."

He didn't have to tell her twice.

Grateful for William's guidance now, she refused to berate

herself for screaming or being scared of the dark. She knew all too well that the predator after her was very real. No, she wouldn't apologize for being scared.

CHAPTER EIGHT

"There you two are. Supper's all ready," Eliza gently scolded when William and Meggie entered the dining room.

Meggie had to sit next to *him*.

The only seat left where a place had been set was next to the stranger.

William pulled out her chair. Meggie hesitated. No one had ever pulled out a chair for her, treating her with such respect, like a lady. Emotion welled in her throat. She swallowed hard, then nodded to William, Eliza, and the Marksons before taking her seat.

The stranger sitting next to her said nothing.

Neither did Meggie. She rubbed her cold, clammy palms together, fighting the urge to check her nape. How could she calmly sit and eat at this dangerous table, made so by the stranger's presence. Her head pounded. She'd no appetite for anything but to get away from him. Self-conscious that everyone could read her thoughts, she stared down at her plate. *I'm a coward,* she chastised silently. *Nothing short of a coward.* Still, she didn't look up.

Oh, faith! She suddenly panicked all over again. What if . . . what if he tells everyone what happened in Denver? That I fainted in the street, that he took me to my room, that I was alone with him, that he'd seen me undressed, that I'd seen him all but undressed this very afternoon. Her thoughts trailed from bad to worse. Once the stranger told everyone at the table about her—that she wasn't a lady—that she wasn't decent—William and Eliza would send her packing for sure! Where to go? What to do? She had no place to go . . . no place.

"Rose?"

Meggie couldn't look at Eliza. She could feel the noose around her neck tighten. The lamplight on the table burned low. She was glad for it. No need for more light on this horrid, deciding moment.

"Rose, I want you to meet Ethan. Ethan Rourke from Denver."

"Ma'am," Ethan said, his eyes on his food and not Meggie.

The instant Meggie heard his name—*Ethan Rourke*—it was familiar. Oddly, hearing his name made her feel strangely akin to him, as if they were connected by distant memories. But how could that be? It could not. Before Denver, she'd never met the man. She took a sip of water to buy time, to better sharpen her wits. None of this made sense.

Neither looked at the other.

Nor did they look at William or Eliza to see the queer expressions on their faces.

"Have you two met before?" Eliza posed; the suspicion in her voice obvious.

Meggie looked at the Marksons, relieved that they were busy eating and seemed oblivious to her predicament. She squirmed in her seat and finally looked at Eliza, then at William, then again at Eliza. Their faces said it all. They knew she was lying. The noose around her neck tightened more. She'd no choice now. She'd have to tell William and Eliza about Denver before Ethan Rourke did. An unmarried woman like her, alone out west, in a room with a man . . . they'd believe her a fallen woman. Maybe that was just as well. Better to think her a fallen woman than—

"Rose," Eliza asked again. "Have you two met?"

"Ye—"

"No," Ethan broke in over Meggie. "No, Eliza. We've never met before. "Pleasure, Miss . . . uh, Rose is it?"

Meggie couldn't believe what he'd said—what he didn't say. She'd be eternally grateful for Ethan Rourke's silence, while at the same time wishing him into eternity.

Ethan looked at her now.

She made herself look back.

His dusky glare accused her of something. But what? He couldn't possibly know anything about her. She'd given little away about herself during their previous encounters. Maybe he was mad she'd been a bother to him in Denver. Maybe he was mad she'd seen him half-naked earlier. Whatever the reason, right now she was unnerved by his eyes on her, undressed by his penetrating regard, and overpowered by his darkly handsome good looks.

Where had she heard his name? Where?

Of course. At Junction House. Martha Wheatley had gone on about someone named Ethan at the stage stop. Meggie felt a little better at the recollection. Still, she felt warm under his continued scrutiny. Too warm. She wiped her sweaty palms on her skirt as if the action might help. It didn't. She had to make some reply to Ethan, to say something before everyone thought things amiss.

"A pl—a pleasure to make your acquaintance, Mr. Rourke," she said haltingly, all the while staring down at her now-full plate of chicken and dumplings. When had food been served to her? The chicken didn't smell like chicken, but like musk and deep woods and new tobacco. She'd no appetite for it.

Ethan began eating, looking away from her now.

The room cooled. Meggie mentally thanked every saint she could think of. His steely presence still unnerved her, but she managed to pick up her fork and take a bite of chicken.

Conversation started up around the table. She was grateful for it; grateful attention had turned from her.

"Ethan, how'd it go today with Simon Pritchard?" William asked.

"Fine. He's got a nice little cabin. All the comforts he needs for an old mountain man." Ethan took a sip of his coffee.

"I'm that happy to know his cabin is sufficient, Ethan. It's the Utes I was asking about."

Ethan took another sip of coffee, the strain on his face less readable in the dim lamplight. "Not a sign of trouble so far, William. Not enough of us up here yet for the Utes to bother with."

"That's good news." William looked relieved. "We haven't had any problems in the years we've been up here. Not yet. We don't see many Indians, but we know they're around. Ever since the Meeker massacre, well, we all worry about what went wrong there. Innocents slaughtered by that goddamn Colonel Chivington!"

"Excuse me, ladies," William apologized, keeping his obvious anger in check.

"Yeah, well, I'm with you on that, William," Ethan intoned. "The territory in these parts is too rugged for the government to worry over just yet." Ethan didn't try to hide the bitterness he felt about the way the government had dealt with Indians so far. "Besides, we've got a treaty with the Utes promising they won't stop any of our stages or bother the settlers up here."

"I know, but I'm still waiting to hear exactly what the Utes are getting out of it."

"You should ask what the Utes are *supposed* to get out of it, William. That's been the problem with other treaties. The government doesn't always come through. It's horses the Utes want mostly. Let's hope Washington follows through and gives them what's promised."

Meggie caught the somber looks exchanged between the two men.

"I hope so, too, Ethan," William said softly.

Nothing more was said.

Ethan got up from the table first.

"Thanks for the fine supper, Eliza. I'll just say goodnight," he said with a polite nod to everyone before leaving the room.

Meggie listened as his booted footsteps took to the stairs, the same stairs leading to the same hallway leading to a room on the same floor as hers. They'd be sleeping close, way too close. Her insides gave a start, forcing her up from her chair. Quickly now, she followed Eliza into the kitchen to help with the supper dishes.

Pure spring water spilled over smoothed rock. Each cascade ebbed and flowed toward the steamy crystal pool at the base of the mountain ridge. Fragrant evergreens protected the little clearing and stood watch over the two lovers. Lying on a meadowy carpet of wildflowers Meggie had never felt so happy, so alive. Pleasure exceeded her wildest imaginings. She lay on her back with her arms above her head, her fingers splayed to gently run over fragrant soft petals of pink and red.

A suggestion from her lover brought a low moan to her throat. Willingly, she waited for him to cover her aroused body with his own powerful frame. In heightened anticipation, she waited for him. Rippled thighs straddled her quivering hips. Sculpted hands came to rest on either side of her head. Ready to be pierced through with those slate shards, she opened her eyes, opened herself to love.

But it wasn't her lover who leaned over Meggie with the offer of his kiss. It was the devil stealing her daydream away!

Meggie struggled to get the villainous weight off her. The fiend had her trapped in his vice-like, painful grip. Its evil laugh, like the blade of the sharpest knife, repeatedly cut through her fear-stricken body. A cold, claw-like hand smothered her mouth and throat. She couldn't cry out for help. The other taloned fingers ripped at her bodice, exposing her flesh to the devil. Molten red embers pointed their fiery glare at her, glowing ever brighter at her alarm, at her panic.

Please. Oh please, God. Let me die! Let me be rid of this monster. Let him not touch me with his filth. She prayed for the sleep of death. She screamed for it.

Awakened from her nightmare by her own strangled cries, Meggie felt powerful arms cradle her trembling body. Terrified and confused, she dared not move. She stilled like the dead. Unable to see anything, she dared not speak. Although her intuition told her the strong hands cradling her now were not the claws of her night terror, she couldn't calm.

If not the devil . . . then who?

She heard nothing but the sound of her heart thudding wildly in her chest, echoing from wall to wall, closing in around her. The room was dark, the tallow gone out. In her worst nightmares she'd always awakened alone. The sisters had never come in. No comforting arms had ever held her before.

Whose arms held her now?

Anxious and disoriented, still terrified, Meggie fought the bizarre, overwhelming urge to lean into the comfort of the unknown, tender grasp. But she didn't dare. This could be evil trickery. In her own defense she began to mutter, "six feet under, six feet away, where to stay safe, the devil must stay!" She tried to get away now, but could not wrench free. Tears of desperation poured down her cheeks.

"Easy now."

Meggie stilled instantly at the deep, reverberating tone. When she felt the warm vibration of the mysterious intruder's lips against her forehead, the shock of his touch stunned her, yet drew her to him. The stranger's words were as gentle as his touch. Whoever he was, he wasn't going to hurt her. She knew it now. If he wasn't the devil then who? *An angel?* Instinctively, she gave herself over to the heavenly embrace. "Thank you, my angel," she whispered. Of course it was crazy to believe an actual angel held her now, but believe it she did. She felt safe now. Who but an angel could make her feel safe?

Ethan cradled the distraught woman in his arms as if she were a child.

But she wasn't.

He couldn't ignore her soft curves, her low whispers against his chest, or her clinging sweetness for much longer. Here she thought he was an angel—and he was thinking like a devil. If only she didn't feel so damn good all curled up and snuggled against him. Needing him. It felt good to be needed again. For longer than he cared to remember, he hadn't let any woman touch him like this and break down his guard against . . . against exactly what was happening. He tightened his hold. He knew he wasn't the answer to anyone's prayer but it felt good to be the answer to Nutmeg's just now.

For long minutes Meggie and Ethan held onto each other like starved animals, giving and receiving the comfort they both sought.

Neither could get enough.

The first to stir, Meggie reluctantly pulled out of the angelic embrace. Unable to see in the darkness, yet no longer afraid, she reached for a tallow on the bedstead and quickly lit it. Now she could see exactly who her angel was.

"You!" Meggie bolted from the bed.

"Yeah, me." Ethan stood now, too.

"Why are you in my room? How dare you?" Meggie, shocked and incensed at Ethan's presence, faced him straight-on. She didn't care that his tall frame towered over hers. She readied for the fight.

But Ethan wasn't ready. In his own battle with the way her shapely breasts rose and fell under her nightdress with each agitated breath, with the way her loosened scarlet braid fell seductively over her, with the way one rosy lip of her sweet mouth nibbled the other, he felt himself sink deeper and deeper into those violet-to-black depths. Right now he couldn't concentrate on any fight that Nutmeg wanted to have with him.

Meggie saw his apparent indifference to her ire, and it fueled her anger.

"What are you looking at? You can't stand there and gawk at me! You have no right to be in here! What made you think that you could march in here and intrude on my privacy to harass me again?"

"Harass you? Jesus Christ, lady."

"Don't you take our Lord's name in vain. You're not fit to—"

"To what? Be in the presence of your precious God? No, maybe I'm not," Ethan threw back. "I wouldn't be in here now if you hadn't screamed loud enough to wake the dead. It seems like you're just fine now. Back to your old self. And we both know what *that* is." As soon as they were out of his mouth, he could see the searing effect of his words. He'd regret them later, but right now he just wanted to put this wildfire out.

Meggie's insides folded at the hurtful, pointed remark. No, she didn't know what *that* meant. Why, he sounded as though he knew something about her when he knew nothing. How could he?

"All I did was have a bad dream." Meggie's anger stayed fueled. "Is that a crime to you? Is that unacceptable to you? I'll have you know I can handle my own nightmares, thank you very much. I don't need you or anybody else barging in here. I don't need your help. I don't need anybody's help."

Now Ethan's insides folded. Nutmeg had got to him again. He resisted the sudden urge to encircle her in his arms, to press her shaken form against his own and take away her fear. Something in her dreams scared her to death. He wished he knew what. He wished even harder that he didn't want to know. The inferno in front of him faded to embers. He'd needed to get out of there before Nutmeg could flare up again. Without another word, he turned and walked out the door.

All the fight left Meggie the moment Ethan left. She couldn't believe any of this. She couldn't believe her wished-for angel was Ethan Rourke. She couldn't believe he'd witnessed her night terrors. They were to be kept secret from everyone, especially him.

Drained by the horror of her nightmare and her confusion upon awakening to find Ethan in her room, she crawled back into bed. It was not yet light out, making her glad for the little candle that burned close by. She turned onto her stomach and gave her pillow an exasperated thump before resting her cheek against its clean softness. Even with her eyes shut tight, everything about Ethan's unwelcome visit was still in the room, from his heart-stopping handsomeness to the traces of his musky essence. Sleep would not come easily.

At breakfast the next morning, Eliza said nothing about last night—about Meggie screaming loud enough to wake the dead. Ethan's very words. Humph. He wasn't at breakfast. Well, good and good riddance! Her meal would be peaceful. No need to worry about seeing him again today. After a few bites of egg, her traitorous thoughts returned to Ethan. Her spirits dampened. Maybe Ethan wouldn't be back. Meggie couldn't ask Eliza and raise her suspicions. Meggie shoved in another bite of egg and tried to tell herself that she didn't want to know anything about Ethan. The next forkful didn't go down well.

What if Ethan had gone back to Denver . . . maybe even for the rest of the winter? Why should she care?

I don't!

Suddenly unable to sit still, Meggie thanked Eliza for breakfast and went upstairs to pack her things. She wanted to get to her cabin as soon as possible and forget all about Ethan Rourke.

Someone rapped on Meggie's door. It was late afternoon. Her heart went to her throat. It could be—no, it couldn't be Ethan. Feeling every bit the fool, she walked to the door and unlatched it.

"I brought you some cherry bark tea." Eliza waltzed in and set the tin on the table.

Glad for Eliza's company, Meggie put the kettle of water over the fire.

"Thank you for everything, Eliza, for the cabin and the rocker and—"

"Oh, tish tosh, Rose. You needed a roof over your head. That's all this is." Eliza looked around the cabin. "It's that plain I'm afraid, Rose."

"Plain?" Meggie disagreed. "Why, not at all. It's perfect, Eliza. Why, it's every bit as nice as Thornfield Hall to me."

"Thornfield Hall? Is it in Ireland? Is it your family home?" Eliza quickly asked.

Too late, Meggie realized she'd been talking about Edward Rochester's estate from the pages of *Jane Eyre*. Furious with herself for not separating fact from fiction, Meggie bit back her upset.

"No. Not my family home, but a friend's. A family friend." It wasn't a total lie, Meggie thought. She did consider Edward and Jane family friends.

"I'm sure you miss your friends and family, but I've got some news to perk up your day," Eliza said brightly.

Curious, Meggie waited to hear what news.

"What would you say to a shindig held this very eve? I forgot to mention it to you before, what with all the excitement over your arrival and the stage coming in. Never you mind. We'll all gather together at tonight's shindig," Eliza said, her merriment obvious.

Meggie had never heard of a shindig. Not wanting to show her ignorance, she kept silent and waited for Eliza to continue.

"Folks will come to town tonight to celebrate the end of haying and the harvest before winter sets in for good. I expect every ranch family in these parts will be here. How lucky for you." Eliza reached over and gave Meggie's arm a little squeeze. "You can meet everyone and everyone can meet you. My neighbors are already chomping at the bit to see the new schoolmarm."

"Is a shindig like a church meeting, Eliza? Will we thank our Lord for our bountiful blessings?" Meggie asked. It would be nice to attend a church meeting.

"A chur—?"

Eliza didn't seem to know what to say. She had a funny look on her face. Meggie shifted uncomfortably in her chair, knowing she must have spoken incorrectly.

"Why, no, dear. A shindig is a social, a party. There will be lots of good food, visiting, and dancing." She gave Meggie's arm another squeeze. "You know, you've certainly given me an idea though. We don't have a church yet. We've all been so busy trying to carve out a life in this wilderness, we haven't made the time to put up a church. Parson or not, it's high time we did," she declared.

A church couldn't be built quickly enough to suit Meggie. She'd much rather spend tonight in prayer than at any shindig, any social—*with dancing—with men.*

The water was ready. Meggie made haste and set about brewing their tea, happy for any task to end talk of the upcoming social. After they'd enjoyed their tea and before Eliza left, Eliza advised Meggie to save her appetite for the evening ahead and to be at the hotel before dark so everyone could go to the shindig at the smithy's together. Eliza's advice wasn't necessary. Meggie had no appetite for food or barn dancing. And who exactly did Eliza refer to when she said *everyone* would walk over? Did *everyone* include Ethan? Meggie didn't have the stomach to see him again, either. She walked over to the hearth and plopped down in her rocker. Out of habit, she pulled out her crucifix from the neck of her dress and held onto it tightly. Her insides tensed as she thought about the night ahead.

Ethan didn't want to go to any shindig, either, but if he refused William and Eliza were sure to ask questions. He didn't want personal questions thrown at him any more than he wanted to make an appearance at Zeb Kinney's. Only one thing kept him in Hot Sulphur Springs now: his worry over the Utes. Otherwise he'd be over the pass in the time it took to roll a smoke. He'd ridden all day, and there wasn't a sign of Indians or of any trouble.

Still, Ethan needed to make sure things were quiet, what with that poor Ute girl raped and killed. Ethan wished those bastard trappers were still alive so he'd have a chance at them. Every time he imagined what they did to the Ute maid, no revenge satisfied. Revenge is what worried Ethan about Chief Showah-can. Had Simon Pritchard been right? Had the Utes already exacted their revenge, or was there more trouble to come? Ethan decided to spend one more day in the mountains and do his best to find out.

Nightfall came all too soon, and with it the social that Meggie and Ethan both dreaded.

Meggie, relieved Ethan wasn't with them, followed William and Eliza down the street toward Zeb Kinney's barn. As they walked, the music and laughter grew louder. The three passed through a maze of wagons and buckboards along the way. Meggie couldn't believe she was going to a social with dancing and drinking.

Dancing and drinking are tools of the devil, Meghan Rose Mc-Murphy.

The sisters' warning rang in her head like the clanging of church bells. The wrathful clanging shut out the lively music coming from the barn. All Meggie could hear in her head was the droning liturgy of the sisters:

Tools of the devil! Tools of the devil!

Someone took hold of Meggie's hand. Immediately Meggie knew who it must be: Sister Mary Catherine.

Don't worry, Sister Mary Catherine. I won't do anything wrong ever again. I won't. I'm good. I'm good. I wash my sins away every day.

Struck by the sudden overpowering need to cleanse her hands, Meggie tried to wring them together.

"Rose? Rose, what's wrong?"

Eliza! It was Eliza and not Sister Mary Catherine. Meggie had been imagining things again. She was always imagining Sister Mary Catherine, the strictest of all her teachers, telling her to pray for forgiveness every day, to live a chaste life, and to steer clear of sin and wrongdoing. Meggie hastily untwined her fingers from Eliza's.

William walked on ahead, unaware the two women had stopped.

"Whatever is wrong?" Eliza said, alarmed.

Think, Meggie girl. Make sense of it.

"It's just . . . I just haven't been to a social in a long, long time. I'm that excited, I am. You startled me, Eliza. That's all. I startle easily. I always have." Meggie looked at Eliza, hoping she hadn't sounded too ridiculous.

Eliza only smiled. "Come now, Rose. We don't want to be late."

Meggie felt so relieved that Eliza had paid no mind to her odd behavior, she wanted to hug her. But of course, she did not. How pretty Eliza looked with her blond hair coiled softly atop her head and a yellow ribbon to help hold it in place. Her matching yellow frock was just as lovely. Meggie hadn't thought about dressing up for the social until now. She'd given no thought to her own attire and wore the same gray woolen she'd had on all day. What she had on made little difference. It never mattered to Meggie that she should look pretty to anybody.

The next thing she knew, they'd arrived at Zeb Kinney's place. The barn was all lit up. Countless lanterns hung from the rough walls. Meggie lingered in the doorway while William and Eliza went inside. She should leave. This wasn't any place for her. This place must be sinful. Without realizing what she was doing, however, one of her booted feet began to tap in time to the lively melody.

Two fiddlers stood on a raised platform, while couples danced round and around to the tune they played. Children scurried past, chasing one another through the sea of dancing couples. The children's innocent laughter struck a chord in Meggie. She began to relax. Besides, none of this looked sinful at all. She noticed two children in particular who'd joined hands and were trying to step in time with the adults. The little boy and girl failed miserably in their attempt to follow the dance. They broke into peals of laughter and held their tummies.

"Come on in, Rose." Eliza broke into Meggie's thoughts, taking up her hand again.

This time Meggie let her.

"Everyone's here, Rose. Well, almost everyone," Eliza muttered, all the while scanning the crowd. She turned back to Meggie. "I can't wait for you to meet folks," she said excitedly, then tugged Meggie across the dance floor.

Eliza didn't seem to mind an occasional bumping from the couples swirling by, but Meggie sure did. They couldn't reach the other side of the barn quickly enough.

"As soon as this set is over, Rose, you have to meet the blacksmith and his wife. There's Zeb Kinney now on one of the fiddles. Clovis has to be somewhere about. And then, let's see, I'll find . . ." Eliza's voice trailed off as she again scanned the crowd for someone else to introduce.

Meggie looked around the huge barn and spotted two long tables laden with sumptuous food. Delicious aromas of baked apples and cinnamon floated through the air. Desserts of every kind, pies, cakes, and cookies covered one red-checked tablecloth, while the other was barely visible under all of the meat dishes, platters of fried chicken, and baskets of fresh-baked breads. She noticed another, smaller table with liquid refreshments, pitchers of water, lemonade and something else.

Bottles of spirits!

"The devil's drink," Meggie whispered out loud. "I'll not let it pass my lips," she vowed to Sister Mary Catherine in the same whisper. "I'm good. I'm good."

"What, Rose? What's that you say?"

When will I learn to keep silent? Meggie berated herself, wondering how many more times she could fool Eliza. "The food looks good. Very good."

"Well, of course it does," Eliza agreed. "You must be hungry. Go. Go and get something to eat. You can meet the Kinneys after you've had a plate of food," she clucked, much like the mother hen William had described.

At just that moment, a plump woman wearing a smile nearly as broad as she was approached them.

"How do, Eliza? Idn't this quite the gatherin'? I declare, my Zeb's as happy as kin be, gittin' to play that fiddle of his. Only thing he loves more than his fiddle is his horses. The kids and me fit in somewheres." She laughed heartily at her own words.

Meggie couldn't help but smile. The woman's round, dumpling cheeks, double chin, and honey-colored, twinkling eyes reminded her of one of the warm apple pies waiting on the dessert table. Her mop of curly hair, fastened in a haphazard bun atop her head, looked to Meggie like lumps of maple sugar all stuck together. Dark blue, long-sleeved homespun adorned the woman's ample frame.

As soon as Clovis Kinney was introduced to Meggie, the jolly woman near bubbled over with excitement.

"Pleased to meet you, Miss Rochester. I fer one am pleased as kin be to have you here," Clovis said as if Meggie were a long, lost friend. "If I kin ever find my Emma, I want her to meet you. She's six and full as kin be of pure vinegar." As if weighing her words to the new teacher, Clovis added, "well, just mebbe there's a touch of sugar in there somewhere."

"It's nice to meet you, Mrs. . . . Clovis," Meggie quickly corrected. "Please call me Rose. I'm learning I don't have to stand on such formality in the West."

" 'Course you don't," Clovis replied, hesitating, as if Meggie's words made her contemplate the thought for the first time. "And idn't it wonderful? Why we're all just plain folk needin' to stick together to git by up here."

"Mama! Mama!"

An adorable little maple-sugar, mop-headed girl ran up to Clovis and threw her tiny arms around the woman's skirts. The child clutched a rag doll tightly in one arm. Clovis placed a hand on the child's head while the little girl sobbed.

"Mama! Mama! Mama! Ole' Willie says he's gonna throw Nellie in the river. He says . . . I'm just a baby and . . . he's

114

gonna throw my dolly in the river. Don't let 'im, mama. Don't let mean ol', stupid ol' Willie hurt my dolly."

"There, there, Emma. Don't you worry none 'bout Willie. I'm shore he'll do no such a thing. No one is gonna toss Nellie in the river. I'm shore Willie's fergotten 'bout Nellie by now," Clovis soothed, and kept patting her daughter's head.

"No, Mama! He's bad, and he's gonna do it!" Tears poured down the little girl's face.

Meggie's heart went out to Emma—to Emma and her treasured rag doll. She knew what it felt like to have such precious things ripped away.

"Now Emma, you dry them tears and meet the new school-marm."

The child instantly quieted. Then she slowly turned around to peek up at Meggie. Holding her doll close, she offered up a curious stare. Except for a few lingering dry sobs, her tears faded.

"Say hullo, Emma," Clovis gently urged.

The little girl said nothing.

Meggie knelt down to be at eye level with Emma. "My doll's name was Belle. She could have been Nellie's sister."

Seemingly at the mere mention of her precious Nellie, Emma smiled.

"May I meet Nellie?" Meggie asked.

Apparently needing no time at all to make such a decision, Emma held Nellie up in front of her.

"How do you do, Nellie? I'm happy to know you and to know Emma."

At this the little girl began to giggle.

"Yer funny, and yer nice to talk to Nellie. Prob'ly you don't know she's just my dolly. She's not really real. I mean really, real, like us an' all."

"Is that so, Emma? Well, now who's the teacher? Why, you

are!" Meggie tickled Emma's tummy, which made the little girl giggle louder. "You know, Emma, I can't wait to have you and Nellie at school. It will be so much fun with you and the other boys and girls."

Emma frowned. "Not mean ol' Willie. Anyways, he's stupid ol' Willie and won't learn nuthin'. He just fights and does mean things."

"I bet together you and I can teach Willie a thing or two. What do you think, Emma? We'll make a good team."

Emma seemed to consider Meggie's words.

"We'll learn mean ol' Willie not to be mean ol' Willie." Emma giggled again. As quickly as she'd appeared, Emma, with Nellie in tow, disappeared into the crowd.

"That's my Emma. Always somethin' goin' on. Always. All the time. You was very good with her, Rose. You shore are good with little 'uns."

"She's a darling. If all the youngsters here are like her, I think I'll pick vinegar every day," Meggie gaily offered, borrowing from the mother's own words.

Caught up in their own laughter, none of the women noticed the man who stood nearby, near enough to hear and see everything that had taken place.

CHAPTER NINE

Ethan had slipped in the back door of the barn. He'd promised Eliza he'd make an appearance and that's all he'd do. One pass through the barn, say his hellos to Eliza and William, and then he'd leave. He sure as hell didn't want another run-in with the unpredictable redhead.

But no sooner had he gone inside than there she was, right in front of him.

The small cluster of women had their backs to him. That was something, at least. Eliza and the smithy's wife were talking to Nutmeg. Ethan leaned against a nearby post. He'd wait for the conversation to break up and for Nutmeg to walk away. He should have been the one to keep walking; then he might have avoided hearing the exchange between Nutmeg and the young tyke.

Like two little girls together. Ethan had already seen it in Nutmeg—childlike one minute and full-blown female the next. The tenderness he'd just witnessed, the way she was so easy with the little girl, threw him. He thought of Nutmeg's scars, amazed she could be so tender and gentle despite them. He got mad all over again about her scars. Then he got mad at himself all over again for caring.

The longer he watched Nutmeg shower sweet affection on the youngster, the more his insides got twisted up. He remembered how Nutmeg had reached out to him last night, how she'd pressed into him, needing him to protect her. Was that the child in her or the woman who had reached out to him?

Ethan had no idea why Nutmeg hid her incredible shape. Most women, he knew from experience, would put themselves out there to be seen if they had Nutmeg's body. Most women wouldn't cover up so. He'd seen Nutmeg uncovered, and that was part of his problem. Smooth, white, creamy skin all sprinkled with nutmeg and flavored with spice. He could almost taste it. *Damn.* Ethan knew he should turn-tail and leave Zeb Kinney's barn, but he didn't.

Fully dressed now, Nutmeg looked the same as she did when he first saw her in Denver, all buttoned up to her neck in that dratted wool gown, hair wound so tight it could bring tears, spectacles trying to hide all the allure in those violet eyes, and a cross hanging around her neck like an albatross. She looked the same. He should feel the same. He shouldn't give a damn one way or the other about her. Instead of getting out of there, he charged over to the refreshment tables, suddenly needing a drink more than he needed to leave.

Meggie hadn't seen Ethan pass by. A small group of young ladies had approached her and drew her into conversation.

"Why, how do you do, *Miss* Rochester? We all had to come over and meet the new schoolmarm. And well, here we are," one of the young ladies said and held out her hand.

By now Eliza and Clovis Kinney had wandered off, leaving Meggie alone. She tried to smile at the dark-haired beauty's introduction, but something about the young woman made Meggie recoil. She read insincerity in the young woman's cat-like eyes and heard it in her syrupy tone. It took effort for Meggie to take her outstretched hand.

"I'm happy to make your acquaintance, to meet all of you," Meggie said.

The young woman in question looked to be about seventeen

or eighteen. She didn't let go of Meggie's hand. Her hostile grasp triggered unwanted memories. Meggie had known unfriendly, untrustworthy, and unkind people like her before.

"And you are?" Meggie asked out of politeness, wresting her hand free.

"Of course. How very rude of me."

Meggie didn't miss the young woman's condescension.

"I'm Olivia Tritt." She glanced about her group of friends, evidently needing to make sure of their attention before locking gazes with Meggie again. "I'm up here visitin' for a spell. I'm one of *the* Tritts of Denver. My father's an important banker in Denver. Likely you've already heard of him."

Struck by Olivia Tritt's conceit, Meggie shook her head no.

"Come along, Livi." One of the other girls tugged at her arm.

"In a minute, Flossie," Olivia snapped. "I haven't finished meetin' *Miss* Rochester."

Meggie was finished. She'd no desire to spend another moment in Livi Tritt's mean-spirited presence. "Very nice to have met you all." She managed a smile. "I'll just go now and get my supper."

"Of course. You go right ahead. Not me. Certainly not me," Livi avowed. "I just couldn't eat a bite. A girl has to keep her figure, you know. With all the gentlemen here, I'm just too busy to eat. I declare they all have me dancin' so, I've just been runnin' and runnin'."

Meggie felt the sharp edge of Livi's pointed words.

"What did I tell you? Here comes Zachary Cleary," Livi proclaimed. "That boy just won't leave me be."

Relieved when the young man whisked Livi Tritt onto the dance floor, Meggie thought it a shame that someone so beautiful on the outside could be so unpleasant on the inside. The rest of Livi's little group disappeared when Livi started dancing. Relieved to be alone, Meggie turned toward the refreshment table . . . then froze.

Somewhere between arriving with the Byerses and fending off Livi Tritt, she'd actually forgotten Ethan Rourke might come to the social. She should leave right here and now, but she stayed rooted to the spot. *Damn and Tarnation!* Meggie forgot to appeal to the sisters for forgiveness for cursing. She watched Ethan. He was talking with an older man and sipping a drink of . . . spirits!

"How very apt," she muttered to herself. "The devil with the devil's drink." Certainly she thought of the sisters now. Humph. Only last night Ethan had been her angel. Devil or angel, she determined to keep a safe distance from him. Just then Livi Tritt walked up to Ethan. Meggie's instincts told her to leave, but she didn't. Livi said something to Ethan. In the next moment the dark-haired beauty was dancing in Ethan's arms. Meggie watched them swirl past.

She hated to admit it, but Livi Tritt looked radiant in Ethan's arms. Meggie hadn't noticed before how lovely the green muslin was on the young woman, or how its scooped neck revealed more than a hint of Livi's endowed bosom. Shocking, Meggie thought. Livi's shining, black tresses, partially pulled up in a green ribbon, fell over the hand Ethan had around her back as they moved over the dance floor. Envious, Meggie couldn't take her eyes off the pair.

They look so well together.

Both dark.

Both attractive.

Both perfect.

Without her volition, Meggie's hands began to smooth the worn folds of her woolen dress. She ran her fingers down over her waist and hips before raising them to straighten the tightly fastened collar of her baggy garment. After a touch to her wire rims on the bridge of her nose, she checked each hairpin that held her hair tightly in place. It did no good to try to tuck loose wisps into the pins. They never stayed. Nothing more to be done here, Meggie girl. No perfection or beauty here. Meggie didn't like having such wicked thoughts—imagining being attractive. Such thoughts invited trouble. Then why did it bother her now to feel so plain and unattractive?

Meggie had only to look at Ethan Rourke for her answer.

The tune was over. Ethan escorted Olivia Tritt off the dance floor. He'd been surprised to find Angus Tritt's daughter in Hot Sulphur Springs. The banker's daughter was a beauty, but Ethan knew her type. Soured his stomach every time.

"Ethan, would you be kind enough to get me a glass of that cool lemonade. I'm just as warm as can be," Livi said, sugarcoating the words, and then turned to her friends.

Damn, he was bored with women like her. He'd had his fill of them. Samantha was like them in some ways, but he was used to his mistress of four years. He liked their easy, uncomplicated relationship. Neither wanted to satisfy anything other than physical need, not demanding any commitment or love. He'd never give either to any woman again. He'd danced with Olivia Tritt, but he wasn't going to do any fetching for her. About to walk away, her next words stopped him.

"Isn't she just the plainest thing you've ever seen, girls? Her hair is a fright. And those silly little glasses over those silly little freckles. Have any of you ever seen such a dress? Why she's ready for All Hallow's Eve!" Livi cruelly giggled. "No wonder she isn't dancing. Who'd ask an old maid schoolteacher like Rose Rochester to dance?"

"Ladies and Gents! Choose your partners fer the next reel!" One of the fiddlers yelled over the noise of the crowd.

"Well, Ethan Rourke, I suppose you and I are destined to have this next dance." Livi reached out and took hold of his arm.

"Sorry, Miss Tritt, but this one's promised." Ethan extricated himself from the shocked young woman, then worked his way over to an even more shocked Nutmeg.

Dumbfounded, Meggie stood stone cold still, her eyes fixed on Ethan.

The fiddlers began playing.

"Well, come on, woman," Ethan said the moment he'd reached her.

"Come on? Come on what?" she asked, still in shock.

"Sam Hill, Rose. Dance, that's what."

"I don't."

"You don't?"

"I don't," she said louder.

"You don't what, *Rose?*"

"What's wrong with my name? Why do you say it that way?" Upset as she was, Meggie hadn't missed his pointed intonation when he said Rose.

He didn't answer.

Meggie knew somehow that he wasn't going to. She couldn't think of anything to say to him now but the truth.

"If you must know, Mr. Rourke, I don't dance."

"Is that so?"

"Yes, that's so. I told you, I don't dance." She raised her voice in self-defense.

Ethan grabbed her hand in his. "You do now," he insisted, and hauled her onto the dance floor.

Meggie tried to hold her ground and free her hand from his vice-like hold.

"I can't! Please. It's a sin." Meggie knew she shouldn't say sin—especially to him—especially after last night. His bitter words at the mention of her "precious God" still made her flinch inside. She didn't know much about Ethan Rourke, but she suspected he wasn't a man of God.

"A sin? A sin to dance? We'll see about that," Ethan ground out, not letting her go.

"I can't! Don't you see? I've never—" Tears of utter anguish and humiliation streaked down her flushed cheeks. She hated herself for losing control. She hated that Ethan Rourke saw.

"Never danced?" He eased his hold on her, but didn't let go.

Was it her imagination, or did Ethan give her hand a squeeze? She trembled inside at his touch, at his nearness. It didn't make any sense that she reacted so to him. The only answer for her was to run away as fast as she could, and as far as she could, from Ethan Rourke. She tried to bolt, but he wouldn't let her go.

"Tell you what. You don't cry anymore, and I won't step all over those little black boots."

It was the way Ethan spoke, all husky and soft, that gentled her, that made her flesh tingle. The rich timbre of his words trailed down her spine, dissolving her tension. Any urge to run away dissolved, too. Suddenly it was last night, and Meggie ached to nestle in his strong embrace. She'd felt safe there. Would she again? Drawn now into his masterful arms, she had to know.

"Just keep your eyes on me. Don't look anywhere but up at me," he quietly commanded.

Meggie obeyed. Even if she'd wanted, she couldn't look anywhere else but at Ethan, or be anywhere else but in his arms. She eagerly sought the refuge he offered, warming under his dusky glance. On a level she wouldn't let surface in her mind, she knew that whatever he wanted of her she'd do. Meggie willingly let him guide her around the dance floor without a thought that she was committing a sin in doing so.

She fought the overwhelming urge to look down at her feet and see how they managed to be dancing. She'd never danced in the whole of her life. She'd never been in a man's arms before . . . well except for last night. It felt deliciously wonderful. To be light on her feet in Ethan's arms felt wonderful beyond wonderful. She'd spun around like this before, but not to dance, for an altogether different reason. Meggie refused to let her spirits dampen and to dwell on the past. She refused to consider her fears. Not right now. Right now she danced in Ethan Rourke's safe, strong, angelic arms.

How wonderful Ethan is—just like Jane's Edward.

Ethan's magnetic slate gaze pulled Meggie closer. His thick ebony locks begged for her touch. His playful mouth, hinting of dimples at both corners, turned into a mesmerizing smile revealing even, white teeth. She remembered how warm and soft those very lips had felt against her skin last night. Something truly magical about Ethan beckoned to her from the top of his dark good looks, down the entire length of his hard-muscled body. Without realizing it, Meggie danced in Ethan's arms right onto the pages of *Jane Eyre.*

Meggie had never dreamed of such arms. Strong yet tender . . . capturing yet letting go . . . awakening every part of her slumbering womanhood. Now she knew why Livi Tritt looked so radiant and alive in these very same arms. Unfortunately, Meggie also knew something else now: how it felt to be jealous.

Ridiculous!

Me, jealous?

Utterly, completely ridiculous!

She refused to acknowledge the green-eyed monster rearing its ugly head in her thoughts at the moment.

Ethan pulled Meggie in closer each time they circled the floor, sinfully close. His masculine essence misted over her, soothing, stroking, and arousing every inch of her. When she detected a hint of alcoholic spirits mixed in, she ignored it. Nothing mattered now, nothing but the way a few dark, curly hairs peeked out from the open neck of his chambray shirt, the way the corded musculature of his neck pulsed in time with the fiddles, and the feel of his strong fingers splayed wide across her back. She'd never felt anything like this before. Wanton pleasure stirred deep within her, moist, tingling pleasure.

It has to be a sin to feel this way.

But right now, under his spell, Meggie didn't care.

The music stopped. Meggie didn't want the music or this moment with Ethan to end. His gray, silky gaze held her spellbound in his arms.

He smiled.

She melted all over again, still holding on to him.

"Well, there you two are." Eliza approached. "Why, Rose Rochester, you're all flushed."

Embarrassed, Meggie quickly pulled out of Ethan's grasp. Her hands immediately went to her flaming cheeks.

"I . . . I guess . . . I guess I'm not used to dancing," she stammered uncomfortably.

The way Ethan smiled down at her didn't help cool the situation. Her face burned all the hotter. Eliza must have noticed. How could anyone not?

"You look just like a blushing bride, Rose."

No sooner were Eliza's words out than Meggie saw the smile leave Ethan's face. Her spirits plummeted along with it. His eyes hooded over until they were unreadable. The fragile, silken strands that held her body, her spirit, so close to Ethan only moments before, severed.

"Ladies." Ethan nodded an abrupt goodnight before he dissolved into the confluence of folks already leaving the shindig, which was soon to end.

Meggie turned toward Eliza, more self-conscious than ever under her watchful eye. At least no one else was watching her. No one else saw her behave so foolishly in Ethan's arms.

She was wrong. Livi Tritt hadn't missed a thing that went on between the homely schoolmarm and the wealthy, handsome westerner. Fierce jealousy and resolve joined forces to elicit a vow from Livi. *No one will have Ethan Rourke but me.*

Ethan didn't want to have anyone right now. After cursing his way back up to his room at the hotel, he also made a vow. He'd stay one more day to make sure all was quiet with the Utes, then he'd head for Denver. There wouldn't be any danger waiting for him there in Samantha's arms. In the arms of his mistress, he'd be safe from the danger that Nutmeg's were sure to bring.

The events of the evening weighed heavily on Meggie as she took the moonlit path to her cabin. She'd forgotten her lantern and was glad for the companionable light of the moon. Cold breezes easily penetrated the thin wool of her clothing. It did little good to pull her old burnoose more tightly around her shivering shoulders. No matter. She shivered more on the inside than the outside. Meggie didn't want to think why. She didn't want to think, period.

The rest of the way home she didn't worry about the distant howls of night creatures, or their predatory eyes following her, or the deep, black waters of the river that surged by so close that one slip could be the end of her. She wasn't worried about arriving to find an empty, dark cabin, either. All Meggie wanted was to curl up under her covers. She couldn't get home soon enough.

Surprisingly, Meggie slept well. She felt strangely at peace. She hadn't had any nightmares. This surprised her the most. She couldn't think why. Surely the absence of nightmares had nothing at all to do with being in Ethan Rourke's arms last night. There could be no connection between her sleeping well and Ethan Rourke. None at all.

She scooted out of bed and kindled a fire in the hearth. Next she slipped her bare feet into her cold boots and grabbed up the bucket next to the door. In no time she was outside and around back of the cabin, fetching spring water. She looked forward to a hot cup of coffee and intended to have it this morning, quicker than she could say her Hail Mary's. Water spilled out of the bucket as she hurried back inside. The air wasn't just cold, it was bitter cold. The graying sky and frigid air could only mean one thing: winter was close.

Meggie readied herself for the day ahead while she waited for the water over the hearth to boil. Not thinking about her actions, she didn't follow her practiced routine this morning. She didn't wash her hands a second time. And then, when she took her long, thick hair out of its braid, she coiled it loosely at her crown instead of in a tight bun at her nape. Several coppery wisps softly draped her face and fell lightly over her neck. She didn't even try to catch them back up in their pins. She'd no mirror to catch her reflection even if she'd wanted to. Then she might have noticed how she'd styled her hair differently in an attractive manner. The rest of her morning ablutions remained the same, save for one thing. During the past five years she'd never forgotten to place her wire rims squarely on the bridge of her nose. Today she did.

Someone knocked at her door. Ethan! Could it be Ethan? Before Meggie could cross the room and open it, her visitors did. Her heart sank. It wasn't Ethan.

"Good morning, Rose." Eliza charged in with Clovis Kinney and Mrs. Grady in tow. All three women carried armfuls of goods.

Meggie swallowed back her disappointment that Ethan hadn't come to see her. She remembered meeting Mrs. Grady, from Grady's Mercantile, the night before. Mrs. Grady's salt and pepper hair matched the gleam in her friendly, speckled eyes. In contrast to the other women, Mrs. Grady was as plain as Eliza was lovely and as tall as Clovis was round.

"Your hair is very pretty that way. The style is most becoming," Eliza declared, a bit winded from the walk with her packages.

Whatever is Eliza talking about? My hair? My hair is the same. Meggie ran her fingers over a more fashioned chignon. How could she have done such a thing this morning? She didn't have a chance to ponder the reason, with company in front of her.

"We've brought you some gifts from town, Rose. Items that folks thought you might need," Eliza explained.

"Of course, please come in. Please set down your burdens," Meggie said, caught off guard by their kind gesture. The women set their armfuls of goods down on the puncheon floor. Meggie warmed to their generosity, despite it being charity. After the merry group enjoyed coffee together, the trio left Meggie to put each donated article in its rightful place.

She carefully laid the colorful, thick patchwork quilt on her bed, then put the hand-sewn lace curtains on the cabin windows. She added the supply of tallows to the pail on the hearth mantel. And wood. Not only did she have new stacks of wood outside her cabin, but she had a brand new ax, too. Compliments of Mr. Grady. He'd actually brought the wood. Meggie'd never heard him. She must have been sleeping too soundly. She studied the ax. Never one to be afraid of work, she looked forward to learning to cut and split wood. Mrs. Grady had brought two bolts of calico from the mercantile. Meggie set both bolts of cloth on the sawbuck table.

Before, Meggie wouldn't have cared about the cloth.

Before yesterday, she wouldn't have cared about new clothes.

But something about yesterday changed things. She refused to reason why.

Today she was eager to make herself new dresses. She ran her fingers over the lovely calico cloth. Eliza, she remembered, had a lock-stitch machine. Maybe Eliza would let her use her sewing machine. There was one package yet to be opened. Meggie knelt down and uncovered the last of the boxes of donated goods. She couldn't believe it! A winter coat. The heavy gray wool coat looked brand new. And a pair of winter boots. The boots were worn, but still in very good condition.

Grateful tears spilled down her cheeks.

In the short span of one morning, she'd received more presents and more thoughtfulness than in the whole rest of her life. It felt like all those Christmas mornings as a young girl when she'd wished hard for just one package, just one surprise, but now the whole of Hot Sulphur Springs made her wishes come true. Silently she offered a prayer to heaven for each and every one of the townsfolk.

Meggie didn't know quite what to do with William's gift. At least not yet.

Eliza told her it was a Colt .45 peacemaker when she handed over the box of bullets with the pistol. When William had time, he'd show her how to use it, Eliza had said. Everyone in these parts should know how to defend themselves, she'd added.

Meggie didn't argue with Eliza about the gun. Until she'd come west, Meggie hadn't thought of protecting herself in such a way—with a gun. Now the thought of having a weapon seemed a necessity. She hid the gun and box of bullets behind the pail of tallows on the hearth mantel. The idea of learning to shoot the Colt .45 suddenly seemed more important than fashioning any new dresses.

Meggie's hand flew to the back of her neck. For the first time since her arrival in Hot Sulphur Springs, the hairs stood on end. Something was coming. Something evil. No matter that she'd moved to remote Hot Sulphur Springs. The evil from her nightmares would come for her, and she could do nothing about it. Instead of panicking, a bizarre calm settled over Meggie. In that moment she resolved to be ready when her demon came—ready to kill or be killed.

So much for living an ordinary, normal life among the ordinary, normal townsfolk of Hot Sulphur Springs.

The afternoon passed uneventfully.

It would be dark soon. She'd been invited to eat supper with Eliza and William. With no lantern to guide her, she'd best get going. And she'd best remember to collect her lantern from the Byers' porch where she'd left it the night before.

At supper Eliza talked exuberantly about last night's shindig.

The Marksons talked exuberantly about the hot springs.

"The mister! I declare, Miss Rose. The mister is that much better from the springs."

Meggie could see that Mr. Markson did look improved. She was happy for their good spirits and good health. So far all the hot springs had brought her was an uncomfortable encounter with Ethan Rourke. She was glad Ethan didn't dine with them. Wasn't she? And wasn't it a blessing no one brought up his name? By the end of the meal, she'd almost convinced herself of it. Almost.

Throughout supper, Meggie's agitation with herself for thinking about Ethan grew. She said her goodnights and charged out the front door of the hotel, scooping up her lantern as she did. The winds had picked up. She didn't notice. The temperatures had fallen. She didn't notice. She forgot to light her lantern. Only when her hair pulled loose from its pins and blew across her face did she realize she couldn't see where she was going. Her lantern fell from her hand. When she bent to pick it up, her shawl nearly flew away. The cold air began to bite.

Somewhere in the recesses of her mind she realized she should have on her new coat instead of her worn shawl. She'd be warmer now, and a coat wouldn't try to fly away. Managing to catch up her shawl, Meggie straightened and tried to pull it back around her shoulders. Heaven sakes, where had the gale come from?

The bitter night was pitch black. No guiding moonlight. Not even one star to give her direction. She didn't think she was that far out of town yet. Even if she hadn't forgotten to light her lantern, she doubted it would stay lit in such a windstorm. Meggie didn't want to return to the hotel and to thoughts of Ethan Rourke. She determined to head for her cabin and make it home in spite of the turn in the weather. Confident of the way, she took deliberate steps down the path.

An eerie noise pierced through the howling winds. Meggie stopped short. It wasn't the wind. Gulping hard, she listened again for the unearthly sound. She peered through the black night in the direction of Zeb Kinney's stable. It wasn't horses. Horses didn't make that kind of noise. Something wild— *something wild might!* With no weapon or defense against whatever lurked in the darkness, it would be foolhardy for her to go after any predator that might lay chase. But then, it would be foolhardy for her to continue down the lone trail to her cabin, where any moment her attacker could strike.

Meggie girl, you're letting your imagination run wild.

It has to be horses, you ninny.

Needing to convince herself of that, she grudgingly left the path and started up the hill toward Zeb Kinney's stable. She'd only gone a few steps in the darkness before she stumbled, losing her footing and her unlit lantern.

"Jesus, Mary, and Joseph!" Meggie stayed where she fell and listened hard through the tempest around her for any sounds from the stable. Nothing. Relieved and convinced she had let her imagination get the better of her, she tried to get up. Her first attempt failed. So did her second. Searing pain shot through her ankle whenever she tried.

"Oh faith!" she spat out through lengths of her hair now blowing wildly across her face.

"This a habit of yours?"

Meggie froze.

She knew that voice.

CHAPTER TEN

"Give me your hand."

That Ethan had found her, fallen and freezing, suddenly made her mad instead of scared. Painful spasms gripped her ankle. Angry at herself and at him, she tried to get up but failed. Her pride hurt every bit as much as her ankle. No matter what, she wasn't about to accept the help Ethan offered.

"Rose, give me your damned hand."

Of all the nerve, cursing at me again.

Ethan reached for her.

"No! You don't need to help me. You don't need to come any closer!" Meggie screamed and tried to scoot away.

Ethan hesitated at her words—the same ones she'd first spoken to him in Denver. He knew she was afraid of him. He just wished he knew why. At least this time he didn't think she'd faint on him. Quite the contrary, Nutmeg wanted to snap his head off. He picked her up anyway, managing first to conceal his Winchester in a nearby rock crevice.

"Let go of me!" Meggie squirmed in his arms and pummeled his chest with her fists. "Put me down! You can't just pick me up whenever you've a mind. I don't need to be picked up when I fall. No one's done it before. No one needs to start now, least of all you! I've done fine all of my life on my own, thank you very much." Angry and upset, Meggie wasn't aware she'd revealed anything about herself.

Ethan's chest tightened. He didn't feel her fists, but the

impact of her words hit him hard. He believed her all right, the part about being alone. He didn't like the thought of her being alone or hurt or afraid of anything or anyone, him especially. Despite this thought and despite the female kicking and screaming in his arms, he kept on down the trail.

He knew where Nutmeg lived. William had volunteered as much the day before. Ethan had just finished stabling Nugget when he'd heard something out back of Zeb Kinney's. Thought it could be a wildcat. Turns out it was. The mountain storm gathering around him didn't compare to the storm in his arms. He couldn't get to Nutmeg's cabin and get rid of her fast enough.

Meggie kept up her struggles. She'd stopped yelling. It did no good. The fool man refused to listen. Glad for the cloak of darkness, she didn't want to see him any more than she wanted him to see her. She knew they headed down the trail toward her cabin. She realized the sound she'd heard before was a wild predator after all—Ethan Rourke. *Angel, my foot!*

They'd reached her cabin.

Ethan kicked the door open and deposited her on the bed.

Meggie was mad at him all over again. Why, he'd no right to break her door latch. No right at all!

Ethan bent over the hearth and lit a fire.

Meggie watched him. She shouldn't. She should be telling him to go away. She didn't. The longer she watched him, the less angry she felt. Something replaced her anger, something as powerful as the hold he'd had on her the entire way from town. She tried to concentrate on the kindling fire and not Ethan. What was happening to her? She didn't understand why being alone with Ethan in her cabin on such an ominous night didn't scare her to death.

Meggie stared at the blaze Ethan had started.

He stood up and turned to her.

She looked at him and not the fire. Time stood still. He walked toward her—right out of her daydreams of Edward Rochester and romance. She didn't feel afraid or threatened, and stared at the flickering tallow in Edward's—*in Ethan's*—hand, she mentally corrected. She watched as he set the candle on the nearby washstand, quivering inside when he sat down on the edge of her bed.

Hypnotized, Meggie let Ethan's masterful hand come up to push the hair off her face; the cuff of his slicker gingerly grazing her cheek. She sucked in a breath, taking in the heady scent of deep woods and tobacco. His masculine essence drew her closer. Waves of excitement pulsed through her. The fine line between fact and fiction, between reality and fantasy, blurred.

Was he Ethan Rourke or Edward Rochester?

She didn't know. She didn't care.

Her handsome angel was one and the same. All she wanted was to be in this man's arms again. Aroused now, her passions stirred, Meggie didn't know what to do next.

Ethan did.

In the glow of the candlelight he read the mounting desire in Nutmeg's dark, luminous eyes. Unable and unwilling to stop himself, he needed to taste her full, rosy mouth, feel her softness against him, and to hear her moan his name. From the first, when he'd witnessed her passion for somebody named Edward, Ethan wanted to hear her cry out his name . . . *Ethan.* Her lips were made to cry out for him, not for some Edward. Jealousy shot through him and a fierce, unexpected possessiveness grabbed hold. He clamped his hands around her slender arms and pulled her closer; demanding what was his to take.

Lost from the first sip of her mouth, Ethan couldn't get enough. No woman ever felt like this, tasted like this, like cool mint melting into sugar and spice. The way she shyly opened to him and touched his tongue with her own set off an unstoppable reaction in him. He covered her mouth with his, doing his utmost to restrain himself until she wanted him as much as he wanted her.

When her arms went around his neck and he felt her delicate fingers entwine in his hair, the pleasure of her artless caress threatened what little control he had left. He needed to feel more of her against him, although he struggled to go slowly. He wanted to shed his coat, but that meant having to let go of her. He thrust his tongue again and again, deeper and deeper into the sweet recesses of her delicious mouth. He could feel her now, coming to him, hungering for him the same way he hungered for her.

Ethan suddenly broke their fevered union, but kept his hands at the back of her head. No woman had ever issued an invitation like this before—matching his passion with her own intense ardor—giving back immediately what he'd just taken. He trailed little kisses across one satiny cheek, over a succulent earlobe, then down the fine softness of her throat. If she were another kind of woman, he could rip her bothersome dress off so he could taste the rest of her fragrant sweetness. But she wasn't. This almost made him stop what he was doing. Almost. Ethan thought again about the way she'd moaned for Edward, and knew Nutmeg couldn't be completely innocent. But then, why did he sense that she was? Right now he couldn't concentrate enough to think of a reason. He couldn't think, period.

He eased her down on her pillow. Her luminous eyes, smoldering with passion, held him, wanted him, trusted him. Never in all his life had he seen such a look. In the candlelight her coppery hair spread over the pillow and down around her shoulders like a raging wildfire. He wouldn't try to put it out. He couldn't, feeling his own control slip even more. He'd never had a female like Nutmeg in his arms, one minute child-like, the next a sensual woman, vulnerable yet wanton. Ethan knew what was about to happen, what had to happen. He just didn't know what price they'd both pay for it. Already losing his guard, he was about to lose his heart.

"Please." The soft moan escaped her lips.

All he desired was in her simple, whispered plea. He needed to hear her moan for him. He felt the wall so long built around his heart, begin to topple.

"Please Edward . . . love me."

Ethan's heart went stone cold. He let go of her. She'd said Edward's name and not his. A knife would have been kinder, a gun more merciful. He needed to get out of there.

"If I were you, I'd get this latch fixed and keep it locked," Ethan said the moment he reached the door. "You never know who or what might try to get in." Then he left her cabin. He'd leave Hot Sulphur Springs at first light.

Meggie didn't know how long she'd lain there, exactly as Ethan left her, staring at the door he'd pulled shut. The tallow was almost out. It didn't matter. Nothing mattered. Her ankle throbbed terribly, but she didn't care about the pain. Her hurt went much deeper. If only she could make it go away. She felt empty inside, save for the pain in her heart, as if something had just been ripped from her. She curled up in a tight ball beneath her quilt. Fumbling under her pillow for *Jane Eyre*, she pulled the book against her chest. It mattered little to her that she hadn't undressed or removed her boots. All she wanted was the comfort the childhood posture always gave her. Feeling for her cross, she hugged it along with *Jane Eyre*.

Meggie hadn't wept, really wept, for years. She did now. She wept now for all the torment and misery forced on her long ago, wishing she didn't have to relive that one horrible day that had left her in ruinous remains for the rest of her life. If only she could explain to Ethan. Dear God, how she wanted to tell him everything. How she hated that he'd just left her. If only she could tell Ethan what happened to her all those years ago, why she behaved the way she did around men, why she dressed the way she did to hide the woman inside, why she had such wretched nightmares, why she kept *Jane Eyre* close by, why she had trouble telling fact from fiction, and why she'd had to flee Boston. If only she could tell him all of those things that she dared not tell him or anyone else. Pru knew. The Sisters of Charity knew. But no one else must know.

Meggie clutched *Jane Eyre* closer to her breast. Jane would explain to Edward, surely, if such things had happened to her, would she not? In truth, Meggie wasn't sure. Like everything else in her life these days, Meggie wasn't sure about much of anything. She set her book down for a moment and leaned over to replace the tallow on her bedstead that had just gone out, wanting to read about Jane and Edward again, hoping to find the answers she needed.

No, that wouldn't do. Candlelight wasn't sufficient for this serious task.

Meggie got out of bed and limped over to the fireplace, re-stoking it for more light. Her ankle almost gave way. She managed to get to the sawbuck table and sit down. Her boots had to come off. She unlaced both and bit through the pain when she pulled the shoe off her now-swollen foot. At last successful at removing her boots, she lit the kerosene lamp on the table, then limped back across the room to fetch *Jane Eyre*. Once done, she placed the book next to the lamp and sat back down, opening the pages as if the novel were a Bible.

The more she read, the more upset she became and closed the book. Jane was worthy of Edward Rochester's affection, but she didn't feel worthy of Ethan's. Jane was good and pure and unscathed. She was not. Reluctantly, Meggie reopened the book. Despite her misgivings, she had to find some way to reach out to Ethan now, some way to share the intimate details of her life, or surely she'd go mad this night.

Wide awake, fighting desperation, she all but forgot the pain in her foot and leafed through the pages, reading but not reading, wishing something would touch her, talk to her, and tell her what to do. One hand kept her page while the other wandered off the page and mindlessly traced along the tabletop, stopping at her newly-put-together box of writing materials. Her fingers fiddled with the latch on the box, then opened it. At once she shut *Jane Eyre* and then slowly, almost reverently, began taking out her writing materials. First a precious sheet of paper, then the bottle of ink, then her steel-nib dip pen. Pulling the lamplight closer, she knew what she could do to reach out to Ethan. She'd write to him. She'd pour out her heart and her troubled soul to him. It would be safe to do so in a letter. In person, it would not be safe, but surely in a letter it would be all right. She could pretend that he listened, that he cared. Her letter would be fictitious, like her romance novel. There would be no harm in it, and maybe a letter would help her heal from her past, if only a little. She felt the better for it already, as she considered telling Ethan everything about herself; no matter that he'd never know.

The hour was late. Meggie had no idea of the time, nor did she care. Filling her steel-nib with a full complement of ink, she first thought of assigning her letter a title: *Meggie's Remains*. Of course that wouldn't be fair; she must begin at the beginning for Ethan to understand.

Dear Ethan,

What I am about to tell you is private. It is all too real and too horrible, but I must tell you so that you will know. I want you to know the truth so that you will not think so badly of me. In truth, too, my reckoning is near, and I fear that I will not live to old age. Do not feel sorry for me. This is just fact and no more. Of course, you will never see this letter, as I've no plans ever to give it to you, but I must write to you now because of the pain in my heart at your leaving me tonight. The look on your face stays with me. I do not understand. What did I do, what did I say to make you turn from me? Oh Ethan, how I wish I knew what was in your heart. How I wish I could tell you what is in mine. I must, dear Ethan, I must tell you, if only in this letter. I must tell you everything now.

Meggie sighed heavily. Where to begin?

Part of my life has been just like Jane Eyre's. You've likely never heard of this beloved romance novel, but there are similarities between my life and the life of Jane Eyre. Orphaned at a young age, I was sent away by unloving relatives to live in a strict, often cruel orphanage, not unlike Lowood where Jane had been sent. At the orphanage I was befriended by Prudence Utter, who surely is my Helen Burns. Helen was Jane's friend at Lowood, but unlike poor Helen, Pru, thankfully, did not succumb to the ravages of consumption. That's where any possible similarity between Jane's life and mine is finished. Jane ended up in the loving arms of Edward Rochester—not in the fiendish grasp of Benjamin Howard.

I had just turned seventeen on the dreadful day I encountered Benjamin Howard at the orphanage. The son of one of the philanthropists that supported the orphanage, I thought nothing odd at all in his tour of the schoolroom that day. Family members of the wealthy often did the same thing. Always feeling a little uneasy at their snobbish scrutiny, I should have been more on my guard, the way Benjamin Howard leered at me. But I wasn't. All I saw was an attractive man walk by, smile, and leave.

Oh Ethan, would to God it had ended there.

Bile caught in Meggie's throat. She swallowed back the bitterness, determined to keep to her task. Taking a moment to refill her pen, she continued with her letter to Ethan.

I was summoned to the headmistress's office several days later, and told I would have the privilege of riding in a carriage to deliver important documents to the office of one of the orphanage's benevolent supporters. I was also told that I should be very grateful for such notice and feel fortunate indeed to travel in such a conveyance. All I really heard was that I'd leave the orphanage and see something of the outside world. The mere thought of such adventure thrilled me. And then to be gifted with a beautiful ivory linen dress to wear for such an outing! I couldn't hide my exuberance from Pru, rambling on to her while she pulled up my long hair with the ivory ribbon provided. I'd never been so dressed up. I wished that Pru could come with me. Maybe there would be a next time and Pru could go instead of me. That would be just perfect, I'd thought.

Pru was suspicious, but I didn't listen to her. She didn't agree that my beautiful dress was any good fortune. She thought the headmistress was up to something, reminding me the matron was ever cruel to me, but I didn't listen to Pru. I so looked forward to my outing that I paid no mind to the dark turn of my dear friend's thoughts. I also paid no mind to the way my low-necked bodice revealed . . . so much of me. No, I didn't listen to Pru but hurried outside the front door of the orphanage, and to my awaiting carriage.

When the carriage stopped in front of a row of prestigious-looking buildings, I thought it had to be the grandest place in all of Boston. Then, when the kindly coachman helped me down, I felt like a royal princess with one of my trusted footmen. The moment I saw the attractive man come toward me, I recognized him from several days before at the orphanage. I smiled at Benjamin Howard and didn't object when he took my arm and escorted me through the elegant, carved front door.

But Ethan, once inside, when I heard the lock click shut behind me . . .

Utterly exhausted, unable to stay awake, Meggie let go of her pen and laid her head down on her hands, needing a few moments of rest . . . just a few moments before she could continue her letter to Ethan.

Someone rapped hard on her door, waking Meggie. She lifted her head with a start, needing a moment to recover her thoughts. At first she wondered if she'd been sleepwalking again in her nightmares. Her ankle throbbed. She remembered her injury. She remembered it, and everything about last night all too well. Her letter to Ethan—her unfinished letter—lay on the table before her. No, she hadn't been lost in nightmares, but in daydreams of Ethan Rourke.

Another rap, this one harder.

Meggie had no idea who it could be. Certainly not Ethan, never Ethan. He'd left her last night. He wouldn't be coming back. She had no idea who was at her door now and didn't really care. No matter that her ankle hurt, she got up from the table and managed to cross the cold puncheon floor in her stocking feet to open the cabin door. She remembered now that the latch was broken. She'd have to fix it.

The door suddenly pushed open. It was one of the children from the social. Meggie recognized the little boy immediately. Ready to rap again, his little fist stopped in midair when she opened the door wider. He grinned at her. The moment she saw his two missing front teeth, she couldn't help herself and smiled back. Brightened by his innocent smile, Meggie squatted down to be level with him. Searing pain shot through her foot but she maintained her posture.

" 'Lo," the little sandy-haired, dirt-smudged scamp greeted her. "Lo. My mama sssays when's ssschool, booksss 'n ssstuf?

When kin I larn ssstuf?" he whistled out through the gap in his front teeth.

Meggie warmed even more to the boy.

"I'm Billie an' I'm . . ." Frowning at his hand, it took him a moment to hold up his fingers to her. "An' I'm thisss many."

"Oh, so you are five years old. My, what a big boy you are. Well Billie, you should come inside. It's too cold for you to stand in the doorway." Still crouched down, she'd no sooner issued her invitation than the youth ran past so fast he set her off balance. Meggie smiled, but had trouble standing back up and pushing the door shut. With effort, she set about rekindling the hearth to make the child something to eat. For a moment she longed to sit back down, not just to ease the pain in her foot, but to continue her letter to Ethan. She felt better this morning for the telling so far. It was as if Ethan had been listening to her and was willing to hear more. *I will tell you,* she silently promised, but wondered if she truly would.

Meggie believed herself lucky to have only twisted her foot the night before, finding that she could bear weight without too much pain as the day wore on. She didn't even need to fashion a cane for support by the time she determined to visit Eliza. Yes, a bad twist was all. Far worse was the pain left in her heart at Ethan's sudden departure. Meggie found out from Eliza that Ethan had left Hot Sulphur Springs that morning without so much as a cup of coffee. Eliza couldn't believe it. Meggie could.

It still hurt that he'd walked out of her cabin last night. It hurt plenty. But being able to set down her thoughts to him on paper soothed her pain, if only a little. Right then and there, Meggie resolved to put Ethan from her thoughts as best she could in the real world during the light of day. But at night, when it was safe, she'd write him, until her story was finished.

In the ensuing days, Meggie stayed busy teaching her pupils

reading, writing, and ciphering, while they taught her about life in the mountains. What the students didn't cover, Eliza, William, and Clovis Kinney did. No task was insurmountable to Meggie. Every day she went to the spring out back and hauled in the water she needed. She learned to chop wood, quickly discovering it would be a daily task and a necessity. Soon she could make her own tallows and knew which remedies and nostrums from Grady's Mercantile she'd need to keep in stock. Eliza lent her the lock-stitch machine, and Meggie fashioned herself a few simple dresses. She learned to knit spun trunk goods and refined her skills at cooking over an open hearth. Finally only one task remained. The very thing she'd intended to do first ended up being last.

The Colt .45 lay hidden behind the pail of tallows on the hearth mantel, exactly where she'd placed it. Meggie had yet to touch the gun. She took it down now along with the box of bullets. It was time to learn to shoot. She'd ask William to teach her this very day.

The snows came to stay in the little town of Hot Sulphur Springs and with them the frigid temperatures of winter. Meggie kept true to her promise to put Ethan from her thoughts during the day as best she could. On days when his handsome face got in the way, she dug harder and trenched out the pathway covered by new snowfall. When his masculine scent of musk, new tobacco, and deep woods hung in the air, she'd put the kettle on for a strong cup of cherry bark tea. If nothing but the memory of his powerful arms around Livi Tritt occupied her thoughts, she'd grab up her ax and split them apart along with the firewood.

With fewer chores to do in winter, more children attended school. Meggie looked at each and every one as little gifts when they walked through her door. Even "mean ol' Willie" showed up on occasion. Turned out he wasn't so mean after all. With a little attention from both her and Emma, the boy actually warmed so to them, and to school, that he was the last to leave every day.

On those nights when the darkness pressed too close against her, Meggie used two tallows. In the stillness she'd sort out lesson plans, go through recipes she would soon try, and think of everything she'd write to Pru when the Express started. Meggie had done everything she could think of at night except continue her story—her letter—to Ethan, since the night he turned away from her, leaving her alone in her cabin. She'd broken the promise she'd made to herself to finish her story to him, and she knew the reason why. She didn't want to feel close to him, to need him to listen, to need *him*—because he didn't want her. He didn't need her. The pain of his leaving was still raw.

At times, like tonight, Meggie could hear the strangest sounds travel across the night from somewhere far off in the distance. It wasn't the howl of wolves or the cry of the mountain lion. Those sounds she knew. She'd dismissed the sounds before, but now she listened hard. This was more like drums, the hum of beating drums. It had to be the Utes. Meggie wasn't frightened. She thought of the boy she'd seen alongside the stream on her trip up to her new home. She rolled over onto her back and stared at the burning tallow. The dancing flame, ever her companion, still burned brightly. Out of habit, she ran her hand under her pillow to ensure that *Jane Eyre* was with her, too. As she listened to the beating of the drums, she was amazed she hadn't paid particular attention to them until now. Her heart picked up the same beat. She didn't think of Indians now, but of Ethan. She flopped onto her stomach and thumped her pillow, kept awake by the aching beat of her broken heart.

In the next moment she snuffed out her tallow and lit the kerosene lamp on the table. Quickly, she took out her writing materials from their box and found her place in her letter to Ethan, to see where she'd left off . . . *But Ethan, once inside when I heard the lock click shut behind me . . .*

. . . I spun around and stared at the closed door, suddenly afraid. When Benjamin Howard took hold of my elbow and turned me back around, all polite and friendly-like, I relaxed, embarrassed at my childish behavior. Ethan, I remember every word exchanged vividly. I will recount all to you, just as it happened.

"Here are the documents I was told to bring," I said to Benjamin Howard, and held out the entwined bundle of papers for him, wishing my hands didn't shake.

"Thank you, my dear," he said. "As your reward I invite you to enjoy a glass of sherry with me." He took the papers from my hands and immediately replaced them with a goblet of the rosy liquid.

"No, really. I couldn't." I tried to give him back the glass, all the while struggling to hold it steady in my trembling fingers.

"Just one toast, my dear. Surely you can't deny me that," he insisted, and refused to take the goblet from my outstretched hand.

His smile captivated me, calmed me. Steadier now, I obediently clicked my glass with his. Mr. Howard seemed ever the polite gentleman. I sipped more sherry. The forbidden spirits tasted wonderful. I was on edge, of course, being away from the orphanage, and alone with a man. I became more nervous then; so much so, that I gripped my glass tight, breaking the stem. The sherry spilled all over my beautiful gown and my glass fell to the plush carpet! Humiliated and scared, I bent down to pick up the broken glass.

"Never mind, pretty girl," Benjamin Howard said, and took my elbow again, guiding me to a stand.

This time I didn't relax or calm at his politeness. I knew I was really going to catch it from the headmistress. She'd punish me for sure. I was used to the thorny switch across my back. Sometimes the demented headmistress didn't need a reason to hit me. Wishing I hadn't just given her one, I dreaded going home to the orphanage. Home, my foot! The orphanage wasn't any kind of home.

Right away, Benjamin Howard gave me another full goblet of sherry. I shouldn't have taken the glass or taken another sip, but I did. Then I took another. I felt warm and wonderful and didn't worry over the horrible headmistress anymore. The sherry was delicious. I forgot all about the broken glass and my spoiled dress and the fate awaiting me when I returned to the orphanage.

Benjamin Howard showed me to a nearby settee and re-filled my goblet of sherry. My senses began to dull. I didn't notice at first when he took a seat next to me. Even when he inched closer and draped his arm behind me, I didn't notice. I should have, Ethan. I should have. Instead, I let myself drift into the magical world of fairy tales where the prince and the princess meet and fall in love and live happily ever after. I let myself drift into a world of daydreams, when I should have seen the nightmare coming.

I felt something at the back of my neck . . .

Embarrassed at what she was about to write, Meggie stopped for a moment. To say such things to Ethan, no matter that he'd never see them, proved difficult. She'd come too far now to stop. She must go on, for her peace of mind.

. . . I felt something at the back of my neck . . . the light tugging lulled me deeper into my dream world. My hair, I remember, fell about my shoulders, loosened from its tie. Still, I wasn't alarmed. When the gentle, stroking fingers moved to splay through my hair, I dared not move and break the magical

spell cast by my Prince Charming. But too late, Ethan, I re-
alized the spell wasn't magic at all. Suddenly my head felt like
it was being ripped from me. I tried to reach up and break the
evil grasp that had hold of me, but I could not! Oh Ethan, I
could not!

Meggie let the pen fall from her hand. The ink needed replenishing but so did she. Besides, she'd said enough to Ethan for one night. Before she put out the lamplight, she went over to the washbasin and poured water into it from the half-filled pitcher. She washed her hands once, then again. Never could she wash away Benjamin Howard's filth. Never!

CHAPTER ELEVEN

Ethan rolled off the voluptuous beauty. Usually he found satisfaction in Samantha's arms, but not tonight.

"I've missed you, Ethan." The blond temptress pouted and ran her fingers through the downy mat of dark, curly hairs on his chest. "You don't come around like you used to. It's not like you." She settled her naked curves even closer against him and trailed her fingers over his chest, then lower.

Ethan caught her hand.

"Go to sleep, Sam. It's late." He let go of her and put his arm across his forehead. Relieved when Samantha fell asleep, he listened to her even breathing and wished he could do the same. But he couldn't sleep, not with Nutmeg's unmistakable image consuming his thoughts. Six weeks had passed, and still he couldn't get her out of his mind. Kept awake by chameleon eyes, one minute full of violets and the next in passionate shadow, by the invitation of her soft, full mouth, by the mounting desire he'd recognized in her yielding body—no, no restful sleep for him.

It was Christmas Eve. Meggie had difficulty getting her pupils to settle into their class work. The children were all smiles and giggles. Invariably they would put down their slates and chatter on, excited about the festive season. Finally Meggie gave up. Instead of continuing their lessons, she distributed colored paper from her precious store of supplies and let the children

149

make cards to give to their parents on Christmas morning.

Shouts of glee heaped onto all the giggles. Meggie's included. Thrown into the spirit of the holiday, she got out corn for popping, and made sure there was enough not only for her little tree, but also for each student to take a string home to decorate their own. All too soon the festivities ended. Meggie gladly accepted hugs from the children as she watched each one take the familiar footpath home. Dark clouds moved in overhead. A storm was coming. The children needed to hurry.

With the last student safely on his way, Meggie went back inside her cabin and shut the door. She felt like she'd already had her holiday celebration, what with all the happy faces and gaiety in her classroom. It was the closest to any real Christmas she'd ever had. There was no church and no church service for her to attend, no midnight mass. But she'd been invited to Eliza and William's tomorrow for Christmas dinner with others from town. Grateful, indeed, for such a celebration ahead, she'd thank the Lord in her prayers tonight for such newfound friends.

Meggie put more wood on the hearth, then eased into her rocker and closed her eyes. It had been a wonderful day with all of the children. She wanted to savor the memories, the wonders of this day. But her traitorous thoughts returned to yesterday and to Christmases gone by.

The Christmas season came and went at the austere orphanage with no celebration. The headmistress and her matrons celebrated with sumptuous food and presents, but there was never anything for the orphans but a single orange placed in the exact center of their carefully made beds. Meggie tried every year to eat the orange, but it always made her choke. So did the unfair, unkind words the lunatic headmistress leveled at them every Christmas: "You forsaken foundlings should be grateful for the roof over your heads and the bread on your table. No need for any more gifts for the likes of you!"

Meggie knew the rest of the orphans had to hate the headmistress as much as she did. She'd seen the evil woman hit others, but she felt singled out. The headmistress hated her in particular. Humph. She finally gave up wondering why.

Meggie and Pru found ways to celebrate the Christmas season despite the cruel matron's watchful eye. They managed to steal a bit of food from the kitchen when they were helping to clean up, quickly stuffing uneaten pieces of bread and leftover sweets in their empty pockets. Then, with everyone in the dorm asleep and the patrolling matron gone, Meggie and Pru would slip out of bed and huddle on the floor, emptying their pockets to share for Christmas dinner. They would whisper and pretend they were in a cozy, warm home with their own family for the holiday. Sometimes they'd pretend they were sisters in the same home, and other times they were friends who lived on the same street. But always, their bond of friendship was their best Christmas gift to each other.

Meggie remembered how she'd imagined normal, ordinary people must celebrate Christmas. She shifted in the rocker, trying to find a comfortable position. She'd imagined ordinary people in their colorful, decorated homes, with family and friends around the holiday table. And tomorrow *she*, Meghan Rose McMurphy, would be sitting at a Christmas table with a merry group of friends—her very first ordinary, perfectly wonderful Christmas! She knew just what presents she'd give her new friends: sweets. And she'd best hurry. Christmas wasn't going to wait for her, for mercy's sake.

She needed to get busy. Yesterday she'd gone to Grady's Mercantile and made careful purchase of the necessary ingredients. She didn't want to have to traipse through the blizzard-like snow now coming down outside. Ignoring the howling winds, Meggie set to work making Christmas sweets, more light-hearted than she could ever remember.

An hour later, there was a heavy rap on her door. Startled, Meggie was glad for the repaired latch. Could it be one of the children in all of this weather? They must have forgotten something. My, oh my. Meggie couldn't get to the door fast enough.

It was William. Snow-covered, he looked like he could be Father Christmas.

"Come in," Meggie greeted with a smile. "Come in, William, before you catch your death."

He shook the snow off and stomped his booted feet on her doorstep, then came inside and pulled the door shut behind him.

"Is it Eliza?" Meggie asked, suddenly losing her smile. What else could bring William out in such a storm?

"No. No, she's fine," he reassured. "Mmmm . . . something smells mighty good in here. Couldn't be mince pie now could it?"

"Whatever it is, you'll have to wait until Christmas dinner tomorrow," Meggie lightly rebuked, relieved that Eliza was all right.

"I came over about tonight, Rose. Folks are coming for caroling and cider around our tree. Eliza flat-out ordered me to fetch you."

"I'd love to, William. I'll come straight away as soon as I'm done with my pies."

"All right, Rose, but don't be too long," William warned. "This weather's turning into a bear. You might want to stay the night at the hotel. In fact, plan on it," he ordered good-naturedly.

"All right. All right, I will," she readily agreed. "Tell Eliza thank you and to expect me soon."

"One more thing, Rose." William hesitated before he turned to leave. "You might do something else, too."

Anxious to finish her pies, Meggie waited to hear what.

"Your Colt .45. Bring your pistol along," he advised, dead serious now.

Meggie nearly dropped the pie she had in her hands. Her insides flinched.

"You can't be too careful," William said. "The bears may be asleep now, but not much else is. In all this snow you can't see what critters might be around."

Ethan's very last words to me before he left.

"And don't forget to latch your door good and tight," William added.

Ethan's same warning.

She didn't want to remember anything Ethan had said. She quickly set down her pie and put her hands over her ears much as a child might when they don't want to listen.

"You all right, Rose?"

"Yes. Yes, of course, William." Meggie, self-conscious now of her action, pulled her hands down. "I just have an earache. I'm sure it will be gone as quickly as it came," she fibbed, and shot William her brightest smile, all the while giving the sisters a mental apology for her lie.

William seemed satisfied with her reply and hoped she'd feel better soon. After giving her one more caution to hurry before the weather got much worse, he was out the door.

Anything but satisfied herself, Meggie's spirits plummeted at the mere thought of Ethan Rourke—the man she shouldn't, but couldn't stop, thinking about. The man she shouldn't, but couldn't stop, writing her letter to. He didn't want her. She hated remembering that he'd rejected her. *I can't let this first special Christmas turn to ruin. I won't!* She forced her attention back to her mince pies and to what she'd need to pack in the worn satchel she kept tucked under her bed.

★　★　★　★　★

Ethan's Christmas, Meggie couldn't know, already teetered precariously close to ruin, too.

"So what do you say, Ethan? Come on. It's Christmas Eve." Uriah tried his level best to drag Ethan from their office. "Ma's got a big dinner all ready. Sis worked all day last month to make you her special fruitcake. I can't go home empty-handed this time. They probably won't feed me if I do."

Now that he'd sifted through the paperwork on his desk, Ethan finally looked up at his old friend. "Naw, you go on now. Please tell your family I'm much obliged for their invite."

"Ethan, you can't just sit here and work. It's Christmas. For once in your life, pry yourself away from work and join us." In spite of knowing what shaky ground he trod, Uriah didn't want to leave Ethan alone on Christmas Eve.

Ethan knew what his friend tried to do—what he always tried to do. Uriah meant well.

"I can't right now, but maybe when I get all this cleared up." Ethan gestured over his desk. "You'd better head on home or that goose will be all gone," he joked, then hunkered down over his papers once more.

Uriah hated to see Ethan turn his back on anything or anyone that might get through that tough hide of his. Ethan had had it rough; that was for damned sure. He'd likely never get over the loss of his family so many years ago, and remembered it like it was yesterday. Uriah, too, would never forget that fateful day.

Riding well ahead of the rest of the wagon train, Uriah and Ethan helped to scout out the jagged, ascending landscape. Stopped in their tracks by the shrill neighing of horses and the piercing screams of folks in the back wagons, they both turned in unison to see what had happened.

Ethan's wagon.

Ethan's family!

Long as he lived, Uriah would never forget the horror and disbelief on Ethan's face. By the time they'd reached the overturned wagon, it was already too late. A rut had caught one of the wheels and thrown the huge Conestoga fatally off balance, sending it tumbling down the steep embankment. Ethan's father and little brother lay crushed under the heavy weight of the wagon. They must have died instantly. Folks were ministering to Ethan's mother and sister by the time Ethan and Uriah reached them. The disastrous accident left his mother pinned inside the wagon and his sister pitched out the back. His sister lay dead in a pitiful heap while his mother gasped for breath in Ethan's arms. The life drained from her as she struggled to reach up and embrace her son one last time.

"I'm sorry, Ma," Ethan cried, holding his mother close. "I'm so sorry I wasn't here. I should've been here. I'm so sorry." He clutched his dying mother ever closer. "Please, God." He turned his tear-stained face to the heavens. "Please save Ma." It took the help of the wagon master and two other men to pry Ethan away from his mother's bloody, lifeless form.

Uriah had no doubt Ethan still blamed himself for that dreadful day.

"If only I'd been there with them," Ethan had said. "The accident wouldn't have happened." It was *his* fault his family died. His job was to look out for danger. "I should've seen it coming." He hadn't protected them. He'd let his family down—but so had God.

The years passed, and Ethan's pain over the loss of his family eased but never went away. Hard work helped, sheer physical exhaustion the best balm for Ethan's troubled soul. But Uriah knew Ethan kept his pain hidden deep inside. Deeper still lurked all of Ethan's guilt over not protecting his family from harm. Not a day went by that Uriah's heart didn't go out to his good friend. Ethan, he knew, mistakenly believed that his love had brought nothing but injury to his family; that his love had destroyed them.

When Ethan met sweet Rachel five years ago, Uriah thought things were about to change. Somehow the spirited young woman managed to penetrate that crusty exterior of Ethan's. Head over heels in love, they planned to marry. Ethan began to live again. But it wasn't meant to be. Tragedy struck. Like many others that year in Denver City, Rachel fell ill with the typhus. There was nothing to be done. Uriah watched Ethan suffer through the same pain and loss he'd been through years ago. He'd see Ethan overturn the snow globe on his desk—the globe Rachel had given him—and he knew Ethan churned with regret. He saw the wall go up even higher around Ethan's heart, and harden him against love and against God. Uriah knew that Ethan believed his love for Rachel had killed her, not the typhus. Ethan would never forgive himself or God for letting her die.

"My family . . . was . . . God-fearing," Ethan had said, his throat tight with emotion. "Rachel was . . . a good Christian woman. Where did that get her . . . or my parents, Uriah? Dead, that's where," he finished bitterly.

Just when Ethan needed to turn toward God, Uriah saw him turn away.

For sure, I'll be an old bachelor, Uriah mused to himself, but he prayed that one day Ethan would find the love he'd lost, the love he needed. Uriah had no way of knowing if that day would ever come.

"Well, Ethan, forcin' me to go home empty-handed anyway, are you?"

"You still here?" Ethan smiled up at Uriah.

"Merry Christmas, Ethan." Uriah tried to smile back but couldn't. He hated leaving Ethan in the cold, empty office.

"Merry Christmas to you, Uriah. And to your whole family," Ethan said. "Tell them . . . well, please give them my apologies and thank them again for their invite."

"Ethan, are you at least headin' home soon? It's the holiday. You gotta get outta here," Uriah pleaded.

"Sure. Sure am. Why, Nettie's got supper ready for certain. Good night now, Uriah."

"Merry Christmas," Uriah repeated one last time before he opened the door and left Ethan all alone.

The same Christmas blizzard swirling outside Meggie's cabin raged down the mountains and across the foothills, reaching Ethan's door . . . the pathway between them rapidly covering over.

The holiday storm passed, but not before Meggie had her long-wished-for Christmas. She'd trudged through the weather to spend Christmas Eve and Christmas Day with friends who felt almost like family to her now. A merrier Christmas there could never be. Everyone in town who could come was at the Byers' Hotel. Children ran underfoot, carols rang throughout, the aroma of Christmas turkey filled the air, candles flickered on the tree with presents piled beneath, and everyone joined in to deck the halls. Meggie slept better that night than in the whole of her life, at long last having "visions of sugarplums" dancing in her head.

After Christmas and the New Year, the townsfolk in Hot Sulphur Springs went back to their routine, back to the rigors of surviving the harsh days of winter. Less isolated than settlers on outlying ranches, the residents of Hot Sulphur Springs had the advantage proximity brings. Companionship lifted flagged spirits, with townsfolk often running into one another at Grady's Mercantile.

Meggie's heart felt light as she turned the knob and went inside the mercantile.

"Mornin', Miss Rochester. Haven't seen you for quite a spell. How's everythin' down at the school?"

"Oh, things are going quite well, Mrs. Grady," Meggie answered the friendly, tall, salt-and-pepper-haired shopkeeper. "The children come when they can. They show up more often than not. I can't expect more than that," she added, enjoying the pleasant exchange.

"You are a true blessin', you are. Our Nate has smartened up plenty since you've been his teacher. Quick as a jackrabbit with his sums now. His father's that pleased."

"Nathan is a very bright pupil, Mrs. Grady. He always comes to school wanting to learn and to work. He sets a very good example for the other children." Happy to have a parent take note of the progress in her child, it gratified Meggie to see Mrs. Grady beam so.

"Now just what is it I can get for you today, Miss Rochester?" Seemingly intent on waiting upon her customer now, Mrs. Grady straightened a burlap apron strap that had fallen down over one arm, then looked up, giving her undivided attention.

Meggie was just about to answer when the door to the mercantile opened behind her. The blast of cold air sent an unwelcome shiver through her. She didn't have to turn around to recognize the voice.

"Why, good mornin', Mrs. Grady."

The syrupy tone of Livi Tritt sent another uncomfortable shudder through Meggie. She knew Livi stayed up in Hot Sulphur for the winter, although she couldn't imagine why. Other than an occasional spotting from a distance, luckily Meggie had been able to avoid any conversation with the unpleasant young woman. Until now.

"Oh, and a very good mornin' to you too, *Miss* Rochester."

Livi's pointed emphasis on *Miss* hit its target. With a smile she didn't feel, Meggie turned around to face her.

"Hello, Livi," Meggie said flatly.

"Mrs. Grady?" Livi directed her attention away from Meggie

in dismissal. "I just came in for some molasses and sugar. But I . . . well, I have somethin' I need to ask you. It's about the Express. When exactly are you expectin' the mail from up Breckenridge way?"

"Likely it'll be here first of the week. The weather's breakin' up some, so I suspect it'll be arrivin' real soon," Mrs. Grady explained. "Won't be long before we'll have a regular Express schedule. With the stage comin' through, we should have service as much as three times in a week. That sure will be somethin'."

Meggie had tramped through the snow to inquire about the very same thing, so she was glad to hear this. She could finally send off her letter to Pru.

"I'm so very happy to hear that, Mrs. Grady," Livi dripped out.

The young woman's insincere intonations made Meggie cringe yet again.

"You see," Livi continued. "Well, I suppose I shouldn't be sayin' things of such a personal nature to you, but I'm expectin' a very important letter." Livi looked directly at Meggie now.

Uncomfortable under Livi's glare, Meggie forced herself to glance anywhere but at the dark beauty. She studied the bottles of colored liquid lined up on the mahogany shelves behind Mrs. Grady. A few of the labels were in Latin. All the squinting in the world couldn't help her read them. Her gaze stopped at two larger bottles labeled in English. Carbolic Acid and Iodine. Both were good for cleaning wounds. Next she turned her focus from behind Mrs. Grady's counter to the wooden barrels stacked along the store's back wall. Several of the barrels had a large spigot near their bottom. The first contained VINEGAR, the next MOLASSES, then PICKLES, and lastly WHISKEY— *the devil's drink.*

Livi spoke louder.

Now Meggie stared hard at all the bolts of cloth neatly set

out on a nearby counter. The colorful fabrics cheered her somewhat.

"Well, Mrs. Grady, let me know right away when I get my letter from *Ethan Rourke.*"

Ethan! Meggie couldn't ignore Livi any longer. The young woman's pointed glower bored a hole clean through Meggie's heart. Jealousy filled it when she heard Ethan's name on Livi's lips.

"He promised me he'd send somethin' on the very first Express that got through," Livi whined. "I'll just have to be patient, won't I?"

Livi's smug grin broadened.

Meggie's frayed nerves had no defense against Livi. Out of habit, Meggie reached up to straighten her spectacles. They weren't there! They hadn't been for weeks. But now, if she could just have the comfort of hiding behind the lenses, maybe then Livi wouldn't see through to her hurt and her dashed hopes. She felt as if Livi could read her thoughts and knew that at night Meggie wrote to Ethan in secret. Painful, jealous stabs began cutting right through Meggie's tense limbs. Looking down at her arms, she expected to see them cut and her sleeves shred to ribbons! She didn't know how much longer she could hold her composure.

"Well, bye now, Mrs. Grady. And bye to you, *Miss* Rochester," Livi threw over her shoulder as she was leaving. "You two have a real nice day." The young woman left without taking her molasses pail or the sack of sugar she'd come for in the first place.

Meggie held on to her composure, despite her upset. Why should she be surprised that Ethan was taken with Livi Tritt? *She's young, beautiful, and perfect. I'm none of those things. I'm old, plain, and the most imperfect of all God's creatures.* Meggie wanted to cry, to scream, to lash out at something, anything to stop the pain—the pain of knowing there would never be any storybook romance for her and Ethan—they would never end up "happily ever after" like Jane and Edward. The truth of it hit Meggie like a cruel slap. It shocked her. *I do love Ethan, I do.* No matter how hard she'd fought against such feelings, she realized now that she was in love with Ethan Rourke. Frightened by this revelation—by its powerful hold on her—Meggie's insides folded. She'd no defense against Ethan. Not anymore. She stiffened her spine. What did it matter now anyway, since Ethan obviously cared for another?

"Now, what may I do for you, Miss Rochester?"

At first Meggie didn't hear the kindly shopkeeper.

"Miss Rochester?" Mrs. Grady repeated.

"Oh, yes. Please forgive me." Meggie struggled to hide her upset. "Actually . . ." She choked back her tears. "Actually you've . . . already helped me. I have a letter here." Swallowing hard, she reached inside the pocket of her heavy coat.

"Are you all right, Miss Rochester? Do you feel poorly?" Mrs. Grady gently asked.

"I'm fine, Mrs. Grady. I've just taken a bit of a chill. Soon as I get home I'll be fine. Would you mail . . . mail this with the first Express?" She could barely speak above a whisper. She placed her letter to Pru in Mrs. Grady's outstretched hand, then reached back inside her coat pocket and withdrew money to pay for the mailing.

"Oh, no need for that now. The rate hasn't been figured yet. You can pay me when I know exactly," Mrs. Grady lightly protested.

Ignoring the shopkeeper's objection, Meggie carefully counted out the estimated coins and put them down on the counter. With little energy for anything but a weak goodbye, and despite Mrs. Grady's concern and her puzzled expression, Meggie turned and walked out of the mercantile. No matter what, she'd avoid any more contact with Livi Tritt.

But that night, despite her efforts not to, Meggie took out her writing materials to continue her story to Ethan. She didn't care that she didn't have the right because he belonged to someone else. Her story was unfinished. She owed him the rest. She owed herself the rest.

Taking out her writing materials, she found the place where she'd left off in her letter to Ethan . . . *I tried to reach up and break the evil grasp that had hold of me, but I could not . . .*

Ethan, it was as if something from the fiery pits of hell rose up and shackled me, laughing at my efforts to break free. The fiend yanked harder on my hair, twisting it and tangling it around his fist. The more I fought, the worse my pain.

I stopped fighting. Maybe this wasn't real. Maybe it was the sherry tricking me. Maybe it wasn't the devil and black magic. If I stayed very still, like a good girl, maybe nothing bad would happen. I shut my eyes tight and wished with everything in me to be gone from the horrible place. Maybe, if I wished hard enough, Benjamin Howard would be six feet under, six feet away from me . . . dead in the ground and my nightmare over. I kept my eyes squeezed shut and conjured my wish, a childlike rhyme born out of fear, to chase away the evil that was upon me: Six feet under, six feet away, where to stay safe, the devil must stay!

When I dared open my eyes, Benjamin Howard wasn't dead but very much alive. I tried to scream. Nothing came out but my hoarse whisper, "Six feet under, six feet away, where to stay safe, the devil must stay!"

My vision clouded. I tried to stay alert, desperate to find a way to escape the monster that had me. When Benjamin Howard's hand sickeningly encircled my breast, a new fear struck me, one I'd never imagined. I thought I knew then what he might do to me before he killed me. The stench of death hung

*in the air—molded gray, dank, rotting. My breaths came quick.
My heart hammered in my tight chest.*

*Then, in one rapier move, Benjamin Howard ripped the front
of my dress open to my waist, leaving my bare flesh exposed to
his loathsome perusal. When his fingers made their clammy as-
sault on me, I fought him with everything left in me. The more I
fought him, the more aroused he seemed. I knew nothing of
men, but instinct told me this monster enjoyed my fear, enjoyed
doing awful things to me. His breaths came like the dragon fire
of nightmarish tales. Then he began . . . he began to whisper
horrible, unconscionable things in my ear . . . while he . . .
while he pressed himself against me . . . against my . . .*

Meggie put down her pen. She fought the urge to get up,
fling open the cabin door, and plunge into the river outside,
desperate to wash away Benjamin Howard's filth. Instead, she
refilled her pen and continued.

*. . . against my innocence. I could never have imagined such
vileness. I wanted to die. I prayed to die. How could I let him
keep touching me and saying such things? How could I ever
have thought him handsome? How could the headmistress have
delivered me up to the devil? Why did she hate me so much that
she would do this? Why? Just when I thought things couldn't get
worse, they did. After the first blow, Benjamin Howard pulled
me from the settee and threw me to the floor, ramming his fist
into my jaw a second time. When he hit me next, I fell into
unconsciousness.*

At this point Meggie didn't want to go on, at least not for
tonight. She'd said enough. She'd relived enough. She turned
her lamplight low and readied for bed.

Meggie knew the exact moment spring arrived in the mountains.

She could hear the change in the flow of the mighty Grande right outside her cabin window. It was just before dawn. She lay in bed and listened to the unmistakable sound of ice breaking free of the swift currents beneath its mullioned layers. Less fearful to her now than it used to be, the powerful force was more companion than foe. She closed her eyes to better listen.

Good things, blessings indeed, had come into her life since she'd arrived in Hot Sulphur Springs. She had a home of her own, friends, and the chance to teach in her own schoolroom. She had everything she could possibly want, everything she'd dreamed of, didn't she? It was the closest she'd ever come to normal and ordinary, and she was content. No, she didn't have Ethan in her life, but she did have her letter to him, and she did have Edward Rochester. Her venerable romance novel would never abandon her, reject her, and find her wanting. Here in Hot Sulphur she could lead a safe life, a life without love but still, a safe life. Meggie opened her eyes at the word *safe*. She thought of Benjamin Howard and suddenly didn't feel safe.

He was still out there. He still wanted her dead.

Meggie shut her eyes again, concentrating hard on the sounds of the river. Its force stroked and soothed her fraying nerves. She felt better, if only a little. Humph, if only she were a child again. If only her life had taken a different turn and she'd never met up with the likes of Benjamin Howard. If only she'd had loving parents to protect her from such evil.

Meggie understood that she'd never know what happened to her parents. The matron at the orphanage told her they were dead and she had no family left. The matron refused to tell Meggie what had happened to them. Meggie remembered lashing out at the matron, trying to kick her and hurt her the way she'd just been hurt. That was the day the matron began to impose undue cruelty upon Meggie. "How dared the little ungrateful brat strike the one who was her protector now? How dared she!" That was when Meggie felt the first switch on her back.

Tears stung her eyes. She rolled over in bed and gave her pillow a thump. She hated feeling sorry for herself. That's exactly what this was. But she couldn't help it right now. Ever and always beset by worry over what happened to her parents, hurting for them, grieving for them, she drifted back into uneasy sleep.

The ice outside the window crashed against the riverbank. Meggie bolted awake. Bright sunlight streamed across her face. Blinking against the unforgiving rays, she sat up in bed and pulled her cross out from beneath her nightdress and put the cross to her lips. Whatever her parents' fate, she knew they were in heaven. Meggie prayed to God to keep them always in His loving arms. She prayed, too, that one day she'd be worthy of a place in heaven with them.

CHAPTER TWELVE

Meggie at last ventured to the hot pools. She'd shied away from them ever since she'd encountered Ethan there. But now she was of a mind to test the waters herself and find out if they were truly healing. They'd certainly helped Mr. Markson. Soon the Marksons would be leaving Hot Sulphur Springs. Meggie would miss them, but she understood. Life in the mountains was too rugged for the elderly couple on a full-time basis. For her, life in the mountains was just what the doctor ordered: anonymity, isolation, good friends, and a good job. There was still one thing that plagued her, one thing for which no doctor had found a cure. She'd yet to feel purged of her sins. Not a day went by that Meggie wasn't constantly reminded of her sin and ruin at the hands of Benjamin Howard.

She picked up her step over the footbridge and hurried toward the field of rising steam. When she reached the water's edge she couldn't help it, and thought of Ethan. This was the very spot where she'd seen him naked and coming toward her—

Meggie couldn't get away fast enough. She ran past the steaming pool. She'd find another one ahead.

Running from her memories of Ethan, she pushed deep into the woods, searching for another bed of hot springs. Out of breath she stopped, finally realizing it would be unwise to keep going, especially without her Colt .45. Besides, the hour grew late. She tried to remember the way she'd just come. Soon it would be dark. Instead of sensibly turning back, something made her keep going. She did, until she heard voices, male voices. She couldn't make out what they were saying. Their language was foreign to her.

Utes!

So many nights she'd lain awake listening to their drums. In all that time, Meggie had never actually seen a Ute, sometimes forgetting in the daylight hours that they even shared the same woods, and sometimes forgetting the danger they presented. She'd listened to their drums at night, often lulled to sleep by them, not really afraid. Yet she'd no desire to actually encounter the Utes in the flesh, especially now, far from her cabin and without the protection of her gun.

Strangely more curious than afraid, Meggie crept quietly and carefully toward the large crop of boulders, in the direction of the voices. If she climbed to the top of the rocks, she might get a glimpse of the Utes. The prospect intrigued her.

She easily made it over the first set of rocks, but the next ones proved more difficult. Hand and footholds were harder to find, but Meggie was too curious to turn back. At last climbing to the top of the rocks, she stayed low to keep out of sight. The voices were louder now, but she couldn't see anyone and edged closer. Horses whinnied and neighed. Meggie crawled out farther onto the precipice, far enough so she could see.

She'd found another bed of hot pools, all right, Utes and all! At least a dozen Indians were gathered next to a large, steaming pool. Two of the men led their horses into the hot springs. Meggie's heart drummed in her chest. Mesmerized, she watched the Utes minister to their animals. The Utes were dark, their skin reminding her of the deep, rich bark of the surrounding pines. Dressed in hide shirts and breeches, with their long black hair caught up in braids, they looked magnificent to Meggie. Just then a man and a woman approached from the edge of the thicket.

Meggie thought the couple looked more like characters out of a romance novel than dangerous Indians. This man, unlike the other Utes, wore his hair loose. The gentle breezes ruffled it and reminded her of a wild stallion. He was taller than the others, and Meggie could see how darkly handsome he was. He wore no hide shirt; he was set apart from the others in that way, too. He held the woman's hand as they walked. The picture tugged at Meggie's heart. She studied the exotic-looking woman. Something seemed particularly odd about her.

Why, she's white!

Not a captive, not a slave, but a white woman hand-in-hand with the handsome Ute.

Meggie's fanciful imagination stirred. She hung out farther over the precipice, fantasizing about the couple's possible romantic beginning.

The woman was beautiful with long, thick, dark braids reaching down to her waist. Her olive complexion, in contrast to the dark skin of her companion, glowed with happiness. In her hide dress and moccasins, despite her skin color, the woman looked like an Indian maid to Meggie. So caught up in her romantic notions about the pair, Meggie paid little attention to her own ever-increasing, precarious position atop the rocky cliff.

One of the men led his horse out of the curative springs. Meggie switched her gaze away from the romantic couple to watch. Once the horse was out of the water, another Indian began to apply a yellow paste to one of its legs. The horse must be injured. Busy thinking about what the potion might contain, she inched a little closer. Disaster struck.

Meggie screamed when she fell off the rocks and onto the unforgiving ground below. She stayed where she lay. She dared not move. The fall didn't kill her, but she suddenly wondered if the Utes might. Dizzy and hurting, she waited for them to approach. Afraid of them now, she lay still and thought of what they might do. Maybe scalp her! Maybe torture her! *Jesus, Mary, and Joseph, Meghan McMurphy!* She didn't think what the sisters might say now about her choice of words.

Above all else, she thought of Benjamin Howard at this moment. At least she could take pleasure in the fact that he'd be robbed of the opportunity to kill her himself. Her head pounded and her arms and legs ached. Her foot felt like it had been severed. Helpless and dazed, she watched as the Utes closed in. Determined not to shut her eyes against them, Meggie prayed she'd be brave.

The Utes circled around her. None of them looked too murderous. They didn't draw their knives or wield tomahawks. Instead they seemed as curious about her as she was about them. Just then the beautiful white woman broke from the circle of men.

"Nu Raven, piwa-n tux Showahcan. Tami kac paqxa-ki umu."

The woman's gentle tone and lyrical-sounding language reassured Meggie, though she couldn't understand the words. When the woman leaned down and began examining her, Meggie wasn't afraid.

"Tami astii-sapa tux pua-rii umu." The woman's touch was as gentle as her voice. She turned briefly away from Meggie and began speaking to a nearby Ute.

"Kui musutkwi-vi. Nawa mama-ci's pura-n napa naaga yaqxi. Musutkwi-vi turusi paa-pu."

At her words, the Indian broke from the group. In his place stepped the tall, handsome Ute who'd arrived with the woman. Now she spoke to him.

"Maku-ta nu rugway muruka mama-ci musutkwi-vi num pavi-ci kui mama-ci kani."

He nodded in apparent agreement with her and then stepped out of sight, but not before touching his hand to her cheek.

The other Ute returned with a hide pouch of yellow paste.

Meggie recognized it as the paste they'd used on their horse. The sleeve of her dress was suddenly ripped open. Meggie gagged at the sight of all the blood that oozed from her arm. No bones stuck out. The woman bathed Meggie's injured arm in water from the warm springs, then applied the yellow paste. The pain subsided immediately. Next the woman worked on Meggie's damaged foot, rotating it first one way, then the other. The examination hurt, but Meggie didn't dare protest. The paste when applied had the same effect as before, and Meggie's pain went away. She smiled at the caring woman, hoping her expression would convey her gratitude.

One of the Indians gathered round her suddenly reached down and scooped Meggie up in his arms. Meggie didn't have time to react or to be afraid. The man promptly put her astride a horse, while another arranged a blanket around her shoulders. Meggie felt weak and unsteady, but held her own. She couldn't believe the kindness being shown to her. Just then the man who'd put her on her horse climbed onto his, snatched up the guide rope hanging around her horse's neck, and then began leading her away. She turned and smiled again at the lovely maid, suddenly happy the woman was living her fairy-tale romance. Meggie thought of Jane and Edward, envious of both them and the Ute couple. Reluctantly, she turned away from the maid and faced the trail ahead, riding in silence behind the stoic Ute, knowing he was guiding her home.

Meggie didn't recognize the trail. Of course, she couldn't exactly recall the trail she'd taken anyway. On the journey home, she thought of the handsome, romantic couple back at the hidden hot springs, likening them more than once to Jane and Edward. Romance like theirs was meant for others. Not her. Before she could have another unhappy thought, she was home.

The silent Ute lifted her down off her horse and carried her inside the cabin. He put her down on her bed, and then, without as much as a nod, he left. Too exhausted to wonder how the Ute knew precisely where she lived, Meggie closed her eyes and fell into an immediate, exhausted sleep.

Weeks passed. Meggie healed so fast she almost forgot she'd ever been injured, but she'd never forget the kindness of the Utes. They had been kind and not dangerous. She'd be forever grateful to them. She decided not to tell anyone about her encounter with the Utes, and hid the blanket they'd given her under her quilt. Not knowing exactly who she was protecting, the Indians or the townsfolk, she decided to keep things secret. Some things were best left alone.

Meggie was out walking, enjoying the warm day, when one of her pupils suddenly ran up to her.

"A letter's come fer ya, Miss Rochester."

"You mean come *for you,* Sally Ann," Meggie slowly corrected, excited at the news. "What letter do you mean? Is there a letter at the mercantile for me?"

"Yeah, the Express just arrived. Ain't . . . I mean, isn't it excitin'!"

"Yes, Sally Ann, it is very exciting, but for heaven's sake take a breath."

"Yes, ma'am," the girl said, but kept on. "We have a letter, too! Gotta git home! Ma and Pa ain't there just now, but they'll be home soon and I have to read what it's all about. Couldn't do so good 'ceptin' you helped me, Miss Rochester. Gotta go!" With that, the girl turned and scampered back up the trail toward town.

Meggie was close behind her.

Pru was coming west! She would arrive in Denver in a month's time, and would Meggie be able to meet her train? Overjoyed,

Meggie began immediately to make plans to do just that. She and Pru had both survived Boston—so far, that is.

When Pru managed to leave the wretched orphanage, she'd secured a job working for the wealthy, first as a cleaning woman and then as housekeeper. Her job kept her away from charity's door. It was charity, however, that had reunited Pru and Meggie. The family employing Pru had sent her on an errand of mercy all the way across the city, to the Sisters of Charity, to deliver donated goods to the convent school. On that visit Meggie answered the bell. The two long-lost friends fell into each other's arms.

Pru couldn't believe Meggie was alive, and Meggie couldn't believe Pru had broken free of the hellish orphanage. Pru had been afraid to find out about Meggie, and Meggie had been afraid to find out about Pru. Reunited now, both vowed to never lose their friendship or each other again.

So excited about the prospect of seeing Pru again, Meggie forgot all about the prospect that she might run into Ethan in Denver.

"Thank you for the ride, Mr. Sykes." Meggie let the salty driver help her down from the huge Concord. His touch didn't rattle her. *Progress indeed,* she thought.

"You shore are welcome," Bill Sykes said, and let go of her arm. "You stayin' here long? I'll be makin' the route nigh on to three times a week startin' Monday next. Still work needin' to be done on the pass, but it won't be stoppin' me. No, sir."

Meggie smiled at the veteran driver's bravado.

"I'm not sure how long I'll be in Denver, Mr. Sykes. I'm going to meet someone coming in from the East on the train. As soon as my plans are certain, I'll book passage back up to Hot Sulphur Springs."

"Good enough, Miss Rochester. Say, do you need any help

gettin' your things to where you're stayin'? Be dark pretty soon." He handed her satchel down to her from the top of the coach.

"Thank you, but no, Mr. Sykes. It's such a nice evening, I plan to enjoy my walk to the American House Hotel. If I remember correctly, it's not too far."

"Yes, ma'am, if that's what you want. Well, you have a real good stay, and I'll be seein' you soon." Bill Sykes tipped his hat in her direction and climbed back into the driver's seat.

Meggie watched him pull away. She was alone now, on her own again in Denver. She'd thought of Ethan during the journey, but then did her utmost *not* to think of him. With all her heart, she hoped she wouldn't run into him again. She prayed she would not.

At first glance, Denver looked very different to her. It was late April now, not October. The street was muddied still, but no ice and snow remained. No ice and snow to slip on. Meggie stiffened her spine. She thought of Ethan, determined not to have any slips this time in Denver.

Meggie, admittedly, had spent so little time in Denver before that she could hardly form an opinion of the busy city now. Wagons drove past. People walked past on the crowded planked walkways along Fifteenth Street. Good, the less likely to be noticed. Meggie thought of Benjamin Howard and tightened her grip on her satchel. Her Colt .45 lay snugly tucked inside. She'd never used it except in practice. But if she had to, she would.

Meggie took care in negotiating the busy street, stepping between the loaded wagons rolling by and all of the riders on horseback. She was glad to walk among so many folks, so many men, with such a degree of ease. By the time she reached the other side of Fifteenth Street, the hem of her skirt was caked with mud. Paying little mind to this, she took off down the walkway, thinking this was the right way to the American House

Hotel. She began to doubt herself. Maybe she should have let Bill Sykes escort her. It was getting late. She didn't relish the idea of being out after dark, lost or otherwise.

There was an alleyway up ahead. That couldn't be the right way, yet she headed straight for the unfamiliar passage. Turning down the alleyway, unsure of the wisdom of her direction, she followed her instincts and kept walking in between the two large brick buildings. She stopped dead in her tracks when she heard music—*dance hall music!*

She'd never been to a dance hall, but there was no mistaking the lively plunking of the piano keys. The sisters had certainly warned her enough about such places. Meggie hesitated, trying to decide if she should continue or turn back.

It grew darker. Meggie turned on her heels to retrace her steps. Whatever was she thinking, coming this way? Just then she heard a woman scream, eerily audible over the loud piano music. The woman's cries reached out to Meggie. Whoever it was, Meggie needed to help her. She forgot her own fears. She couldn't let the woman face her terror alone!

Wary yet determined, Meggie started back down the dark passageway. The screams grew louder. Meggie followed them into one alley, then another. There were no streetlamps to help light the way. It was almost impossible now to see where she was going, so she used the woman's pitiful screams as her guide.

The nauseating scene Meggie came upon made her want to turn and run. Enough light filtered through a nearby open doorway for her to see several men circle around a woman. Bile rose in Meggie's gorge. The stench of death hung in the air. Her breaths came quick and shallow.

With their prey trapped, the men moved in closer. They didn't seem to notice Meggie's approach.

The young woman had no escape.

Meggie knew how that felt, almost every night in her terrifying dreams.

One of the fiends stepped from the predatory circle and pushed the woman against the wall. He ripped at her clothes while the other men cheered. The men seemed drunk, all four of them. Their slurred shouts and stumbled movements were a dead giveaway. Meggie knew the men were going to rape the poor, trapped woman. Avenging anger boiled up inside of Meggie. It had waited eight years for just such a moment.

One of the drunken louts slapped the ambushed woman. Meggie pulled her loaded Colt .45 out of her satchel and shot it into the air. Then, with her pistol in both hands, she pointed it directly at the group of ne'er-do-well inebriates.

That's got their attention!

Now they see me!

"Hell, boys. Looky here now," the man who still held onto the young woman said. "Ain't nuthin' but another little piece of cherry." He looked right at Meggie now. "Betcha you wanna a lil' of what she's gonna git, don't you, girlie?"

Keep your wits, Meggie girl. She had to save the poor waif from this scum. The girl, pinned miserably against the wall, sobbed uncontrollably. Meggie kept her gun pointed at the men. She dared not take her eyes off any of them.

"Will, you and Randy git her now." The same cur spat out the drunken order. "I'll just keep lil' Clemmie here and you two git Miss Cherry. We kin all have ourselves a time. We kin all poke 'em both."

Were they all too stupid and drunk to notice she had a loaded Colt .45 peacemaker pointed at them? Drunken, stupid louts. Miserable scum of the earth.

Two of the men were actually coming toward *her* now.

"You both better stop right there unless you want a bullet clear through those thick skulls of yours," Meggie warned. Upset as she was over this nightmarish situation, she didn't want to really shoot anyone. The men stopped short and she relaxed a little, waiting, keeping her weapon on them.

"Do I have to come over thar myself, boys?"

Despite his drunkenness, Meggie could tell the man was getting good and angry. She recognized his demonic tone.

"Git the bitch now!" he ordered.

When his men started for her Meggie didn't hesitate.

The one she shot in the leg shrieked out. "Boss, she's done shot me! I'm gunshot!"

Meggie didn't drop her sites on the other men.

"You men had better take your friend here to the doctor, or you can let him bleed to death right here on the street," she spat out. "That is, unless you would *all* like to take a bullet. I've got plenty here. You just let me know how it's going to go." Meggie couldn't believe it was her talking and her holding the gun, but it felt darned good to be doing it.

Finally, the pathetic drunkard started to move away. The other men took hold of their injured friend and helped him hobble back inside the saloon. Only the one was left. The worst one.

Slowly, he let go of the young woman.

Gripped in obvious fear, the woman didn't move.

The fiend waited, glowering at Meggie.

Meggie waited, too.

Neither spoke.

Just when Meggie thought the miserable excuse for a man was going to come at her, he began stumbling along the wall toward the saloon door, using the wall to help support his drunken limbs. At the door he turned around and glared at Meggie.

"You miserable . . . bitch," he slurred at her. "Woman like . . . you . . . ain't . . . no fit woman at all." He spat on the ground and then disappeared inside the saloon.

Relieved when all the drunken fiends were gone, Meggie uncocked the hammer of her pistol. It hadn't hit her yet that she'd actually shot someone. Still holding her Colt .45 at her side, she approached the frightened girl. The poor thing didn't look more than fifteen years old. Meggie hadn't been much older herself when she'd been brutally attacked.

The girl stared wide-eyed at Meggie, her body still wracked with sobs.

"Miss." Meggie spoke softly. "You're all right now. Those men have gone. You're safe now," she reassured.

The girl looked away from Meggie and down at her torn clothing, pulling the edges of her ripped bodice together to cover her nakedness.

Meggie's heart went out to her.

The pitiable creature tried to gather together the tattered remnants of her soiled dress before she turned her tear-streaked face back to Meggie.

Meggie looked into the girl's puffy, bloodshot eyes. There was enough fear and pain there to fill a lifetime. Worst of all, she read utter defeat in the unfortunate girl's eyes.

"Here now, you're shivering. Wait just a moment," Meggie softly consoled her, and reached down to pull her shawl from her satchel while replacing her gun there.

"This isn't much, but it'll help warm you," she said, and draped the worn garment around the girl's shoulders.

"Please," the girl finally spoke. "I cain't take it." She tried to pull it off and give it back to Meggie.

"Nonsense," Meggie insisted. "You can take it. I won't have it any other way. Now please, come along with me. Let's get you out of here." Meggie took the girl's arm to guide her out of the dark alleyway to a main street, but the girl suddenly pulled away.

"I cain't! Thank you for all yer help. Saved me for shore. But

I cain't leave."

"You have to," Meggie implored. "Those monsters were going to rape you. You have to get away from them." The girl's declaration left her dumbfounded.

"If'n I leave, I'll be sacked for shore. I need my job. Don't have nuthin' else."

Meggie knew enough about the troubles women faced out west to know the girl didn't exaggerate. Despite the unfortunate ring of truth in the girl's words, Meggie beseeched her to leave.

"*Please* come with me. Those drunkards are still in there. You can't go back inside. You can't let those foul-mouthed brutes touch you ever again. You mustn't let anyone do that to you. Please, I beg you. Come with me. I'll do whatever I can to help you." On some level, Meggie felt as if she were trying to save herself.

"No, ma'am. Thank you anyways, but I cain't let you help me," the girl said with an unnatural calmness. " 'Sides, it's nuthin' what ain't been done a'fore to me."

Meggie let go of the dejected young girl and watched as she made her way toward the open door at the back of the saloon. Meggie wanted to cry. The girl's life was no life at all.

"My name is Rose Rochester! Uh, I mean Meghan . . . my name's Meghan McMurphy!" she called out before the girl disappeared inside the building. "I'll be staying at the American House Hotel if you change your mind! If you need anything . . ." Meggie let her words trail off as the girl vanished from sight, unmindful she'd used her real name, too.

Alone in the dark, more afraid for the unfortunate girl than herself, Meggie picked up her satchel, gun and all, and started to walk in the direction she thought would lead her back to Fifteenth Street. At last finding her way, Meggie made it to the American House Hotel and stepped inside. She'd no idea of the time.

"Well how do, Miss . . . Miss Rochester. Yes indeed, I remember you. How do, Miss Rochester," Mr. Cottswell greeted enthusiastically from behind the registration desk. "Haven't seen you all winter. Been up in the mountains, have you?"

Flabbergasted that he remembered her and uneasy at his evident personal knowledge of her whereabouts, she fumbled for words.

"Yes . . . yes, I just came down over Berthoud Pass this very afternoon," she answered. "I hoped to find a room at your hotel. Do you have one available?"

"Sure do. For you, Miss Rochester, sure do."

Puzzled by Mr. Cottswell's solicitous manner, Meggie was too tired to think on it now and snatched up her room key the moment the little bald clerk tossed her key onto the register. If she could just get some sleep she'd sort everything out tomorrow.

But no such easy slumber awaited her upstairs.

Any moment the fiend would catch up to her. Only seconds away, death followed close behind Meggie in the maze of passages in the dark alleyway. Breathing was impossible. Which way? She must find the way out before it was too late. She prayed as she felt her way along the cold brick of the unforgiving wall. Surely she would not be delivered into the hands of the devil again. Then she felt something. A corner. This must be the way out. Very carefully she followed the turn with her hands. She saw a light in the distance and ran toward it, ecstatic she'd found her way out—her escape! Thank heaven she was almost there. Steps led up to the opening. Only a short climb now. One step. Two steps. Three. Only a few more and she'd be safe. One to go. Just one.

The devil reached her!

He had her!

She screamed and fought, to no avail.

The claws of death pulled Meggie back down, away from salvation. Thrown against the cold jagged wall, the demonic fiend rent the fabric of her bodice in one sharp tear. She didn't want to open her eyes and look at the evil that was upon her, but she did. She would face death. She wouldn't give Benjamin Howard the satisfaction of watching her lose consciousness.

Then he was upon her.

Meggie woke up in a cold sweat. She'd no idea of the time. It was still dark. Climbing out of bed, she lit the nearby lamp, needing it for companionship. She wanted—no, she needed—to continue her letter to Ethan. It would ease her upset. Reaching into her satchel, she carefully felt around for *Jane Eyre*. In it, she now kept the pages of her unfinished letter to Ethan. Taking out her letter, she carefully smoothed out the folds. Glad she'd thought to go back downstairs earlier and retrieve pen and ink from the registration desk, she'd placed it nearby on the bedstead. As it was, the bedstead would do for a desk. She pulled it and the lamp closer, and then quickly filled the steel-nib pen with ink. Once done, she found the place where she'd left off in her letter to Ethan . . . *when he hit me next, I fell into unconsciousness . . .*

After Benjamin Howard was through using me for his perverse pleasure, he dumped my body into an alleyway in the poorest section of Boston. As far as I know, no one bore witness to his foul deed. I guess he thought I was already dead, or at least would be by morning.

Ethan, it would be two years before I had any clear memory of that horrible day. A local constable, I found out, discovered me, still unconscious, and took me to the state asylum. I was barely alive, I'm told. The constable might just as well have taken my dead remains to the asylum, for I was as good as dead inside. My mind had shut down, but not my body—not yet, anyway. I think now that maybe it was Providence that kept me out of my mind, so that I could not remember my brutal violation. When my wits did begin to return, it was Providence again, perhaps, that led the visiting Sisters of Charity to discover me at the asylum. I was to spend the next six years at the convent of their order.

The benevolent sisters put me to work as a teacher in their school, tutoring me daily in strict religious instruction. This simple, spiritual life brought me order, peace, and contentment. It also brought me daily reminders that I must bear the burden of my shame for the rest of my life. The good sisters, unintended though it might have been of them, made me feel I was the guilty party, and not my attacker. My wickedness—allowing myself to fall victim to sin—could be purged through good deeds and living a life in the service of God. I was content to do just that until the day I saw Benjamin Howard again.

I recognized him immediately. His furious, fiery glare burns me still. The moment he entered my classroom with the philanthropic group touring the convent, the hairs on the back of my neck stood on end. I was so scared, so nauseated, felt so contaminated and assaulted, I wanted to faint. I did not. I remember rubbing my hands hard along the sides of my dress, trying to get them clean. To this day, I have trouble feeling clean. I kept my eyes on Benjamin Howard. His maniacal face said it all. The vile predator, after eight years of stalking me in nightmares, wanted me dead. I didn't mistake his cruel intentions—the devil was coming for me and wanted to send me once and for all into the scorching pits of hell. Benjamin Howard left my classroom then with the others, but I knew he'd be back for me. I booked passage on the very next train out of Boston.

Dear Ethan, I could end this letter now, leaving you to think my story is over. But it is not. There is more I must tell you, more that I wish you to know . . .

Too drowsy to continue, Meggie carefully tucked her folded letter into the pages of *Jane Eyre,* then quickly fell back to sleep.

CHAPTER THIRTEEN

Meggie's night left her exhausted. If her harrowing encounter in the alleyway with the drunken rapists hadn't been enough to wear her down, the night terror that followed was. Of course, there was her letter-writing, ever a boon to her spirits. But all her newfound bravado and all the pistols in the world couldn't protect her from the dark hours of sleep when the demonic fiend stalked. How she wished for an end to all of this. No doubt Benjamin Howard would follow her into eternity, making sure she'd never rest in peace! Upset as she was, Meggie hated feeling sorry for herself. She hated that she cried. She hated that she wasn't stronger. After so many years, she should be stronger. She hated that she wasn't.

Minutes passed before Meggie's tears dried. When they did she sat up in bed, disgusted that she'd wallowed in self-pity. She was alive, wasn't she? She wasn't locked away in any orphanage at the end of a switch or lying crazy in the corner of some asylum. And, as for romance . . . lots of women never had it. She should be grateful for what she had, not regret what she didn't have.

Meggie thought of the waif from last night, the girl in true need. She wondered how the girl had fared when she went back inside the saloon. If only Meggie had been able to convince the poor creature to leave with her. She was afraid for the girl. How many more run-ins with such no-accounts could the poor thing survive? *It's too late for me, but maybe not for her.*

Meggie hopped out of bed and reached for her clothes. She had to find the girl and convince her to abandon her dangerous life. If she didn't, the girl might not live to see her sixteenth year.

"Train's been delayed, Miss. Should be here tomorrow," Harold said. The wiry stationmaster never forgot a face. Red hair. In her twenties. The McMurphy woman that son of a bitch Pinkerton was looking for last year. Probably still was, Harold thought.

"Thank you. I'll be back tomorrow then," Meggie said and stepped away from the stationmaster's queer scrutiny.

Harold hoped the surly Pinkerton was well out of the Colorado Territory by now.

Meggie started down the street, disappointed the train was late and anxious to see Pru. Nothing was to be done for it. Besides, she had time now to try and find the girl from last night. If she had to, she'd search every saloon in Denver to find her. Meggie could hear Sister Mary Catherine's lecture. A young woman could be lost forever in such a place! But if Meggie didn't go in "such places," it was the poor girl who'd be lost forever.

Meggie reached the same back street, the same alleyway she'd taken the night before. Sure of her steps this time, she knew she had one turn to make and then she'd be at the rear door of the saloon. Once she made the turn, Meggie stopped short. There were at least a dozen doors in view. Which was the right one?

The first door suddenly opened, startling Meggie.

A plump woman with a washbasin in her hands stepped outside and dumped its contents onto the dirt by Meggie's feet.

"Oh sorry, dearie. Didn't git you, did I?"

"No," Meggie said, doing her best not to stare at the partially-clad woman's dressing gown, open down to the waist. Why, she had absolutely nothing on underneath, not a chemise or corset or anything! A lit cigarette hung from the woman's overly-rouged lips. Her blond hair was a tousled mess.

"Whatcha doin' back here at this hour? If'n yer lookin' fer Hannah, you have to come back later. Hell, most ain't even up yet."

"Hannah? No, I'm not looking for Hannah. At least I don't think I am. What does Hannah look like?" Meggie strained to remember the girl's name from last night.

The robust woman burst into laughter. "Look like? Everybody knows Hannah. Ain't nobody has to ask who she is. Now I git it," the buxom woman said, an idea seeming to dawn. "You be lookin' fer Hannah to git hired."

"Well, yes," Meggie lied, knowing she needed to meet this Hannah. Maybe Hannah knew the girl. "How can I find Hannah?" Uncomfortable under the floozy's once-over, Meggie straightened her back.

"Looky here," the blonde turned serious. "Don't wanna be tellin' you what fer, but you could use a bit of fixin' up if'n you be expectin' Hannah to put you on the payroll."

"What do you mean, fixing up?" Meggie didn't know what the woman meant.

"No offense, dearie, but if you want men to be gawkin' at you, you have to give 'em somethin' to gawk at. Why if you got a woman under all that gitup, it shore ain't showin'."

Oh. Meggie was wearing one of the calico dresses she'd made. It was plain but nice, Meggie thought. Obviously the floozy didn't think so. No matter. Meggie didn't want men gawking at her, pawing at her. No, she didn't want to look nice for men.

"Listen, dearie. If'n you want, I'll help you git fixed up a mite so's Hannah'll hire you straight out," the woman offered with a smile.

"Thank you, but no." Meggie felt embarrassed. The woman

was just trying to be kind. "If I do need help, I'll know exactly where to come," she said and smiled back. "Could you tell me when I should return, when things open up?"

"Suit yourself, dearie." The blonde shook her head. "Anyways, best to come back later, in the afternoon. Then you kin be shore to see Hannah and a passel of young bucks. All them men is real men if'n you know what I mean?" The woman laughed and winked at Meggie before turning and disappearing inside the saloon door.

Meggie was back at the saloon in the afternoon, this time at the front entrance. She'd go inside, find Hannah, find the poor waif, then leave. It shouldn't take long. The moment Meggie pushed through the heavy, swinging doors, she stopped short. The doors poked at her back, forcing her to take a step forward. She'd just entered a forbidden world—a world she'd been warned against by the good sisters—a smoke-filled world of drunkards, gamblers, and debauchers! She didn't want to be afraid but she was, if only a little. A lively tune played in the background. She concentrated on the tune rather than her upset.

I can do this.

I can.

Meggie began threading her way across the room, past tables of men playing cards, talking loudly, drinking, and smoking. At some of the tables, women sat in the men's laps. Meggie tried to look away. She tried not to notice how the men touched the women. She tried not to notice how the women touched the men. Hit with the overwhelming urge to vomit, she put her hand over her mouth and kept going. The stench of heavy perfume in the smoky room didn't help. Every breath made her feel sick. She hurried across the room in the direction of the scantily clad brunette she'd spotted at the bar. Maybe the brunette was Hannah.

Meggie's hand dropped from her mouth. Any other time she might have laughed at all the colored feathers stuck in the brunette's hair, reminding Meggie of a stuffed parrot. But Meggie didn't laugh. Nothing about this afternoon was a laughing matter. A man standing near the woman grumbled something and then left. Meggie was alone with her now.

"Are you Hannah?"

"Hannah ain't here now," the brunette droned as if she'd answered the same question many times before. "I think she's down the street at the Blue Spruce." The overly-rouged and powdered woman didn't appear interested in talking to Meggie and turned her back.

"No, please." Meggie caught the woman's arm. "Please, that's not who I'm looking for. Well, not right now."

"You ain't? Well then what in blazes are you doin' here? Ain't no other reason any gal would be here. Hannah does all the hirin'. For dancin' and for . . . and for, you know."

"Yes, I know." Meggie tried to sound nonchalant. She felt sick to her stomach at the thought of the men and women upstairs and what they were doing together right now. "I'm just looking for a girl I met yesterday. She came in the back door of this saloon and I want to find her. If I describe her you might be able to tell me where she is."

"Here now." The woman put her hands on her hips and faced Meggie squarely. "Everyone's business is private round here. Ain't none of us tellin' nuthin' 'bout other girls to no one. I ain't gonna say nuthin' and git one of my friends in trouble with the law or anybody. That includes the likes of you. I don't know who you are, but I ain't sayin' nuthin'," the brunette spat out, then turned on her heel and walked away.

Left alone at the mahogany bar, Meggie stared down at its worn, scratched surface. *Like me,* she thought. She ran her fingers over the grooves instead of putting her hand to the back of her neck. She didn't have to. She could feel the hairs at her nape bristle and knew she needed to get out of there. But not yet; not until she had a look around the whole place. Meggie stiffened her spine, wincing at all the uncomfortable stares boring through her. She turned from the bar and looked beyond the stares. There was no sign of the girl. Disappointed, Meggie wasn't sure what to do.

Should she go upstairs to the rooms and look for the girl? Just how would she do that? Go into every room with her gun pointed? No, her best course was to search other saloons, try to find Hannah at the Blue Spruce, and only come back to this saloon if she failed. Hurrying now, Meggie crossed the floor once again, and then pushed out through its heavy, swinging doors.

The afternoon dragged on and Meggie along with it. The hair at her nape bristled more than once. Hannah wasn't at the Blue Spruce. Try the Gem, someone had suggested. Well, Hannah wasn't at the Gem either. Neither was the girl. Every saloon had been the same. Uncooperative answers, men who stared so hard they poked holes clear through her, and lewd remarks shouted at her back. Still, she kept up her search.

The Primrose. Meggie liked the name. Such a pretty name for such a disreputable place. Meggie found this saloon far more elegant and ornate than the other saloons, and it surprised Meggie. Gilded furniture glittered against red-striped satiny wall coverings in the immense room. This saloon had a stage with half-naked women dancing in front of a group of men who'd gathered to watch. The women's bodices swooped dangerously low as they gyrated for the leering men, and when they pulled up their skirts, their legs were bare! Meggie thought she'd seen everything in the saloons, until now. Just then she spotted a beautiful woman dressed in purple finery standing near the stage. Her clothes were different from the other dance-hall girls, and so was her demeanor. Everyone approaching the woman seemed solicitous, men and women. This had to be Hannah.

"Damn and tarnation." Meggie tripped over something. The hair at her nape put her on edge. She paid little mind and looked down at the spittoon she'd just run into. Luckily, its contents didn't spill all over her feet. She set down her satchel to collect herself.

Someone grabbed her from behind.

Big, rough hands clamped around her waist.

Meggie instinctively went for her satchel and her gun but couldn't reach either. Already exhausted from hours of searching for the poor waif, she'd run out of energy to be afraid. She should be scared to death now, but all she wanted was to get away from the drunken brute and get to Hannah. The foul stench of hard liquor assaulted her every bit as much as the man's groping hands.

"Well, what have I got here? You feel real good. Spend a little time with me, honey, and I'll put a smile on that pretty face of yours."

The drunken brute pulled her closer. He was disgusting. And so were all the rest of the horrible men at the table. They kept playing, oblivious to her plight. *All spawns of the devil!*

"Gents," her captor announced to the other card players. "I'm taking this little lady upstairs for a bit. Deal me out of the next couple of hands."

The disinterested faces of the group around the table upset Meggie as much as the lecherous brute who held her. Now she began to panic. She couldn't let him take her upstairs! Bile burned her throat. It hurt to swallow. Her vision started to blur. *Six feet under, six feet away, where to stay safe, the devil must stay!* Miserable and utterly alone in the crowded room, she knew no one was going to help her. If only she could reach her gun. Her head buzzed. Any moment she might pass out and be at the mercy of the devil!

"Yes, sir, you feel real good. Hannah has you gals dressed in all sorts of interesting things lately. Don't worry, honey, you'll be undressed soon as I get you alone," the brute promised offensively against her ear. His hot breath made her sick.

"Let me go." Meggie hated that her voice sounded so weak. "I'm not one of Hannah's gals. You're making a terrible mistake. Let me go. I do *not* work here. I beg you, let me go."

Her pleas fell on deaf ears. The gamblers at the table still didn't look up from their cards. The man holding her got up from his chair and pulled her closer against him, tightening his hold around her waist.

"Come on, honey." He put his foul mouth against her ear again.

When he ran his tongue inside it, it was the last straw for Meggie. The fetid odor of his breath, like rotted meat set too long in the sun, made her gag again. If she'd had anything in her stomach, it would have come up. Cruelly dragged into her nightmares by this ghoul, this misshapen evil, disoriented now, she wanted to keep fighting, to flee, but her shaken limbs went limp. It took everything left in her to keep her head.

"Let go of her, Ned."

The brute held fast to Meggie.

"*Now,* Ned."

"Aw, come on, Ethan. I'm just gonna have a little fun with her. You're welcome to her when I'm through, if that's what's got your dander up. Hell, she's woman enough for us both."

Ethan!

Meggie's head began to clear.

Had she heard right?

Had she heard *Ethan's* name?

Everything happened fast. The next thing Meggie knew,

Ethan had hold of her, and not her vile captor. Her captor lay sprawled on the saloon floor, knocked out cold. Meggie stared at the man. It was wrong to wish him dead, but she did. Then, as if it were the most natural thing in the world, she turned into the safety and comfort of Ethan's strong arms. She could feel his heart hammering in his chest against her cheek. Her knees went weak. Shutting her eyes, she snuggled closer and held on tight to him. The force of the moment hit her—the bond she felt, the strong, intimate connection to Ethan because of her secret letter-writing to him. She snuggled closer still. But then she thought better of it and pulled away. She'd no right to feel this way about Ethan. No right at all. He didn't want her. He wanted another.

Embarrassed that she'd fallen into his arms in the first place, Meggie stared down at her feet and not at him. She cared for him. She didn't want him to see. The last thing in the world she wanted now was for Ethan to see how she felt about him. Despite the unconscious man lying at her feet, all she could think about was keeping her feelings for Ethan hidden. Ethan cared for Livi Tritt, not her.

"Let's go," Ethan said huskily.

Meggie couldn't move and couldn't look up at him. Her feet stayed nailed to the very spot that only moments before she prayed to escape.

Ethan muttered something under his breath.

A curse, Meggie thought. She looked up and met his dark, good looks. The next thing she knew, he had her in his arms, heading for the saloon door.

"Ethan!" She wanted to admonish him for cursing but all that came out was, "my satchel!"

He stopped abruptly then turned around with her in his arms. She held on for dear life.

"Grab it," he told her, lowering her enough to pick up her satchel.

She did, hanging onto Ethan and her worn case while he carried her out of the saloon.

"Ethan, you can put me down now," she said the moment they were outside.

He ignored her and kept walking.

"You don't need to carry me down the entire length of the street! Ethan, did you—"

He stopped short and set her on her feet. "Did I what, *Meghan?*"

Stunned, Meggie stared wide-eyed at him. Surely she'd heard wrong.

"*Meghan R. McMurphy,* isn't it?" he said accusingly.

Jesus, Mary, and Joseph! She hadn't heard wrong.

"Ethan, how did you find out? Tell me. Please," she asked far more calmly than she felt. She looked down at his shirtfront. Exposed for the liar she was, Meggie couldn't look him in the eye. On top of everything else, she couldn't take his disapproval.

He said nothing.

She felt like nothing.

"Don't make me beg, Ethan," she finally whispered.

"I don't make women beg, Meghan, unless they want to."

His words upset her, and not for the obvious reason. The coldness in his voice made her want to crawl under the wooden planks on which they stood.

"You can rest easy, Meghan R. McMurphy. Your secret's safe with me."

Somewhat relieved at his spoken assurance, still, Meggie wanted to hide. She couldn't face him yet and kept her gaze cast downward.

"How did you find out about me, Ethan?" She didn't like this conversation any more than he appeared to, yet she had to know. "Tell me, please," she begged, despite her intent not to.

"From the train station when you first arrived in Denver. The list only had one woman's name on it, and it wasn't Rose Rochester. Don't worry, it's destroyed," he said, emotionless.

Bless you, Ethan Rourke. She wanted to say it out loud. She ached to, but she didn't dare. He mustn't find out that she cared for him. And worse, he mustn't find out why she was running under an assumed name—he mustn't find out her dark secret.

"Ethan, will you promise me you won't mention my true identity to anyone? I can't explain now, but I must have your promise," she softly pled. Every nerve in her body stood on end.

"On one condition," Ethan at last answered.

Meggie couldn't imagine the condition. She held her breath.

"It sticks in my craw to call you Rose."

"To call me Rose?" Meggie gulped hard. Although relieved, her nerves were on end for a very different reason than her mishap inside the Primrose just now. She forgot all about Livi Tritt. "Then call me Meggie," she said shyly, at last meeting his tender gaze.

"Nope. I'll call you Nutmeg," he said, his voice husky.

"If you like." She barely spoke above a whisper. Her face flushed. She could feel it, but she didn't care. "Thank you, Ethan, for what you did back there. I really don't get in a fix all the time, you know. I'm actually rather good at taking care of myself now," she said, her heart still racing.

Ethan smiled.

Her heart raced faster. She couldn't take her eyes off the dimples at the corners of his attractive grin.

"I'm sure you are," he said, his tone even more husky than before.

Meggie's spine tingled.

"But the fact is, Nutmeg, I couldn't leave you in a tight spot, now could I? It wouldn't be gentlemanly."

She shook her head in mute agreement; unable to think on anything but the way he'd said Nutmeg.

"If you can't tell me why you don't use your real name, at least explain what in blue blazes you were doing in the Primrose?"

Ethan wasn't smiling now.

"I can't. I'm sorry, but I can't." Meggie wanted to tell him but she couldn't. He'd only have more questions, questions that might lead him down her same deadly path. She didn't want him to know anything about her past, except in her letter, which she would destroy when it was finished. It was too dangerous for her and for Ethan. She wouldn't put him in such danger.

"One thing about secrets, Nutmeg," Ethan spoke low. "They have a way of getting out."

Her insides coiled. The truth of his words tied her up in tighter knots. Secrets did have a way of getting out, but she'd likely be dead before he found out about hers.

Ethan jerked his Stetson off and ran tanned fingers through his dark cropped hair. He slowly replaced his hat, as if searching for just the right words to level at her. "Listen. At least promise you won't go back in there. You know what would have happened to you with Ned. What if I hadn't been there? Do you think for a second any of the others would have stopped him?"

She shook her head no.

"Nutmeg, just promise me. Tell me you won't go back inside any of these places," Ethan insisted.

She didn't want to lie to him again. If she said nothing, it wouldn't exactly be a lie. She stared up into his dark countenance, trying to gauge his opinion of her. The longer she looked at him, the harder it was to concentrate on anything but the memory of his lips on hers and his strong arms around her. She shut her eyes against him.

"Nutmeg, look at me."

She opened her eyes. The moment she did her knees went weak for a second time. Nothing was close enough to grab for support, but Ethan. She hung onto his arm.

He didn't move.

As soon as she had a steady footing, she let go.

"Nutmeg, don't," Ethan strained.

Meggie folded inside, wanting with all her heart to grab hold of him again.

"Hey, Ethan!"

Meggie saw the man shouting from across the street but couldn't clearly make out his face.

"Hey, Ethan!" Uriah called again.

"Be right there!" Ethan yelled, then looked at Meggie again. "You take care of yourself down here in the big city," he said, lightly cupping her chin.

Meggie wanted to lean into his touch but dared not.

"Goodbye, Nutmeg," he said, and took his hand away.

His eyes had hooded over, the tenderness there only moments before gone now. His dismissive look hurt. Meggie swallowed against the pain of it. She watched him join the man across the street, all the while putting her hands to her chin where Ethan's fingers had just touched her.

Uriah hadn't missed the exchange between Ethan and the unknown woman. His eyes were pretty good. The redhead was a looker, plain dress and all.

"So who was that, Ethan? Haven't seen her around before."

"No one," Ethan said curtly and kept on down the street.

"On second thought, she looks familiar. Think I've seen her before?" Uriah wasn't going to leave this alone just yet.

"No," Ethan grumbled.

Uriah felt like celebrating. He wished Ethan cared for his sister, but wishes didn't cut it. Whoever this woman was, she sure got clear under Ethan's tough skin. Good. For the time being he'd let Ethan off the hook. Right now he needed to talk business. The final phase of construction on the pass was coming up soon.

It took heroic effort for Ethan to pay any attention to what Uriah had to say. All he could think about was Nutmeg. Why did he have to run into her again? What was she doing at the Primrose? She just had to go in his favorite saloon and stir things up. Ethan fumed. He thought of Ned Hooper's hands on her soft curves. It made his skin crawl.

No one should touch Nutmeg.

No one but me.

Ethan stopped dead in his tracks at the turn his thoughts had taken.

"Ethan, what's wrong?" Uriah stopped, too.

"Oh, nothing, old pard," Ethan covered up. "Thought I'd forgotten something back at the Primrose is all."

"Did you?"

"Did I what?"

"Sam Hill, Ethan. What did you forget?"

Aw, hell. He couldn't admit to Uriah what he'd just found out himself. He wanted Nutmeg. He didn't want anyone else to have her. He didn't want to want her. No good could come from it. No good could come from his loving anybody. His stomach churned. *Love.* The word rang in his head like a death knell. Where had his love gotten his family and his Rachel?

Killed, that's what.

What if he'd given in to the look, the unmistakable passionate plea he'd read in Nutmeg's stormy, violet eyes? He had to stay away from her. It would be hell to pay for them both if he didn't. At last he remembered Uriah.

"You know what I forgot at the Primrose, old pard? The drink I need to buy us both. What say we go back and have a whiskey?"

"Right, Ethan," Uriah agreed, smiling inwardly. It has to be a woman bothering Ethan. And Uriah knew exactly which one now. It wasn't Ethan's mistress, Samantha, no sir.

Meggie stood in front of the train station waiting for Pru. It was late in the evening.

"Like I said, the Kansas-Pacific won't roll in till tomorrow," the kindly stationmaster reminded her.

"Tomorrow?" she repeated, embarrassed by her mistake. "Yes, of course, tomorrow." She tried to smile. Surely the stationmaster must think she'd lost her wits. Too downhearted to care, Meggie tramped back to the American House. Her run-in with Ethan, more than the disgusting man at the Primrose, had upset her to the core. The moment she closed her hotel room door behind her, she made a beeline for her bed. She needed to rest. Yes, just a few moments rest and she'd feel better. Just a few moments . . .

A knock on the door woke her.

Meggie tensed and lay motionless in bed. Still fully clothed and on top of her covers, she looked around the dark room. She'd no idea of the time.

Another knock, louder this time.

"Who's . . . there?" Meggie tentatively called out.

"It's me. Clementine. Clementine Adkins," the girl answered through the door.

Clementine? Meggie remembered now—the girl's attackers had said, Miss Clemmie. Meggie scrambled off the bed, crossed the darkened room, and opened the door.

"Please come in," Meggie invited. "I'll just light my lamp." She couldn't help but wonder how the girl found her. What name had she used? It had to have been Rose Rochester. That's

197

the only way, she reassured herself.

"I'm sorry to bother you, but I didn't have nobody else," the girl blurted out. "And you said . . . you said you could help me. You was so kind to me, savin' me from them varmints. I was a thinkin' . . . I was a thinkin'—" Clementine dissolved into tears.

"There, there," Meggie soothed and guided the girl to sit down. "Of course I'll help you."

In the hours that followed, Clementine recounted her pitiable plight. Stories of sweaty, pawing men and laudanum forced down her throat upset Meggie the most. Finally the poor girl fell asleep. It would be dawn soon. Meggie sat in the rocker by the window and planned exactly what she'd do to help Clementine.

What money Meggie had brought from Hot Sulphur Springs was now safely tucked in Clementine's pocket. After filling the girl's stomach at the hotel restaurant, Meggie walked her to the train depot.

"Miss Rose, you've been nuthin' but kind. I'll never forget what you done for me. Never." Clementine threw her arms around Meggie's neck and hugged her tight. Meggie hugged her back. To any onlookers, they might be sisters parting, or best friends.

"Clementine, when you get home, everything will be better. From what you've said, your aunt and uncle will be that glad to see you. Here, I'll sit down and wait with you. Your train's due in soon."

"Miss Rose, you go on now. I'll be fine."

A bit of rest would be good before Pru's arrival. Meggie and Clementine had been up most of the night. "All right, but you get in touch with me if you need me," she said, and pushed a paper into the girl's hands. On it Meggie had written her

Express route in Hot Sulphur Springs. "Promise me, Clementine."

"Yes, ma'am. I promise," Clementine said, and then waved as Meggie left the depot.

Meggie walked briskly back to the hotel. Pru's train was due in at three o'clock. She stepped lightly, grateful to have helped Clementine get away from her attackers and save her from a life of ruin.

One life saved, Meggie thought, and felt much the better for it.

CHAPTER FOURTEEN

Excited to arrive in Denver, Pru stepped down from the huge steaming locomotive onto the station platform. When the thick smoke cleared enough to see, she looked around for Meggie. Meggie was nowhere in sight. Garbed in her only travel outfit, shoddy carpetbag and all, Pru sat down on the bench outside the station.

She couldn't wait to see her dear friend again. *Twin of my heart.* Well, not exactly twins. Pru laughed at any comparison. Her hair was mousy brown where Meggie's was vibrantly russet. Her dull olive complexion didn't glow like Meggie's creamy skin, nor did her brown eyes hold any luster compared to Meggie's violet gaze. As for their figures, Meggie was all willowy curves while Pru felt like a stumpy hickory. She never resented Meggie's good looks. It wasn't in her nature.

There was one more difference between the two. Pru had never experienced the terror that Meggie had. She'd trade her soul to erase all of Meggie's suffering. So much pain caused by the monster Benjamin Howard. Pru didn't think she would have survived the same ordeal. Nor did she think she would have survived the crazed matron's switching year after year the way Meggie had. To this day, Pru marveled at how Meggie had withstood such punishment. Meggie possessed an inner strength that Pru did not. Suddenly anxious to make sure Meggie was all right, Pru got up from the bench. Thirty minutes had gone by and still no Meggie.

She tried to recall the exact wording in Meggie's telegraph message: *Will arrive on stage from Hot Sulphur Springs to meet your train.* Rather than worrying over Meggie's late arrival, Pru's practical side spurred her to action. She went inside the depot to ask for directions to the stage line office, believing Meggie's stage from the mountains must have been delayed.

THE COLORADO OVERLAND STAGE COMPANY. Pru read the bold letters on the sign above the impressive looking office door. With her bag clutched tightly in hand, she stepped closer and peered inside. A man sat at a large desk. His back was to the street. She rapped on the window to get the man's attention before realizing how silly it must be for her to do so. The man turned his head to her then got up and walked over.

My, he was big. When he opened the door Pru took a step back, feeling awkward and perfectly ridiculous.

"Hello there, ma'am. Can I help you?"

Why, he was the most incredible man she'd ever laid eyes on. Her nerves shattered. She felt like an idiot just standing there gawking at him.

"Y—yes. I hope you can." Foolish or not, she'd address this Adonis. "I'm looking for someone, a friend. Has the stage arrived yet from Hot Sulphur Springs?" she asked, smiling up into the beautiful eyes of the stranger.

"I believe so, ma'am," he answered with a grin of his own. "Fact is, it came in two days ago."

"Two days ago," Pru parroted, beginning to worry now. She let the handsome stranger usher her inside the stage office.

"How do. My name's Uriah Taylor," Uriah offered and held out a large brawny hand to her.

Pru placed her own small fingers in his, but said nothing.

"And you?"

Oh, Heavens. "I'm Prudence Utter. Actually, Pru. Yes. I'm actually Pru."

"Well, actually Pru, it's good to meet you," he teased.

"It is? I mean, it is nice to meet you, too," she managed, despite her quivering innards. She managed also to remember why she'd come in the first place. "My friend was supposed to meet me at the depot but she wasn't there. I thought it best to check here next."

The moment Uriah saw the appealing brunette, he felt a jolt clear down to his toes. And now, with those large doe eyes looking up at him, it was all he could do not to get lost in their soft, fawn depths. Smitten, he forced himself to concentrate on helping her.

"Don't worry your pretty head, Pru. I'll get the docket from the stage and we'll see if she arrived day before yesterday." Uriah walked over to another desk and grabbed up the docket, only then realizing he'd said *pretty* to a perfect stranger. Funny, for some reason she didn't seem like a stranger. Did he really say pretty head?

"Sorry, Pru, the only woman listed is a Rose Rochester. "I'm that sorry," he added sincerely.

"No Meghan McMurphy? Look again please, Uriah," Pru beseeched, oblivious to how easily his name rolled off her tongue. "She *has* to be on the list."

He did and she wasn't.

"The next stage is due in tomorrow. I'm sure she'll be on that one. Why don't I walk you over to the American House Hotel and help you get a room for the night?"

"Yes, tomorrow," Pru replied absentmindedly. He must be right. *Meggie will be on tomorrow's stage.* "Thank you for your kind offer of escorting me to the hotel, Uriah." In truth, she was glad to have his company for as long as possible, despite her worry over Meggie.

Uriah pulled his hat down from the rack and then opened the door for Pru. When she passed through it, he took the carpetbag out of her hands.

She didn't protest.

They walked side-by-side down the street toward the hotel, their sheepish grins each a mirror image of the other.

"Pru!" Meggie screeched when she saw Pru enter the hotel. She couldn't reach Pru and put her arms around her fast enough. "Oh, Pru, I'm so happy you've come. Forgive me for not meeting your train. I—"

"Fiddle-faddle, Meggie." Pru hugged her back. "I found you all right, didn't I?"

"Yes, you did," Meggie said as they pulled out of each other's heartfelt embrace. "In fact, how—"

Pru stopped her in mid-sentence. "Meghan McMurphy, I'd like you to meet Uriah Taylor," she said and smiled, gesturing toward Uriah who remained close by.

Meggie hadn't noticed the man standing there. She was too mortified that Pru had used her real name. It wasn't Pru's fault. She didn't know about her masquerade as Rose Rochester. The tall, brawny man's kind expression didn't threaten Meggie. For the briefest of moments, she thought she recognized him, but was quick to put this thought from her mind. She tried to smile at him. This man knew her true name now. Soon another would, and then another. The hourglass had turned.

"How do, Miss McMurphy. It's a pleasure," Uriah greeted. *Why, she's the same gal that Ethan was talkin' with earlier, the one that got under that tough hide of his. I'll be doggoned.*

"Yes . . . yes, thank you," she forced out. "And thank you for helping Pru find me," she lied, wishing against wishes that Pru had come alone.

Uriah blushed. "Shucks, wasn't nuthin'. Well, I best leave you two ladies now." He started to back away then hesitated. "Miss Pru, I hope we can visit while you're here. Uh, I mean—"

"Yes, I'd like that, Uriah." Pru blushed back.

"Fine and dandy then." He grinned ear to ear and shuffled his feet, reluctant yet again to leave. "Yes, well, fine and dandy," he repeated. "Evenin', ladies," he touched the brim of his hat, then turned and walked away.

Meggie put her arm through Pru's. "Come upstairs and tell me all about this Uriah Taylor of yours."

"Fiddle-faddle, Meggie. He's not my Uriah Taylor," Pru admonished.

"Not yet," Meggie teased.

The pair spent hours catching up. Of course, Meggie would never mention her private letter to Ethan to Pru. She intended to destroy the letter. When she did tell Pru about using the assumed name of Rose Rochester, Pru was upset that she'd revealed Meggie's true identity to Uriah. "Don't you worry," Meggie told her, while worrying herself. She knew that secrets have a way of getting out, Ethan's very words to her earlier.

Pru wanted to know if she should caution Uriah about using the name Rose Rochester, but Meggie said no. To do so at this point would only bring more attention to her. Besides, Meggie would be returning to Hot Sulphur Springs, leaving Denver and anyone who learned of her true identity behind. "Everything will be fine," she lied, worried that she'd upset Pru.

Pru, however, wasn't at all upset to learn about Meggie's affection for Ethan Rourke. Oh, Meggie didn't come right out and admit it, but Pru could read between the lines. She was glad that Meggie had met someone—that Meggie had let the handsome westerner break through her defenses. *High time,* Pru thought. Maybe this Ethan Rourke was the very one to help rid Meggie of her nightmares of the monster Benjamin Howard. Since Meggie's future happiness depended on it, Pru determined to find a way to bring Meggie and Ethan together.

The opportunity came sooner than expected.

Pru and Uriah discovered they had more in common than their obvious attraction for each other. They had Meggie and Ethan in common. It didn't take long for Pru and Uriah to come up with a plan. Uriah would, by hook or by crook, talk Ethan into throwing a big doin'. Pru would attend and bring Meggie. Over Pru's protests, Uriah insisted on buying both Pru and Meggie fancy dresses for the event.

"What party? What on earth are you talking about, Pru? You know how I feel about such things. We're supposed to leave for Hot Sulphur Springs first thing tomorrow." Flabbergasted, Meggie stared openmouthed at her friend. They'd already stayed longer in Denver than she'd planned. Out of deference to Pru's fondness for Uriah, she'd consented to remain a while. But a party? What nonsense!

"Oh, Meggie, fiddle-faddle. You've not been out since I arrived. You can't stay cooped up here in this hotel room for fear you'll run into Ethan Rourke. You *are* going to attend this party with me tonight. Besides." Pru played her trump card. "It's the last chance for me to see Uriah before we leave, Meggie. Won't you please go to the party with me?"

"Prudence Utter, that's pure nonsense." Meggie huffed back. "I'm not trying to avoid Ethan Rourke or anybody else."

"Oh, Meggie," Pru gasped. "I'm so sorry. I forgot about . . . you know . . . about—"

Meggie took up Pru's hand. "It's all right. Don't fret, please. It's just that I'd rather be in my cabin in Hot Sulphur Springs." Meggie's tone softened. "Be sensible, dear Pru. Even if we did want to go to this party of yours, we don't have the right clothes. So you see, it's impossible." Meggie plopped down on the edge of her bed, glad to see Pru smiling again.

"Oh, but we do." Pru grinned mischievously, thinking more

about Ethan Rourke now than Benjamin Howard. "I'll be right back."

Before Meggie knew it, Pru was out the door and back again with two large parcels wrapped in brown paper and twine. She placed one in Meggie's lap.

"Open it," Pru said excitedly.

Meggie didn't want to open her parcel. She didn't want to go to any party. Reluctantly, she undid the twine, then parted the wrapping, unable to resist sliding her hand over the violet satin gown inside. It was the stuff of fairy tales.

"Pru, where did th—"

"Where and how isn't as important as your wearing it," Pru insisted.

Again unable to resist, Meggie stood up and let the gown's loveliness fall in front of her, shoulder to floor. "It's the most beautiful dress I've ever seen," she whispered, and began to twirl around, holding the satin gown close.

"Meggie, you look beautiful," Pru gushed.

Uncomfortable with the compliment and with her dress front, Meggie ran her fingers from her neckline over her bodice and down to her waist. The lace ended just at the top of her bodice, joined there by violet satin. She felt naked, exposed beneath the patterned lace. "I can't show this much of me in public. It's indecent, Pru!"

"Fiddle-faddle, Meghan McMurphy. There's nothing indecent about your gown. You're the picture of fashionable elegance," Pru went on as if she'd been at the very center of Boston society.

Humph. Fashionable elegance. Such words for such an outing. Meggie's scars began to aggravate her back.

Pru couldn't wait for the party, anxious to see what would happen between Meggie and Ethan when they saw each other.

She and Uriah had everything planned, at least as far as they could. The rest was up to Meggie and Ethan.

"Pru, even if . . . I mean . . . this dress . . . the only other time I wore such a dress . . . you know the disaster, the consequences of revealing . . . of showing—" Meggie could feel Benjamin Howard's leering, demonic regard strip her naked. He might as well be in the room with her now. Swallowing hard, she shrugged her shoulders and ignored the hairs bristling at her nape. It felt like Benjamin Howard was walking over her grave, back and forth, to make very sure *she* was the one six feet under.

"Meggie." Pru knew full well the dark turn Meggie's thoughts had taken. "For tonight put that monster out of your thoughts. He's gone from your life. He can't hurt you here."

No, Pru, you're wrong, Meggie thought.

He'll come for me.

I can feel it.

"Meggie." Pru gave her a quick hug then let go. "I need you to help me dress—or don't you want me to look lovely, too?" she teased and gathered up her fawn-colored gown.

"Bless you, dear friend," Meggie said, brightening. "Of course, I want you to look lovely. Why, you'll take Uriah Taylor's breath away," Meggie declared the moment Pru had slipped into her gown.

Pru's olive complexion glowed with happiness. Her brown eyes sparkled. "Oh Meggie, he's . . . I—" She couldn't finish.

Thrilled for Pru, Meggie wished with all her heart that tonight would be perfect for her. Pru deserved to be happy, to have her dreams come true. And if Pru wanted her to go to some dreaded party, then she would, whether she felt like it or not. It was the least she could do for her dear friend. Turning around to collect the rest of her things, Meggie found herself facing the full-length mirror. She didn't like mirrors. But instead of turning away—very unlike her—she stepped closer to the glass and studied her reflection.

All her life she'd imagined this, dressed up for a ball. Yet she'd never imagined having such clothes or having her hair done up so beautifully. Pru had pulled her thick russet hair up, coiling it attractively at her crown with pins, then violet ribbon. Loose tendrils escaped, the soft wisps framing her face, ever soft, ever lovely. Meggie stared at her flushed cheeks. She'd not stared at her reflection in a very long time. Funny, she'd forgotten she had a light peppering of freckles across her cheeks and the bridge of her nose. She'd forgotten her eyes were such a deep violet, almost matching the satin of her gown. Staring now at her full mouth, pinked on its own, she didn't think she'd need any lip rouge. *Lip rouge!* Quickly now, she yanked her gaze away from her face to her bodice. Despite concerns about her modesty, Meggie felt like a princess in the satiny, puff-sleeved gown. The soft material drew in tightly at her waist before tumbling in delicate folds to the floor. The bustle ruffled out stylishly in back.

"Ready, Meggie?"

Meggie stiffened, and then straightened the folds of her gown. "Yes," she answered, dread over the evening ahead settling hard over her. With a bravado that she didn't feel, she turned on her spool-heeled shoes, snatched up her drawstring reticule, and followed Pru out the door.

Ethan wished he hadn't let Uriah talk him into throwing a party tonight. He wanted to go downstairs now and tell everybody to go home. He'd let Uriah convince him it was important for business and important for the new stage line. It wasn't like Uriah to be all-fired up about such things. Ethan had agreed to the party to get Uriah off his back, but he remained suspicious.

In his bedroom, delaying going downstairs, Ethan poured

himself a whiskey, then sank down in the leather chair by the fireplace. The fire crackled and hissed. Ethan didn't care much right now about his business interests, and he didn't care at all about any party. In fact, since he'd run into Nutmeg at the Primrose last week, he hadn't felt like doing much of anything.

Damn her.

And damn me for thinking of her.

He poured himself another drink and finished it in one swallow. He set his glass down and picked up the snow globe Rachel had given him. Oddly, he'd brought the globe upstairs last week. It had been sitting on his study desk for years. After a few shakes, he righted the glass, then studied it, holding it up to the fire. The little skater spun round and around amid fire and ice.

Fire and ice—Nutmeg and me.

Ethan promptly set the globe away from him and lit a smoke, pondering the bitter irony of it all. Kept separate, fire and ice thrive. Brought together, neither can. Aw, hell. He shot out of his chair and tossed his smoke into the fireplace, then headed down the back stairs.

Meggie and Pru stepped inside the foyer of the grand house. Meggie had yet to ask Pru exactly who was giving the fancy party. It mattered little.

"Exactly as I'd imagined Thornfield Hall," Meggie whispered aloud before she thought better of it.

"Thorn-what?" Pru replied absentmindedly as she stared up into the flickering lights of the tiered chandelier overhead.

Meggie couldn't believe she'd let her imagination get the better of her once again, thinking about her romance novel and not the reality of the moment.

"Meggie," Pru faced her now. "Thorn-what?"

"You misheard me. I said what a grand hall. Now you must go inside and find your Uriah." Meggie quickly diverted the conversation.

"You come with me," Pru said, and hooked her arm in Meggie's.

"No. Not yet. I'll be along in a minute." Meggie tried to hide her mounting discomfort. She should never have agreed to come.

"Meggie, are you all right?"

"Yes, I'm fine." Meggie lied, removing Pru's arm from hers. She didn't want to do anything to jeopardize Pru's evening with Uriah. "I just need a moment, Pru. That's all, really."

Pru knew this wasn't easy for Meggie. But Pru held steadfast to the plan she and Uriah had made for Meggie and Ethan to see each other tonight. Surely all of this would be worth it for Meggie. "You take all the time you need," she reassured, then reluctantly turned and left Meggie alone in the foyer.

Discomfort crept up Meggie's body, inch by distressing inch. She didn't belong here. Now that Pru had gone inside the party to be with Uriah Taylor, she'd seize the opportunity and leave. Quickly pivoting, she put her hand on the ornate door handle.

"Miss?"

Someone called from behind her. A man. She let go of the door handle and slowly pivoted back around, coming face-to-face with a kind-looking older man in a vested, dark suit and starched white shirt.

"Miss, is there somethin' I kin do fer you?"

Mutely, she shook her head no. The man didn't appear sinister.

"Pardon me fer sayin' anythin', miss. It's none of my business, but didn't you just git here?"

"I . . . yes . . . I did," she answered, flustered. "But I forgot something very important back at my hotel. I'll just run and fetch it," she said, relieved to have thought of anything at all to reply. She'd lost count of her lies.

"Well, if'n you don't mind my sayin', miss, a lady as purdy as you should stay and give all them nice gents inside a chance to dance with you."

Meggie smiled at the compliment.

"If'n you leave now, you'll be plum robbin' all the poor men here this evenin'."

She began to relax, warming to the company. "How do you do. I'm Rose Rochester." She introduced herself as if to do so was the most natural thing in the world for her, no matter the name she used.

"How do. Name's Ezekiel, Ezekiel Smithers. The wife and I work here, have fer years. You don't have to run off just when this evenin's gittin' goin'. Be a shame fer you to miss it."

His trusting eyes held her at the entry. Suddenly she wanted—she needed—to be honest with Ezekiel Smithers. "I don't really belong here, Mr. Smithers. I came with a friend but I can't stay. I'm in a fancy gown, but I'm not fancy like all of the folks in there." She nodded in the direction of the ballroom. "I won't feel easy among them. I have to leave. Goodbye, Mr. Smithers." She smiled regretfully and turned to leave.

"Young woman, you belong here more'n most," Ezekiel said.

"Mr. Smithers." Meggie turned around again, wondering what he meant.

"It's Ezekiel," he corrected.

"Ezekiel," she said with ease. "You're too kind, but I don't belong here. You don't know me, who I am, where I'm from. I don't belong here." She choked back sobs, utterly embarrassed.

"Oh, but you do, Miss Rose."

Meggie didn't agree and turned to leave.

Ezekiel stepped in front of her and pulled both of the heavy carved doors closed, shutting her back inside.

"Off you go, young woman. It's the only way now. You won't be gittin' out this door till you've at least had a waltz."

Meggie's stomach churned as old fears stirred. She hated that she was so easily frightened. She hated that Ezekiel Smithers wouldn't let her leave. With no recourse now, she tossed Ezekiel a defeated smile, then slowly walked past the grand central staircase toward the ballroom. If she'd but turned, she might have seen the mischievous look of satisfaction on Ezekiel's aged, caring face.

"There you are!" Pru declared the moment Meggie stepped into the ballroom. "We were about to come and look for you." Uriah was right on Pru's heels, his thick-mustached smile practically ear to ear.

"Hello, Mr. Taylor," Meggie quietly greeted.

"Uriah," he corrected, his blue eyes twinkling. "Well, what do you think?"

"What do I think?" Meggie quizzed back.

"About all this? The house? The party? The—ouch!"

Pru stuck her elbow in his ribs hard, afraid of what he might reveal to Meggie. "We'll be back in a minute," she told a suspicious-looking Meggie, then grabbed Uriah's arm and quickly dragged him into the sea of dancing couples.

"Back in a minute, indeed," Meggie muttered. Those two were up to something. She'd been a schoolteacher far too long not to notice when mischief was afoot. Well, she'd wait just that: a minute. Then she'd leave, certain she'd get past Ezekiel this time. Against her better judgment, knowing she'd do better to leave this very second, she chanced a look around the ballroom.

It was all magical, storybook magical. The waltzing couples revolving about the dance floor to the stringed orchestra made her think yet again of Thornfield Hall and *Jane Eyre*. She couldn't help it. It was all so romantic . . . and definitely time to leave! About to do just that, suddenly a swirl of emerald green and charcoal danced by and caught her eye. She recognized the couple.

Livi Tritt and Ethan.

Humph, *Blanche Ingram and Edward!* Meggie's insides turned. Greedy, malicious Blanche Ingram, trying to keep Edward from Jane! One of the passages from *Jane Eyre* that Meggie had committed to memory came to mind, the passage where Blanche humiliates Jane in front of Edward, knowing Jane hears her, and knowing Jane is little Adele's governess. *Why, I suppose you have a governess for her; I saw a person with her just now—is she gone? Oh, no, there she is still behind the window-curtain . . . you should hear mamma on the chapter of governesses. Mary and I have had, I should think, a dozen at least in our day; half of them detestable and the rest ridiculous . . .* Then Blanche went on to speak of Jane's appearance to Edward. *I noticed her; I am a judge of physiognomy, and in hers I see all the faults of her class.* Humph. Faults, phooey! Meggie hated Blanche, and she hated Livi Tritt!

Furious with herself for not leaving before this, Meggie couldn't believe her bad luck at seeing Ethan again. Here at this party of all places. Hadn't she been worried about this very thing since she'd seen him at the Primrose saloon? And of course he would have to be in the arms of Livi Tritt. Emotions warred inside Meggie. She wanted to leave, yet needed to stay. The scars on her back hurt. Her head hurt. The longer she watched Livi dance with Ethan, the worse she felt. She felt plain and ugly and utterly ridiculous, even in her fancy satin gown. Blanche Ingram had won.

"A pretty lady like you oughta be dancing."

The raspy voice cut down Meggie's spine. Taller than her by a head, the unwelcome man's presence unnerved her. He stood too close. The hair at her nape stood on end. The pockmarked devil took a step closer, the smell of garlic and cigars assaulting her. The man's glassy, bloodshot leer turned her stomach.

"Name's Bart, little lady. Bart Gentry." He nodded in feigned politeness. "How 'bout you and me having a turn together?" he whispered suggestively, and stroked her cheek with his oily fingers.

She wished she had her gun. She'd shove it right in his stomach and dare him to touch her again!

"Gentry," someone called out.

"Can't you see I'm busy with this pretty lady, Tritt?" he spat out when the pudgy, middle-aged man approached.

Two devils, Meggie thought.

"Bart, we have to talk now," Angus Tritt declared nervously.

"Can't it wait, Tritt?"

"No."

Bart scowled at Tritt then turned back to Meggie.

His lascivious, crooked, yellow grin undressed her. Mentally, she cocked her Colt .45.

"Well pretty lady, looks like you'll have to wait a spell for ol' Bart. Don't you move now," he warned. "I'll be right back."

Meggie had no intention of being around when ol' Bart returned.

CHAPTER FIFTEEN

"Gotta find out who that redhead is, Tritt. Let's make this quick."

"She's sure a looker," the banker volunteered, obediently following in Bart's footsteps.

"This'll do." Bart stopped at the open door of Ethan's empty study. "Let's go in here where we can talk in private."

Once inside, Tritt closed the door behind them. He wanted to get this conversation over with before Livi noticed anything. He'd do anything for his daughter, anything. Home from the mountains no more than a day and she'd let him know yet again that she wanted to be rich and a member of Denver's elite society. "If you love me, Daddy," she'd said . . . "If you love me, you'll make us rich." His bank was their ticket to good fortune. If getting rid of Ethan Rourke would allow his bank to flourish, then so be it. If murder meant his daughter would be happy, then so be it. Angus swallowed hard and faced Gentry.

"All right, Bart, when's it to be?"

Bart pulled a cigar from his vest pocket and struck a match to light the tobacco. After a satisfying puff, he leveled his gaze on Tritt.

"In two weeks they're gonna work on the last of the pass construction. Rourke and Taylor will be up on the summit themselves to supervise the blasting. It'll be perfect. No one will suspect a thing."

"Humor me, Bart. Exactly how perfect and exactly how will

it all get carried off without anyone knowing or suspecting a thing? Nothing can go wrong here. We both have too much at stake."

Bart wasn't about to let anything go wrong. Tritt didn't have to worry. He'd waited too long to get his revenge to make any slip-up now. He and his brother should have reaped the benefits of the gold discovery in Breckenridge, not Rourke and Taylor. They'd all been working claims close to one another. The fact that Rourke and Taylor's claim paid off stuck in his craw. Had for years. That and his brother going to work for the sons of bitches, then up and dying while setting dynamite in one of their shafts. All for what? For Rourke and Taylor? Not hardly. A pine box is too good for 'em. He'd bided his time long enough. Two weeks and it'd be finished.

"I still want to hear the *how* of all this." Tritt broke into Bart's murderous thoughts. Tritt had never liked Ethan Rourke. Rourke was too powerful and well-liked in Denver. From the start, he and Rourke never got along. Rourke spirited away too many of his customers to Moss's Savings and Trust. When Tritt hooked up with Bart Gentry, it was his lucky day. His financial problems would be over. Livi would be happy. No one would be the wiser. No one would suspect him of any wrongdoing. He was a respectable banker in Denver who was in on a business deal with Rourke. Besides, he wouldn't have to do the killing. Bart would do the killing. Despite this fact, Tritt could feel his guts turn, out of fear.

"Like I said, nothing to get nervous about, Angus," Bart assured. "I'm going up myself to set off charges of my own. I'll take my men and we'll get the both of 'em in one nice little blast. Parts of 'em will be all over Berthoud Pass." He smirked. "I've waited a long time for this." His pitted face turned dead serious. "A long, long time." He took another deep puff on his cigar.

Tritt pulled out his pocket handkerchief and wiped the nervous sweat from his brow. "I'm counting on you and your men to take care of everything, Bart. Nothing can go wrong. If anything does, well, then—"

"Relax, will you? If you're so damn nervous about it all, then get out now. I can figure another plan, another time. I'm sure you can afford to have things stay the way they are for a long time to come yet, now can't you?" Bart taunted.

"No. No, Bart. We have to move on it now. You know I can't let Rourke flat-out ruin my business. No. Move according to your plan. I don't want out. No, sir." Tritt dabbed his sweaty face one more time then looked around for a whiskey decanter. He needed a drink.

Meggie spotted Pru and Uriah across the dance floor. They were not looking her way. Good. She would slip out now. Her only hope was that Ezekiel was not at the front door. She had to leave before Ethan or Livi saw her. Worse, before that disgusting Bart Gentry returned! Quickly mapping her best escape route she backed up against the nearest wall. All she had to do was follow it to the arched entry. Turning to her side, inching her way along the damask rose-papered wall, Meggie wished she could sink into it and disappear. She glanced behind her. No one followed. Relieved, she kept on. Only a short distance now and she'd make a clean getaway.

A charcoal arm suddenly came down in front of her, blocking her way. *Jesus, Mary and Joseph!* Meggie stared in disbelief at the tanned fingers splayed over the silken wallpaper. She didn't have to look up to know who they belonged to.

"Leaving so soon, Nutmeg?"

Meggie shut her eyes. At least it was Ethan and not Bart Gentry. Still, she couldn't look at Ethan. Pressing her back to the wall for support, she suddenly felt unsteady from head to toe. The evening had already taken its toll. She didn't have much left in her, especially to deal with Ethan.

Ethan put his hands on either side of the wall, holding Meggie to the spot.

"I don't know how you got here, Nutmeg," he said in a husky whisper. "But I'm not letting you go this time."

Jolted by his words as much as the moment—just like when they'd first met in Denver all those months ago when she'd felt instantly trapped—so she felt now, held suspended in his intimate web as silken strands threaded round and around her shaken form, each one tighter than the next, each more penetrating than the next.

"It'll be all right, Nutmeg. Open your beautiful eyes and I'll prove it to you," he promised softly.

Meggie swallowed hard, yet kept her eyes glued shut. What a time for her mind to play tricks on her, imagining Ethan saying such things to her. They were the stuff romantic dreams were made of, not the real world—not her real world. Grudgingly now, with little choice, she opened her eyes and looked into his.

The moment she did, she read the raw emotion on his face, and she knew she hadn't conjured his words from any romance page. This was real. Ethan was real. Her knees buckled.

His hands found her waist, steadying her. "See?" he gently teased. "Just like I said, everything will be all right. I'm here to prove it to you."

His words held her steady every bit as much as the masterful span of his strong fingers at her waist. The idea that Ethan cared for her, really cared for her—and maybe wasn't in love with Livi Tritt after all—thrilled yet scared her. She didn't know what would come next, what should come.

Ethan did.

For the second time in his life, he was in love.

The moment he spotted Nutmeg tonight, he had to face the

truth of it. This time he couldn't let her walk out of his life. He needed to have her—to love her. It was selfish and he knew it. He'd battled with his feelings, with the haunting memories of his family and Rachel, and knew the right thing would be to leave Nutmeg alone. She'd stay safe if he left her alone. But the moment he saw her tonight, he knew he'd lost the battle warring inside him.

Nutmeg took his breath away. She looked beautiful. *For me,* he thought. *Only me.* She'd always been beautiful to him, despite the plain way she dressed. But now . . . in the fancy gown . . . the fragrance of wildflowers all around . . . her lustrous hair softly bound, yet waiting for his touch . . . her luminous eyes drawing him in ever deeper with each flutter of her silky lashes . . . her inviting mouth asking to be tasted—damn! He fought the urge to take her right there in front of everyone.

"Dance with me, Nutmeg."

Ethan had asked her the same question before. This time she wouldn't refuse. She couldn't. Was this the night for dreams to come true? Was it possible? The instant Ethan took her hands in his, the instant she felt his steady warmth pulse through her own tremulous fingers, she knew it could be. Dreamily, Meggie let him lead her into the circle of revolving couples, her troubled past fading with each step taken.

Oblivious to all but each other, neither noticed the beady pair of eyes tracing their every move. Bart Gentry spied them the moment he'd returned to the room.

"Damn that son of a bitch Rourke. Who does he think he is, taking my redhead?"

Tritt shrank from Bart's malevolent tone.

"I'll give you two weeks with her, Rourke. Two weeks, then she's mine. I can wait," Bart grated out under his breath. "C'mon Tritt, how's about I buy you a drink."

Ever obedient, Tritt followed and kept silent.

Other eyes watched Meggie and Ethan. Two other women wanted to get Ethan, and to get rid of the woman in his arms.

Livi seethed with jealousy. *Ethan Rourke is mine.* In the time she'd known him, none of her attempts to snare him had worked. Married to him, she'd be rich and powerful. She'd be the toast of Denver. Livi was running out of ideas to get Ethan, and now she could see that she was running out of time. Something needed to be done about the plain schoolmarm, and fast!

The pain of seeing her man in the arms of another, hit Samantha like a bullet. Instead of anger, she felt gunshot. She knew, as only a woman could tell, Ethan cared for the redhead.

Dancing in Ethan's arms, Meggie was unaware of the two women who carefully scrutinized her. For eight years she'd gone down the only path open to her, not having anticipated or desired anything but to get through her days and nights. Well-practiced in keeping fanciful thoughts just that, tucked away in wishes and romantic daydreams, she was afraid of what might happen if her dreams truly did come true. The prudent thing to do would be to pull out of Ethan's powerful arms. But her passions ruled her now. Afraid or not, there was no turning back.

Round and around Meggie spun in Ethan's arms. Unaware of everyone else in the room, all she could see now were the dimples at the corners of Ethan's strong mouth, the way his cropped, dark hair just reached the collar of his formal, white shirt, and the way his rugged, masculine physique fit perfectly into the charcoal fabric of his jacket and waistcoat. All she felt was the pull of his dusky gaze, the lure of his roughness drawing in her softness, and his clean, deep-woods scent misting over her. Heat sparked wherever he touched her, and from every place she imagined he might. Her senses reeled.

The music stopped.

Ethan didn't let go of her.

Meggie didn't let go of him.

He smiled down at her then took his arms away, only to take up her hand and pull her along behind him across the still-crowded dance floor.

She let him. How could she not?

He was her Edward.

Ethan led her up a narrow stairway, then down a wide hall, and then into a bedroom. She wondered whose bedroom, whose house, but then didn't care. She should care what the sisters, especially Sister Mary Catherine, would think of her now, seeing all their years of strict teaching going out the window in one passionate moment, but she didn't. In this room with this man she'd at last find happiness and love.

Still, she must take care and not reveal her hard-kept secret to Ethan. Only in her letter. Ethan knew her true name, but he must never know about Benjamin Howard—that he'd left her ruined and a sinner. She could bear anything but seeing Ethan's look of revulsion if he discovered the dark secret in her past . . . anything . . . anything but that.

Ethan took her in his arms.

She forgot all else but him now.

His mouth found hers.

The ecstasy of his lips on hers again fanned the flames already burning in her. She opened for him and let him taste and explore, reveling in each stroke of his tongue. The fire he stirred in her ignited and spread throughout her body, daring any part of her to deny him. She wouldn't. She couldn't. His expert hands slid down her back, lower and lower, until he rhythmically pressed her hips hard against him. Even through all the layers of their clothes, she felt him against her, his hardness seeking her softness.

She tightened her arms around his neck, fearful that any moment he might break their kiss, any moment he might stop what he was doing to her. She never knew such things could happen between a man and a woman, never in any of her imaginings. Completely lost now in a mist of earthy woods and sheer masculinity, she disappeared against him, into him.

Suddenly he broke their kiss.

Shocked, Meggie went cold.

"Oh, my sweet love," Ethan whispered. "You were made for me, only me," he murmured, then trailed kisses down her throat.

Meggie grew warm again. She was afraid of what was about to happen between them, yet her aroused body cried out for him.

Ethan knew it.

"Don't worry, Nutmeg. I'm here. Don't be afraid. I'll show you how to love a man, to love me. I'll show you," he said in a husky whisper as he took up her hand and led her toward his bed.

Meggie let him guide her to the bed. Mutely, she stood and waited beside the massive bed. She didn't have to wait long. Ethan's hands reached for her again, this time deftly loosening her hairpins and untying the ribbon, freeing her coppery tresses, letting them spill down her back and over her shoulders. Ever so lightly, he traced the length of one tendril along the side of her face, past her throat, over lace and then satin, down to her waist. Her heightened senses left her raw with anticipation.

His dusky scrutiny stayed on her.

Spellbound, she waited.

Ethan put his arms around her again, this time to find the top hooks at the back of her gown. At first his fingers gently rubbed and circled overtop the metal stays. His hypnotic touch made her yearn for something more. The instant his skilled fingers unfastened the first clasp Meggie realized what it was. She wanted it, too. When the back of her gown was undone, she gave in to the dreamy magic of the satin slipping off her shoulders, her scars forgotten. When Ethan bent to gently nuzzle one bare shoulder, then the other, she watched him, mesmerized. When his fingers moved to the top of her chemise to slowly untie her bodice, the uncertainty of what was about to happen didn't frighten her. She was living her fairy tale. She was with the man of her dreams, the man she loved, the man she would now willingly give herself to, body and soul.

But something went terribly wrong the instant her breasts were exposed to Ethan—the instant he touched her skin. The desire and pleasure she'd felt in Ethan's arms turned into something else—something *monstrous.*

Ethan was gone . . . replaced now by Benjamin Howard!

Her worst nightmare had come to life!

Piercing cold swirled all around her, penetrating every part of her nakedness. Like a frozen blade the frigid air sliced her heated passion into bits and pieces. Utterly defenseless now, Meggie hadn't seen the devil coming! She was petrified . . . for Ethan!

Where was he?

What had the fiend done to Ethan!

Benjamin Howard could do what he wanted with her, but not with Ethan. She couldn't let him hurt Ethan! Desperate, dizzy with fear, she struggled for some clarity of thought, some way to save Ethan. None of this was Ethan's fault. He must stay safe!

Repelled when the fiend reached out for her with its clawing talons Meggie fought back. "No! No! Let me be! Why can't you let me be? I don't want you ever to touch me again! Get away! Get away from me!"

Amazingly, her attacker backed away from her. Meggie couldn't believe it. The dark fog in the room began to lift. Her vision began to clear. Benjamin Howard's image faded . . . replaced by another . . . *Ethan's!*

At once, this moment was the best and the worst of Meggie's life. Eternally grateful Ethan was all right, she knew that she wasn't. Her second worst fear, above Ethan's safety, had been realized. She'd lost her mind—she'd lost her mind in Ethan's arms, mistaking him for Benjamin Howard! *I must be mad,* she accused herself. *Only a madwoman would have behaved so just now.* Suddenly Meggie felt as if she deserved everything she'd ever gotten, every switching from the cruel matron, and even what Benjamin Howard had done to her. All of it and more . . . for what she'd just done to Ethan.

"What's the matter, Meghan? I'm not your Edward?" Ethan gritted out, his voice cruel and full of loathing. He'd stepped far away from her now.

Edward? Meggie couldn't believe what Ethan had just said. Why would Ethan suddenly conjure Edward's name? Edward, her secret romantic hero? Ethan couldn't know such a secret! The weight of kept secrets at once burdened her. Edward was one more secret, one more lie. Self-conscious about her nakedness, she pitifully pulled the ties of her bodice back together, wishing he'd called her Nutmeg and not Meghan.

"Ethan, please," she whispered, putting all her despair she felt in that one word.

"Please what, Meghan? Please get out? Please go away? Please don't touch you?"

Meggie could hear all the hurt in Ethan's harsh words, the harsh words she'd just leveled at him when she believed he was Benjamin Howard.

"Ethan, I can explain," she said without thinking. She knew she could not. "Please, Ethan," she begged, hating herself for the liar that she was. Scalding tears spilled down her face.

Ethan slowly walked toward her.

Each step seemed to take him farther away, instead of bringing him closer. Deathly afraid of what he might say next, Meggie's tears dried to hushed shudders. She stood her ground.

"No need for explanations, Meghan McMurphy. Or is it Rose Rochester? Which one of you is here now? Which is the liar? Which one of you belongs with Edward?" By now he'd reached her, towering over her, looming, ready to strike. "Whichever you are, neither belongs here with me. I don't want you. Go back to your precious Edward. Play your tricks on him. Play him for the fool."

It was the finality of Ethan's tone more than what he'd said that landed the killing blow. She stood before him in her coffin of silence, stone cold still. Strangely removed from the moment, Meggie tried to make sense out of what had just happened. She tried to make sense of her mixed-up thoughts.

Everything changed in her when Ethan undid her chemise. The moment he brushed the sides of her bare breasts, she was lost, not in the arms of passion, but in the claws of her night terrors. Never did she imagine that so long after her devastating rape, her mind would still be in such a state. *For good reason I was left in that asylum for two years!* This thought hit Meggie hard, this and the knowledge that she couldn't tell fact from fiction. And, just as bad, Ethan believed she loved another.

Edward.

Jane Eyre's Edward.

If her situation were not so dire, Meggie might have laughed at such an association. Ethan was right. It was too late for explanations. Too many lies stood between them. She'd hurt him enough with them. At the end of it all, Meggie knew it was better for Ethan to believe her a liar who loved another man, than to learn of her sinful ruin and uncertain mental state. Ethan deserved someone unscarred, clean of mind and body, and truthful.

"Get out, now."

Ethan's painful dictate held her to the spot a moment longer.

Fighting new tears, she reverently studied his face, wanting to remember every detail of his dark, handsome features.

"Get out of my room, out of my house, and out of my life," he ordered coldly.

"*Your* room? *Your* house? I didn't—"

"Oh, you're good, Meghan McMurphy," Ethan said in a scathing voice. "I'll give you that. Now you want me to believe that you didn't know you were coming to my home tonight. That you didn't line up like all the others who're after my money. Really, Meghan, you surprise me with this last failed attempt at trickery. I won't ask you to leave again," he warned.

He didn't have to. Meggie bolted for the door.

He slammed it behind her.

She fell back against the unforgiving wood, feeling every bit as evil as her tormentor, Benjamin Howard. She'd just hurt the one person who mattered more to her than anyone else in the world. Her punishment was deserved. Never would there be enough penance for her wicked deeds.

Someone was coming.

Suddenly Meggie remembered the party and all the people about. She had to get out of there. *Jesus, Mary, and Joseph! My clothes!* When she looked down at her state of disarray, at her nearly bare bosom, she straightened her bodice then did up the back of her dress. By some miracle she managed to hook most of the metal stays. Quickly now, she worked on her hair, smoothing it as best she could. She looked up and down the hallway, unable to remember where the back stairway was. She had to get out of there now, the back way or the front. Hurrying, she used both hands to wipe away any telltale tears then prayed no one would be there when she reached the grand staircase.

Not all prayers are answered. Ezekiel Smithers once again stood between her and any easy departure.

"Ezekiel, I'll be leaving now." Meggie strained to sound as

matter-of-fact as she could.

His look of genuine concern held her at the bottom step of the staircase.

"Are you shore you have to leave just now, Miss Rose?"

"Yes. I'm very tired. I'll just say goodnight." She fought more tears. He was so kind.

"Well, yer not leavin' by yer lonesome." Allowing her no chance to protest, Ezekiel took her by the arm and ushered her out the front door to one of the waiting carriages. "Here now, step on up, Miss Rose."

Once she was seated inside, Ezekiel asked her where she was staying.

"Brewster," Ezekiel said to the driver. "Take this fine young lady to the American House Hotel."

Meggie's heart snapped in two the moment Ezekiel closed the door of the carriage—the carriage that would drive her out of Ethan's life forever. When she returned to the mountains she'd finish her letter to Ethan, and their story—their precious time together—would come to an end.

CHAPTER SIXTEEN

Benjamin Howard tore the Pinkerton's message to bits and tossed them aside. Getting rid of the red-headed bitch wasn't going to be as easy as Howard had thought. She'd been scarred when he had her, scarred! If only he'd known, he'd never have wanted her. The cursed headmistress should have told him. He'd have found another, unmarred, and perhaps more willing, more beautiful.

Still angry over it all, Benjamin Howard studied his notes from Samuel Perry. The Pinkerton had tracked Meghan Mc-Murphy as far as Denver, to the American House Hotel. A gal fitting her description and the time-frame had registered there under the name of Rose Rochester. Perry didn't know much beyond that. She'd flat-out disappeared, not working in Denver, far as Perry could tell. Might be she's turned to whoring, Perry had said. Or might be she's somewhere in the mountains. The Pinkerton's message went on to say that he didn't think the gal had left Denver and gone somewhere else, leastways not by train. The note ended with Perry's request for more time and more money, certain he'd find the gal soon.

Benjamin Howard wasn't giving the no-good Pinkerton any more time or money. He didn't have any more time. He'd worried enough over the bitch and the damage she could do to him, to his social position, to his career. He'd go to Denver himself. If she'd turned to whoring, he'd find out. If she worked anywhere in the city, he'd find out. Hell, if she was anywhere in the God-forsaken new state, he'd find out. He knew he could. He knew he would. Failing wasn't an option.

Howard grabbed up the rest of Meggie's file with both of his hands, gripping and rubbing the file as if she were inside it instead of just the paper. *Full of surprises aren't you, my girl? Will you have any left for an old acquaintance?*

MEGHAN ROSE McMURPHY. The name printed on the file stood out in bold letters. Howard already smelled the chase. His nostrils flared. His blood sang. An almost inhuman appearance came over his handsome features, exposing his dark side, uncaging the evil changeling. Upon a closer look, one could imagine such a metamorphosis. One could imagine Benjamin Howard shedding his human form to take on the devil's. One could imagine shiny, dark hair transformed into oily scales. Black eyes yellowed. A square jaw rounded and thickened into his neck and coiling shoulders like a serpent readying to devour its prey. His viperous fangs shot out to inject its venom. He held Meggie's file in his talons, disgustingly licking until the ink of her name disappeared. *Just like you will my girl.* After, that is. After he'd had her one last time.

In a few moments his composure returned, but he needed more. Lucy. Always he could count on her to do his bidding. She'd proved a most willing secretary indeed. Although she was a little past her prime, he still enjoyed her. With uncanny quickness, he was out of his office and standing behind her seated form, with his hands around her neck. Her office was empty, the door closed. They were completely alone.

"Don't turn around, Lucy. Don't move." He began to stroke and massage her soft neck. Already he'd grown hard. At first he only tugged at the neckline of her dress letting his fingers move just inside the collar. When she started at his touch, he chastised her.

"Now, Lucy girl, you know better. I told you not to move.

You don't want me to have to tell you again now do you?"

"No," Lucy whispered obediently.

Deftly he removed his fingers from her neck and ran both predatory hands down over her collarbone before he traced the sides of her bodice, then encircled each of her full breasts. But as always, it wasn't enough. With eerie swiftness he again found the neckline of her dress before he ripped it open to her waist. When he'd exposed her naked breasts, he quickly spent himself against the back of her chair.

Ah, she's sweet. So sweet.

He'd keep Lucy a little longer in his employ, as long as she could pleasure him like this.

"Fix yourself up now, Lucy." He dropped a few coins on her desk for new clothes. It wasn't the first time. "We've got work to do. I need to leave at the end of the week."

No orphaned, impoverished, red-headed bitch was going to ruin him! The fact that he'd ruined her never occurred to him. All that occurred to him was that Meggie was still alive and could talk.

"Please, Meggie. Please don't leave."

Pru's appeal fell on deaf ears. Meggie threw the last of the few items she'd brought with her to Denver in her satchel. It was almost six o'clock in the morning. She'd have to hurry or she'd miss the stage to Hot Sulphur Springs.

"Talk to me Meggie, please. I know you're angry about last night. Uriah and I should have told you about Ethan. I'm sorry but we . . . thought . . ." Pru stammered under the heat of Meggie's burning glare. "Whatever happened last night with Ethan? You don't have to tell me. But please give things time. Don't rush back to the mountains before you've had a chance to see him again, to work things out. I know you lo—"

Meggie railed at Pru's intended words.

"Don't you say it! Don't say that I love him! If I never do another thing in this world I will forget that I ever met Ethan Rourke! This subject is closed. Forever." She wouldn't cry. All her tears for Ethan had dried sometime during the long, fitful night. She'd head to the mountains where she'd find sanctuary from the ache, the pain, the finality of losing Ethan . . . after she finished her letter. At once guilty over her harsh words to Pru, she softened her tone.

"Everything's there, Pru," Meggie said, nodding toward the bed where she'd laid out the violet satin gown and the raiment that went with it. Just like for a funeral, Meggie thought, since that's how she felt. Her own.

"Are you sure this is what you want?" Pru quietly asked, her voice filled with all the sadness she felt.

Meggie looked at her dear friend, and then set down her satchel and crossed the room to embrace Pru.

"Yes, this is what I want," she whispered as she hugged her. "This is how it *has* to be."

"Do you want me to come with you, Meggie? I can be ready in two minutes' time."

Meggie let go of Pru and bent down to pick up her satchel.

"No, Pru, my wonderful, dear friend. You've only just found your happiness with Uriah. You must cherish it always. I'll be the happiest of all knowing you're with the man you love, the man who loves you."

"But—"

"No buts, Pru." Meggie insisted, and started for the door. Once there, she put her hand on the cold knob and then hesitated. "Promise you'll come and visit me."

"Of course, friend of my heart, of course," Pru swallowed back her tears.

With that, Meggie was out the door. She'd no tears left.

"Are you awake, honey?" Samantha softly cooed against Ethan's back. "Ethan, honey?"

"Go back to sleep, Sam." He wasn't in the mood for conversation. He wasn't in the mood for lovemaking. And he most certainly wasn't in the mood to admit that thinking of Nutmeg prevented him from wanting his mistress.

After Nutmeg left last night he'd stormed downstairs and abruptly ended the festivities. Everyone filed out except Uriah and Samantha. Still angry, he told Uriah he'd see him tomorrow. He should never have asked Samantha to come to the party. Stupid idea. She'd readily accepted. He didn't care about the appearance of things in Denver society, where respectable folks didn't associate with mistresses and the like, at least not outside of parlor houses. Hell, none of that mattered. Right now he didn't want to be with Samantha or anybody else.

Not only did Ethan not want his mistress, he couldn't make love to her. Always before he'd easily lost himself in her waiting arms. Her voluptuous body never ceased to fascinate and satisfy him. His failure to perform with Samantha helped fuel his anger at Nutmeg.

Damn her.

Damn her deceptive, lying ways.

Damn the wildfire she started, and damn me for not being able to put it out!

The fact that Nutmeg loved someone else hurt the most. Hell, pretending to want him, when all the time she wanted *Edward*. The name gave him a headache. Ethan suddenly thought of the conversation he'd had with Livi Tritt last night. He was still put out with Uriah for inviting Tritt and his daughter to the party. Ethan didn't refuse when Livi wanted a dance, although he should have. As he'd danced with Livi, she'd tried to convince him that Rose Rochester was really a brazen hussy chasin' after all the men in town. And Livi didn't want to be the one to tell him, but she's just playin' everyone for a fool.

Yeah, fool is right, Ethan berated himself.

Maybe Livi had Nutmeg pegged right. He knew Nutmeg *was* a liar, living under an assumed name, in love with another man. Maybe, the way Livi told it, Rose Rochester loved a lot more than one man. No, Nutmeg wasn't worth any more of his heartache.

But another part of Ethan wasn't entirely put out with Nutmeg. On some level too deep and painful to acknowledge, Ethan was relieved he'd made her leave his bedroom last night. She was safe from him now. Safe from the love he mistakenly would have given her—the same love that had killed his family and his Rachel. The past had taught him that much.

Just then Samantha's hand came around to stroke his cheek.

"Not now, Sam." Ethan's back was to her.

"But Ethan, honey. I want you so. I need you to touch me, to feel you inside me." Her hand moved from gently stroking the side of his face, down over his shoulder and arm, before coming to rest against his side. Slowly she splayed her fingers and massaged his stomach then moved her hand down farther.

Ethan grabbed her hand and stopped her. Anything but stimulated, he didn't want Samantha touching him. Right now he could kick himself for bringing her upstairs after the party. He should have sent her home along with everyone else. None of this was her doing.

"Sam," he said with a gentleness he didn't feel, his back still to her. "Not now. Go to sleep. We're both tired."

"I'm not tired, Ethan, and I won't go to sleep." She raised on her elbow. "You can't just dismiss me like this! Something is different. I can tell. Women know these things. Why you . . . you don't *want* me, do you? That's it, isn't it?" She broke into tears and sobbed against his back.

Joanne Sundell

He hated this. To have Samantha upset and crying wasn't what he wanted. He turned over, intending to hold her and calm her down. But she was quicker than he was, and scooted over to the other side of the bed before he could touch her. She gathered the covers up and buried her face in them.

"Sam, please don't cry. Come here." Even as he said it, he knew she wouldn't. Once she'd set her mind to something, there wasn't any way to change it. Her tear-streaked faced looked so forlorn. He wished things were different. He wished he felt different.

"Sam," he whispered, unable to think of anything to say to console her.

"When, Ethan? Who?"

Her simple questions took him by surprise. "I don't know what you're talking about, Sam." He really didn't want to get into this.

"You know *who*. I know *who*. And I know *when*. That red-headed woman last night. That's who and that's when. I saw you together. I know."

Not about to get into a discussion with Samantha about Nutmeg, he kept silent. Besides, what good would it do to say anything? It certainly wouldn't help Samantha right now.

"You don't have to say a word to me, Ethan. I know she's the one you'd rather be with right now. She's the one you care for. Not me."

Now he *really* hated this. He and Samantha had never used words like "care" before. He hated himself for what he was doing to her. She didn't deserve to suffer because of him.

"If you only knew what practically all of Denver was saying about her, maybe you wouldn't think her so wonderful."

He let Samantha talk. At least he could do that. Thankfully, she'd stopped crying.

"The whole city is laughing at her. Her going to all the

234

saloons and dance halls, trying to rescue some girl from *evil* drinking, and *evil* gambling, and *evil* prostitution! What a joke she is, Ethan! Hannah and I had a good laugh over her and her saving that girl from the clutches of all the 'horrible, wicked men' in town." Samantha paused and took a breath, just long enough for her sarcasm to take full effect. "Why, do you know she helped the girl leave town? The really funny part is that she thinks she saved the girl from the grips of a few gentlemen who only wanted to have a little fun one night. Pulled a gun on them all and shot one in the leg. Can you imagine? She shot one of the customers! She must be crazy. Keeping men from their pleasurin' time."

Nutty Meggie. Ethan pictured the scene. His hat went off to Nutmeg. But when Samantha said crazy, Ethan thought of that first time, when he'd seen Nutmeg spin around in her bare feet in the middle of the snowy night. He'd thought her crazy then. The next day when he'd so much as intimated she might be nuts, she near tore his head off. Crazy or not, nothing Nutmeg said or did would surprise him now that he knew she was full of lies and deception.

He shrugged off the nagging possibility that she might really be a temperance-sign-toting, Bible-thumping, schoolmarm. Aw, hell, what difference did it make? It didn't change the fact that she was a fraud and a liar. So what if she could use a pistol? He fought his grudging admiration that she'd pulled a gun on some bastards to help out the young woman in question. If Nutmeg took a shot at one of the bastards, he must have deserved it. Feeling the fool again, Ethan realized Nutmeg probably didn't need him saving her from the likes of Jake Hooper. *She must have had a good laugh on me over that,* Ethan fumed silently.

"And plain as she can be," Samantha kept on with her tirade. "Why, that's what just everyone says. The fact that *you* find her interesting, Ethan, is the exception. I can assure you." Samantha dripped the words out then scrambled out of bed and hurried to dress.

Ethan didn't try to stop her.

"Well." Samantha wasn't finished. "I won't have any part of you, Ethan Rourke! Four years is long enough. Four wasted years with a man who doesn't want me. There are plenty of men in this city who do want me. If you think you're the only man around here that I want, then you're sadly mistaken."

Ethan said nothing to Samantha. He had nothing to add. Unless, of course, he chose to tell Samantha that Nutmeg didn't want him. What was it Nutmeg had said? *Let me be! I don't want you to touch me again! Get away from me!* Her words still echoed against the steel wall he'd rebuilt around his heart.

Hell, Edward can have her. I don't want her.

Pulling his attention back to Samantha, he didn't stop her from leaving. She deserved better than he could give her now. She'd find it. Of that, he had little doubt. They'd shared an association for four years, and even affection, but no more than that. He'd make sure she had money. At least he could do that much.

With Samantha gone, Ethan's efforts to fall back to sleep failed. He threw off the covers and edged himself out of bed. Still naked, he yanked up his charcoal trousers from the floor where he'd thrown them, and pulled them on. His head pounded. He felt like he'd been up drinking and carousing all night. Hell. Maybe that was the problem.

Ethan reached for the nearby decanter of Scotch whiskey. He poured a stiff drink and downed it in one swallow. He poured another. It didn't matter that the clock just struck six in the morning. He lit a smoke and wracked his brain, but for the life of him, he couldn't come up with one thing in his life that did matter right now. Not one thing.

★ ★ ★ ★ ★

Uriah couldn't believe his eyes when Ethan stumbled into their office at eight o'clock. Ethan was corned! Ethan *never* overdid it. In the fifteen years he'd known Ethan, this was the first time he'd seen him all liquored up.

Ethan barely had a nod for Uriah, and flopped down in his desk chair.

Something's got Ethan's gut. Uriah had an idea what it was. "Want some coffee, Ethan?"

"Don . . . wan . . . no . . . damn . . . no . . . damn coffee," Ethan slurred out.

"How in blazes did you get here like this?" Uriah was incredulous.

"I'm fine . . . jus fine." Ethan's eyes closed.

"Oh, yeah, fine. If you're fine I'm President Ulysses S. Grant," Uriah chided. "I know I'm not Grant, and I know you're not fine." Before Ethan passed out altogether, Uriah got him to the cot in the back office. He pulled the blanket up over an anesthetized Ethan, wondering if Pru would be more successful in talking with Meghan. Maybe Pru would have more luck in finding out what happened between Meghan and Ethan last night.

Meggie had been on the stage for two hours now. She'd taken the last seat open. Six other passengers traveled with her. Three women and two men were seated inside the coach, while one man rode outside with Bill Sykes. It was a bit crowded, but Meggie didn't care. She paid no mind to the fact, either, that she sat in the coach in close proximity to two men, strangers to her. She couldn't get home to her cabin fast enough.

All greenhorn tourists from the East, Meggie quickly decided. She wondered if any of her fellow passengers knew what they were in for, journeying into the rugged mountains. The men sitting opposite her looked like true dandies in their bowler hats, Chesterfield overcoats, and spats. One had long, Dundreary sideburns and wore full, cloth gaiters buttoned right down over his ankle-high spats. Meggie remembered the big Saratoga trunks she'd seen piled on top of the stage. Greenhorn tourists, indeed, she thought, turning her attention to the ladies. All three wore lace cornet head coverings. They had to be uncomfortable over the miles, what with fancy bustles attached to the backs of their travel outfits.

Suddenly the group inside the stage struck her as funny—the thought of this green group sojourning into the wilds of the Colorado Territory in their ever-so-fancy clothes was hilarious. She began to laugh, at first chuckling to herself and then out loud. It felt good to laugh, to think about something besides her troubles.

She laughed so hard her stomach hurt. Never mind the aching spasms; she didn't care. And never mind the odd stares from the passengers. They just made her laugh all the more. Meggie knew they all thought her touched. She didn't care. For the first time in her life, she wasn't self-conscious about what others might think of her. What did it matter?

What did anything matter anymore?

Ethan didn't want her. He didn't even like her. He'd never love her. At that sobering thought, her tears of joy turned to a flood of heartache. She mistakenly thought she'd cried her last over Ethan. More low-spirited than ever, Meggie slumped against the hard leather seatback. The presence of the other passengers unnerved her now. She ached to be anywhere but in the coach with them. It felt to her as if every detail of her pathetic life was written all over her tear-streaked face. Self-conscious now, she choked back her sobs and did her best to regain some degree of composure.

★ ★ ★ ★ ★

Livi stormed into the sheriff's office, driven by jealousy, and overcome with the fear of losing Ethan Rourke to that red-headed hussy! She couldn't let Rose Rochester get Ethan, and she wouldn't. Sure that she could drum up charges against the nuisance schoolmarm, Livi intended to do just that. She'd accuse Rose of stealing from her father's bank, and get her father to help her prove it. Her father would do anything she asked. Besides, the Tritts were important in Denver. Rose Rochester was a nobody—a thieving nobody!

Someone else already had the sheriff's attention. Although fuming inside that she had to wait to be heard, she studied the tall stranger and liked what she saw. He was handsome, all right: dark and handsome, and looked like he came from the East in his expensive clothes. Interested in the look of the man, she was interested, too, in what he had to say. More patiently now, she waited to report Rose Rochester's thievery to the sheriff, listening instead to the conversation between the sheriff and the good-looking, obviously wealthy stranger.

"Sheriff." Benjamin Howard tried to stifle his anger at the poor excuse for a lawman. "Let me spell it out for you again. The woman I'm looking for is in her twenties, has red hair, arrived in Denver within this past year, stayed at the American House Hotel for a time, might be a prostitute, might be a schoolteacher, might have even married one of your locals by now. There's no record of her leaving Denver, Sheriff. She's still around, I'm sure."

The sheriff eyed Benjamin Howard with suspicion. He didn't like people coming in and telling him how to do his job. This eastern dandy had no idea what he was a talkin' about. Denver had thousands of residents. If nobody broke the law or caused a ruckus, no way he'd know about 'em. "Listen Mr. . . . . Mr.—"

"Howardton."

239

"Yeah, Mr. Howardton." The sheriff smoothed his mustache as he spoke. "Did this young woman do anything wrong? Why are you lookin' for her anyways?"

"You damned right," Howard snapped back. "She's a liar and a fraud. Back east she stole from me, and I'm going to find her and take her back to face justice." Howard knew his charges were weak, but he wasn't about to tell the truth of it. This stupid sheriff didn't need to know anything beyond finding Meghan McMurphy for him.

"Broke the law, you say?" The sheriff was still suspicious. "Just what was it the woman stole from you?"

Benjamin Howard knew to hold his temper. It wasn't a good idea to draw undue attention to himself and to his visit to Denver. He kept his conversation easy. "Listen, sheriff, all I'm trying to do is to find a young woman going by the name of Rose Rochester, and see that she faces the consequences for her thievery. That's all, sir."

The sheriff didn't miss the "sir" part. This citified easterner was trying to pull a fast one on him, and he wasn't gonna have any part of it. Could be a spurned lover or some such? Anyways, the sheriff didn't want to help this suspicious stranger find anybody.

Livi sure did. She couldn't believe her good fortune. She knew Rose Rochester, and she'd be most happy to lead this Mr. Howardton right to her. Most happy, indeed.

The sheriff interrupted Livi's excited thoughts.

"Listen, Howardton. Think you'd best get on outta here. 'Fraid I can't help you."

"I'll go now, Sheriff," Benjamin Howard gritted out, "but you can bet I'll be back." Then Howard stormed out, much the same as Livi had stormed in.

She turned on her heel without a word for the sheriff, and caught up with Benjamin Howard. "Mr. Howardton! Mr.

Howardton!" she panted, near shouting at his back.

Benjamin Howard stopped and turned to face the woman. He recognized her from the sheriff's office.

"I know where Rose Rochester is," Livi blurted out, gleefully. "I know exactly where she is."

Howard smiled at Livi, and tipped the edge of his hat.

Junction House couldn't come soon enough for Meggie. She'd grown weary listening to the other passengers chatter on and on. The women talked of nothing but the latest fashions, while the men bragged about how many elk and buffalo they would kill. Meggie understood hunting for food, but she didn't agree with hunting just for the sake of it. It was wasteful and cruel. The group planned to meet their guides in Hot Sulphur Springs and from there on, journey into North Park and the Gore range. *Good riddance,* Meggie thought, before thinking better of it. The sisters wouldn't take too well to her unkindness. But the sisters didn't have to sit here and listen to these callow fellows. She leaned back in her seat and shut her eyes. Despite the bumpy rocking of the lumbering coach, and despite her agitation, she actually fell asleep.

When the Concord pulled into Junction House, Meggie was the first to disembark. Filled with melancholy, without a word to anyone, even for Martha Wheatley, she dashed inside and straight up the stairs to be alone. It was wrong of her not to speak to Martha. She should go right back downstairs and apologize, explain. But what could she say to Martha besides "I'm sorry." She couldn't tell Martha the truth. She couldn't talk about Ethan or about losing her wits in his arms. To help escape the moment, Meggie soon fell asleep.

Her melancholy was worse the next morning. If Martha hadn't come in to rouse her, she wouldn't have gotten up at all.

"Poor little thing," Martha cooed as she helped Meggie sit

up. "No wonder you was in such a way last evenin'. If'n I'd known you was feelin' so poorly, I'd been up here and helpin' you fer shore. You just come downstairs and I'll git you some hot tea and a hearty breakfast. It'll fix you right up."

"Thank you," Meggie said weakly, and got out of bed. She had to. "You're very kind, Martha. I'm just tired. Don't worry over me."

" 'Course I'll worry over you if'n I want," Martha said, ever the mother hen. "Now come on. You need some vittles in yer stomach."

Meggie followed Martha down the steps, each one hard taken. Her legs felt like lead. She dreaded facing everybody and couldn't imagine how she'd get any food past her lips.

Meggie was the first to depart the stage in Hot Sulphur Springs. Satchel in hand, she practically ran all the way to her cabin. Once inside, she set her satchel down and leaned against the door, glad to at last find refuge.

"Rose! Rose! Are you all right?"

Jolted by the pounding vibrations at her back, Meggie stepped away from the door.

"Rose!"

Meggie opened the door for Eliza.

"My dear girl," Eliza exclaimed, her concern obvious. "I'm that worried over you. Whatever is wrong, Rose?"

Meggie wasn't prepared to reveal anything to Eliza. She had to make up something and quick. "I've come down with the ague, I think. I felt like I was going to lose my breakfast when the stage arrived, and, well . . . I just needed to get here fast as I could," Meggie hurried with her lie and made haste to sit on the edge of her bed. She didn't bother to ask the good sisters for forgiveness.

"There, there." Eliza sat down next to Meggie. "The trip to

Denver must have taken it all out of you."

If you only knew, Eliza, Meggie thought.

"You rest, dear. I'll just make you a nice cup of tea. You'll feel better then," Eliza gave Meggie's arm a squeeze and got up.

Meggie lay down on her bed and pulled the quilt over her. For the first time in a very long time, she gave no thought to the whereabouts of *Jane Eyre* or her letter to Ethan or her cross. She didn't bother to undress or take off her boots. Oddly, she took comfort from Eliza's presence, watching her light the hearth, and then set about making a pot of tea. She didn't feel quite so alone now. Her eyes soon closed.

When she awoke, it was dark out, and Eliza was gone. The fire still burned brightly. Eliza must have only just left. Forcing herself up and out of bed, Meggie went over to the table and lit the kerosene lamp. She found her satchel, and then *Jane Eyre,* and then her folded letter to Ethan. It was time to finish it while she had the energy to do so. She found her place, her last words in her letter . . . *I booked passage on the very next train out of Boston. There is more I must tell you, more I wish you to know . . .*

This will be my last account to you, Ethan. My letter will soon end, but there is more I wish you to know. I have been fearful since that dreadful day at the hands of Benjamin Howard that I would lose my wits again, never to regain my sanity. As you know by now, I've been left in ruins, my remains a bitter pile of ashes that will soon blow into dust, and I'll be gone. At the outset of this letter, I told you as much. I am not seeking pity, and only want to state the truth of it all. Benjamin Howard will come for me, as he must. I'm alive and I can talk. He's very prominent in Boston, and I'm nobody—an orphan, a woman without position or means. No one would believe my story over his. He must kill me. This I know and this I accept. I intend to be ready for him, but if I am not, this is as it must be. To repeat, I accept my fate. I deserve my fate.

Let me tell you now that the reason I chose the name, Rose Rochester, instead of using my God-given name, Meghan Rose McMurphy, was to help shield myself from discovery. I chose Rose Rochester because Jane Eyre married Edward Rochester in the beloved novel that I keep close to me always. I am not in love with any Edward, as you believe. Edward is a made-up, fictitious character. He's Jane Eyre's Edward, not mine. I keep Jane and Edward close for companionship and to help take away some of the pain from my past. Whenever I feel scared and alone, I find comfort by slipping into the fanciful world of Jane and Edward and Thornfield Hall. Here I can imagine a different life. Here I can imagine I'm heroic Jane who's fallen in love with dashing Edward. But in the real world, I've wanted little to do with men, until you, Ethan. Until you.

The fear I gave mention to earlier, the fear of losing my mind, proved true when I was with you in Denver. For a moment, when you touched my naked flesh, the fine line between my daydreams and nightmares, between fancy and fact, blurred in my head. For a moment I thought you were the devil, the fiend Benjamin Howard. I was frightened that he'd killed you. So frightened for you, Ethan. I tell you this now so you will know that I love you and that if there were any way for me to show it to you, I would. I fear I will ever be tainted and repelled by the touch of a man, ever afraid, ever lost in my nightmares. This is not your fault. I want you to know. I hate that you think ill of me, that you think I'm a gold-digger who loves another. I am surprised beyond anything you might imagine that I've been able to fall in love with you, a flesh and blood man, when I thought I never would. At least I have this gift from you, Ethan. I do have my love for you. I will keep it with me in this world, and on into the next.

I will always love you, Ethan Rourke. Always and forever. Your Meggie . . .

Her pen was dry. She waited now for the ink to dry, for the words she'd just set down on paper to dry. Her tears, too, had dried. She'd none left. The fire still burned. Slowly, she carefully folded the last page of her letter and put it with the others. All folded, all finished, she looked again at the fire, intending to toss the whole letter into the blaze, but she did not. Almost unwittingly, she tucked her folded letter safely back inside the pages of *Jane Eyre*.

There would be time enough tomorrow to destroy her last connection to Ethan . . . time enough tomorrow.

CHAPTER SEVENTEEN

The next morning Meggie felt better than she had in days. The sunshine across her face warmed her whole body. She lay in bed, stretching her awakening arms and legs, able now to come to terms with the reality of her life. She'd live it without the promise of love, without Ethan Rourke. Sitting up in bed, Meggie decided then and there to focus on all that she had instead of what she didn't have. She'd told herself as much before, but this time she meant it.

I have a good home, good friends, and a good position. I've been blessed many times over.

Irritated at herself for wallowing in self-pity for the past two days, Meggie scrambled out of bed. In the next moment she had her pail in hand and was out the door and around the cabin to fetch fresh, spring water, her hair a tumble, her feet bare, and in her nightdress.

"Rose Rochester!" Eliza scolded, coming round the side of the cabin. "Are you out of your mind? No shoes? Not dressed? How is a body to get you well with such behavior? You give me that pail and march inside this instant!"

The out-of-your-mind part was already forgiven. So was the lecture. Meggie handed over her full, water bucket and obediently padded inside her cabin.

"Eliza, don't fret so over me. I'm fine, really."

"Well," Eliza conceded, "you do look much better this morning." She set Meggie's heavy pail by the hearth and put her pot of chicken broth on the table. "But you should take more care."

"I will. I promise," Meggie acquiesced. "Thank you, Eliza. Thank you for caring and for being my friend."

"You've nothing to thank me for," Eliza said. "And now, Rose, since you're feeling so fit, you must tell me all about Denver, every little detail."

Meggie would share some of her news from Denver, but certainly not every detail, and most certainly not one word about seeing Ethan again.

It took two full days for Ethan to recover from his drunken binge. His body sobered up, but his heart and soul were still plagued with anger at Nutmeg, at himself, and at the world. He tore into Uriah the moment his old friend entered their downtown office.

"You're late. Where the hell have you been? You think everything will get done for next week all by itself?"

Uriah had expected this. Ethan wouldn't be right until he puzzled things out, one way or the other, with Meghan McMurphy. Until then, he'd have to put up with Ethan's ill-tempered moods. It wouldn't do any good just now to bring up her name. Nope. He'd already discovered from Pru that Meghan, it seemed, wasn't ready for any kind of talk either. A shame. It was all a shame. Here he'd finally found happiness with Pru, and Ethan seemed to have lost his chance for it with Meghan. Didn't seem fair. Not fair at all.

"Reckon I'm a little late," Uriah conceded.

"Damn straight you are," Ethan barked back. "Here," he shoved a stack of papers into Uriah's hands. "Here's all the shipping orders for the explosives and new equipment. Want to have a look before I pay them?"

This was bad. Really bad. Uriah never did any bills or looked at any payments. Ethan always did that. But Uriah accepted them anyway before turning them right back over to Ethan. "Nope, don't need to see 'em. I'm sure it's all down in black and white just fine."

"Well, all right then, I'll send them out this morning and we can get busy with plans for next week. If you round up our crew and get them ready, I'll get the explosives squared away."

Explosives! In your foul mood! Uriah hoped that Ethan would feel a lot better come next week. Nobody should mess with dynamite unless his head was clear as a bell. Not even Ethan. Uriah knew he'd have to worry about Ethan all week and into the next.

Meggie, on the other hand, endeavored to worry about nothing at all. Not even Benjamin Howard.

I'm a brand new person, she told herself every morning. *This is a brand new day filled with brand new moments. My life is ordered and peaceful. I'm content. I have everything I want or need.* As she busied herself about her cabin, she almost had herself convinced. Almost.

Back to taking no more than ten minutes to get washed and dressed, Meggie located her wire rims and put them on. She pinned her hair up into its usual tight bun. Her wooden cross went around her neck to stay. But *Jane Eyre* suffered a different fate. Meggie had taken her beloved romantic tale out from under her pillow and hidden it in the bottom of her satchel. She didn't feel like keeping the romance novel as companion anymore, and she shoved her satchel way under her bed. She thought herself done with Edward Rochester, too.

The days passed. Meggie resumed school hours and gladly taught any children who could attend. She visited Eliza and William most evenings and Clovis Kinney most mornings. Whenever she thought of Ethan—of how little he must think of her now—she chased him from her thoughts. Sometimes it worked. Some scars were harder to heal than others, she realized.

Ethan had scars, too. Not a day passed that he didn't feel the loss of his family and his dear Rachel. All dead because of his love for them. At least Nutmeg hadn't lost her life because of his feelings for her, but there was something else that cut at him. He'd been played the fool. Nutmeg had deceived him. She'd lied to him. That wasn't the worst of it. She loved someone else. She didn't want him and dammit, he didn't want her, either! No, he wouldn't play the fool, ever again. Nutmeg wasn't worth it.

Late in the afternoon, Ethan put his mind back on his work. He'd leave on Nugget at first light. Itchy to get to work on the wagon road over Berthoud Pass, tomorrow couldn't come soon enough. Uriah would follow with the supply wagon and their crew.

Right then, Uriah had other things on his mind.

Still trying to figure how good fortune found him, Uriah stood away from the counter at the Broadway Clothing and Dry Goods while Pru waited on a customer. He remembered a conversation months ago when Ethan asked him about fancying a shop girl at the mercantile. At the time, Uriah couldn't imagine such a thing, but now here he was, thirty years old and ugly as ever, in love with a shop girl at the mercantile. For the life of him, he couldn't recall what anything was like before Pru.

In the morning he'd leave for Berthoud Pass, but tonight he'd spend with the woman he loved.

"It's all set then?" Angus Tritt removed a handkerchief from the breast pocket of his tweed jacket. He wiped away the nervous sweat on his brow before he pressed Bart for more details.

"You know, Tritt, you worry too damn much about everything," Bart snarled. "You should start thinking about how you're going to do all your celebrating when the two of 'em are blown to bits and scattered all over the summit," he joked.

Tritt wiped away more beady sweat. "You enjoy this whole business a little too much." The cold-blooded look Bart shot him shut down any more talk. If he wasn't careful, Bart might back out of the plan.

"Yep, your troubles and mine will be over by noon tomorrow," Bart said with a sneer. "My brother can rest in peace, and Rourke and Taylor can burn in hell." He poured a whiskey and belted it down. "You're right about one thing, Tritt. I *will* enjoy this." He set his empty glass down hard on the polished mahogany desk, then left the banker's office without another word.

Tritt stared at the ring of moisture that formed around the bottom of Bart's glass. His handkerchief still in hand, he hastily wiped his desk before dabbing the telltale perspiration still trickling down his face. After tomorrow, he didn't want to have anything more to do with Bart Gentry.

Friday morning and not a cloud in the sky. Glad for it, Ethan was almost at the summit of the pass. The weather wouldn't hold things up today. Good. The sooner he could get to work and get his mind off his troubles, the better. The storm inside him over Nutmeg, instead of quieting over the past two weeks, raged on. Spicy swells of nutmeg and cream splashed over nearly every thought, threatening to drown him in their wake. Soft arms reached out for him. Rosy lips opened, waiting for his kiss. Luminous, violet eyes rimmed in sooty lashes lured him into their passionate depths. Flames of scarlet aroused wherever they touched.

"Aw, hell." The day had already grown too hot. The repressive heat easily penetrated Ethan's clothes, itching and irritating every part of his body. He couldn't find a comfortable position in the saddle. Long swallows of water from his canteen couldn't quench his mounting thirst. A tap on Nugget's haunches quickened their pace. If he didn't think it would harm the huge, lathered animal, he would run him straight up the rest of the pass.

In ten minutes' time, Ethan reached the worksite. Uriah and their crew weren't too far behind. He slid off Nugget and gave his fatigued horse free reign, then ripped off his Stetson and wiped his forehead with the thick cotton of his sleeve. Like it or not, it was going to be a long, hot day. Accept it or not, Nutmeg was the reason. She was driving him to distraction. A distraction he couldn't afford now. Working with explosives was serious business. He needed to think straight.

Nugget had already wandered away. Two items Ethan should never have parted with were still attached to the saddle: his canteen and his Winchester. If he'd been thinking clearly, he'd have them both in hand. But he wasn't, and he didn't. Instead he absent-mindedly shuffled toward the thicket of pine at the edge of the wagon road, intent on surveying the job ahead.

Out of nowhere the unmistakable cold muzzle of a rifle jabbed hard into his back. Ethan didn't have to turn around. He had a good idea who held the gun. His sharp instincts told him as much. "Well, Bart, didn't expect you up here today," Ethan said coolly, not moving an inch.

"Aw, shucks, Ethan, I was hoping to surprise you. Damned if you're just too smart for ol' Bart," Gentry said sarcastically and buried his rifle harder into Ethan's back. "Tell you what, though. I don't think you're smart enough for ol' Henry here."

The moment Ethan figured to get the scattergun from Bart, Bart was too quick for him, and stepped out of reach.

"No you don't," Bart gibed, his rifle on Ethan.

The two men faced each other now.

251

"Can't get out of this one, Ethan. Won't be that easy. No, sir. You're going to die today, my friend. And there's nothing you can do about it."

"You want to let me in on what's going on here, Bart?" Ethan stood stock still, his muscles tensed.

"Smart as you are, Ethan, I think that should be plain as day. I have the gun. You don't. You're going to die. I'm not," he spat out.

Ethan took care to keep his eyes leveled on Bart and his temper in check. Angry with himself for getting into this slippery situation, he wouldn't react to Bart's warped sense of humor.

"Oh, I suppose I could fill you in a little," Bart said, smirking "Try remembering a few things. Try remembering how you and Taylor killed my brother. Try and think back on how you two stole my claim. Left ol' Bart with nothing, nothing at all."

Ethan knew he shouldn't be surprised, but he was. All these years he'd wanted to help Bart. He'd always felt bad about the accident that killed Bart's brother, but it had been his brother's own doing. Ethan had always felt bad that Bart's claims never panned out, and had tried to bring him in on deals to help him along. But this? This he didn't see coming.

"Boys!" Bart suddenly yelled out.

Three surly hombres appeared from the nearby crop of boulders.

Not moving a muscle, Ethan watched and waited. They looked like comancheros, mean and dirty and spoiling for a fight. All wore cartridge belts crossed over their chests. All had pistols strapped on. All had danger written on their hard, no-good faces. Ethan realized his odds just dropped.

Bart nodded to two of the comancheros. "Get him and tie him up good and tight over there." He pointed to the edge of the tall timber. Just as his gang started to drag Ethan away, Bart stopped them. His face was only inches from Ethan's.

The watery film over his beady eyes glistened. Spittle formed at the corners of his crooked smile. Ethan could see how much Bart enjoyed this.

"You're going to get to watch us kill Taylor and your men. You'll be able to see them all blown to bits before we kill you," he growled. "I want you to see all of it, old friend. Every little piece of every one of 'em scattered all over this goddamn mountain!"

Ethan's mind raced over his options—over his lack of them.

"Take him, fellas, and gag the son of a bitch," Bart spat out and stepped away.

Trussed up like a damned Christmas bird, they tied him all right. Ethan was pure pissed at himself all over again. Dammit! His arms and feet were stretched and lashed between two trees, Indian style. Blood already seeped from his wrists where the tight hide bound them. The bastards had pulled off his boots. His bare feet and ankles started to swell just beneath their leather ties. The rag stuffed in his mouth tasted like it had just been pulled out of something dead. He watched, helpless, while the comancheros set the ambush, their bundles of dynamite ready to blow. Then he watched Bart and his gang of low-lifes slither into their hiding places to wait for their kill.

Ethan heard horses. Then the lumbering wheels of the supply wagon. In a bizarre blur, the vision of a wooden cross dangling over a buttoned dress clouded his panicky thoughts. He thought of Nutmeg. One shake of his head, and her image faded. He thought of praying to save Uriah and his men, and then thought better of it. He didn't believe in God. God had given up on him a long time ago, and he'd given up on God. There wasn't anyone to help now, no one at all. Hopeless and helpless, Ethan shut his eyes against what was about to happen.

In the next moment someone from behind was cutting him loose, first his hands, then his feet. Ethan yanked the gag from his mouth and turned. Whoever it was had already disappeared, quicker and quieter than . . . *an Indian*. Nugget was near. Ethan gave a quick whistle. He'd no time to wonder who'd just helped him. Uriah and his crew had reached the summit.

Bart and his gang were not looking Ethan's way, but crouched down, ready to fire their explosives. They didn't hear him call Nugget, and they didn't realize he was free.

Ethan, bootless, took his pistol from his saddlebag and shoved it in the waist of his trousers, then grabbed his loaded Winchester and fixed Bart in his sites. His first shot hit dead on. Bart keeled over. All three comancheros came for him at the same time, pistols blazing. Despite their flurry of bullets, Ethan got every one of the sons of bitches.

Uriah jumped down off the wagon and ran over to Ethan. "Jesus Christ! You all right? What the hell's going on?"

Ethan was glad to see his old friend alive. "Bart meant . . . to kill . . . us all, Uriah," Ethan panted out. "Dynamite's all set over there." He gestured with his Winchester. "The bastard meant to blow us all to kingdom co—" Ethan didn't have a chance to finish. The bullet in his back silenced him. He slumped forward against Uriah.

Bart Gentry wasn't dead yet. Despite the gaping wound in his chest, he'd somehow managed to get his hands on his rifle and point it at Ethan. In a last gasp, dying the cowardly way he'd lived, he put a hole in Ethan's back before he slumped to the ground.

Meggie sprang out of her rocker. A sudden, searing pain had shot through her back! *Jesus, Mary, and Joseph!* Her empty rocker creaked back and forth. She instinctively looked it over, but found no spider or viperous critter that might have bitten her. She looked behind her, but found no one lurking with a knife or a bullet. Then she felt the back of her neck. No hairs bristled there.

Only then did she remember her pupils. Some giggled at her. She tried to smile back. On impulse, agitated now, she dismissed the children for the day, knowing she couldn't concentrate on their lessons. The children whooped with glee and happily obeyed her. Meggie sat back down in her rocker. Instead of the comfort she usually found at the soothing movement, her nerves refused to settle. She got up and began pacing. That didn't help either. She sat back down and closed her fingers around the cross resting over her bosom. Her cross grew hot in her hands! She abruptly let it go. Something was wrong, very, very wrong. Suddenly she didn't want to be alone. Grabbing up her shawl she rushed out the door so fast, she didn't bother to latch it shut.

Meggie woke the next morning, the uneasy feelings of yesterday waking with her. She'd stayed the night with Eliza and William, and slept in the same room she'd been given her first night in Hot Sulphur Springs. Restless and on edge, she was surprised she hadn't had any nightmares. She'd expected to, what with her uneasiness. Maybe it was her imagination yesterday and nothing more, her mind playing tricks on her again. Still, she wished she felt better. Just then she heard a voice, a man's voice. Jumpy, she glanced quickly around the room but saw no one. It was definitely her mind playing tricks on her now. She quickly climbed out of bed. But the voice, at first a whisper, called to her again, this time louder. Meggie's heart stopped. She knew that voice.

"Nutmeg, where are you?"

Ethan! It was Ethan's voice.

Her very next thought was of *Jane Eyre*. Edward had called across the moors to Jane in just such a way when he was—

"Nutmeg, where are you?"

"I'm coming, my love," Meggie called back, just as Jane had. "I'm coming."

Petrified for Ethan—knowing the very instant that something had happened to him yesterday—Meggie fumbled with her clothing, her hands so shaky they felt useless. She didn't cry. She didn't have time to cry. Desperate now, she fell to her knees before God. "Please, dear God, keep Ethan safe. He is good. I am not good, but Ethan is good. You've no call to listen to a sinner, but please listen to me now. Please save Ethan." Meggie stayed on her knees, unable to rise and face her fear. She'd been afraid before, terrified for herself. But this fear, this oppressive fear for Ethan, ripped at her, gutting her very soul.

"Luckiest man I ever saw," the aging doctor muttered to Uriah while he checked Ethan's bandages. Ethan, still out cold from all the laudanum, lay unconscious on the narrow bed.

Uriah had spent the night in the doctor's office with Ethan. He'd sent word to Ezekiel and Nettie Smithers to reassure them he'd be over as soon as there was any news. Then he got a message to Pru. She came immediately and stayed. Neither one slept. They'd both jumped like scared rabbits the moment the doctor returned in the morning.

"How's he doin', Doc?" Uriah asked, anxiously watching the rotund surgeon look Ethan over. The strong smell of ether and rubbing alcohol permeated the room.

"Better," the doctor mumbled. "Don't see any new signs of trouble here. Got the bullet out of his back, but it did its damage all right. Tore him up more'n usual. Damn scatterguns are mean and nasty. Yes sir, Mr. Rourke is one lucky bastard," the doctor repeated.

Uriah let out the breath he'd been holding.

Pru did the same.

"Infection," the gray-haired doctor spoke more clearly now as he inspected his unconscious patient. "Infection is something to worry over. Infection and the chance he might start to bleed again. But Rourke here is a big, strong fella. He ought to do just fine." Finished, the doctor draped the sheet over Ethan and pulled up the blanket at the foot of the bed. "Did he wake during the—"

Ethan stirred. His eyes remained shut, but his lips moved.

The doctor, Uriah, and Pru hovered close.

"Nutmeg . . . where are you?"

"Just rambling," the doctor said. "Typical after all he's been through." He stepped away from Ethan's bedside. "Folks, I've got some house calls to make, but I'll be back in an hour. You two be here when I get back?"

He didn't have to ask. When the doctor left, Uriah and Pru took a seat on the wooden bench where they'd passed the night.

"Pru, could you make any sense of what Ethan said?"

"Nutmeg, Uriah. He said nutmeg."

"He's wantin' to know where *nutmeg* is?" Uriah was bewildered.

Ethan moaned again.

Uriah and Pru rushed over to him.

Ethan didn't open his eyes, but stirred nonetheless. He appeared to be waking, restless and agitated. When he started to thrash from side to side, rattling the narrow bed, Uriah and Pru worried about the exact same thing at the exact same moment. Ethan could start to bleed again if he didn't keep still.

At once, Ethan settled, his eyes still closed. "Nutmeg . . . you're coming," he muttered, then fell back into a deep, drugged sleep.

Uriah and Pru sat back down and stared at each other, their thoughts a mirror image: Nutmeg is coming? It made no sense. No sense at all.

★ ★ ★ ★ ★

Meggie hurried down the back stairs of the Byers Hotel. She found Eliza crying in the kitchen and William trying to comfort her. Much as Meggie wished she could hurry right past the distraught pair and find Ethan, she could not.

"Rose, there's been trouble," Eliza said weakly. "At the top of the pass. Shooting. Men were killed. Ethan—"

The whole of Meggie's life balanced precariously in that unbearable, agonizing moment. *Don't say it, Eliza! Don't you say it!*"

"Ethan's still alive, Rose," Eliza was quick to reassure, too upset herself to notice Meggie's particular upset over Ethan. "Uriah's taken him down to Denver. He was shot. Shot in the back," Eliza got out before she again dissolved into tears.

Ethan's still alive.

Meggie forced herself to stay on that thought, and that thought only.

Ethan's still alive.

She had to get to him before—swallowing hard, unsteady on her legs, she put a hand against the wall for support. Her heart hurt so bad, it was hard to talk.

"Eliza . . . William . . . I'm . . . I've got—" Meggie rushed out the kitchen door. She had to get to Denver any way she could. She ran down the footpath to her cabin. Once there, she rushed through the open doorway so fast she didn't notice she'd left her door unlatched the day before. All she could think of now was Ethan. She'd go to the Zeb Kinney's stable and get a horse. She made a dash for her bed and scrambled underneath it to retrieve her satchel and pack the few things she'd need for the journey.

"Well, well. Is this any proper way to greet an old acquaintance?"

Meggie froze. The instant the voice slithered across the floor toward her she knew who it belonged to.

Benjamin Howard!

Too late, the hair on the back of her neck bristled until it hurt. Too late. The monstrous evil snaked closer and closer until it found her under the bed. She knew one day the devil would find her—that someday he meant to finish what he started all those years ago. But dear Lord, why now when she had to reach Ethan!

Lord, please, Meggie silently bargained, *if You just help me get to Ethan, then this fiend, this evil can have me. Just save Ethan. Save my love.* It was as wrong to bargain with God as it was to parley with the devil, but she couldn't help it.

"Come on," Howard whispered above her. He'd reached her bed now. "Be a good girl and come out from under there and give me a proper welcome."

Meggie's stomach heaved. She threw up all over her stretched-out arms, somehow managing to keep her knotted fingers on the handles of her satchel. Just why she held onto her satchel for dear life, she had no idea. Stone-still under her bed, she squeezed her eyes shut and tried to combat the sick smell of her own fear. With little air and even less light in the small space, it felt like her tomb.

"I'm losing my patience with you, Meghan. And just when I planned to be nice and polite."

She didn't move. She'd fallen into a snake pit. Escape was impossible. Meggie waited for the serpent to strike. She screamed when his taloned fingers shackled her ankle and he began to drag her out from under the bed.

"I *told* you. Time's up."

"Let go . . . of me . . . you spawn of . . . Satan," she gritted out between painful gasps.

"Now, now, Meghan, my dear. Name-calling. Not nice. Especially from a good Christian girl. Not nice at all," he cuttingly admonished, unhanding her but not stepping away.

Meggie pulled herself up to a seated position. She silently chanted, out of habit more than any defense, *Six feet under, six feet away, where to stay safe, the devil must stay! Six feet under—* Meggie saw Howard's boot coming. Before he could kick her in the stomach, she gathered her satchel in front of her to take the blow.

"Bitch!" He yanked the satchel from her and threw it on top of her bed. "Look at you. You're a mess. I didn't come all this way to find you so soiled."

Soiled! Soiled! The irony, the agony, of having the very person who'd ruined her calling her soiled when he—

"Stand up and let's have a look at you."

With no choice but to obey, Meggie slowly got to her feet.

Garbed in a masquerade of western attire instead of an eastern suit, Benjamin Howard looked like a ridiculous store-window dummy. In another time, in another life, she would have laughed, but not in this life with this menacing predator waiting to swallow its prey. Howard covered every inch of her body with his serpentine leer. If there had been anything left in her stomach, it would have spilled out now. As it was, she choked back bitter bile and held her ground.

"You've grown into quite the young woman, hideous scars and all, haven't you?"

His use of the word "hideous" was even more ridiculous than his outfit. That he called *her* hideous made her even sicker. She dry-heaved again.

Howard started to back away from her.

She watched him take every step, wishing he'd keep on going, out her door, and out of her life. But wishes were wasted on inhuman snakes like Howard.

He shut and latched her door. "We don't want anyone disturbing our little reunion, now do we?" he cynically intoned.

260

Keep your head, Meggie girl. She didn't want to give Howard the satisfaction of seeing her afraid. *If it's the last thing you do, keep your head.*

"Yes indeed, quite the young woman."

So close now the fetid odor of his hot breath singed her cheeks, Meggie held herself still as a corpse.

"You need to clean yourself up." He began circling her. "First things first." Like a viperous strike, he yanked her hair out from its bun, not bothering to loosen any of the pins. "Yes, yes," he whispered excitedly. "Much better." He jerked and pulled on her hair until it fell down her back, then Howard came around to face her. His next strike took her wire rims.

"I don't like you in these, my dear," he announced, twirling them in front of her face before he dropped them beside his foot. One pivot and they were crushed. "And as for this—"

Meggie's insides recoiled at his touch but she willed herself not to move. His scaly hand brushed her bosom when he reached for her cross, tearing it from her. Little pieces of the chain that held the cross against her breast fell to the floor. As if he were battling an enemy, Howard threw the wooden crucifix hard against the back wall of the cabin. It made an eerie crackling noise when it hit and splintered in half.

Meggie stared at the broken cross in disbelief. It was as if her faith, her God, lay in pieces on the floor. Meggie fought to stay calm, to think straight. *God is unbreakable. God is forever. God is watching over Ethan. God will keep him safe,* she reassured herself. The devil Benjamin Howard could destroy her, but he couldn't destroy the power of God.

"Why, Meghan, my girl, you look a little frightened," Howard taunted. "You shouldn't be scared of old Benjamin. Not yet." He waited for his meaning to sink in, aroused by its apparent victimizing effect. Then he shoved her toward the washbasin and pitcher.

"Now wash off that putrid stench."

The pitcher was empty.

"I . . . I can't—"

"Dammit, girl. Don't cross me," he threatened, grabbing hold of her hair and twisting it to the point of pain.

Meggie struggled to speak.

"No . . . water. I can't. There's . . . no water."

His mood altered. He let go of her hair.

She added *demented lunatic* to *monster, fiend, rapist—Lucifer.*

"Well, well, you'll just have to fetch some water, now won't you?" he snidely informed her, and clamped his cold fingers around her elbow. "Get it. Now!" He released her and shoved her away.

Meggie stumbled over to the door and picked up her bucket. Slowly, reluctantly, she unlatched the door. In one step she'd be outside . . . and free! Maybe she could run. Maybe she could escape. But the moment she put a foot outside, Howard caught up with her.

"No, no, you don't. Not without me, my girl."

It wasn't just his fetid breath that sickened her. His whole body reeked of decay, an odor that clung to her now like thousands of parasites, each one wanting her blood. When he pushed her outside, she stumbled again, but managed to keep her footing.

"Hurry up." His mood worsened as he scanned the area.

Meggie mutely walked around to the back of the cabin. Howard was right behind her. She bent down and filled her bucket with spring water, fighting the urge to plunge into the nearby river. Utterly downhearted, she stood up and turned around—into the gleaming blade of a knife.

"Just so you won't get too feisty on me, missy," Howard warned. "Now get back inside." He jabbed her with the knife, not enough to cut, but enough to embolden him.

Meggie feebly washed herself, knowing she'd never get clean. She didn't have the energy to worry over it.

"Change of plans, my girl. We're not staying here. Too close to town. To intruders."

Intruders! She wanted to laugh. She wanted to scream at the bizarre irony of it.

Howard threw a linen towel at her.

Meggie dabbed at her face and clothes before she faced him again.

"Here." He grabbed her satchel from off the bed. "Fill this with supplies to last a few days."

A few days? Meggie stiffened inside, steeling herself against such news. She took the satchel he thrust at her and forced herself to walk to the kitchen area, aimlessly pulling food items off the shelf.

"That's enough!" Howard yelled.

She clamped the bag shut.

"All right. Let's go," he snarled. "Don't worry about anything else. You won't need anything else."

Meggie let him shove her back out the door, but refused to show any fear. She knew what he meant by his sick comment. She knew she wasn't coming back.

CHAPTER EIGHTEEN

Ethan blamed himself for not figuring the bastard Bart Gentry out earlier. Yellow belly. Gutless son of a bitch coward! Ethan went over every detail of the incident again in his head. All of the sons of bitches, comancheros to boot, were dead now. Or were they? Another face loomed in front of him: *Angus Tritt's.* Whenever he'd brought Gentry in on a deal, Tritt was in on it, too. Both of them were heartless, greedy bastards. Deep in his gut, Ethan knew Tritt was a part of all this. Ethan tried to get up. He didn't belong in this sick bed. Not while Tritt still breathed the same air as he.

"Hey, where do you think you're goin'?" Uriah bellowed out from across the room.

Mindless of the pain slicing through him, Ethan rolled onto his side then tried to swivel off the bed.

"Dammit," Uriah cursed, barricading Ethan's way. "You want to start bleedin' again? Doc said you had to stay still and rest. An' I'm here to make sure you do," the big man ordered.

"It's Tritt, I know . . . Tritt." Ethan groaned, rolling back onto his side. He closed his eyes and breathed against the pain. "I know it, Uriah." Ethan opened his eyes, leveling them on Uriah. "Tritt was in on this. I know it. I have—"

He tried to get up again but Uriah stopped him.

"All right. Ease up," Uriah said, and pulled Ethan's covers over him.

Pru approached.

Embarrassed, Uriah blushed at the chance she might have seen Ethan's nakedness.

"Mr. Rourke," Pru shyly addressed. "I'm . . . we're . . . grateful the Lord above returned you to us."

Who in blazes? Then Ethan remembered her. Nutmeg's childhood friend.

"I'm Pru. Prudence Utter," she explained. "I'm Meghan's friend and . . . Uriah's."

Ethan didn't need Prudence Utter telling him she was Nutmeg's friend, what with her bringing God in on things right away. Shifting his attention back onto Uriah, Ethan couldn't think about Nutmeg now.

"You have . . . to find . . . Tritt, Uriah," he sputtered through the pain, grabbing Uriah's shirtfront.

"I'll find him. Don't worry." Uriah eased his hands from Ethan's. "I'll take care of it. You sleep. Pru's stayin' in case you need somethin'. But rest now."

Ethan tried to fight the laudanum, but he couldn't. He was out before Uriah left the doctor's office.

"Afternoon, Uriah." Angus Tritt stood the moment Uriah entered his office. "Glad you're all right. We all heard about the trouble up on the pass yesterday. Sorry for it. Just glad you're all right. And Ethan. He'll be all right, I'm sure. Yes, glad you're both all right."

"You said that one too many times," Uriah said levelly, and then shut the door. They were alone in the banker's office, the tellers and customers on the other side of the door.

Tritt didn't bother to pull out his handkerchief. He wiped away nervous sweat with his bare hands. "Come on in, Uriah. Have a seat," he offered anxiously, then sat back down at his desk.

Uriah coolly took a chair, but not for a second did he take

his eyes off the jittery banker. What he'd thought might be a wild goose chase, started smelling like a sure-as-shootin' hunt.

Tritt ran the sleeve of his shirt across his sweaty forehead. "What . . . can I . . . do for you?" he stammered.

Uriah couldn't hold his temper.

"Now that you mention it, you son of a bitch, you could start with why you and Gentry tried to kill us." Uriah watched and waited for Tritt's move.

"Don't . . . know wh-what you . . . mean, friend." The perspiring banker tripped over his own words.

Uriah knew anything could happen now. Tritt was getting jumpy on him fast. He had to be ready when the bastard tried something. But Uriah couldn't resist baiting him, just a little.

"You know, it's a funny thing how the truth always manages to crawl out from under even the biggest dunghill. Gonna be real interestin' to see what all the nice folks on the other side of your door will think of you once they know their trusted banker is a lyin', murderin' son of a bitch. Yep. Real interestin'." Uriah wanted Tritt to squirm.

He was squirming. Tritt dragged open a desk drawer.

Uriah waited. He was ready if the bastard tried to pull a gun on him. Would be real satisfyin' to put a hole right through his crooked head.

Tritt found his pistol all right, but he didn't point it at Uriah. With slow deliberation, he placed the nozzle of the Smith and Westin in his mouth and pulled the trigger, scattering bloody bits of his head all over his nice, clean desk.

Justice was Uriah's only thought at the scene in front of him. *An eye for an eye.*

"May you rot in hell, Tritt," Uriah pronounced disgustedly, then left the dead man's office.

That same night, Livi Tritt's lifeless, beaten, brutalized body was found in an obscure Denver alleyway.

Forced to walk for hours with Howard prodding her on as if she were a stray cow, Meggie willed herself not to give in to exhaustion and hopelessness. Without knowing Ethan's fate, she was going crazy. Each step was madness now. Soon it would be dark. Other predators would stalk besides her perverted captor. Deeper and deeper, they headed into unfamiliar wilds. Unsure of her exact bearings, she was very certain Howard had no idea where they were going. The only path he cared about was the one putting as much distance as possible between her and any salvation.

To Meggie's misfortune, they wandered through an area even the Utes rarely trod. She knew the Indians only sojourned in this direction to bury their dead deep in the rocky crevices. She felt more alone than ever now. When they reached the next clearing, Howard pushed her so hard she fell to the ground.

"We'll stop here," he rasped out, spittle dripping from the corners of his uneven grin.

Meggie pushed herself up and scrambled to her feet. Blood seeped from the hand she'd put out to catch her fall. She wiped it on her calico skirt, wincing against the pain. When she saw the spittle at the corners of Howard's malevolent mouth, she knew he smelled her blood. Like a snake ready to swallow its victim, whole.

"Well, my dear, let's open that bag of yours and have our supper." His mood altered, evidence of the changeling that he was.

Supper! What kind of game was he playing? Meggie's thoughts raced. What was he waiting for?

"Sorry we can't have a nice warm fire for you, my dear," he said in feigned apology. "But someone might find us. We don't want that to happen, do we?"

Find us! He stupidly believes someone could find us here, in the middle of nowhere? Without a fire, animals might attack. She didn't worry over herself, preferring death by wild animals to death by the devil. Suddenly the satisfying picture of Benjamin Howard caught in the jowls of a ferocious mountain lion, or better still, a bear, picked up her spirits. Fine then, no fire.

"Now be a good girl and pull something out of that bag of yours for me. I'm hungry enough to eat—"

Meggie's insides seized at his unfinished words. His lascivious leer was the ugliest expression she'd ever seen on any human. But then, Benjamin Howard wasn't human. Quickly, she opened her satchel and pulled out whatever her hand found. A hunk of cheese. Biscuits.

"Here," she offered angrily.

His claw-like fingers snatched the food up immediately.

"Thank you, my dear. Now let's get comfortable and enjoy our little respite together."

She waited. For what, she couldn't know.

"Come on now, sit. Sit!"

Filled with unease, she slowly dropped down to sit by him. She refused to eat.

Finished with his food, Howard reached into a coat pocket and pulled out a circle of rope. "Bedtime, my dear."

Meggie stared wide-eyed at the rope. She hated that she was afraid.

He was behind her in the next moment. He tied her wrists in back of her, giving the rope an extra, painful tug when he'd finished. Then he snaked around in front of her and pushed her over to bind her ankles.

Meggie didn't expect this—to be tied up. A knife or a gun would be better. Quicker.

"Ah . . . I can tell by that look on your pretty little face that you don't know what I have in mind for you. I can't have my beautiful Meghan worrying so, now can I? Do pardon my rudeness, but you're going to have to wait a little for my pleasures. The anticipation of it will have to do for now. You'll soon learn. It's always better when you have to wait."

Keep your wits, Meggie girl. Despite the dark closing in all around, she couldn't avoid the unearthly gleam in his eyes.

He grabbed up her satchel then shoved it under her head.

"There. Isn't that better? Snug as a bug."

She didn't take her eyes off him. He slithered over to a nearby pile of boulders and coiled down before pulling the brim of his phony cowboy hat down over his eyes. It took little time for him to fall asleep.

But for Meggie, there would be no sleep. She'd stay awake to keep an eye on the devil while she prayed for her angel.

Ethan was awake when Uriah arrived back at the doctor's office.

"How'd you sleep last night?" Uriah asked, coming over to Ethan's bedside.

"Fine. How'd Tritt sleep?" Ethan asked, worried at Uriah's somber look. Something must have gone wrong.

Uriah exhaled sharply. "Tritt's sleepin' for good. Shot hisself, he did."

Ethan wasn't surprised. Tritt was a coward, just like Gentry. Ethan still didn't like the look on Uriah's face.

Just then Pru rushed through the door. "What's . . . happened, Uriah?" she panted. "I heard . . . about Meggie at . . . the Express office—"

Ethan grabbed up his sheet, wrapping it around his waist as he bolted off the narrow bed. He knew now why Uriah looked so worried. It wasn't over Tritt's death. It wasn't over him. It was over Nutmeg!

"Ethan," Uriah took hold of Ethan's shoulders. "Get back in

bed. You'll injure yourself this way."

"I'll injure you if you don't tell me what's going on? What's happened to Nutmeg?"

Nutmeg? Uriah and Pru immediately exchanged looks, the same name on both their minds. Both knew now who Ethan had been calling for in his drugged state.

"Out with it, Uriah," Ethan demanded.

Uriah let go of Ethan. "All right. All right. Just take it easy. It won't do any good to get all riled."

Pru stood next to Ethan, and they were both tense and waiting for Uriah's news.

"Word got down from Hot Sulphur Springs a while ago. The town's all in a dither over their missin' schoolteacher. She disappeared into thin air. Folks think maybe it was Indians."

Pru's heart dropped to the floor.

"What else, Uriah?" Ethan demanded.

"Wadn't anythin' more."

Ethan fought the picture of Nutmeg being raped and tortured at the hands of the Utes, exacting their revenge on her innocence for what the white man was doing to their people. None of it was justified . . . white man or red. No matter what Nutmeg had done to him, or to others, she didn't deserve this!

"Where the hell are my clothes?" Ethan barked out, frantic to get dressed and find Nutmeg. But the moment he took a step, flaring pains in his back sent him to his knees, sheet and all.

Uriah helped him to his feet.

"Dammit. You're not in any shape to ride. I'll go."

"No," Ethan gritted out between clenched teeth. But he knew Uriah was right. He couldn't sit a horse now. He leaned back against the side of his sick bed and waited for the pain to ease so he could speak.

"We'll go, Uriah. Get Sykes . . . to hitch up the stage . . . and meet me here. We can switch teams . . . at Junction House."

"You're not going without me," Pru insisted.

Within a half-hour all three were on the stage bound for Hot Sulphur Springs.

Meggie had no idea how far from town they were. She hadn't slept a wink all night. Howard had. Thank God he had, and left her alone. He'd untied her as soon as he woke up, and hadn't molested her . . . yet.

Worry over Ethan and not over herself kept her going. She didn't want food, but she was so thirsty now it pained her to swallow. She'd never give Howard the satisfaction of asking for a drink. Near a stream, Meggie tossed her satchel by its edge, and plunged her face into the rushing creek to gulp down mouthfuls of blessed water. She shrieked when Howard grabbed her hair and yanked her head up.

"I never gave you permission, missy," he declared venomously. "You have to *ask* first. You didn't ask me, so you can't have any more," he hissed and dragged her away from the stream.

Her time was running out. Meggie knew it. Completely insane, her maniacal captor couldn't go on much longer. Any moment now, his next move could be her last.

A bright moon guided the heavy Concord over Berthoud Pass and on to Junction House, where Ethan got fresh horses. Hardly a word was exchanged among the threesome the entire journey. No one wanted to say out loud what each feared most—that Meggie was already dead.

The Concord pulled into Hot Sulphur Springs just before dawn. Lights flickered from inside the Byers Hotel. William and Eliza must have heard the stage pull up. They were out the front door before anyone had a chance to climb down.

"Ethan!" Eliza rushed to him. "Thank God you're all right!"

Ethan braced against her hug.

"Oh, Ethan. I'm sorry. Did I hurt you? I'm sorry," she apologized, tears welling in her eyes.

"Eliza, I'm fine. Don't cry over me."

"But Ethan . . . Ethan, you . . . and then Rose. Oh Ethan, Rose is gone," Eliza blurted out to him before sobbing into William's chest.

Ethan and Pru knew who Rose was. Uriah didn't.

"Rose? Wh—"

Pru interrupted before he could finish.

"I'm Prudence Utter, *Rose's* friend since childhood," Pru pointedly directed more to Uriah than to the Byers.

Rose's friend since childhood? Meggie. Nutmeg. Uriah understood. Exactly what, he wasn't sure. But he understood enough to hold his tongue.

Eliza pulled out of William's arms. "You're Rose's friend," she said reverently before taking both of Pru's hands in her own. "Oh please, come in. All of you. I'll make some coffee."

The trio followed William and Eliza inside. Bill Sykes wanted to unhitch the horses before he'd join them.

Ethan didn't feel like drinking any coffee. The trip up had given him time. Too much time. Enough time to realize that if anything happened to Nutmeg, it would be his fault—for loving her. The last to enter the kitchen, Ethan lingered a moment just outside the door. His wound had opened. He could feel the warmth of his own blood oozing from it. Aw, hell. He made sure of the buttons on his leather vest, hoping the vest would help stem the bleeding. He needed to get out of there before anyone noticed.

"What's the matter?" Uriah asked; his eyes on Ethan.

"Nothing, pard," Ethan said. "Just a little ache is all." He dropped into one of the kitchen chairs across from Eliza and William, needing to hurry with this. "Eliza, what happened?"

"Rose went missing two days ago. She'd spent the night with us and then rushed out the next morning when she heard you'd been hurt. She didn't say where she was going, Ethan, but she must have headed for her cabin."

"I went right away," William spoke up. "There wasn't any sign of her at her place. Nothing seemed disturbed. It smelled bad though. Like someone had been sick."

Ethan's stomach turned at this. He didn't want to imagine any of it.

"We've not had a lick of trouble here in Hot Sulphur with the Utes. I don't think it was Indians. Why would they up and all of a sudden do something to Rose?" William kept on. "It doesn't make any sense."

Ethan didn't know whether or not to be relieved. "Then what, William? Who?"

"Don't know. Can't come up with anything. No suspicious strangers in town and nothing unusual happening before Rose went missing. We've combed the area. Can't come up with a thing."

"Maybe I can," Eliza whispered, an idea striking her. Without another word she left the kitchen only to return with the hotel registry. "Here. The answer might be in here."

"What do you mean, woman?" William asked. "What's in there?"

"A suspicious stranger. Last week. Don't you remember? The easterner in the brand-spanking-new western clothes. Remember I told you how odd he looked and acted? All the questions he asked about our town and the folks in it. Like he was looking for someone."

"His name," Pru struggled to stay calm. "Find his name."

Eliza opened the registry to the last entry. "Here, here it is." She pointed to the name. "B. Howardton."

Benjamin Howard! Pru turned white as a ghost.

"Pru? What is it?" Uriah asked anxiously.

"I can't. I can't tell you. Any of you. I promised Meggie I never would. I can't." Pru put her hands over her face and dissolved into tears.

Caught up in the moment, Eliza and William didn't even hear her say Meggie instead of Rose.

"You can tell me, Pru. You have to tell me." Ethan rose from his chair.

"But I promised," Pru sobbed into her hands.

With a gentleness that he didn't feel, Ethan reached out and pulled her hands away. "Pru, you have to tell me. We don't have much time. Tell me," he urged.

Pru knew he was right. Whatever happened, there could be little time left for Meggie. If Meggie hadn't already been murdered, or worse, at the hands of Benjamin Howard, she soon would be. Maybe Ethan could save Meggie. Maybe he wouldn't be too late.

"Only you, Ethan. I'll tell only you."

Ethan sat back down.

Eliza, William, and Uriah, without protest, quietly slipped out of the kitchen and left them alone.

Pru swallowed hard before she began.

"Ethan, I have to tell you some things. Things about Meggie's past. I warn you. It's hard to hear."

"I'm listening," he encouraged.

"Meggie grew up in an orphanage. Did you know that, Ethan?"

"No."

"I was there when they first brought her. She was only four years old. We took to each other right away. I was scared, alone, and young, too." Pru wiped new tears from her cheeks. "God only knows why, Ethan, but over the years, the head matron at the orphanage grew to hate Meggie. I don't know why. Maybe she was jealous because Meggie was so kind and so beautiful. At every opportunity—the matron didn't need a reason—she'd switch Meggie."

The scars. Ethan remembered them on Nutmeg's back. He'd never wanted to kill a woman before, but he wanted to kill the brutal matron.

"Meggie never cried. She'd come back to her bed and crawl in without a sound. She never complained. I'd try to get her to say something . . . but . . . she never did," Pru choked out. "And then . . . then," Pru dissolved into tears yet again.

Ethan put his hand on one of Pru's shuddering shoulders, trying to console her.

"It was just after her seventeenth birthday when it happened." Pru suddenly stopped crying and straightened her back. "Meggie was seventeen when hell came calling."

Ethan couldn't believe Nutmeg had more to suffer, beyond the beatings and the scars. He dreaded hearing the rest of this.

"The matron delivered her to him, you know, to Benjamin Howard. Right up to his door. Meggie had thought herself so lucky to be given a beautiful dress to wear and taken in a carriage. She actually thought the cruel matron might have had a change of heart about her. All Meggie had to do was carry documents to the orphanage's 'most prominent and generous contributor.' " Pru spat these last words out. "Delivered right into hell she was . . ." Her thoughts traveled back to the awful episode.

"Pru." Ethan insides caved, but he had to hear the rest.

Snapped back to the present, Pru continued. "That one day, that one horrible day has terrorized and haunted Meggie for eight years." Pru looked right at Ethan now. "Benjamin Howard locked her in a room and then viciously beat and raped her. She was knocked unconscious. Who knows what else the fiend did to her, or for how long!"

Oh, God, Nutmeg! No! No! The horrible scene flashed in front of Ethan. Now he knew why she'd recoiled from him when he tried to touch her. She had reason enough.

"When Howard was through with her," Pru whispered, "he dumped her in an alleyway like so much garbage and left her for dead. I'm sure the fiend believed she'd die before the morning. But Meggie fooled him. Fooled the devil, she did." Pru almost smiled at this.

Ethan saw Nutmeg's ravished, beaten body, alone, lying cold and alone in that dark alleyway. The disturbing, impossible picture of the horror she'd suffered tore him up inside. Right now he hated his own sex, every man who could have hurt Nutmeg so.

"When she didn't return to the orphanage, I was so frightened," Pru kept on. "I tried to find out what happened to Meggie, but no one spoke of her. At the orphanage they acted as if Meggie never even existed. They acted like her life had no importance. It was horrible. I didn't know what to do. Finally, I gave up. I'd no choice, or I'd be put out on the street. Ethan." Pru looked hard at him. "I should have left then. I was a coward. I should have left."

Ethan kept silent. He could neither condemn nor applaud how she'd behaved.

"Two years," Pru said. "I found out Meggie was in the asylum in Boston for two unbearable years. Out of her mind. No identity. No memory. Nothing but haunting nightmares for companionship."

Ethan's heart lurched in his tight chest. Nutty Meggie. He remembered that he'd once called Nutmeg crazy. How it must have sounded to her when he'd called her that.

Unmindful of Ethan's thoughts, Pru continued. "A blessing for sure, the Sisters of Charity rescued her from the asylum. They took her in to their convent and nursed her back to sanity.

That's where Meggie learned to be a teacher, and to let God back into her life to bring ease to her tortured soul."

Her cross. Ethan understood now, and shut his eyes as if he'd just been hit. He could still see the wooden crucifix draped over her bosom—like a hand on a Bible. He'd condemned her for wearing the symbol of a God he no longer believed in. Ethan could still hear her pleas for his understanding that last night they were together, and he could hear what he'd said to her: "You don't belong here with me. I don't want you. Get out! Get out of my room, out of my house, and out of my life." Nutmeg had wanted to explain. She'd said she could explain. *I wouldn't give her the chance.*

In the whole of his life, Ethan had never hated himself more than at that moment, nor loved any woman more than his beautiful, courageous Nutmeg.

"Meggie fled Boston the very day Benjamin Howard saw her at the convent school." Pru hadn't finished. "She feared for her life, Ethan. He thought she'd died. Meggie said she knew he wanted to kill her. And every day that she's been here in the West, she's known he'd come for her. He couldn't risk Meggie telling anyone what he'd done. Meggie traveled under an assumed name to protect herself. She knew he'd find her one day." Pru looked Ethan dead in the eye. "And he has."

The truth of Pru's words hit Ethan worse than any bullet. The blood seeping from his own wound felt like Nutmeg's. He shot out of his chair. He'd find her or die trying.

Chapter Nineteen

"You're not goin' anywhere without me," Uriah said, at Ethan's heels the moment Ethan charged past him, then out the Byers Hotel. Uriah didn't need any explanation. The look on Ethan's face said it all. Meggie's life was on the line. Ethan's was, too. Right now Uriah would have to put that worry aside. He followed Ethan to the Kinney's stable. The stage was there, their rifles inside. Once Ethan had his gun, he grabbed a saddle and slapped it on the nearest horse. Uriah followed suit.

Ethan climbed painfully off his horse as soon as they arrived at Nutmeg's cabin. Damn. He still bled. The second Uriah's back was turned Ethan pulled a bandanna from his hip pocket. He hastily undid his vest, shoved the neckerchief inside the back of his shirt, pressing hard against the sticky ooze, and then reclosed his vest.

"The cabin door's still open, Ethan," Uriah stated the obvious.

"Yeah," Ethan acknowledged, dreading what he might find inside. It was the hardest walk of his life. Gaining entrance, he stopped in the cabin doorway and glanced all around.

William had been right. It smelled bad, but there wasn't any sign of trouble. Everything seemed in place. But Ethan knew better. He looked around the space again, this time letting his gaze linger over Nutmeg's bed, the kitchen area, her rocker by the hearth, and the rows of desks. All of a sudden an image hit him—an image of Nutmeg being dragged out of here and taken

God knew where. He could see it happening in every corner.

"Ethan, where are you goin'?" Uriah followed him back outside. "We haven't finished lookin' here."

"I have," Ethan said, and then crouched down to study the ground. "Footprints, Uriah. Two sets." His wound still oozed. Gritting against the searing pain, Ethan got to his feet.

"You don't look so good, Ethan. Let's take a breather before—"

"No," Ethan growled, then grabbed up his horse's reins and hooked his boot in the stirrup. Somehow he managed to hoist himself up. "Uriah, we can't give that bastard any more time with her. You understand? No more time. Now c'mon. Let's get going. At least they're on foot and left us a trail to follow," he said, more for his own benefit than Uriah's, before turning his horse upriver.

Uriah didn't know where the bastard Howard had taken Meggie, but he'd follow Ethan into hell to help find them.

Near her wits' end, Meggie aimlessly plodded on through scruffy thickets and over craggy rocks. By now she'd come to expect the harsh blows her captor landed on her back each time he thought she'd slowed down. Blows on top of scars. She didn't feel them anymore. Foggy memories plagued her. She thought of all the years at the end of the matron's switch. Right now she didn't care which devil was after her. She'd tried to hold onto precious thoughts of Ethan, but even he slipped from her mind. Yesterday. She might have cared yesterday. She'd had something left yesterday. But after another chilled, sleepless night, bound up at the feet of Satan, waiting for the moment he'd fatally strike, she'd no life left in her. One feathery thought kept her in this world, holding on to her and preventing her from slipping into the next.

Why hadn't Benjamin Howard killed her?

What was he waiting for?

Whatever evil he intended, why did he hesitate?

Two days and nights had passed. She'd expected him to kill her, or worse, by now. Unable to think clearly, Meggie prayed for an end to this madness. *Finish it! Finish it! Put* me *six feet under, six feet away!*

Without warning, as if the devil heard her silent prayer, Benjamin Howard shouted from behind her. "Here! Stop here!"

Disoriented, Meggie stopped. She struggled to hold herself steady.

"Turn around. Now!"

When she managed to do so, her first impulse was to laugh at the unkempt state of the illustrious Mr. Benjamin Howard. Like a snake having trouble shedding its skin, his rumpled, ill-fitting, dirt-streaked clothes hung as if they'd soon slide off his brittle bones. But his contorted face, his cruel mouth, and his eyes— she couldn't laugh when she looked straight into their yellow-ing, beady, aroused depths. The serpent was preparing to strike.

"This looks . . . good to me . . . my sweet," he hissed between shallow breaths. "What . . . do you think? Will it do . . . for us? Will it provide a suitable end . . . for our unrequited love?"

Meggie stared blankly at his lecherous, crooked smile, and then at the surrounding area. The river caught her eye. It rushed by, escaping downriver. For some inexplicable reason, the fact that they were going downriver and not upriver suddenly energized her.

"Answer me," Howard demanded, coiling a taloned hand around her throat.

"Wh-what?" she choked out, needing time to concentrate.

He tightened his grip on her. "Oh, feisty now . . . aren't we?" he whispered. "Well, well. You can't know . . . how much that pleases me . . . Meghan," he said in between excited gasps.

His breath sickened her more than the claw-like hand at her neck.

"I suppose you've . . . wondered what's kept . . . me from all this beauty for so long?" With viper-like speed, his other hand moved over her body, touching her, assaulting her.

Meggie thought she'd be ready for what he would do. But she wasn't. Not for this.

As quickly as he'd grabbed her, Howard abruptly let her go.

Meggie fell back and tripped over her satchel. She hadn't remembered setting it there.

"Good," her captor oiled out. "Now I have your . . . full and undivided . . . attention. I told you before," he wheezed. "It's always better . . . when you have . . . to wait. And since . . . we only have . . . this one last time, well . . . I wanted it to be . . . perfect for you . . . and for me."

Meggie didn't miss any part of his sick meaning.

"I couldn't enjoy our little affair . . . if I thought . . . we'd be interrupted. You understand . . . I'm sure. We had to get farther . . . away from town. But alas . . . my sweet . . . I've grown weary of our journey. Our time together . . . sadly . . . must end," he panted unevenly. "You do understand . . . don't you girl?"

She dare not take her eyes from this dementia, this bedlam.

"Now be a good girl . . . and come back over here . . . to me. Aren't you happy I'll have you . . . hideous scars and all?"

Meggie pulled to a stand, once again putting her satchel between herself and this monster.

"Very well . . . bring your little case . . . if you like."

The moment she was within reach, he snatched her satchel away and threw it on the ground. "Sorry. Changed my mind."

Desperate for any kind of comfort, she eased her foot against her case. Facing Howard now, she could see the river over his shoulder, rushing past them downstream, toward home. Meggie wanted to laugh. She wanted to scream out to this stupid, maniacal idiot that they'd gone in circles and were likely close to Hot Sulphur Springs!

"I've an appetite for you . . . for your . . . delicious apple-sauce cake . . . my dear," he wheezed, gasping harder for each breath.

His silly, bizarre attempt at any kind of civility made Meggie want to laugh at him all the more. She knew his sick meaning, but still she wanted to laugh.

"I want . . . one more piece," he said, sliding his razor-like tongue over his salivating lips. "Now look . . . in your little bag . . . and get it for me!"

Finish it! Finish it! Finish me! She wanted this to end. Now. Angrily, she bent down and fastened her hand onto the worn handles of her satchel.

"Fetch it, missy," he spat out then turned away from her a moment.

Meggie jerked her satchel wide-open and peered inside. She wanted to find the remaining cake and shove it down his venomous throat and choke the life from him!

Jesus, Mary, and Joseph!

Her loaded Colt .45! There it was—beneath the cake, and right next to *Jane Eyre*! She'd forgotten that she'd put her beloved novel inside her satchel and that she hadn't removed her gun since returning from Denver. Meggie shot a quick glance at Howard. He wasn't looking at her. Deftly, she retrieved the cloth wrapping with the cake inside and closed her valise partway.

"Give it to me, missy." He'd turned on her again.

She held out her hand with the cake in it. As soon as he'd snatched it away, she replaced her satchel beside her on the ground.

Howard licked his fingers, taking his time, doubtless to

prolong her fear. "I'm not really . . . as satisfied as . . . I'd expected," he whined lasciviously through gasps for air.

Is there no end to his sickness?

"I think you know . . . what I need now," he oiled out.

Demon seed! How many times had she got down on her knees and thanked heaven above that she hadn't conceived his devil child when he'd raped her.

All at once he came at her, clawing at her neck with both of his taloned hands!

Buttons flew!

Cloth ripped!

Meggie willed herself to stay still as she could. She would only have one chance. She couldn't afford to lose it.

Howard hooked his scaly fingers into the top of her chemise. In one swift movement he ripped open the white cotton, exposing her breasts to his leering glare.

The instant he reached for her, Meggie dropped to the ground and pulled her satchel over her nakedness.

It made him laugh. "Time's up, my girl. I told you."

Slowly, with great care, Meggie put her hand down inside her bag and felt for her gun. Curling her fingers around the cool steel, she pulled to a stand, tense and waiting for her only way out of this nightmare.

"Now just what do you have in there? Something for . . . old Benjamin in your . . . little bag of tricks?" His maniacal panting swallowed his words. The broken vessels in his eyes gave off a reddish glare, burning from the very pits of hell.

Meggie pulled out her gun and fired at his chest. At such close range, Howard's blood splattered over her bare breasts before he slumped to the ground. The look of disbelief on his distorted face should have been proof enough that she'd avenged herself. But it wasn't. Meggie waited—waited for him to pass out of this world and right into purgatory. Her bag slipped from her hand, hitting the ground near him.

"You . . . bitch," he slurred at her before he gasped his last breath.

The instant he died, Meggie felt it.

He couldn't hurt her ever again. The nightmare that her life had become was over. She shut her eyes. All the fear and evil that had sent her running from life so many years ago lay dead at her feet. Despite the cruel matron, despite Benjamin Howard's villainy, she'd survived. Meggie felt victorious standing over Benjamin Howard's dead body. She'd slain her dragon. She'd killed the demonic fiend from her nightmares!

That's exactly how Ethan found her. Half naked, long coppery tresses blowing in the afternoon breeze, covered in blood, with a pistol still smoking in her hand. He never thought he'd find her alive, but the brave woman in front of him was very much alive.

Thank God. Ethan let out the breath he'd been holding. Yes, thank God. He might be a believer again, after all. His love hadn't meant Nutmeg's death. Awestruck at such a realization, Ethan wondered now if he'd been wrong about God all these many years, and decided maybe he had been. The weight of such a moment, suddenly lifting his troubled past from him, lifting away his guilt humbled him to his very soul.

Meggie still hadn't looked up. She didn't hear anyone approach. She stared at the dead man lying in a pathetic heap at her feet. *Fooled the devil, I did. Fooled you, Benjamin Howard. Fooled you right back into the tormenting flames of hell where you came from!* Meggie didn't think the good sisters would mind her pronouncement over the lecherous rapist and attempted murderer's evil, lifeless body. She heard a twig break and looked up.

"Ethan!"

The Colt .45 fell from her hand and thudded to the ground.

Instinct made her want to run into his arms, but her stubborn limbs didn't move a muscle. Frozen to the spot, she waited breathlessly for him to come to her.

Ethan slid off his horse and quickly reached her. He hooked his boot underneath the dead body lying between them, and rolled it out of the way with one shove.

Meggie fell into his strong arms and held on for dear life.

So did Ethan.

Even if they found the words to express what they felt at that moment, neither could speak. For now it was everything just to be in each other's arms. To know that life still breathed through the one they each loved most in the world.

Uriah backed up his horse and directed his eyes away from the pair to give them privacy.

Long moments passed before Ethan or Meggie attempted to pull away from each other. Ethan was the first. He had to see it in those luminous violet depths of hers. He had to see it written all over her lovely, brave face. He needed to see for himself that she was all right.

"Oh, my love," he whispered, and gently brought both his hands around to reverently caress her tear-stained cheeks. The dark smudges under her eyes hinted of the hell she'd just come through. Blotches of dirt marred her cream and spice complexion. Tiny cracks in her lips had filled in with dried blood. Twigs and pine needles were tangled in her hair, snarling and matting down much of its length. His heart broke for her, for all the fear and misery she'd endured at the hands of that son of a bitch. He'd give anything to take the misery away. Ethan silently prayed that Benjamin Howard hadn't raped her again. The thought of her facing such terror a second time—

"Nutmeg?" he started to ask. He had to know. But when he let his gaze drop down over her delicate throat and saw the cuts and marks her attacker left, then to her bare breasts and all the blood there . . . he didn't have the heart to make her tell him. Wanting to protect her any way he could, he ripped off his vest and placed it around her to help cover her nakedness.

"Ethan!" Meggie panicked when she saw his blood-soaked shirt. Instinctively she pressed both her hands against his bloody shirtfront.

Ethan, consumed with worry for Nutmeg, had forgotten about his own wound.

Uriah jumped off his horse and got to them in seconds. One look told him Ethan had already lost way too much blood. How in blazes he'd managed to stay on his feet this long, Uriah had no idea.

Dazed with new fears for Ethan's life, Meggie barely noticed Uriah's presence.

"C'mon partner," Uriah ordered, carefully taking hold of Ethan's arm. "Let's get you on your horse and back to Hot Sulphur while you still have a little life left in you." Uriah tried to keep the worry out of his voice.

Meggie tried to help Ethan, to support him.

It all finally caught up with Ethan. Dizzy from blood loss, he struggled to keep his blurring focus on Nutmeg. "No, Uriah. Get Nutmeg on my horse."

"She can have my horse," Uriah assured. "Now, c'mon."

It was getting harder and harder for Ethan to talk. "Not . . . not till she's . . . mounted," he gritted out.

Meggie didn't need to hear another word. She carefully let go of Ethan, gathered up her satchel and her gun, then climbed on to Uriah's horse.

Uriah guided Ethan's boot into the stirrup and helped lift him onto the waiting animal. He didn't have to take the reins away from Ethan. It was all his old friend could do to hold on to the saddle horn. Before he led Ethan and Meggie out of there, almost as an afterthought, Uriah turned and looked down at the dead man.

"What do you want me to do with this varmint's carcass, Ethan?"

Ethan had little trouble getting his answer out. "Leave it for the wolves."

The trio made it back to town before Ethan lost consciousness. Bill Sykes was out front of the hotel when they rode in. He hurried over to help Uriah get Ethan up to one of the rooms, with William right behind. Eliza left "Rose" in Pru's hands just long enough to run to Grady's Mercantile to fetch needed bandages, nostrums, and its proprietor. With no doctor in town, Grady was the next best thing.

Within the hour, Grady had rebandaged Ethan's wound and assured everybody he'd likely recover. Things looked pretty clean. No signs of an infection setting in. Not yet, anyways.

Meggie wasn't satisfied.

"He'll wake up, won't he, Mr. Grady? Won't he wake up soon?" she asked anxiously.

"Don't you fret," the kindly apothecary reassured. "He's lost a lot of blood, but he needs his sleep now."

Meggie breathed a little easier. The only chair in the room was a rocker. She pulled it over by Ethan's bed and settled down into it. She'd wait for as long as it took for him to regain consciousness. No amount of persuasion from Pru or Eliza could make her budge. Nothing could make her leave Ethan's side. She pulled his vest tighter around her, giving no thought to the fact that her tattered clothes were covered in dried blood. When she felt a shawl being draped around her chilled shoulders, she mumbled a weak thank you, hearing the door shut from behind as Pru and Eliza left her alone with Ethan.

CHAPTER TWENTY

Her gun forgotten, Meggie took *Jane Eyre* from her satchel and carefully tucked the book under Ethan's pillow. She'd slept with Jane and Edward under her pillow through many of her dark years. They'd brought her hope, companionship and love. Surely they'd do the same for Ethan.

Shedding Ethan's vest, she placed it lovingly over the back of the rocker, pulled the shawl securely around herself, and then settled back down in the chair. She leaned her head against Ethan's vest, and then quickly fell into an exhausted sleep.

Pure spring water spilled over smoothed rock. Each cascade pulsed toward the steamy crystal pool at the base of the mountain ridge. Fragrant evergreens protected the little clearing, standing watch over the two lovers. Lying on a meadowy carpet of wildflowers Meggie had never felt so happy, so alive. She lay on her back with her arms above her head, her fingers splayed to gently run over the fragrant, soft petals of pink and red. A suggestion from her lover brought a low moan to her throat. Willingly, she waited for him to cover her aroused body with his. In heightened anticipation, she waited for him to cloak her trembling limbs with his powerful frame. Hard thighs straddled her quivering hips. Powerful hands came to rest on either side of her head. Ready to be pierced through with those slate shards, she opened her eyes, opened herself, to love, to Ethan.

"My Ethan."

She met his steel gray gaze before she let hers travel lovingly over his well-formed brow, then down past his sculpted, straight nose to rest on a strong, firm mouth. His lips twitched ever so slightly. Her insides seized. A telltale dimple appeared at one corner of his mouth. Her inner tremors spilled over into heated waves of pleasure. The waves grew as she drank in his handsome features.

"I love you so, Ethan."

How she longed to have his gentle, hungry lips press against her waiting mouth. To have his body against hers, to have the two of them melting together into one. His dusky scrutiny worked its spell, slowly, deliberately, exposing her, fascinating her.

"Oh, Ethan, you are my passion, my life. Touch me. Love me."

Mounting desire exploded into blissful ecstasy.

"Ethan. Oh, Ethan."

In that instant Meggie shut her eyes and prayed that nothing would ever harm him again.

"Hope that's for me this time."

Meggie woke with a start at the sound of Ethan's voice, her dreams suddenly real. Scrambling out of the rocker, she grabbed his hands up in hers. "Oh Ethan, you're . . . I—"

Ethan tugged on her hands until her face was only inches from his.

"Get in."

"Get in?" Stunned, Meggie tried to pull away. "You need food and medicine and rest. You don't need me."

"You're wrong, woman. You're just what I need," he whispered, shutting off her protests with his kiss.

She kissed Ethan back, wanting him, loving him. But then she remembered the situation and abruptly pulled out of his reach. He was still ill, and she must look a fright.

"Ethan, I'm a mess. Please don't lo—"

"Nutmeg, you're the most beautiful woman I've ever seen. Lie here next to me. Please. There are things I have to say." Deep dimples formed at both corners of his gentle mouth. "I can't do it unless you get your schoolmarm, temperance, sign-toting, Bible-thumping rear end in this bed with me right now."

His disarming grin teased every part of her insides, taking away her shyness of him and her self-consciousness over her looks. Maybe she should ask him exactly what he meant by his rather unflattering description of her, but instead she climbed into the bed and snuggled against his warm strength.

"You need to ask William to send for the circuit judge."

"The circuit judge?" Meggie rose on her elbow and looked straight into Ethan's mischievous, dark eyes. He must be taken with the ague. Suspicious of fever, she placed her free hand on his cheek.

Ethan laughed and turned his face just enough to give her hand a quick kiss.

"You think I've got the fever, do you? Aw, Nutmeg, the only fever I have is you—in my blood, in my heart, in my soul." His grin faded.

She held her body tense, trying to make sure of his words.

"Marry me."

His husky whisper sent shivers racing everywhere. Those two simple yet powerful words at once gathered up her entire life and held it within their tender grasp. They issued a promise of happiness, days of dreams, nights of passion. No more fears. But then, Meggie did have one fear left: Ethan had to know she wasn't chaste. She'd forgiven herself for any sin the moment she killed Benjamin Howard, but she doubted Ethan could ever forgive her. He wouldn't want someone used . . . someone unable to—she couldn't finish the thought. As uncomfortable as it was, she had to tell Ethan about her past.

"Ethan, I can't marry you."

Ethan didn't say anything. He didn't move.

"I'm not good enough for you, Ethan Rourke." Meggie tried to hurry before her nerve left her. "You deserve a woman who's not been spoiled by . . ." She swallowed hard. "Years ago, Ethan, with the man back there, Benjamin Howard . . . he raped me. He did things to—"

"Marry me," he broke in.

"But Ethan, I'm not—"

"Marry me."

They'd had a conversation like this before when they'd danced together at the social. He hadn't listened to her then, either. Was it possible he didn't care about what she'd just told him?

"Ethan, do you mean it? Are you in earnest? Do you truly want to marry me?"

"Yes, my darling. Yes."

"Then, sir, I will marry you," she answered quickly, remembering Jane had given Edward just such a response. Meggie had her own flesh and blood hero in Ethan. She had her own Edward.

Ethan growled out a laugh as he rolled over and collected her in his arms. The sudden movement disturbed the book that had been tucked under his pillow all night. It slipped out in plain view.

"What the?—" Ethan scooped up the leather volume. "*Jane Eyre.*" The instant he read the title, he remembered where he'd seen it before. Puzzled even more now, he handed the book to Meggie. "Why did you—?"

"Put this under your pillow?" She finished his sentence and took the book from him. "Because I wanted them to be close to you all night."

"Them?"

"Jane and Edward."

"Jane and Edward," he parroted flatly. *Edward.* He recalled the name only too well.

"Ethan, it's all in here, in my novel. How poor, plain and

orphaned Jane Eyre grows up to fall in love with the man of her dreams. And then Edward proposes. Edward Rochester loves her, too. Edward marries Jane. Don't you see, Ethan?"

He was beginning to. All this time, and he'd been jealous of a fictitious hero from a romance novel. He didn't feel foolish. Anything but.

"You're the man of my daydreams, Ethan. You're my Edward."

Before that moment, Ethan didn't think there was any room left in his heart to love Nutmeg more than he already did, yet he found some.

The next time Pru nudged the door open enough to check on the sleeping couple, she discovered them wrapped in each other's arms. Ever so quietly she pulled the door closed.

Ethan awoke to find Nutmeg still asleep next to him. It had grown dark out. Someone must have come in and lit the lamp on their bedstead. He was about to douse the light when he saw the book, *Jane Eyre,* set on the table beside it. There was something . . . a letter, he thought . . . sticking out from the book. Curious, without wanting to disturb Nutmeg, he deftly slipped the folded pages from the novel. He probably shouldn't read it, but he couldn't resist the temptation. Managing to gain a better position, with Nutmeg still fast asleep, he unfolded the letter and began to read.

Dear Ethan . . .

It was a letter, all right, a letter to him! He brought his vision into careful focus and read on.

What I am about to tell you is private. It is all too real and too horrible, but I must tell you so that you will know. I want you to know the truth so you will not think badly of me . . .

Ethan clutched the pages hard. Nothing on earth could have taken them from him. He read every word, carefully, no matter how painful it was to continue. Finally, nearing the end of the letter, he blinked hard to keep his focus clear. Tears stung his eyes.

. . . I am surprised beyond anything you might imagine, that I've been able to fall in love with you, a flesh and blood man, when I thought I never would. At least I have this gift from you, Ethan. I do have my love for you. I will keep it with me in this world, and on into the next.

I will always love you, Ethan Rourke. Always and forever.

Your Meggie . . .

Carefully, reverently, Ethan replaced the folded letter in Nutmeg's romance novel so it was no longer visible. He didn't want Nutmeg to know he'd read it. She'd meant to destroy the letter, but he was ever grateful to have seen it. It was the most private, the most special, and the most holy moment he'd ever experienced in the entirety of his life. He'd never felt closer to God, knowing that this amazing woman loved him. He put out the lamplight and drew Nutmeg closer. Being given such a precious gift, he wasn't about to let anything happen to her, ever again.

Tomorrow was Meggie's wedding day. Tomorrow the circuit judge would come, and she would marry Ethan. By noon tomorrow, she'd be married and so would Pru. As if Meggie could be any happier, Uriah and Pru were to get married along with them in a double ceremony. When Uriah had learned the circuit judge was on his way to perform the ceremony for Ethan and Meggie, he'd asked Pru to marry him on the spot, right in front of everyone gathered in the Byers' kitchen. Pru accepted without any hesitation. The next moment had them all exchanging hugs—William, Eliza, Uriah, Pru, and Meggie.

It was right after that when Meggie sat William and Eliza back down at the table to explain her masquerade as Rose

Rochester. Both understood completely.

"You've nothing to be forgiven for," Eliza resolutely declared. "Nothing at all."

Eliza started making wedding plans right away. "One day is hardly enough time to get things ready." But she was determined. Within the hour, she had Clovis Kinney helping to bake the wedding cake, her husband Zeb lined up to provide the music, and Mrs. Grady working to find two dresses at the mercantile suitable for Meggie and Pru to wear on their wedding day. "Weather permitting, we can have the ceremonies under a canopy of wildflowers just beside the bridge out back. The whole town will come. Oh, it will be too lovely," she professed, sighing heavily. "Just too lovely."

Back in her own cabin now, Meggie busied herself with preparations for tomorrow. She'd had her hair pulled up, then down, trying to decide how she should arrange it for the ceremony. For now, she left it down. The dress Mrs. Grady found for her was beautiful. It must have been packed away somewhere in the store. She ran her fingers over the white gingham carefully laid out on her bed. Its gently scooped neckline and puffed muslin sleeves were perfect. Just perfect. Mrs. Grady, she hoped, would find Pru something equally wonderful to wear.

With all the tenderness she'd saved up her whole life to bestow upon the man of her dreams, Meggie reached for her wedding dress. As she held the soft fabric up to her, she began to recite the vows she'd soon make to Ethan.

"I Meghan take you Ethan to be my lawfully wedded husband. To love, honor, cherish, and obey . . . forsaking all others . . . to have and to hold from this day forward . . . in sickness and in health, till death us do part." Something was wrong. *To have and to hold* stuck in her thoughts, conjuring an altogether new fear. This one was for Ethan.

Suddenly scared to death that she'd hurt him again, Meggie threw her dress onto the bed. She dashed toward her rocker and fell into it. Its gentle movement offered no comfort. She shot up and began to pace. Her thoughts raced ahead of her.

What if the same thing happens again? What if I can't bear Ethan's touch? Yes, she'd let him hold her, but she was frightened that there could be nothing more. In marriage, there was supposed to be more. What if she could not?

I can't do that to him. I can't hurt him again!

She remembered the horrible, hurt look on his handsome face when she'd pushed him away the night of his party. She couldn't marry Ethan knowing she might bring him more unhappiness. She couldn't sentence him to a lifetime of hurt—to a lifetime with a woman who couldn't bear his intimate touch.

Suddenly Meggie knew what she had to do.

Much improved after two days of good food and a lot of rest, Ethan itched to get on with his life. First on the list was marrying Nutmeg. After tomorrow they could both get on with their lives together, as man and wife. Just then the very subject of his impatient contemplation rapped on his door.

"Ethan, I have to talk to you," Meggie called through the door.

He had it open in a heartbeat.

"Can't wait for tomorrow, eh? I know, you just can't stay away from me," he joked with a humor he didn't feel when he looked down into her troubled features. God, she was beautiful. He loved that she wore her coppery hair loose and free. It fell down over her shoulders and the front of her simple calico like a flaming waterfall. Her cream and spice complexion beckoned to be tasted. Her beautiful eyes deepened to passionate black. Her soft, rosy lips needed to be kissed.

"Ethan, please," she implored. "I want you to come with me."

"Ordering me around already, are you?" he teased, despite his mounting concern over her anxious behavior.

"Please don't mind that I am. This is important. Very important," she entreated.

"All right then, let's go." Fully dressed, he opened the door and followed her through it.

No sooner had they exited the back of the Byers Hotel then Meggie grabbed up Ethan's hand and practically dragged him along the familiar pathway, to a secluded spot well past her cabin.

"You want to tell me what this is about now?" he asked as soon as they'd stopped.

She let go of his hand, as if she were returning something she'd borrowed without permission. Just as slowly, she let her gaze travel up his muscled chest, over broad shoulders, a sculpted jaw, thick, dark cropped locks, then onto his face, memorizing every detail of his handsome countenance, his firm yet gentle mouth, his straight nose, and his magnetic, penetrating, steely regard. A mist of tobacco and deep woods settled over her. Meggie was frightened she might never behold Ethan again after—

"Nutmeg," Ethan said hoarsely. "What is it?"

The worry she heard in his voice spurred her on.

"Ethan, you know tomorrow we're supposed to marry."

Supposed? The word caught at his chest.

"We can't marry. I can't marry you unless we're . . . we're together first. I can't. It wouldn't be fair to you. We both have to know if . . . if I can—" Flushed with embarrassment, Meggie couldn't finish.

"Nutmeg," he whispered tenderly and took her hands in his, unsure of the moment.

"Ethan, please, let me finish," Meggie gulped out. "We both have to know if your touch . . . if I can be a proper wife to you, Ethan. I have to know if I can be."

"Oh, my love." He brought her hands up to his lips. "You don't have to prove anything to either one of us. I don't give a damn if this is all we ever do together the rest of our lives." Slowly, gently he ran his lips over her fingers and reverently kissed each one.

"But Ethan," she broke in, "I do."

The moment she saw the pair of deep dimples appear at the corners of his slow grin, everything changed. Suddenly Nutmeg couldn't wait to find out if she could be a real wife to Ethan. Unlike so many months ago in Denver, this time Meggie helped Ethan undo the buttons that fronted her cotton dress. Frustrated with her lack of success, she began undoing his shirt. Relieved when his mouth found hers, she leaned into his kiss while he pulled her dress off her shoulders and down to her waist. Her scars were forgotten. Oh, the torment of not having his powerful body crushed against her naked flesh! Anxious for his touch, Meggie ripped her chemise open, instantly reveling in the feel of his magical hands on her breasts.

If either had been able to gather any wits about them at that frenzied, fevered moment, they might have realized the question looming over them had just been answered.

Meggie could, *indeed,* be a proper wife to Ethan.

His sensual, consuming kisses didn't stop as he lowered her to the ground and let the soft, green moss cushion her bare back. Neither did his kisses stop as he slipped her dress down over her hips, catching the ripped chemise with it in his deft fingers. When his skilled hand found her female center . . . the agony of such unexpected pleasure surely would kill her.

Ethan craved the same death. In no time he'd rid himself of his bothersome clothing and held his manhood just over her, before he entered her.

All traces of fear gone, Meggie exalted in the magic of the moment, rising to meet Ethan, ever higher, ever stronger, ever in love.

"Oh, Ethan." Meggie was the first to try and speak. "I . . . I love you."

"Oh, my darlin' girl," he huskily confided. "I've loved you from the first. I just didn't know it. But now we have the rest of our lives for me to prove that I do."

Drawn close to his side now, Meggie rested her head in the cradle of Ethan's strong arms, thinking about what he'd just said. *They'd have the rest of their lives together to love each other.* She felt safe and loved and happy, truly happy. To be in the arms of the man of her dreams and not just conjuring him up from the pages of *Jane Eyre* still felt like someone else's fairy tale. But the moment she felt Ethan's arms tighten around her, his masterful touch was proof this was her fairy tale come true.

Jane and Edward fell in love on the pages of a romantic novel. They'd helped her through so many, many dark years. She'd be grateful to them, ever and always. Now she could tuck her beloved romance novel safely away, no longer needing it for companionship. She had Ethan now. She had Ethan, when she'd thought she never would. She delighted in the feel of his arms around her, and basked in the glow of his love, knowing theirs wasn't a romance to die for after all . . . but one to live for.

ABOUT THE AUTHOR

Meggie's Remains is **Joanne Sundell**'s fourth historical romance. This novel is based on Joanne's love for the first name in romance: *Jane Eyre.* Charlotte Brontë captured Jane's heartbeat, making it her own—making it ours. In homage to *Jane Eyre,* Joanne hopes to capture Meggie's heartbeat, making it her own—making it ours.

Joanne's heroines are women of substance, women of passion . . . women for all time. Her heroines include an immigrant doctor, a deaf printer, a woman born into prostitution, and now a woman trying to keep a clear line between what is real and what is not.

Joanne lives in the Colorado Rockies with one husband, two huskies, and two cats. Her three children are grown and live away, but are ever in her heart.